A Fictional Reimagining of
My Time on Weight Loss Reality TV

Kai Hibbard

Cover design by Rénee Barrat The Cover Counts.com
Interior format by IndieDesignz.com

Thank you to my Js.

Sometimes when you lack the courage or character
to make the right choices, the repercussions of the choices
you did make help you build that courage and character.

12/31/2015

Walking backstage before the final reveal, I can hear clips of me from *home* playing on a jumbo screen for the live studio audience. I have plenty of hate mail letting me know my personality and glib sense of humor don't translate well to TV. So, it shouldn't surprise me when I heard myself in the clip joking, "My recurring nightmare is my main competition running marathons while carrying his entire family on his back, passing me by and flipping the bird; I really hope he is actually home speed-eating ice cream," and having crowd roar with boos instead of laughter. It does surprise me though, and it stings a bit. I really do try not to be a cynical bitch; next time I get offered the "opportunity of a lifetime" I'm probably going to take a hard pass. People will judge and say I should have known better, but there really was no way I could have any clue what I was signing on for. I mean, who in their right mind would have signed on knowing *everything*?

I tried so hard to make the right choices. Once it was explained to me how lucky I was, I was desperate to show people I was worthy of being selected for this opportunity. I put my mind and body through hell and, now, here in this moment, about to walk out, listening to the people I worked so hard to not let down, boo me? Nothing feels right. I look the way everyone has told me I am supposed to now and I hate myself more than I ever have. I am pretty sure that's not how this is supposed to work. I didn't even really buy into this whole concept at first. It all just seemed like an adventure, some cool story to tell a potential grandkid someday. Just a dumb lark. Being fat seemed like a thing that was mostly everyone else's issue with me, and only my issue with me when the world reminded me I was *supposed* to be apologetic for it, and like anyone else, then it would get to me. It wasn't the central reason I am here. This was supposed to be *fun*. I've never in my life hated my body like I do now. I'm hungry; I'm dehydrated; I loathe looking in a mirror; my body physically hurts and I'm being booed by strangers. This is the fucking opposite of fun. This whole shitshow started New Year's Eve last year. Because, of course it did.

Chapter 1

My name is Atisa Aflague, but everyone calls me Tisa. I dig it. I also despise New Year's Eve. I'm not *always* a petulant whiny shit, but this holiday brings out the worst in me. I hate the pressure of how one night is supposed to set the tone for the entire following year. Superstition dictates that if you have a lousy New Year's Eve, the whole year will inevitably follow suit, and I just don't buy it. I hate going to overcrowded clubs or parties, then during the countdown at midnight I stand around like, *yep, don't mind me. I'll just be awkwardly blowing my noisy party favor over here while everyone else happily explores each other's tonsils.* In a way I know damn well that everyone else's celebration is just as full of alcohol infused forced joviality as mine. This year is sure to be more of the same.

No matter what size clothing you wear, you've had that night when you're getting ready to go out, and you can't find anything that fits. Let alone makes you feel good about yourself. This is that night for me and, of course, there's the added holiday pressure. I'm supposed to go out dancing with Britta, my adorable—sure to be in something cute—friend, and a few other close friends who insist that this time it will be fun. Attempting to get ready has me a ball of frustration and fear. Sexy as an aesthetic goal seems almost unreachable at this point. And it's New Year's Eve, the holiday I hate the most. I may have mentioned that.

I'm not allowed access to the exclusive *sexy clothes club* because my number is *too* high. My clothing size or my weight, or a combination of both. Choose which ever number you like. The world has told me in a million ways they're both too high. Tonight's struggle is a case in point, finding cute clothes that fit is a feat on par with climbing Kilimanjaro, for instance. I'm just not an *acceptable* number. For some reason clothing designers seem to think if you're a fat woman, then you must be inordinately fond of polyester or huge floral prints. It is damn near impossible to find anything without those two ever-endearing qualities. Add to that the fact that I live in *Alaska*—not exactly a hotbed of haute fashion for anyone—much less for a fat woman.

I like sleeveless dresses and form-fitting skirts as much as the next girl, so why are my only fashion options housedresses or polyester pants? Are the floral prints meant to help me blend into the sofa? Is that, the natural assumed habitat of the fat woman, thus she can disappear out of sight? I feel either invisible to most of the world, or inversely singled out by people who want to make my body a joke, or by uninformed dipshits who are *concerned for my health*. What they are actually concerned with is how my body makes them uncomfortable and somehow that's supposed to be my problem.

"Crikey Jim, look we have a fat girl in the wild!" I'm not proud of the fact that sometimes I narrate in my head, but at least the voice is modeled after a Hemsworth, so I have *that* going for me. In my mind he's whispering to the cameraman in front of him as he peers…

*"Look how her thighs bulge as she sits, and the giant pink flowers of her housedress blend seamlessly with the fabric of her sofa as she watches Netflix. Shhhh, careful; they're notoriously bitchy when disturbed. If we don't startle her we might just get to see the actual moment where she totally gives up on life and literally becomes the sofa. Wait, her thinner, attractive best friend has called and needs cheering up, she doesn't give up on life today Jim, **not today.**"*

I don't understand it. I like to go out dancing just like anyone else-- especially not wearing something made of highly flammable fabric that looks like tired curtains at the local hospice. Maybe that's the point of fat girl clothes, to send a message: Flammable. Stay away. Watch out for this one. My size might be contagious. Looking at me might burn your retinas.

In what I am sure will come to be known as my annual New Year's Eve mental breakdown, I settle for a black polyester shirt, slacks and a pre-game shot of vodka. Sometimes a girl needs liquid courage.

Nothing goes with vodka quite like highlighter, so I brighten up my favorite parts of my face with quick pats. I'm going to cling to my pretty, highlighted face like a talisman tonight. Unfortunately, short of wearing a tarp wrapped around my whole body with the words *look up here*, and an arrow pointing to my face, there is only so much highlighting of a face that is possible. If I had a dollar for every time someone told me, "But you have *such a pretty face*," I'd be celebrating New Years in Dubai, not Anchorage, Alaska.

It's ten o'clock when we arrive at the club. The place is dark enough for dancing confidently but light enough to still feel cautious. Amongst the sweaty throngs of dancers and drunks is a mirrored wall. I kid you not. An entire wall, of *mirrors*. It's like the least enjoyable fun house ever built, with the added bonus of beer-soaked floors, and sweat smell. The bar pulsates with current pop hit remixes from whatever random white girl is currently appropriating black music for her *bad girl* phase album, before returning to *innocent ingenue* for her next one, to make a buck. *Lucky me.*

There is nowhere a single girl in her twenties wants to be more on New Year's Eve than at her local dive bar. Clad in layers of girdle-like clothing and polyester that doesn't breathe. Surrounding herself with skinny friends gives her the opportunity to use the go-to move on the dance floor, the *fat girl shuffle*. Don't pretend you don't know what dance I'm referring to. You've done it or you've seen it happen. I try to suck my horribly offending already *Spanx*-clad stomach in, hold my arms down so that they don't jiggle and knock innocent bystanders to the floor, causing fatalities. I tuck in my multiple chins and shake my booty. In my heart I'm shaking everything my mama gave me. In reality, however, I want to be anywhere else in the world—like on my couch with a good book. I hate New Year's Eve.

Every woman has two voices in her head, if she's lucky. I have more. The voice taking over tonight is the one I hear more often than not lately. She criticizes and points to the *wrong*. Louder and more affirmative, the voice comments when I catch a glimpse of myself in the mirror. I resent the shit out of this particular voice, it's not sexy like the Australian one. I begrudge the fact that I don't feel comfortable because I'm dressed like an eighty-year-old woman. I'm shoved into shapewear when I don't *want* to be, all for the purpose of avoiding judgment. Is it too much to ask to dance without a fucking care, and pretend

New Year's Eve is awesome, like the rest of these assholes who don't get nutrition and diet tips from strangers?

As this was going through my mind I thought back to a conversation I had with my bestie, Britta, the previous week. She's a fitness competitor with a body you could bounce a quarter off of, and a habit of counting the calories in my glass of wine while discussing squats. She said, "Tisa, I love you but you are really fat right now." *Brutal.*

Why do people find it important to remind fat people that we are fat? I promise you, it's a known fact we carry our bodies with us—*everywhere*. I have mirrors in my house and I have a pretty good grasp on what I look like, just as any fat girl you point out their weight to. We are reminded daily everywhere what the world thinks of our bodies. I can't even watch television without a weight loss ad every five minutes this time of year. If I hear the phrase *New Year, New You* one more damn time during a break from *Black-ish* I'm going to scream. Discussing my body with others seems like a waste of time.

Britta had seen the finale of a weight loss reality TV show called *Less Is More!* Ah, now this is starting to make sense. "You can win it," she told me while setting consecutive personal bests on lunges *and* pitching me the idea of applying.

"Mmmph," I replied through a mouth full of—what was no doubt—lettuce.

"Really Tisa, they're in desperate need of a female winner, and I've seen you before… uh…" She threw me a critical glance between wall sits in the living room while I looked on from the kitchen table, "well, before whatever this is that you have going on here. You lose weight almost as fast as any guy can."

The shock of her suggestion caused me to choke on a particularly feisty bite of salad that was clearly out to get me. I wanted to tell her that I don't care about losing weight right now. What matters is taking a break from the constant homework, two jobs and the endless aerobics classes I was teaching until I got my Bachelor's degree. I was rather proud for killing it on the LSAT after studying for months, and having been awarded a full scholarship to law school in the fall. It's like she thinks I've been doing nothing but speed eating Snickers for the past six months and binge-watching Netflix. Didn't I deserve a break?

"Did I mention there is a two hundred and fifty-thousand-dollar prize?" she continued.

She looked at me while I looked at the lettuce I was eating and decided firmly that Ben and Jerry's ice cream, while avoiding this conversation, would've been a far better choice.

Two hundred and fifty thousand dollars—sure, that's not *too* shabby. However, I've never been motivated by money or competition. When someone insists they are better at something than I am, my initial reaction is to tell them *congratulations* and move on.

I glanced over at Britta. "Hey there bestie of like, forever…when have you ever seen me give a shit about money or *winning* anything?"

She stopped planking long enough to meet my face with a defiant glare. "Yeah, you may not care about money, but you know who does? The holder of your student loans—Uncle Sam."

She had a point. I was concerned about the debt, but was postponing it for now. "I'll worry about that after law school." Britta realized she had lost me to Ben and Jerry's and resumed her Romanian deadlifts instead. Whatever she was doing looked painful.

My reflection in the mirror at the club brought me back to the moment. I looked spent by the beauty routines I had gone through just to come out tonight, in an effort to not have my humanity and sexuality dismissed because of my size. All the squeezing and waxing, painting and plucking were exhausting. Not to mention, all those products and my drinks cost money that I legitimately, as a student, did not have. I feel sexy, I feel amazing, I'd like to be treated as such and I would also like to not be in crippling debt after law school. What if I did do the show? I made a command decision right then and there: The next morning I'd bust out a video camera and make a taped audition of myself to send to the show. And that choice called for vodka.

Vodka and I also wouldn't scoff at getting laid tonight. I abandoned the mirror wall along with my ruminations, and head to the bar. The hot girl who saw my sexy version of shuffling was there, talking to another girl, but still threw the occasional glance at me. I guess those nuances were coming off me in droves, because she seemed to be picking up on them. I was working my magic. I got a vodka water from the bartender and surveyed the woman while I sipped my drink. She was tall, blonde, and from what I could tell, probably never missed a Workout of the Day at her CrossFit box. To be fair, she *was* wearing a t-shirt with the local Box's logo on it tipping me off…which only irritated me slightly when I thought about the nap she probably took before just throwing on that t-shirt, while I wrestled in war paint and a push up bra, and yet she *still* looked delicious. I imagined her on top of me, and I guess I got lost in that thought for a second, because suddenly I realized I was staring at her, and she was looking back at me. I caught myself. Then I smirked, both in my embarrassment at directly staring at the woman I was fantasizing about, and because I knew I looked damn good tonight (regardless of the annoyance it took to get there, and how it might have been even more spectacular with other wardrobe options, the finished product was still pretty damn hot). I wanted to flirt. I sipped more vodka and soda, aiming for highly suggestive and completely willing vibes while I continued making eye contact with her. She flashed a crooked smile that didn't hurt her chances any. I was already moving toward her before I thought much of it. She looked mildly surprised that I was gutsy enough to approach her. She recovered from the surprise, and fixed me with an anticipatory look that suddenly made me resent my lack of wardrobe options even more, I wanted to be wearing the cutest curve hugging little black dress right now with the way she was looking at me. I wanted those eyes to see more of me. And mine more of her because what I could see was tall, broad, tan and very well built.

"Hey," I said, sidling up to her. "Come here often?" There wasn't ever a time where corny didn't score points, plus I can tell she's already about me and pretty much anything intelligible is going to do the trick here.

"I never leave. They glued me to this chair three years ago; I've lived on bar nuts and appletinis ever since," she replied, and I couldn't help but chuckle. Touché, hot girl. Touché. She cracked another crooked smile, and I noticed her lips were full. Tall, with full lips *and* wit. So far, so good.

I segue into the standard half hour-ish of small talk that social decorum demands when you're out and spot someone you want to take home and ring in the New Year with, by riding them like a carnival ride but would be scolded for saying so directly. I ask questions about her and should be listening closer to the answers, but I'm lost in the sexual vibes she's giving off. She has tattooed forearms attached to a pretty well sculpted form—which is quite alright with me. While she cast the occasional glance at my shape, I felt out the prospects for the rest of this night. I was right, she was into me and she was definitely as hot as she appeared from across the bar.

I order another vodka soda and bought her a drink too. I move closer to her to hand her drink to her, and I notice her thigh brushes mine. I casually place my hand on her thigh. She puts her hand on my mine, and I squeeze. Our eyes meet and we both wordlessly agree where things are going tonight. My hand is pretty far up her thigh, giving her the courage to reach up and cup my face with one hand and glance at me with admiring eyes. For starters, I want her tongue in my mouth. As I lean in, I push my body against hers and our lips meet. Her arms embrace me, as she holds me close. My hands are still on the top of her thighs, and I feel the immediate response in her intensity to our kiss. She is a good kisser. Those full lips—definitely worth it. The kiss alone is doing things to me as well, and when we finally separate, I ask her if she wants to go somewhere else.

We weren't far from the countdown when I find Britta and tell her I'm leaving.

"What? Leave? It's ten to midnight." she said, looking at me like I'm doing it to personally offend her.

"I know! I'm sorry, but, uh, something's come up." I replied. She keeps staring at me for another few seconds, until it dawns on her.

"Oh right, I see. Well, a girl's gotta do what a girl's gotta do." she quips. "When you have the chance, jump at it."

"I am. I'll see you later." I said, as I start to move away from her and the other girls we had met up with for the night. The hot girl was outside finding us a cab and I wanted to get to her as fast as possible, lest she might disappear like a fairy, or the cusp of a dream almost remembered.

"You will. Happy New Year." she calls after me.

"Oh, it's going to be." I shout back, and then I'm out in the dark cold Anchorage night, trying to search for the girl who made the night interesting. There she stood at the curb with the door open to a Lyft. As I make my way over to her, I shuffled in, and scoot over. When she slid into the seat next to me, I tell the driver my address and we were are on our way. Once we were moving, I wasted no time. I leaned over and told her what my intentions were for the rest of the evening. She confirmed hers matched mine with the hottest look I've ever seen in anyone's eyes. I put my hand in her lap and massaged her as we started making out. She put her hand on my thigh, and I curse internally because I know the shape wear underneath my clothing is going to require scissors, or gymnastics to get out of later. As she runs her lips down my neck I can feel my skin begin to prickle with excitement. The need for more slams into me like a piano falling from a ten-story window, but I know we must get home first. The breaths escaping my chest are more, pants at this point. I slide my fingers under her shirt and, holy fuck, the feel of her abs, coupled with the slight curvature of her body, is incredible. She had taken her hand off my thigh and was tracing my curves with her finger tips.

The driver was surprisingly nonchalant about it all, then again, he was doing the bar run on New Year's Eve. I'm sure he's seen more than I could imagine. We had arrived at my house and I got out of the car with her following closely. I was at the door unlocking it when she caught up with me, wrapped her hands around my body while pulling me back against her, kissing my neck again. Her hands found me once more and I sighed.

"You feel amazing."

"Let me unlock the door, and you'll get to feel more." I unlocked the door and we stepped into the dark room. She flipped a switch and looked around before settling her eyes on me. I felt like she was devouring me with that look, and it made me ache for more. I wanted more, but I wanted to be forthright about tonight.

"Look, I don't want you to get the wrong impression," I said, knowing I might break the mood. But I wanted it to be clear right away. "I am leaving in a few months for school, and I'm not looking for anything serious. I want this, and I want you to do it well enough for me to enjoy it," I said and smirked with playful snark, "If you do that, perhaps we'll have encores later on, but that is literally all I am looking for right now." She looked at me with fascinated eyes.

"Challenge accepted." she said, simply.

"Good." I retorted and moved toward her.

What followed was a lights-on fierce frolic with a woman who reveled in my curves as much as I reveled in her angles. Not bad for a NYE hookup. She was attentive, respected my boldness in bed, and didn't object when I had gotten mine and was happily depleted.

"I'm spent. You're gonna have to finish the race carrying me," I said. She wrapped her arms around me, and I felt her abs again as she took control to meet her needs. I slid away from her and we lay there for a bit, the pleasure still resonating silently in the air with us both. She got on her elbows and caressed my body, as she looked it over with the same devouring look from earlier. Slowly tracing my curves. It felt good, but I was halfway asleep already. I got up and tugged at the covers. She got up and asked about the bathroom. I crawled deeper into bed, briefly considering if she would leave now if I called her a cab, so I could sleep in my preferred diagonal bed-hogging position, then decided I didn't mind being touched a little more. Plus calling a cab seemed like an insurmountable amount of effort right now. I was already so close to sleep. When she came back, she was still naked, crawled in bed with me, and her hands resumed their body cartography. This will do.

"Did I qualify for encores?" she questioned while chuckling after a few minutes, as her hand was brushing against my thigh.

"You did adequately." I teased.

"I'm glad I measured up." She snickered. Her hands were gently massaging me. I was slipping into sleep. "I'm Jane by the way." she said suddenly. I hadn't thought about names really, I wasn't searching for depth in this Goddess, just some fun.

"I was Tisa. You enjoyed meeting me, I promise." She laughed again.

"Happy New Year, Tisa." she said as she laid down.

"Happy New Year to you..." I mumbled passing out before finishing the sentence.

1/1/2015

Happy New Year. This morning I awoke with the intent of recording the audition video for the weight loss show Britta had mentioned. Well, as hellbent as someone with a persistent headache, and morning breath that could kill an entire barnyard of farm animals- never mind the hot girl from the club sleeping next to me that needed to be addressed.

Ever multi-tasking, I grabbed water, ordered a Lyft and spent three minutes with my mouthwash. A morning after drinking and debauchery always called for a thorough cleanse, or something like that according to GOOP and Gwyneth Paltrow. It was time to face the truth—weight loss reality TV might be an adventure, plus my schedule is open before school in the fall. And herein lies the added bonus, this future grandma will have a hell of a story for the grandkids—imagine the possibilities!

Jumping into action, I borrowed a camcorder from Britta, pressed play and readied my best, *you should hear more* face. I shared the little tidbits of information about myself that I imagined producers typically wanted to know, without really having a clue what that might be while dancing for the camera.

Against my better judgment, I shipped off the video in all its hung-over glory. Was this almost a feeling of excitement—or impending doom? Despite the odds being slim-to-none that anybody found what I'm offering interesting, I felt mysterious, and a bit *adventurous.*

3/21/2015

In customary style, I had promptly forgot about sending the video until I heard back from the producers. The email I received from the production department jogged my memory. *Did I really send a video of me hung over with leftover make-*

up on? Will I end up in some sort of intervention? Holy Jesus, will it be shown... publicly?

The email was pretty much like you'd expect from somebody in the reality TV world, aloof and weirdly impersonal.

"Tisa, we received your video. Could you give us your sizes?"

I was both surprised and instantly annoyed with the tone, and I was pretty clear about my annoyance in my reply.

"Dear Sir/Ma'am, I have lots of sizes. My eyes are medium, my wit is grand, and my mouth is big enough to compliment them both. What do you need exactly? With Eternal Affection, Tisa."

There. *That about did it.*

The next day, I received a response email, completely unfazed, and without acknowledging my brilliant wit and humor.

"Could you give us your shirt size, pant size and shoe size?"

Just as short as the first, and with hint taken, I replied.

"Sure. My pants size is 26, I wear an extra-large shirt, and while I have no idea why my shoe size is relevant to my weight, I wear a size 7."

I looked over their email, and pondered who the hell was sitting there writing these; whomever it was replied within the hour.

"Wow, you wear a size 26 pants *and only a size 7 shoe? That's a small shoe size.*"

Spunky, that one. I'm being judged on my shoe size by a faceless LA reality TV drone. My shoe size was really freakishly small in proportion to the rest of my body; that it was the first thing in this absurd email chain that warranted comment? At this point, I was incensed.

"Yeah, a size seven, I guess that is small...maybe you can see now why I find it a problem that my ass is so big that I sent in a video to be on a weight loss reality show."

Perhaps they agreed, which is why the next email was a detailed request to film a *goodbye video* at the airport, and an itinerary for my flight to Los Angeles. This is happening... I was pretty excited to have a cool story to tell, I mean how many people did I know that had been on reality TV? *Zero.* Britta was predictably ecstatic, and already spending my prize money on a tummy tuck and new boobs for me later. I was more focused on the fact the that I still didn't believe this was happening. Weren't my odds of being kidnapped better than the odds of being selected for a reality TV show?

4/16/2015

While filming the goodbye video at the airport, Britta was not above some friendly gloating. "This is going to be the best thing ever," she started with a giggle. "Just you wait. You'll get to LA and your life will *completely* change."

"Um, I like my life already."

"Of course you do, Tisa. Of course you do!" talking to herself about my *changing life* and obviously not hearing what I had just said, Britta's excitement was practically coming out of her pores. "Look at the camera. Wave."

"Britta, I don't even know why we are filming this shit, and I think my trip to LA will be short lived. A trip just short enough to learn what being rejected from reality TV feels like. I mean, the odds of being selected to actually appear on reality TV are something like one in two hundred thousand, just being flown out for an audition didn't guarantee me a spot. The odds are not good." Forever the optimist, Britta ignored my words.

"Either way, it's a trip to LA and they said to film you leaving. Maybe you could look like you miss us a little?" She was asking for a lot.

"Shut up and give me the damn camera, I have a flight to make. Besides, I'll see you in a week anyway." Friends push, that's what we do. We push for each other to have better lovers, better lives, and we push while we know we resent the pushing. I didn't resent Britta, not yet and not over this. While her optimism was puke-inducing, I loved her outlook.

I crossed the steps from carpet to plane and found my seat. I needed a seat belt extender to fit comfortably, and yet again I get the message loud and clear, world. My body doesn't fit and I'm exhausted by it. I guess that's why I'm on this plane in the first place.

I had no idea what I was signing up for. I probably wouldn't be abducted and killed, but I really have no idea what joining reality TV is like. On what felt like an endless flight to LA, spent avoiding the fifty-year-old woman next to me that wanted to show me her 500 photos of her vacation to Berlin (with 498 of those photos consisting of her posing in front of structures), I thought about how I didn't even really know what this particular reality TV program was about.

The only thing familiar was the opening theme song, and exactly three minutes of a very cute girl contestant named Tammy standing on a giant scale doing a Rockette-type leg kick. *Seems harmless enough.* Maybe this could be my opportunity to fit in, without having to think about it. To board a plane and not have to think about how I had to hit the call button for the seatbelt extender, making my body safe like everyone else's.

What do I have to lose? The money didn't *really* motivate me, but the thought of being able to shop with ease, not warrant the *health* advice of strangers, and have a bitchin' story to tell my grandkids, did. *Let's do this.*

I arrived at the holding pen, *um, hotel* in LA, after a ride filled with the sounds of *Dog Days are Over* being crooned over the car speaker. I tapped my foot and hoped it was an indication of things to come.

As soon as I walked in, a production assistant spotted me in all my glory and immediately approached. "You must be here for the weight loss show?" he inquired, sounding somewhat unsure. Perhaps he expected me to arrive, gnawing on a turkey leg, asking where I could get butter to dip it in. Most people see my fat body and make multiple assumptions, all of which boil down to some variation of gluttonous slob who doesn't care for herself, but loves cats and fast food.

True to my nature, I opened with a casual light and friendly tone, with only the smallest tinge of smartass. "No, I'm here for the gymnastics competition," I said with a smile. "Is your job just to sit here and talk to any fat person that enters the lobby looking confused? What happens if you ask the wrong fat person? You could get in a lot of trouble for that, we are stronger than we look."

Of course, he didn't think I was funny. We were off to an excellent start. He and the rest of the tepid production assistants reminded me probably a thousand times in the first few minutes, it seemed, just how lucky I was to even get to go to the *The Spa*, a magical place where fat people's dreams come true.

"There were 200,000 other fat people in line behind you," they all explained with perfectly white smiles. They seemed to say, "and if you so much as breathe incorrectly we will send you home, and you will have ruined the best thing that ever happened to you!" Oh man, what was I in for?

4/25/2015

Yet another humorless production assistant led me into an interview room where more people associated with the show were waiting. I was poked, prodded, interviewed, and measured in every way you can imagine. I had urine and blood taken, was placed in a machine whose only defining feature I could deduce was it looked like an egg, and then on another that seemed like a Xerox machine for humans. People were scribbling on clipboards, peering over half-moon glasses, whispering to each other and looking at me with critical apprehension. For the first time in my life I actually asked myself, "Am I fat *enough?*"

It was hard to know if they hated me with every fiber of their being, or loved everything I brought to the table. What's more, I didn't know which outcome I was hoping for; why the hell am I here?

4/27/2015

I was still myself in occasional moments during the process though, which means as hard as I tried, I couldn't always stop myself from cracking a joke or making a sarcastic observation. I really do realize there is a time and place, I do. But I can't help myself. Other people don't believe I know the appropriate time or place for jokes. Most of them seem to work on the production crew of this reality show.

I made the mistake of asking about flying home to Alaska if this didn't work out. Wasn't that a normal thing to say? *Apparently not.* The evil little female production assistant I affectionately nicknamed *Stalin with the Horrible Teenage Acne Well Into her Twenties and a More Glorious Mustache* lost her damn mind on me. The rigors of ordering fat people around all day must've been taxing her.

This four-foot tall dishwater blond went from zero to spittle rocketing from her pale lips like she was the hose at a wet t-shirt contest. "You better shut your mouth right now, if you let other people know where you are from or anything about yourself, you will be disqualified!" she screeched, "Do you *want* that? Do you want to ruin what is probably the best thing to ever happen to you? Do you want to go home?"

I answered in shock with my *I'm pretty sure people who are genuinely sorry look like this* face and instead of my usual response I apologized. Because, if everyone keeps saying that this is the best thing to ever have happened to me, maybe it *was.*

The production assistant from my arrival—still looking grim, came to fetch me and led me to the room where I was going to sleep. The only thing I could think was, people sure were nicer on TV.

"Here you go," the door opened and I was left without a key. I was locked either in or out- if I left, I wouldn't be able to return. What the fuck is that about? They seemed to like their contestants confused. I had this constant feeling of slight befuddlement that slowly took over my excitement.

People are just superficial enough to keep me doubting their motives, but not so much that I feel like I'm being outright mislead, maybe that's progress. It's like trying to join a clique in junior high all over again. "Tisa, *everyone* is wearing pajamas to school. Join us!" then you're the only a-hole with a side ponytail in footie pajamas at school on a random Tuesday. I won't fall for that shit again, that was uncomfortable.

A few minutes later, this is what I surmised; I have to call someone if I want to leave my room. I wanted to swim badly- so, I called to see if I could have a permission slip to go to the pool. I imagined her clad with a clipboard and frown, scouting ahead and making sure the coast was clear. We clearly were not allowed to fraternize with the other potential contestants. Was this because they didn't want too many fatties in bathing suits all in one place at one time, as that would surely have caused a rip in the space-time continuum, or something just as heinous? All I wanted to do was lay in the sun, read a book and think entirely dirty thoughts about the other night.

"No. You have to stay for your interview." Neat-o. A knock on the door about a half-hour later brought a woman who came to talk to me about how my life was about to change. It was difficult at first, to figure out who this lady was. She had an air about her of somebody who was either important, or *thought* she was.

Her hair was hipster chic, and she wore an outfit so smart that it probably had an honorary Doctorate from Yale. She had these weird beady eyes and was way paler than the women I had seen since being in California.

"Hello, Tisa, we haven't met yet, but I've heard a lot about you. I'm Allison, a producer for the show." I honestly have no idea what a producer does exactly except tell production assistants that they aren't doing anything fast enough. Allison asked briefly about my trip and stay so far, with what was clearly a passing interest. Then she moved on to encouraging me to eat. "You know, they have some really decent restaurants here in LA." she started.

"They do? I haven't really been allowed…" I replied, but was cut off before I had time to let her know I was pretty much a prisoner in this room.

"Oh yes, all the good ones; Carl's Jr. Applebee's. Denny's. Many places to get some solid meals."

I wasn't sure where she was going with this. "Ah right... all the good ones." *As though fast food was the height of my foodie appreciation, because I'm fat.*

She wasn't looking directly at me and after a beat of silence I wasn't sure if I was secretly being filmed for an ad for one of these eateries she mentioned or if she was just holding a pose before fading to black. "Like I mentioned, I haven't had much of a chance to leave my room." This didn't seem to get through to her. She turned to me and fixed her eyes on me.

"Your chances might be better if you ate something, you know before the show starts." The way her elevator gaze surveyed me as she said this, I felt as if John Connor had sent her back in time to either kill me or save me.

"Eat food with me if you want to live." should've been her opening line, with a leather clad hand extended. I understood that she was trying to help, in some twisted reality TV kind of way. I imagined she went to all the potential contestants and ran off this spiel, like she was the Witch from Hansel and Gretel, trying to fatten us up for the slaughter.

"I see," were the only words I could really muster. She seemed to decide that this particular train of thought had arrived safely at the end of the line and switched to less opaque topics some of which seemed weirdly intrusive and others oddly-detached. Like she was trying to assess how cooperative I was or how far I would be willing to go to stay in the game. Sure, her company was welcome, after lengths of time spent alone in my room with little to do, but her suggestions caused more confusion. I'm auditioning for a weight loss program. So far that has meant being yelled at, measured in weird ways and now, encouraged to eat. I should've gone to space camp instead. Freeze-dried ice cream sounded almost as good as sex. *Almost.*

Chapter 2

4/28/2015

Today is actual casting time, or as the producers seem to see it, the fat people parade. We get to go to the Spa today and the grand selection process, and ceremony will commence. We had a taste of *The Spa* yesterday, when we were all loaded up on buses and taken out there. As resorts go, it wasn't as grand as one might think. It *was* however a nice change of scenery from my hotel room, where I had spent too long in limbo between locked in and locked out. Information still wasn't being made readily available to us, and I couldn't help my mind drifting to post-apocalyptic future type scenarios in which fat people would be rounded up and put in gyms where we would never be allowed to leave just to scare the pounds off. *Treat 'em mean, get 'em lean* seems to be the going mantra.

We spent all day loafing around the property, while production shot B-roll. B-roll is all the pieces of film people see that aren't of serious consequence to the show. Fillers, basically. In this case, groups of fat people walking around wide eyed, pointing in awe at the fantastical utopian place called The Spa—where dreams come true and livestock typically reside. Seriously, *horses* live here. After several hours of wide eyes and ooh'ing and aah'ing in the blazing California sun, some of us were getting fatigued and dehydrated. Our arms were tired from all the pointing at our new surroundings. We were herded back onto buses to return to our hotels for the night.

The bus ride was particularly testy because they forgot to feed us when we arrived, or at any time today. Eventually someone in production figured out that fat people need to eat to live just like anyone else and ordered *Subway,* only not enough for everyone.

Here is food. But just enough to get your mouths watering and make you hangry. seemed to be the rationale behind this move. I thought it was a casting ploy. I imagined being led into a rodeo enclosure with a big pile of the subs in the middle where contestants duke it out like rabid wolverines until—under jubilant applause—the last man standing could eat him, or herself to death. Like *Gladiator* only with more fat people and less incest. I think that might actually be how they plan to determine the cast.

The hotel room was a welcome sight after walking around in the sun all day with no discernible point. Was B-roll all they needed? Or did they want to tire us out before the actual process, so we'd be less inclined to riot for food? Or maybe they need us to look like shit on camera to enhance the *look at the poor fatties* effect. It's hard to say because nobody tells me anything, but when the hotel room is a welcome sight, things are getting kind of bad.

4/29/2015

This morning I was woken early as fuck and made to pack all of my belongings. It was *finally* happening. I was going to be doing something productive instead of having weird conversations where I'm encouraged to eat but prevented from obtaining any food. Once again, we were herded into the damn toaster oven buses, and driven to The Spa. We were guided to the big grass field where the horses usually do their thing –I have no idea what their thing is; Dancing? Trotting? Running for office? Something. The property manager of The Spa seemed a lot less excited to have all us fat people on that grass than you would expect.

"Could you please get all these big people off the grass? They are trampling it and damaging it for the horses!"

Nice lady, that manager. She definitely understood physics and I'd be surprised if she hadn't graduated magna cum laude from MIT with a major in weight distribution, I thought sarcastically.

Oddly enough with everything going on, I spent most of my time preoccupied with the fact that I was out of underwear. Yeah, I know, no one wants to hear about my panties, but seriously I sent my shit out to the hotel laundry and it didn't come back before I left with all my stuff. How the hell am I going to get my underwear now that we had to pack everything and were told we might not be going back?

I have this habit of drifting off into fantasy when I'm bored, just like anyone else, and believe it or not taping endless B roll while having to be weirdly silent is boring as all hell. Especially the silent part. So, I spent some quality time letting this adorable dark-haired personal assistant, Daniel, take up large parts of my fantasies. This entire trip might not be a bust after all, regardless of fat camp outcomes. He spent the afternoon with us, mostly just corralling people if truth be told, but there was definite flirting going on. I'm *certain* of it. I understand that having a crush on a production member is a little cliché and a bit pathetic, but what else was I going to do with all my downtime. I'm a woman after all. And he's a cute guy. Plus, the butterflies kicked into action when he came over to talk.

"I'm putting you over here with the good-looking people," he said, as he was guiding people, and indicated an empty area to me. "Don't get any ideas." I had a few before he even mentioned it.

"Will you be coming with me?" I replied, way too coy for my own good but I didn't really care. I was bored and any conversation was better than none, let alone one with the guy I had spent time undressing in my mind. Plus, he handed me a bottle of water. I didn't see him hand *anyone else* a bottle of water. I mean, maybe I looked dehydrated to the point that I might drop dead and thus be bad press for the PA assigned to babysit me. I'm still pretty sure I look sexy as fuck in my Alaska t-shirt. He's about this ass, and that's why I'm now the proud owner of said bottle of water.

"I'll be over here in the area for guys who wish they had spent more time in Alaska." Yup. He was about this ass.

"Well if you can't go to Alaska, Alaska just came to you," I said, as I opened the bottle of water and drank in—what I really hoped was—a seductive way. I was thirsty as fuck and would've poured the water into my mouth faster than Niagara Falls if I hadn't been trying to flirt. On the plus side it was working. I knew this because Daniel took a step closer and started what would be no doubt a clever reply, when his name was screamed by another PA. He gave me an apologetic smile as he rushed off. I felt the familiar rush of attraction flow down between my shoulders but when it lingered, I realized it was just more sweat. I do have the feeling though that if I get to stay at fat camp, Daniel and I are not quite through with flirting.

Well, the trainers made their entrance. I now realize I probably should have watched more of this show before coming here. *Whoops.* The first time the contestant hopefuls met the trainers people went ape-shit. *I really should've at least caught a rerun or two of this show before signing on.* Anyway, when this little blonde trainer Shea showed up, there was this audible sigh of disappointment from the crowd. There had been another brunette trainer previously that was universally adored by fans of the show a guy from Kentucky explained to me, but everyone seemed to instantly forget their disappointment and cheered anyway. You would've thought the Beatles had arrived. The two trainers—the aforementioned blonde and a chiseled tattooed titan named Chad—started immediately putting all the hopefuls through the paces with calisthenics while walking around and surveying us like livestock. I was desperately lunging while waiting to hear about how great my hips were for breeding purposes or have somebody check my teeth to estimate my age.

"I am *NOT* fitness Barbie or a cheerleader wuss, no matter how I look!" Shea, the previously crowd disappointing bottle blonde with a ponytail who looked like she could deadlift a Buick, shouted at us, simultaneously managing to appear insensitive, offensive and narcissistic. *Cute.*

"I don't know what you think you know, but I'm here to get tough on you!" Chad barked. "I will make you work until you can't work anymore! I'm the tough trainer you are afraid of!" Uh, ok, maybe. I'm sure there are tons of tough guys out there who obsessively check their reflections in the camera while making duck face. It's not my go-to intimidating move but you never know, he might be brutal in the gym especially if it looks good for the camera.

Honestly? I was still thinking about my fucking underwear. Strange thing to be preoccupied with, I know, but doing physical activity, it was understandably back on my mind. If you have ever been a fat Alaskan girl suddenly dropped into the heat of California your underwear would be on your mind too, *trust me*. Think weapons grade chafing. I'm pretty sure I'm going to die from it if we keep doing lunges for the camera in this heat. It's a thing. I'm sure that death by chafing is a thing. Where is my underwear? Why didn't I put deodorant between my thighs? What the hell am I doing here?

When casting finally happened I got a brief idea of who each of the fourteen people that were going to be living on the Spa with me were. I think it was useless knowledge because it doesn't seem to be anything like our own ideas of ourselves. It was this weird sort of pageant introduction to one another from the trainers based on what their impressions were of us from watching us on the field doing calisthenics. I don't know about anyone else but I am definitely at my absolute best in ninety-degree heat doing exercises for the camera a billion times in a row. I hope someday to meet the love of my life in those very circumstances —smelling of farm animals and desperation while sounding like a wounded incontinent asthmatic.

Based entirely on what the trainers had to say, my new fat camp Bravo Team opponents were a ragtag bunch, as weirdly desolate and oddly desperate as I was. Desperate to understand what the fuck was going on. I don't remember all their names. Two people stood out though, Shannon from Nevada because I encountered her once before on B-roll day. I felt she had the depth of a balloon animal and she was making moon eyes at the guy from Idaho standing next to her. Farrell from New Jersey, also stood out because that poor bastard tripped and fell going up the stairs. Super awkward. There were four others too, but they didn't do anything significant enough for their names to really make it to my short-term memory.

As far as my team—the Alpha Team—goes, just from listening to Shea describe the team members when she chose us, I can tell *good judge of character* probably isn't a phrase often used to describe her. She strikes me as the kind of girl who would follow a strange man down an alley for the promise of a new puppy. She seems desperate to prove that the brunette trainer from previous seasons was a one trick pony and wouldn't be sorely missed. In my limited observation, she seems clueless from moment one.

"I chose Alaska," she said about me, "because never once did she stop smiling! That is the kind of positive attitude I want on Alpha Team!" Listen, I'm a happy person in general, but I'm not so much what you would call a *smiler*, and I'm sure as shit not a *smiler* while doing jumping jacks in ninety-degree heat with no underwear on. Shea was way off base. It wasn't a good omen. But I had been chosen. I was part of the elite group of lucky fatties that were chosen by the workout overlords to lose weight on almost live TV!

The way the game show works, my fellow Alpha Team members—three guys and three other women along with me—were competing to lose the most weight as a team against the Bravo Team. In addition to working out and weighing in, for added drama we had these things called challenges. Challenges are events where I believe contestants are tasked to do things like jump from cliffs with ropes in their teeth into churning crocodile infested waters to pull a canoe loaded with 800 pounds of ball bearings to see which team of fatties is fastest and therefore less loathsome than the others this week. There are also bizarre contests where we are tasked with eating things to get prizes. I'm not sure that's true, because it doesn't sound right. I'm pretty sure the girl, Dawn from Minnesota, a self-described *super fan* of the show, who told me this in whispered snatches of conversation during fatties on parade B-roll day was just fucking with me. When she mentioned how they kept the team names military style to inspire their troops, I knew she was off her rocker.

Dinner sucked. I realize I'm complaining about the food on what is essentially a fat farm, but it really did suck. We ran off the field triumphantly following our trainers before we were abruptly stopped. Literally just yelled at us to stop and sit down, then the trainers disappeared. The next few hours until dark all ran together for me but they involved one of the worst meals of cold beef and vegetables I have ever had, which says a lot coming from a girl who isn't known for really being a *picky* eater. Also, we still weren't allowed to speak to one another. This was killing me. Even after being chosen as cast members, because the cameras were not yet in place, we had to sit and eat in silence.

When we attempted to say hello to one another we were screamed at and reminded how we could still be "sent home at any time!" The little four-foot drill sergeant from earlier was babysitting us. They had confiscated everything we brought with us except clothing and I hadn't even told my parents what was going on yet, or gotten my underwear.

In an absurdly timid almost cartoonish voice—that I instantly resented was coming from me—I asked about contacting home, "Um, can I call my mom to tell her that I am staying in LA?"

"BE QUIET! We will take care of informing your families! You can STILL be sent home, don't think you're special just because you've been selected, things can change!" I mustered all of the assertiveness I had left after being treated like cattle for a week.

"Ok, well, I get that, but all of my things have been taken and I need to let them know where I am…plus, I'm a little concerned because I'm ninety percent certain that the PA I just saw walking by is wearing my sunglasses that you said had to be locked up for *safe keeping* and I'm not entirely…"

"What did I *tell* you??? BE. QUIET. Eat your dinner and be thankful. Do you know how many fat people want to be where you are? Gawd. How ungrateful." And with that, the last of my courage disappeared somewhere with my favorite sunglasses. *Dammit Tisa, you're lucky to be here,* I needed to remember that.

4/30/2015

I am trapped at this Spa. I'm serious. I. Am. Trapped. There's no phone, no computer, *nothing*. I'm hiding in the dark to write this, because I am damn near certain some asshole is going to yell at me *yet* again. Before my terrible dinner complete with ass chewing from a PA and after the riveting introductions involving some weird zip line antics resembling a cut-rate Cirque du Soleil the trainers chose the official cast. The rest of the hopefuls were sent home to work out by themselves and my fucked-up journey in LA-LA land has officially begun. I'm a little concerned that my tenure here might be short lived because I don't know any of these other people who were selected for this show. Also, I'm pretty sure I'm going to need my underwear *now*. I wonder if it is even stateside anymore or did they sell it to fund this show.

5/1/2015

I like people, don't get me wrong, but if I don't like you? I know right away. As for Becky on my team…we are going to have issues. I don't know about the rest of my fat camp friends but her and I? Nope. I'm not dumb enough to ignore the fact that some of it is envy. I'm pretty sure this girl has never had an obstacle in her life, she literally lives in a mansion and models for a living. I'm certain that while I've had nights full of misery and ice cream, Becky ate filet mignon and had men lined up after a heartbreak. Alright, not really, but that's how it seems to me because I'm petty and hungry.

Shea was on a roll with this whole judge of character thing when choosing people though, and she had this nugget of wisdom about Becky,

"This girl has had her head down the entire time that she has been on the field, and this is the last day she is going to walk with her head down. Because Alpha Team is going to hold their heads high and you are going to be so proud of yourself from this day forward!" With this declaration she proceeded to choose Becky. You know how annoying can come through even without verbal interaction? Meet Becky. But that was how Shea interpreted Becky, shy. Becky. The plus size model and pageant winner.

Becky of the non-stop chatter once we were actually allowed to speak that went something like, "Hey, did I mention I am a plus size model? I don't really like to talk about how I was a plus size model. Remember when I said I didn't want to talk about being a plus sized model? That's true. But I totally am. A plus size model."

Becky, was the girl that told us she mailed her beauty pageant crown in with her application to be on the show and placed a *Don't feed the Plus Size Models* T-shirt above her bed as decoration. This is a girl who so obviously did *not* want to draw attention to herself, or the fact that she was a model. Perhaps her head was down because her pageant crown had permanently damaged her neck muscles? I can totally see how Shea thought this girl had her head down the whole time and had issues with not being able to put herself out there on display. Not so much, Shea, not so much.

On a side note, I've never seen hair as big as on this girl. Do they give awards in pageants for that?

Second side note, Shea is never allowed to set me up on a blind date—I'd end up with a serial killer. "He's great Tisa, he loves long hikes, duct tape art and is something of a home video artiste." Worst judge of character, *ever*.

I'm looking around at my new cast mates and realize I have never seen any of these people before. Not in an interview, a doctor's visit, or a van ride anywhere did

I encounter any of these people before fat people B roll day. I didn't recognize any of these people because of the fourteen of us chosen, thirteen of us were in one hotel and one of us was in another. Take one wild guess who was the fourteenth person is. I am screwed. All of these people know each other peripherally from being in the same hotel and on the same buses or at the same doctor's visits. Obviously, as odd man out, the first weigh-in my team loses, I am fucking toast. They will vote me home before I can get my underwear back. On the bright side, maybe Becky can get over her timidity long enough to teach me how to pageant wave before I go.

Chapter 3

Eventually we were escorted to where the trainers were waiting and had an on-camera moment where we finally got to meet one another properly. Immediately after, the trainers happily announced that it was *weigh-in time*. I'd only seen the show one time when Britta was telling me I should audition. Again, what the fuck was I thinking? I thought for some reason that the scale I saw on TV was real, because it's TV, *right*? Why would they lie? How silly of me. The scale is a giant prop that was rolled out from behind a false wall in the gym. I realized that the show's gym was where my first attempts at acting were going to take place. First lesson, pretend this is actually a gym. It looks like the most luxurious place anyone could dream of to work off that extra 250 pounds you're carrying around on your ass. In reality, it is a temporary structure with no air conditioning in the middle of a desert. Please take a moment and imagine the smell of this gym where fourteen people who take up space will be working out for two to eight hours a day. The odor alone could have violated articles in the Geneva Convention. Guess what else it doesn't have? A *bathroom*. It's a damn good thing I am an Alaskan girl and have mastered the art of the squat.

Tonight, we spent almost seven hours in the so-called gym getting on and off the stupid fake scale pretending to be surprised. The women did this humiliating little farce in spandex shorts and sports bras while the men were allowed to wear T-shirts until their time to weigh-in. It dawned on me during the entire charade that the real scale was the cattle scale they put me on in my hotel room after Mag came to my room and encouraged me to eat. That conversation makes a little more sense now.

I'm amazed at the depth of emotion I'm seeing when my compatriots weigh in. There is shock and tears. Literal *tears*. Are you fucking kidding me right now? Shannon, she of the moon eyes focused on Blake from Idaho was the most ridiculous. She had tears streaming down her face when the number popped up and a look of bewilderment. Seriously though, did you really not know your weight? What in the actual fuck. Give me a break, every fat person here, unless you've made it past regular scales into livestock scale territory, knows exactly what they weigh down to the damn decimal. I don't know about anybody else but I don't exactly forget I'm fat. How the fuck can you possibly forget your size when people are happy to point it out as though it was the only distinguishing characteristic you possess? I'm pretty sure I could get into a tragic yachting accident losing both arms and legs, and half my fucking skull and some bitch would ask me if I lost weight when I ran into them again at a high school reunion. As though everything else was perfectly harmonious in my appearance but the size of my ass was the only concerning matter. Whatever Shannon, when you once again walk amongst laymen, that performance might impress. We're experts in weighing in here, you aren't fooling anyone.

We also stood on platforms as teams while the cameras were rolling to get footage of us watching the weigh in. What was strange about the whole thing was all the filming happened when no one was weighing in. We were staring into space at two in the morning while pretending to weigh-in at least three times and we are all exhausted. Production has us all stand there reacting to imaginary weigh ins. We are not allowed to speak, we are not allowed to move, and we are not even allowed to stand comfortably, which makes for what I have to assume is awesome *bitch face* footage. Lucky, for me I was born with my own bitch face.

I am incredibly self-conscious in nothing but a sports bra and spandex. To top it off, I have a nervous habit where I sweat like a pig no matter what I weigh.

In an attempt to temper my humiliation, I tried to stand with my arms protectively crossed over my chest, because in addition to nervous sweating my nipples are standing at attention in this stupid sports bra

"Tisa! Arms down, *now!*" Became my full name for the duration. I entertained myself with a fantasy that this is how a fat camp rebellion might have been instigated in a parallel universe. "Don't move!", "Put your arms down!", "Stare straight ahead!"—Until some crazed person just says *fuck it* and rampages for a carbohydrate.

I'm a little baffled they're taking hours of footage of us staring into space pissed off and tired with nothing going on at a weigh in. It's two a.m. and I am freezing. It may have been 113 degrees during the day, but it's 50 degrees tonight, which is quite a swing when your only protection against the elements is a sports bra and your body fat. Believe it or not, fat girls still get cold like other humans. My fucking nipples could cut glass, I'm sure that'll thrill the PG audience at home.

Eventually we finished the and moved as a group up to the house where we would really be staying. Time to enjoy the four hours of sleep we will be getting.

5/3/2015

Holy Shit. The first workouts involved a lot of exertion and vomiting. I'm not a doctor but I do know that taking people who have never worked out consistently and having them work out until they puke is probably not a good thing. I'm pretty concerned about my feet bleeding through my shoes. I wonder if that's a problem like the vomiting.

During one of the first workouts this week, the gym is set up for convenient filming but not really for safe working out. Because of this, as Shea was having us do some circuit training, a dumbbell managed to roll under my right foot and I twisted my ankle. Awesome, so not only am I that girl no one knows, I'm also fucking limping now. I wonder if I get to actually see a doc for this shit. Doctors are awesome when your body hurts. You know what else would be awesome. Food. Food would be awesome.

5/4/2015

I am going to cut a bitch. I am so fucking tired and our resident plus size model makes me want to scream. This girl is all naked ambition to parlay this reality show shit into super stardom. She waltzed around introducing herself to every single member of production like they were a possible agent. It was like a minnow retreating from a great white. If it weren't so pathetic it would've been hilarious… or I guess if she weren't so damn annoying it would've been hilarious.

As if that wasn't annoying enough, Becky has another awesome little habit. We are getting next to no sleep at night and Becky has this habit of getting up almost two hours early in the mornings so that she can do her hair and makeup before we go to the gym to work out. Let me just go over that point again for the cheap seats, *she gets up two hours early. To do her hair and makeup. To go to the gym.* She showers, blow-dries and straightens her hair, does her makeup, and then curls the hair she has just straightened. Perhaps I've always been lazy about my hair, but I cannot for the life of me understand the point of this. Then she goes to work out in the not-air-conditioned fake gym in the desert heat. A few days of sharing a room with her and I've had enough of hearing her alarm go off before four a.m., and then hearing her dink around the room to get camera ready, I lost my sleep deprived mind.

I get that people want to look their best. It's TV with millions of viewers, but when you are working out more hours in the day than you are sleeping, sleep is at a premium. I'm not proud of how annoyed I am—and the other girls sharing the room are just as irritated as me, only they are nicer than me. So, last night when she was setting her pre-four a.m. wake up call, I asked her, "What time are you getting up?"

Becky surveyed me briefly, "Early."

I was not pleased with the vague answer and she knew I wasn't. I was not prepared to be the bigger person and let this go. "I get that you are getting up early Becky, you get up early every day, but it is almost one a.m. now. So the question is, how early are you setting that alarm for?" I said, pointing accusingly at the clock she had been fiddling with.

"Mmmshd." Becky replied, turning away to avoid my near homicidal stare.

"I'm sorry? What time was that? What time is Mmmshd Becky?!?"

She turned toward me, trying to muster the little assertiveness she had left. "Four a.m."

It was then that I lost my mind.

"The hell you are. If you set that alarm and wake this room up one second before six a.m. so help me. I swear I will shove that alarm clock so far up your ass Captain Hook will forever fear you!"

She slept in the common room. I'm pretty sure her and I are not going to be running across any dewy flowery meadows hand in hand anytime soon. I wonder whatever will I do with the two halves of a whole heart necklaces I ordered us.

5/8/2015

The troubles with Becky have continued and for a change, I am not the only one annoyed. This whole first week of filming—the days we film the weekly episodes are not a week apart, I've started to lose track of time—there have been issues with her *outside* of the alarm clock fiasco. Becky managed to piss off the entire team at least twice. The first time she worked her magic, we were on a tour of the kitchen. She approached Bruno, a cop from Colorado. I watched casually from the sidelines as the rest of the women on the Alpha Team overheard Becky tell him, "In this game you want to think ahead and you need to pay attention to the fact that there are more girls than guys on our team. If we lose the first weigh-in you better start thinking about what woman you want to get rid of or what woman would make the perfect alliance partner." If she'd had a mustache, I'm pretty sure she would've twirled it here.

I mean, she's right, and that was good advice. It's just that her timing sucks and she sure as shit didn't read the dude before approaching him. Which surprises me not at all from her previous agent hunting on set and being oblivious to people literally scrambling to get away from her. Everyone is still trying to survive the grueling workouts and filming schedule, no one is ready to think about strategy yet. She just comes off like a team splitting asshole with this move. The vibe is a complete focus on working hard and finding a way to cope with how sore and fucking tired we are. I stared at Bruno looking befuddled and unimpressed with Becky when Debbie, one of the other women on the Alpha Team who clearly overheard the conversation too, caught my eye and raised her eyebrows.

Debbie is an intense rugby playing competitive woman with three small kiddos from Tennessee who looks like America and apple pie had a baby. White blonde hair—apparently strategically manufactured by production who had come to her hotel room and dyed her hair before casting, according to her—big blue eyes and a smile full of teeth that seemed impossibly white that helped win her Miss Congeniality at her state fair as a teenager. She projected innocence in that southern white girl way, confusing her prey because she was actually a fierce predator. Her mornings had also been cut short by the sound of Becky's alarm clock chiming off two hours before necessary and it was taking its toll. There wasn't a lot of bullshit surrounding Debbie and although she had that disarming face of a cherub, she had the mouth of a sailor. In my opinion this was a plus. I always trust people who use the word *fuck* more than I trust those that say *fudge* when they're pissed off, so this trait endeared her to me, making her likable in a milieu that made bullshit the rule more than the exception. Debbie had been heavy her entire life unlike some of us who had yo-yo dieted our way here and was preoccupied with a concern about her eating habits. She had a fondness for what she affectionately termed all the *white trash treats*. When pressed for a definition she told me that it meant, *pretty much any of the fine cuisine you can pick up at your local gas station.* She was staring daggers at Becky who was still pestering Bruno, while we listened to some spiel about how the stove worked in this kitchen that cost more than any house I had ever lived in. If Becky's early morning routine had any upside it was, that it brought the other Alpha Team women Debbie, Esther and myself together with our mutual hatred of alarm clocks and plus size models from Georgia who insisted on their use at four a.m. It's hard to believe Becky couldn't have predicted that outcome, what with being so keen on playing the game and forming alliances like she was with her furtive whispering right now. I appreciate the camaraderie forming with Debbie and Esther, regardless of the circumstances that spawned it. After the hotel stay where I was threatened with ritual slaughter if I opened my mouth, it was nice to have some people to talk to who weren't associated with the production or telling you to shut the fuck up all the time.

If you ask Becky she would probably tell you I am the meanest bitch in the world for how I treat her on the Spa, and I can't really argue because I believe Miss Manners probably takes issue when you threaten to shove someone's alarm clock up their ass with a snide comment. Watching Debbie light into Becky tonight when Bruno and the girls of the Alpha Team confronted her about being a *game playing pain in the ass that needed to focus more on running in the gym then running her mouth*, I know if I had been Becky, I probably would have cried. Instead, Becky just hated *me* more for it. Of course, she did.

Esther on the other hand tried to be more diplomatic in handling Becky. Esther was the most religious of the three Alpha Team girls who had bonded, which doesn't take much really. I know houseplants that are probably more religious than me, but she was. Perhaps finding some kind of benevolent deity in your life imbues you with the ability to be diplomatic even in the face of horrendous personalities like Becky. I probably won't ever find out. Esther is from Delaware where she left behind a wife and two kids to be here in Spa heaven with the rest of us. Her path on to the show had been riddled with difficulties. She had to leave care taking of her two her kids to her wife, a woman whose job required a lot of travel. She also had to leave the business she built on her own in her assistant's hands. Getting to *The Spa* required a lot of sacrifice for her, and she wasn't about to tolerate petty crap messing it up. Perhaps being privy to all the small grievances involved in running your own business had given her the necessary means to handle people being shitty. She did her best to stay friendly with Becky, but Becky had pissed everyone off with that damn alarm clock and made it increasingly difficult for anyone to stay friendly with her. Esther sort of happily nodded along while Debbie read Becky the riot act and Bruno looked confused.

We have our first challenge coming up soon. Challenges are bizarre semi athletic events where we humiliate ourselves for prizes as far as I can tell. At this point the Bravo Team is this big cohesive happy family and the Alpha Team fights so fucking much it feels like we are the living embodiment of Katy Perry and Taylor Swift throwing shade on Twitter. While incredibly entertaining from the outside, it's an absolute train wreck for us. On top of all the petty bickering—before you judge, you try being nice while not eating or sleeping for a few days—we don't really click with our trainer, Shea. Shea tries really hard to bring us together by coming up with team cheers or asking questions about us. It's awkward and sort of fails when half of us are staring daggers at one another in mistrust thanks to the plotting and scheming gone wrong of our plus size model extraordinaire. My team is basically Taylor Swift trying to hangout with Nicki Minaj.

Production likes exploiting the living hell out of our discord and constantly seeks to stir shit up. They can tell we are not, at this point, happy with Shea as our trainer. I'm not happy because our personality styles do not mesh well *at all*. Questions like "Why do you think Shea doesn't like how you dress?" asked by production during interviews, while I logically realize they're probably completely made up, don't really help when I like her about as much as I like cotton candy. Cotton candy looks like it's going to be awesome every time but in reality it's just a gross sticky mess. I can be an opinionated, aggressive, bitch and Shea, though it's cute when she tries to be, is not. She looks like she could crush beer cans in one of her palms, but honestly? I think she would bitch about how she might chip a nail if someone asked her to. She might even complain that the angle is wrong for her face type; she is *that* kind of girl. That doesn't mean I'm receptive to the team splitting shit I see subtlety happening in all my private on camera interviews with production. Production deliberately asks questions designed to make me question Sheas commitment to Sparkle Motion. Sorry, Team Alpha. As far as I can tell the rest of my team aren't thrilled with her simply because they had been fans of the show's earlier seasons and expected Jasmine, *the wonder-brunette*, which puts Shea in a tough spot. I luckily have no idea who Jasmine is—having never watched the show —so there are no comparisons from me. I get to dislike her solely for her.

5/9/2015

Today is our first challenge. I'm literally nauseated at the thought. Being in the gym and having cameras on you when you are in your room or sleep is tricky enough when you're used to a life of anonymity. At least it's things I've done before so I can somewhat relax. Doing a challenge—where I have to be on new and unknown ground—involving my physical abilities with others depending on my performance and cameras rolling is a whole other ballgame. Today's challenge is an obstacle course across a bridge. Sounds simple enough, right? means we have to scale a series of walls that become progressively higher as you go. I have no idea who thought running a bridge in ninety-degree heat and scaling twelve-foot walls was a good idea, but I want to throat punch the asshat. I'm sure it was hilarious to watch though. There's nothing like fat people struggling to bring on a chuckle or two. I'm looking forward to a challenge where I am buried alive with rats or have to eat a spider.

My internal dialogue of, *Oh, I'm sure the doctor is here today, cause I'm out of shape and running in 100 degrees while climbing 14-foot walls,* and *please don't vomit in fear* prompted me to look for the doctor as I scanned the bridge. Silly me. Nope. No doc. Why would I think that a doctor monitoring this event might be necessary in a place where people keep telling me my fatness means imminent death? There is however, a sports trainer here I was introduced to when my alarm at not seeing the original doctor from tryouts anywhere on set started to annoy one of the PAs. The trainers name is Malik. *Doc* Malik. Like a Doc Holliday type doc only with no pistols and less tuberculosis, not an actual MD. Probably nicknamed thus as to lull us fatties into a false sense of security, *Doc Malik is here. So, when I pass out in the heat, he will be able to give me a tonic and some leeches to clear me right up.*

He genuinely seems sensible enough but then again, I'm about to run across a bridge in scorching heat while climbing walls, so what the hell do I know about sensible? I was standing around waiting to pee for what felt like the sixteenth time since arriving at the bridge (I'm a nervous urinator, along with the nervous sweating it's almost like a really disgusting superpower) and we struck up a conversation.

"Hi, I'm Doc Malik." he started. As good an opener as any.

"Hello, I'm Tisa. Pleased to meet you." I responded as innovatively. Small talk always starts off really wooden, at least I hadn't mentioned the weather yet. Noticing my anxiety, he continued with a genial smile that instantly comforted me and eased my nausea.

"I know it seems rough out here today." It seemed so unlike how the rest of the crew spoke to me and it kind, of made me forget I still had to pee. "They try to keep you on your toes, and throw curveballs at you a lot. Are you doing ok?"

He made me feel like whatever was coming wasn't going to be something I couldn't do. "I am doing ok," I said half hoping, half believing. "I appreciate you taking time to check on me." I genuinely did. Not a lot of people besides Daniel—the hot PA of my fantasies—had spoken to me as anything but an object to be used as needed so far, so this was nice. Even Daniel had motives that could be construed as less than neutral, but I forgave them as mine were equally as wicked. Doc Malik seems like a person who sincerely cares about us as humans, not just contestants.

"I don't want you to feel like you are risking your health any more than necessary," Doc Malik told me as he flashed a knowing smile. "I am going to be around and now that you know who I am, you should also know that I am always willing to have a heart to heart about anything you feel is going on. I have a few nifty things for that ankle you're favoring and what I assume are nasty blisters causing that blood on your shoes."

It nearly brought a tear to my cynical eye. Feeling desolate and isolated for days upon end, despite being surround by people—people who aren't directly mean but also aren't precisely nice—makes meeting a friendly face a big deal.

"I will! Thank you so much Doc," I answered, fighting the urge to awkwardly hug him. I settled for a weird half fist bump, half handshake thing.

"Of course. Good luck," Doc Malik said as he smiled at me again and moved on. As he left my vicinity I remembered I had to pee again, and while the nausea made a return as well, it felt a lot less significant now.

I had the privilege of meeting A.C. Moss at today's challenge. Moss is the male counterpoint to the female producer that was trying to fatten me up for slaughter in my hotel room. He can sense weakness like a vulture (I think he smells it on people). He sees the potential for drama that the split in our team has, and he worked some Hollywood dark magic at the challenge.

Trainers are not allowed at challenges. So, during the endless wait in vans that is the prelude to every soul crushing challenge moment ahead, A.C. Moss came and spoke to the Alpha Team. I have no idea precisely what this man's job is. I know his title is *producer* but that doesn't really explain things to me. I have only seen him once during an interview before I was cast, then again when we asked where our paychecks were. Those two moments were enough for me to dread dealing with him again. When he is around I swear the temperature drops and something walks over my future grave. His only task seems to be to sow discourse among the contestants, or to claim that *accounting errors* are responsible for whatever no man's land our three hundred-dollar weekly paychecks are currently residing. Today's pre-challenge conversation was all about how he knew we weren't happy with our trainer and if that was true then we should do everything we could to get rid of her. We were all confused, but he said if team members could be forced to leave, *why not vote off your trainer?* You can imagine how this conversation did nothing to unite us *or* encourage us to work with Shea.

Even if we were a dysfunctional team—and we certainly were—with evil wizard A.C. Moss trying to mastermind an epic shitstorm, we kicked ass in today's challenge. Holy shit we were a cohesive team today, it was amazing. Bruno in particular was a star today getting each of us over those walls. I think his ability to focus had something to do with the inherent difficulty in giving significance to petty drama when you're desperate to win. Or maybe Bruno was still pissed off about all the team infighting when his arm was half way up my fat ass throwing me over that fourteen-foot wall and that's what motivated him. So much for the shit talking from Bravo Team that we were lazy, huh? Who is lazy now motherfuckers? Ok, I'm a little fired up. It was nice to actually work together as a team though. And to show Mr. Moss that his drama incitement doesn't fly around Alpha Team. Unless it's our own drama, of course.

5/10/2015

This was weird today. I cannot for the life of me remember anytime at this Spa when I have been advised by my trainer to take a nap or have had the time to take a nap, yet production told us that they needed footage of us going to sleep, so we had to crawl in and out of our beds pretending to wake up and go to sleep today. Why in the world would we need footage of us sleeping during the day when I barely sleep at night? Getting out of bed, stretching and yawning? Or climbing in and getting comfy under a blanket? Makes no sense to me.

As I've pointed out repeatedly, Shea is new and you can tell she is totally trying to figure out how things work around here. Chad seems completely unsympathetic to her. Maybe there is some animosity because he was fond of Jasmine? I don't know but it's like watching *Mean Girls* when they interact sometimes. I'm totally waiting for him to try to make *fetch* happen. Don't get me wrong, I don't adore her either, but damn, I didn't realize how competitive the trainers were on shows like this. Shea seems a bit clueless but Chad has made it perfectly clear to our team and his own, that he doesn't respect her, at all. Despite vastly different backgrounds, we are in this together. I suppose that is what team mentality is about and if it hadn't been for Becky and today's challenge, I don't know if I would have felt the same way.

5/23/2015

Second weigh-in is tonight, it's been twelve days since our first one. I was under the impression that the weigh-ins were exactly a week apart. I can't imagine where I got that impression when production keeps telling us to exclaim how surprised we are at our *one-week* weight loss when we are on the giant fake fucking scale. I guess production says it's something to do with filming schedule so the weigh-ins will be at lots of different times. All this means to me really is that tonight is another night of hours of filming in tight ass super flattering spandex shorts and a sports bra. Our real weigh-in took place early this morning on a cattle scale. It wasn't that bad but we all had to dehydrate, and that was a misery I've never experienced before.

Our trainers forbade their teams from drinking any water for up to 24 hours before a weigh-in, even though we were working out for hours in that un-air-conditioned gym in the desert. Those who couldn't take it would swirl water around in their mouths and spit it out. If I had put any water in my mouth down the hatch it would've gone, so none for me this morning. I have to give Shea credit, apparently, she knew that dehydration had been used in all the seasons before ours to get the desired results at weigh-ins and didn't agree with this behavior. In an attempt to stop this and make this season healthier, I watched Shea try to strike a deal with Chad to not dehydrate. Unfortunately, this agreement lasted only the amount of time it took for Chad to tell her "Yes," then fuck her over.

As the Alpha Team was getting its final workout in, Shea watched Chad working his team out and noticed that he had cut their water intake. She came over and apologized to our team.

"I don't know what to say guys," she started remorsefully, shrugging her shoulders. "Bravo Team has cut their water intake, so you won't stand a chance if you don't also."

What bullshit. It's already 100 degrees in here and there is so much sweat from people working out so hard that it makes the climate of the gym feel like a swamp and we are still cutting water.

"I can't believe it," Debbie mumbled as she dragged her feet back to the treadmill.

Shea looked defeated and I felt a brief moment of genuine sympathy for her, then remembered that I was the one who had to work out with no water. Shea further distanced herself from sympathy when she reminded us that *The Spa* was probably our last chance at a healthy life and if we went home we would all die fat so this was a necessary step, dehydrating. She also hammered home the importance of winning the weigh in, when she told us if we were menstruating to not wear tampons in the morning on weigh-in days for fear it added extra weight.

As opposed to real life at home where I *always* knew what I weighed, I have no idea what it is here and now. When we weighed-in, it was in the morning before the night of actual filming and on a cattle scale where you were not allowed to see the results. The results were displayed on the prop in the gym later that night. When we got to pretend to weigh in three times acting shocked and surprised at the number each time. They could put any number they wanted on that scale, we fatties would never know. It was all part of this being kept in the dark strategy that both spread a murmuring fear of failing among us and kept us always guessing.

The prize we won this week both for winning and not dying during that ridiculous fucking army boot camp bullshit challenge was switching a team member's weight loss amount for a person on the other team's weight. We all sat down and decided that if we were going to choose Becky, then maybe she should drink a lot of water to add weight, instead of losing any. This strategy would fuck over the other team with the added bonus of making Becky look like a lazy asshole on national TV.

Just kidding none of us thought of that. Becky was just not working as hard as the rest of it and we noticed so we went with her.

5/24/2015

The weigh in was the biggest disaster and contained one of the biggest bitch moves I have ever seen. I mean Shea is annoying as fuck, don't get me wrong, but when Becky's weight loss—that we all knew was going to suck by game show standards—dropped, she straight up blamed Shea. Esther proceeded to lose her Mormon mind on Becky for that—it was rather spectacular to witness. I do not believe I have ever seen anyone completely destroy a person without swearing before. It was almost art.

When Becky stepped on the actual scale to weigh in that morning, she hadn't bothered to work out with the rest of the team beforehand and had drunk water to weigh more. Both of these things were sound decisions from the standpoint of playing the game but I think later she felt she had to make an excuse when she got on that scale and her numbers were not as high as the rest of the team. She knew America—who isn't privy to any of what was going on in this insane asylum—would just assume she was lazy. She must have been explaining herself to viewers at home, which is weird cause she did a lot of annoying shit with us and never bothered to explain herself, *You see Tisa, I used the last clean glass without cleaning any for the rest of the thirteen people that share this house because I am deathly allergic to manual labor, and it would've literally killed me.* Just give me something. *Anything.*

The weigh-in was basically pathetic. Our team had some weird sense of fairness and chose to swap Becky's weight with another girl's weight. Why the fuck didn't we choose a guy? Dumbasses. We kind of deserved to lose and to have to send someone home for that choice. I've been reassuring my wounded ego with the idea that Becky was just so damn annoying our subconscious stepped in so that we messed it up so we lost on purpose. Yes. That's totally it. Not us being stupid.

The cool thing about weigh-ins though, no matter what else was going on; the teams were always supportive of each other when we got on that damn scale. Fat people unite!

I stepped on the scale and both teams were whooping and cheering wildly. Even if we quibbled during the days, there were nothing but high fives and support across the board when the numbers clocked in. Shouts of *Go Tisa*! and *Awesome work, Tisa*! rung from both Bravo and Alpha Team and gave me a renewed belief in this process and the people around me. As I got down and rejoined the crowd, I in turn cheered my fellow contestants on.

"You are doing so well!" Blake from the Bravo Team told me with a soft pat on the shoulder. "Really amazing."

"Thanks Blake," I said, suddenly feeling less apprehensive about this whole place. Who would have thought positive reinforcement would work? I almost forgave Bravo Team for dehydrating, costing us some quality H2O. We all understood what each of us was going through, even if our production wardens didn't. Game or no game, we are all fighting the same battle.

5/25/2015

This bitch, wow. Last night when an argument took place between her and Esther—with Shea there—all Becky had to do was own up to the fact that she was afraid of looking lazy on national TV so she panicked and blamed Shea. Instead, in what seemed at this point to be typical Becky fashion, she kept blaming others for her actions. How the hell are we responsible for you not working out? I'm looking forward to going to elimination, voting her fame-chasing ass and infuriating alarm clock home and then taking her far comfier looking bed afterward. I'll work on being a nicer person some other time, right now I want a good night's sleep.

The whole elimination process was more difficult than I anticipated, *especially* with the opinion that I have of Becky. I didn't realize until tonight how much I keep hearing that this is a miracle place designed to save our lives and how I've started to believe it. I also didn't realize until I had to vote to take that away from someone, that I might feel bad about it. I had thought it wouldn't be a problem, but really, I felt sad.

I get that this is a show but why did production do this to us? The room we had to return to after voting Becky home, was full of food. They literally filled the room with fresh cooked comfort foods. Macaroni and cheese, cake, ice cream all you could think of, piled up in our living room. I'm exhausted and crying because even if she was horrible I feel like I took Becky's chance at health away from her tonight. I'm hungry, sad, tired, miss my family and had to do something awful. Then I walk into a room chock full of comfort food. *Fucking everywhere.* Then, when I want to leave I am told I have to sit in this food filled fucking room so the cameras can get footage of the other team talking to us.

"What the..." I exclaimed when I stepped into the room, tears still streaming down my cheeks. The smell and sight of all this food hit me like a freight train. Cakes, both chocolate and vanilla, ice cream by the gallon in big glass bowls with whipped cream, steaming bowls of macaroni and cheese, big plates of burgers and pizza. "You can't be serious with this?" They *were*. I was getting worked up, and couldn't believe this shit was actually happening.

"Please sit down around the table for the cameras," a PA told us while looking directly at me.

"We just voted off a team member and you want us to sit here with all this food? I don't want to do that," I said, not sitting down.

"We have to get shots of Bravo Team talking to you about this," she continued, ignoring my objections. "Just sit down and we'll get this over with. You won't get out of here until we do."

I wanted to drown her in a bowl of mac and cheese. What kind of sadistic asshole does that to sad, tired, fat people?

Chapter 4

I saw a woman cry over potatoes. I'm still processing it today. I am not kidding. I ruminate on the fact that a production team full of sadists put us in a room of comfort foods and I saw someone actually cry because it was so fucked up. I teared up in rage over how bullshit a move it was to do that to us, but the food didn't really affect me so much. While I get the reaction, intellectually, I don't think I am quite as emotionally attached to food. However, I might cry over vodka, or lack of sex. I mean I almost cried myself to sleep over the wasted potential in my encounter with Daniel the hot PA, but I haven't cried over potatoes. I just keep thinking about how utter and complete bullshit it is, that after a really grueling and stupidly emotional moment—like having to vote to send someone home—they send us to a room completely filled with comfort food. That's not an asshole thing to do at all—take a bunch of people who may have been self-medicating with food, mess with their emotions for weeks then taunt them with food. I'm pretty certain any asshole working in reality TV production is a huge fan of that moment when Marley dies in *Marley and Me*, too.

Also, I am annoyed by the smugness of the damn Bravo Team. We're all buddies at weigh in but any other time, they annoy me. We get it, you guys are cooler than us, you get along better, and you sing kumbaya while holding hands at bedtime. Your trainer actually calls you by the right names, and (it's been weeks, plural, and Shea called me Debbie the other day.) They act like they're never going to have to send someone home. Like you can tell in their stupid smug potato faces that they really think that. Ok, maybe the potatoes did get to me more than I realized. At least I didn't cry when I saw them like Debbie did, but now I want some. Fuck this day. A plague on their Bravo Team happiness! I miss tater tots. I really do.

So, I'm limping like a mo-fo and still bleeding through my shoes. I am one sexy fat girl. I'm not even the most jacked up. Chris is way worse off. Chris is a strawberry blond guy on the Bravo Team from Illinois, where he works some cubicle job at an office. He spent his days sitting in front of a computer. Both for work and his hobby. He writes in his spare time and is actually one of the wittiest motherfuckers I've ever encountered. As illustrated by how he handled us trying to get our 300 dollar a week paycheck when he went toe to toe with A.C. Moss.

"Mr. Moss, sir, have you had the chance to look into the case of the missing paychecks?" he quipped in his best Victorian England accent. A.C. looked like he was dealing with a difficult child, that just needed to be patronized a little. That seemed to be how he approached most people.

"You know," he started in a self-important tone, "this show is a huge machine, where every little cog plays a vital part. We want to make sure you guys are doing well and get the proper attention along the way." It was clear that he had not given two fucks about our paychecks. We weren't working for it anyway, just risking our lives for the entertainment of the masses, but *whatever*.

"And we thank you for all that you do for us," Chris went on in a slightly mocking voice, hell-bent on not letting A.C. win this one. "But the thing is, we signed these contracts that put a lot of restrictions on us in exchange for one small thing, a three hundred dollar a week paycheck. It's been a few weeks now, and USPS isn't *that* unreliable." The accusation hung thick in the air. A.C. shifted his defense.

"The show has a certain amount of funding, you see." He was trying to be condescending, but he was on thin ice. "We have allocated the funds to make sure you are looked after here on the show. Accounting is looking hard for funds to allocate for your paychecks. Plus, I think you're undervaluing the lifesaving efforts we are putting forth on your behalf and what an opportunity you have been given here that you cannot assign a monetary value to."

Chris didn't miss a beat, but surveyed A.C. quickly and said, "Have they looked at your shoes? Those Italian puppies could pay two of us for a week." There were a few chuckles, and A.C. laughed along so as to appear with us, but I'm pretty sure he would've gladly sacrificed his $800 shoes for the chance to beat Chris to death with them.

"I'll see what I can do. I'm sure the checks are getting to you soon." He flashed a stiff smile, then went on his way. Even if he decided to go out of his way to tell accounting to delay our checks instead, it was worth it to see that scene go down.

But right now, witty Chris just looks beat down and was walking like a cowboy. Not the cool kind. He's in near constant pain. I think they said it was bursitis or something. Either way, he's not alone. We all pop Aleve like it's Pez when we can get it because it's contraband. Which is hysterical, I'm allowed to do things like dehydrate myself to within an inch of my life and work out until my feet are bloody pulps only kept together by cheap sneakers, but I can't determine if I need an Aleve? I think the workouts don't count if I'm not also in excruciating pain.

It would be cool to see a doc, a proper doc. No offense to Doc Malik, he is amazing. But seeing a doctor who could more thoroughly make sure that a heart rate this high in an almost 300-pound girl really isn't going to kill me, would be cool. I mean if being fat means I am on the verge of death at any moment surely running mountains while trying to vomit my lungs is contraindicated by proper medicine? At least we have Doc Malik. That guy is a God send. I mean we are told to disregard what he says most of the time by our trainers and production because apparently, we will gain weight if we take his advice but he is allowed to give us band aids and this electrical shock thing to our muscles, so that's cool. *I guess.* Mostly his quarters serve as a place to escape and try to talk to someone connected to the rest of the world. He doesn't seem to give a shit about how fast we lose weight like everyone else around here does. A crazy notion I know, someone who actually gives a shit about our health, what a novel concept. Now if only we were not told at every turn that he is evil and trying to sabotage our weight loss by most all of production.

I don't know why they even really keep Doc Malik around, if he's so detrimental to saving our lives. They are the ones paying this guy. Is it like superheroes never killing their nemesis because if they did, there would be nothing left to do. It's tough because I don't know who to believe. They know what makes us healthier. His job is *just* fixing injuries. Everyone says this program is saving our lives and that our trainers are the ones saving us. I don't feel saved, I feel exhausted.

I talked to Daniel, the hot PA guy again today. I've seen him around here and there but they keep him busy, and besides he's not really supposed to socialize with the contestants. I guess they are scared he's going to tell us how to tunnel out or give us the guard schedules or something. But today, he caught up with me coming back from the gym and walked with me a bit.

"Hi Tisa," he started, as I turned around at the sound of footsteps. "I thought I'd never get a moment with just you."

"If I knew you wanted one, I would've walked from the gym alone more often," I responded, glancing sideways into his eyes. He was good looking, with his dark hair and wide smile. I felt a hot bomb go off somewhere in my abdomen as I realized how long it had been since I had gotten laid. If only the walkway between the gym and house stayed deserted a little longer.

"I'd like more than one," Daniel broke my train of thought just as it was getting interesting, but in all fairness, it did involve him, and I shouldn't put the cart before the horse. "They keep me busy here, but I saw you leave and had to see you if only for a second."

His thought train was going down the same track as mine it seemed. "Aren't you ever off work though?" I inquired suggestively. He picked up on it immediately because a knowing smile spread across his handsome features.

"Why yes, sometimes I am," He raised his hand and let the fingers brush lightly down my neck. It was a relatively small gesture and over quickly. But it had the intended effect. I had to focus to gather my thoughts, "But I've deliberately picked up more hours to stay on set, there are, uh...things that interest me here."

"Perhaps there should be more moments then—when you aren't kept busy while you're here?" I wanted more moment's right then. A door opened and closed in the distance. I had obviously been off camera and mic for too long and someone else in production was looking for me so it wasn't going to happen tonight. We *both* knew it.

"I also wanted to give you this," Daniel said while handing me a sugar free peach ice tea. I remembered telling Debbie or Esther how badly I wanted one and spotting Daniel in my vicinity shortly after. I was actually a bit touched and something slightly before turned on. Damn. But that frigging door had opened and somebody was looking for me. I accepted the ice tea and thanked Daniel.

"Don't be a stranger," I said, as I turned back toward the house, flashing a smile at him. I hoped he wouldn't be. And that he could find a time and a way.

I was pretty glad that I had figured out how to disconnect my mic. It's amazing the things you learn after a couple weeks on reality TV. Debbie, Esther and I had figured out what spots on the Spa property were camera free and where the mics were no longer strong enough to send back audio. We had also started to drive production crazy with things like putting our middle fingers up in front of our faces so they couldn't use the footage or to say things like *anal sex* randomly in the middle of a personal conversation making the audio useless. Disconnecting the mic was the trick I was most grateful for in that moment because I wanted no one fucking up my verbal dalliances with Daniel. The adrenaline from those little encounters and chocolate protein shakes were pretty much the only things keeping me from dropping dead from exhaustion.

I headed back to the house and prepared for more of the same shit—hours of working out and no food. Ok food, but not a lot. Cynthia, the show's host—A seemingly nice blonde woman with a history of commercial soap opera success, a loud mouth and excellent taste in shoes—was mostly kept separate from the contestants. She was *talent* while we were cattle...err, contestants. Today when I arrived she was in the house for the first time because we needed to film some extra scenes for the elimination vote and she flipped her shit when she finally got a good glimpse of our entryway *decor* just as I was walking into the house. The entryway was plastered with wall-size, blown up posters of our bodies. These were deliberately shot to be unflattering and reducing us to mere parts, not human beings, just body parts with *offensive* fat on them. Stomachs. Thighs. Upper arms—they were so shocking she literally shrieked in horror, "Whoa! What the fuck? Are these necessary?" Of course, they were, lest we forget how despicable we were to look at. Better to see our own horrible images every day, and feel so ashamed by the sight, so that we went that extra mile in the gym. "Take this shit down right now. What the fuck is wrong with you people? Why would you put these up?" It was pretty bad ass to hear her advocate for us.

Minutes later PAs scampered to take the huge pictures down and replace them with full body shots of us in sports bras and spandex. Sigh. An empty victory, but a victory I guess?

5/27/2015

I'm no longer in a *voting-off-hangover-carb-desperate* fog of resentment and I can actually see how good it is for the members of the Bravo Team to have that cohesiveness. Disregard what I said yesterday about the Bravo Team. I'm obviously just envious. I'm still bitter and I sound like it, but I'm in a mood from having to shoot the intro to the show today. The intro has me standing next to a fence. I was directed to do something *Alaskan*. I have no idea what the fuck is *Alaskan* about standing next to a fence and fake laughing but that's what they wanted. I'm expected to spend time putting on makeup for the intro to a show where I will never look like that again? Good grief.

"I'm confused you guys? I thought I signed on to a reality TV show? Last I checked I didn't wear makeup in any of my interviews, *or* in the 8 hours I spent in the gym yesterday."

"Funny Tisa, just go fix your face."

Silly me for thinking that I looked fine as I was. What was I thinking liking my face? How *dare* I? Twenty minutes later I hauled my sweaty ass back down the hill to the *Alaskan looking* fence ready to go. Nope. I apparently did such a poor job they sent me back to fix my face twice more. If I have to go back up and do it again, I am coming down looking like a Juggalo. I like how I look *without* makeup. I don't understand the problem. I don't normally feel ugly, I mean I have my days but today I felt small and somehow wrong. This place is getting to me.

5/28/2015

We got a surprise this afternoon. Production was disappointed we weren't ecstatic about it. When Shea informed us about our surprise, she spoke with the enthusiasm normally reserved for high school pep rallies.

"Guess what you guys?" she said in a voice usually reserved for those who have had too many energy drinks or suffered from a severe case of the Billy Mays.

"Uh…" somebody started, but before anybody could elaborate on that thought, Shea answered her own question.

"We are going to work out…" pause for effect, "at the beach!" She almost jumped and clapped her hands as she said it. She didn't jump and clap, but I could see the thought flash in her eyes. We all looked at her. I think I heard a cricket chirp somewhere in the distance, before the silence was even too much for it, it took off. Shea's smile slowly narrowed to a look of genuine bewilderment. Nobody wanted to drag their asses to the beach to work out. *Nobody.* There wasn't anything fun or exciting about that thought. I don't know if she got that.

5/29/2015

As we loaded up in the beat to shit old Mustangs production provided we were all excited. Finally, the chance to go somewhere in a vehicle other than vans driven on California highways by twenty-year-old production assistants. Those vans were not the safest I have ever felt in a vehicle. Stories about all those church van accidents went through my head every time we flew down the highway in them. Not to mention they were overloaded with fat people, had no seat belts and hit top speeds of around eighty miles per hour. I guess I was still naïve because I was honestly surprised when production told us we would only be in the cars long enough to get footage of us driving off. Then of course it was back into the vans.

The *ride to the beach* was hilarious. There were camera men hanging out of church vans filming us driving up and down the block in the Mustangs—then one of the hubcaps came flying off. I'm pretty sure there is a *the wheels fell off* metaphor about this whole experience in there somewhere. They actually trucked the cars down to the beach and had us get back in so that they could film us driving up in them when we got there. To recap, production allowed us to drive about 100 yards for the camera, then took us to the beach in church vans while simultaneously trucking the now *empty* mustangs there. Then they filmed us driving the last 100 yards to the beach in them. They have money for that kind of shit but giving us our $300 dollars a week, or getting me my damn underwear back is putting too big a strain on their budget. Makes total sense.

I was especially hesitant about this whole beach thing because I'm still contending with my sprained ankle. I knew running in sand with a sprained ankle was probably not going to be pleasant or safe but I didn't dare disobey what Shea and production demanded. The assumption is that I am here because I am obviously disgustingly lazy and weak willed, if not I wouldn't be fat. I'll be damned if I was going to live up to that image of me. I had talked it over with Doc Malik.

"I'm worried about my sprained ankle, Doc," I told him at one of the few brief checks he was allowed to do.

"Running in sand with it will be tough."

"I know, Tisa. I'm sorry you have to. I will be nearby throughout it all—in case it gets worse—and I will step in and help you out."

"By the time you get to me, if something happens, you might not be allowed near me if it interrupts filming." He knew this. I knew he knew. I just needed to tell him I was worried. At least there was the comfort of knowing one person here wanted me to not kill myself on camera however entertaining and good for ratings that might be.

"You won't kill yourself on screen," Doc Malik said with a smile, as if he just read my mind. "I won't allow you to," His presence was reassuring but I knew he could be overruled by Shea or production. They always had final say and a way of making you understand that if they didn't you were risking everything.

My fears were confirmed. Doc Malik was trying to look out for one of the Bravo Team members. The degree of suspicion his actions were met with was at paranoia levels seen only in that "Aliens" guy on The History Channel. Hunter, a tan brown haired slightly befuddled looking electronics store manager from Georgia was nauseous from the heat and the workout. Doc Malik sent me over to him with a Styrofoam cup full of something to calm his stomach. Doc would have brought it to him himself but wasn't allowed to appear on camera.

"This is from the medical trainer, Hunter," I whispered as I handed the cup to him. His look was the strangest mix of gratitude and distress.

"I can't, Tisa. I'm not allowed to," he whispered back.

"What? You're sick, man. This will make you better," I whispered with exasperation. Chad, Bravo Team's trainer, had come over and was surveying us critically. He looked at Hunter, ascertained what was going down and said, "Do not drink that. You do not eat or drink anything that I don't tell you to," Hunter immediately threw it out. I looked back off camera and saw Doc sigh with frustration. I mean, I don't blame Hunter though. Apparently the best medical and dietary advice from professionals—production constantly told us we were receiving—resided only in the brains of these two trainers. *Do what your trainer says, or you will lose your shot at being here, being healthy and will go home to certain death.* I'm pretty sure Patty Hearst heard something similar from those kindly people that kidnapped her for her own good.

Just then I heard Daniel holler my name from the beach. It was time for the Alpha Team workout. Shea chose yoga. She is getting increasingly frustrated with how we, as a team, aren't giving her the respect she wants and I'm pretty sure this workout isn't going to go well. This was an issue born of a couple of different things. One was that as a team, we felt that Shea's dedication to her team was a lot less than Chad's. Chad was at the Spa more often than Shea and had a knack for relating to his team more easily. He does small things like learn their names for instance, while I'm not entirely sure Shea even realizes who is on her team or that she isn't at Disney World.

Shea, thinks that we are all fat because we are lazy and so she treats us that way. Like one day in the gym, she was monitoring Debbie and I, we had just arrived, and took a second too long getting on the treadmill.

"Come on girls, we're here to work out, not lay about on the couch like you did at home." I think perhaps she thought it was a comically delivered line—a joke between buddies. But we're *not* buddies. It felt pretty clear, that this particular *joke* was founded in her belief that we were just lazy lay-a-bouts who didn't care about anything but food, laying around, gluttony, and sloth. Or whatever other deadly sins people conjure up when they see fat people. She seemed to believe we wanted a magical fix from her that required zero effort and behind this bizarre cheerleader facade, she subtly resented it. I should've known she would think something as unfounded as *they're all lazy* after learning what a terrible judge of character she was. I mean, for fucks sake, Esther had a child under 3, her own business and was very active in her church. Debbie had two kids less than a year apart and played on multiple volleyball and softball teams—and let's not forget that Miss Congeniality title she had earned. I had just graduated with a double major after working two jobs throughout college including teaching aerobics at my current weight. Laziness was not our issue. Shea was too shallow to even bother to think it through any further and it was causing resentment. Add to that production encouraging us to talk about how horrible a trainer Shea was in each of our interviews and it's no wonder the train wreck continued.

Every night we had sequestered interviews in a little closet alone with a camera surrounded by jars of candy. I get why the candy is here but seriously, this was getting ridiculous. We then read through a list of fascinating questions like "What was the hardest thing about today?" or "How did being fat work out for you today?" or "Do you think your team will ever stop looking like the 2008

Detroit Lions?" Then the questions would turn more nefarious, asking things like, "Why isn't Shea as good a trainer as Chad?" or "Why do you think Shea doesn't like you guys as a team?" The questions were so obviously designed to keep us from getting along with Shea because a bickering fighting screaming Alpha Team made for better TV. I was waiting for the inevitable, "Why does Shea wipe her ass with pictures of you?" question. Forget that production had repeatedly told me this woman was supposed to be the only person who could give me my health. She was literally supposed to serve as my medical and emotional guide through a very grueling process. Instead, they spend as much energy as possible mind-fucking the whole team so we don't trust her. All of this shit-stirring made getting through the intense physical days even more taxing.

"Alright guys, today on the beach, we will do yoga," Shea announced with so much fake enthusiasm, you'd think she was doing PR for Charlie Sheen. Perhaps she *had* picked up on our despair, when she originally told us we would be going to the beach.

There was a collective groan and shuffling around but the guys were especially dissatisfied with this turn of events. I took one look at an almost seven-foot-tall Bruno, who couldn't touch his toes, struggling in the sand and I knew this was going to go badly. Sure enough, he was the first one to speak up.

"Yoga?" he exclaimed perhaps more strenuously than he intended. "How is this going to help us lose weight?" Shea looked like she regretted signing on to chaperone us fatties around the Spa and especially at the beach. I thought I also saw a brief flash of annoyance on her face, like a teacher when the lazy kid asks, for the tenth time if this will be on the test.

"Yoga will help you limber up and benefit you in the long run with your training," She considered the matter closed, I think. But Bruno wasn't ready to accept this.

"Long term, perhaps. But one day of yoga on the beach might not be as beneficial."

Shea clearly felt like her authority was questioned. She was steaming and not just because it was ninety degrees. At this point Kevin piped up too. "I don't see what it will do for us either. The other team isn't doing yoga," he pointed left where we could all see Bravo Team doing some sort of bizarre driftwood carrying boot camp in the sand. It looked a lot more weight loss producing than yoga. Shea looked as if somebody had just popped her balloon. Tears were forming at the corners of her eyes and when she spoke it was clear that she was nearing her wits end.

"Just do it. Do the yoga. I'm telling you to do the yoga, so you *do the yoga!*" I half waited for Bruno to say *make me* and Shea to break his neck with her thighs or something but it never happened. He picked up on the desperation in her voice and demeanor and decided yoga probably *was* good enough for us for now.

5/30/2015

Dammit, another fucking temptation. This time I'm staring at a tableau where either a carrot stick, snack cake, or immunity lay beneath little sand castles. I take a moment to thank God that a love of food isn't really the reason that I'm fat. I know you would think that I would have to love food to get where I am but really, it's my lack of regard for food that got me to this beach in the middle of summer, sweating balls, staring at sand castles. I can literally eat the same thing for months and not care. That is a problem when you are too busy to take the time and effort required to choose foods that nourish you instead of eating whatever is at hand. What was mostly at hand in my everyday life was anything cheap someone else had cooked. I just ate whatever was available or easiest to fit in my mouth to kill my hunger. If I loved food—the way Debbie does for instance— these temptations and the food spreads they set up for us after eliminations would have been excruciating as well as enraging for me. Debbie, our *food crier* misses her babies so bad right now that when the ridiculous spreads of decadent foods come out, there are tears already rolling down her cheeks. After witnessing that shit, you can't tell me that weight loss isn't psychological as well as physical. There is no therapist here to help with things like this, just people you are competing against, a trainer that can't relate to the pain you are in, and a production crew waiting to exploit it by catching it all on film.

This particular temptation didn't really tempt anyone. "Does anybody really want to do this?" Esther asked. "I mean the prize *is* immunity."

"You know if it was later in the game I probably would be about immunity," Farrell interjected, "but honestly it's kind of really early in the game for that. I mean they're just snack cakes and carrots if you don't get the immunity but the idea that everybody's going to think that I'm already greedy and gluttonous and stupid for succumbing to this trick makes me really hesitant to think about doing this, don't you guys feel the same? "

We did. Farrell made complete sense. Standing there listening to this and looking at the castles I'm absolutely certain that they're right. We aren't completely stupid. We know there's this idea we are all so lucky to be here and if we play into a temptation that has you eat food your trainer wouldn't approve of we would just be validating that line of thought. I can just see how pissed off Shea and Chad will be if we go back down the beach and tell them we ate snack cakes. I'm not prepared to deal with the wrath of Shea this morning especially after yesterday's yoga debacle. If she was about to pile drive Bruno for not being about yoga on the beach, she might just eat my liver with fava beans and a nice bottle of Chianti for this. The whole thing doesn't seem worth it to me. It's making me anxious. I have a feeling the crew would film this as though I were some carb deprived rampaging Fatzilla tearing through these sand castles if I decided to try for immunity from being voted off.

Suddenly a random disembodied voice from behind the cameras says, "Guys, guys come on. This is a game. You have to at least look like you're considering it. Don't you want the opportunity of immunity? America wants to see you considering getting immunity. It's all part of the fun. If you're not going to actually do the challenge then walk back. Please, come towards the sand castles and at least pretend you're thinking about it so I can get some good footage for fuck sake?" It was A.C. He didn't give a damn what we really wanted to do, he cared about his narrative. Fine, just get the shit over with.

"Golly gee guys, after reading the rules this looks like it could be beneficial to staying at the Spa and meeting our goals, what do you all think?" I'm pretty sure I sounded as wooden as Pinocchio.

"You might be right, Tisa. We should put some serious thought in it," Hunter chimed in, making me realize my acting skills weren't so bad after all.

Time to sleep on the beach. Lulled into a peaceful night of rest by the ocean side. Perhaps we could have a bonfire while Bravo Team sings that fucking Kumbaya shit for *real* this time. Just kidding. That didn't happen. I don't know why I keep getting surprised by this. "Oh, I'm in that tent, ok cool, do we get to shower or anything before we sleep?"

"Don't be an idiot Tisa, no one is sleeping on the fucking beach," Chad scoffs at me. Holy shit, Chad just talked to me. I mean it *was* to point out what an idiot I am but still he usually acts like the Alpha Team has the plague. I'll take it.

We put up gorgeous tents which I am pretty sure are the same ones that were supposedly *given* to us on the first night for *sleeping* in the gym. Then after filming a barbeque—that could be more accurately described as a ground turkey commercial—we spent twenty minutes in the dark, crawling in and out of the tents telling each other good night.

"Ouch!" "Oh, sorry Brody, is that your elbow?" I'm not used to folding my bulk in and out of such a small enclosure. Plus, with an additional four or five *(how many people are in this tent for fucks sake)* fat people this is starting to resemble a circus clown car.

"Good night, Shannon!"

"Night, Debbie!"

"Sleep well, Chad."

"Night John-Boy!"

"Tisa, quit fucking off."

"Sorry."

After twenty minutes of completely sincere bedtime wishes, it was time to load up in yet another church van and go back to the Spa for actual sleeping.

5/31/2015

Oh god, oh god, oh fuck. The worst part of this whole beach week bullshit is going to be this damn challenge. I am staring at two flags dangling from fourteen-foot high poles at six am and my brain isn't fully computing this. It doesn't bode well for a *fun* day. Alright, taking deep breaths, looking at it on the surface it doesn't seem that dangerous when you think about it. We can do this, we need to run half a football field length to the water line, gather wet sand using our hands and bring it back to make a pile that will get one of us high enough to snatch down the flag. This will be fine. Breathe. I used to play on the beach as a kid and I've built more than one nice pile of sand in my time. Surely this is no different.

I spoke too fucking soon. There is nothing safe about a four-hundred-pound man standing on top of a loose pile of sand while jumping blindly over other people on the ground all around him trying to hold up said pile of sand, so he can grab for a flag. Bruno our fearless almost seven-footer has repeatedly jumped from this haphazard pile of sand reaching for that flag. I want to vomit with nerves every time we ask him to jump again.

At one point, the pile of sand was so precarious that we decided the only way we were going to make it hold enough to support Bruno was to use our own bodies as buttresses. We laid around it trying to hold it together while Bruno stood on it. At one-point he accidentally stood on my hand which is on top the pile of sand. I instantaneously got bruises in the shape of his sneaker tread. I think the word *Nike* will be permanently etched into the back of my hand. I was one pink cardigan short of an Umbridge punishment.

They chose prizes that were probably the only thing that would make us damn near kill ourselves to get them—care packages. True to style, they lined them up for us to see, but not touch. Debbie's had her kid's pictures on the side to taunt her, and she burst into tears when she saw them. Hunter teared up too. I imagined us holding Debbie back with dramatic music playing with her arms flailing wildly at the boxes as she goes to tear the throat out of a PA who won't give it to her. Some people missed their families more than others but we were all ready to have proof that people who genuinely cared about us still existed. We hit the challenge with a fierce determination.

"Come on Bruno. Just jump, man," Brody shouted at him.

"But I don't think I can make it, guys. We aren't there yet," He was looking up at the flag. It was still a good 4 feet above him even with his seven-foot frame on top of the sand pile.

We are not having it. We all needed those care packages from home. "Just try. Just jump and try your best," I shouted at him, pushing sand back into the pile with my hurt hand. He sensed the desperation in us and felt it himself too. Letters from our families that we hadn't seen or exchanged a word with for nearly a month, moved our mental needles from standard crazy straight to Gary Busey levels.

"Bruno, you have to just try," Brody nearly begging, tried again.

"Bruno please just jump, it's fine. Just jump," Debbie chimed in.

"I don't know, guys. It's really high up. What if I miss?"

"That doesn't matter, Bruno. Just try. Please!"

He tried. Oh my god how he tried.

When he missed and fell crashing to the sand, I could hear Esther sniffling next to me. We had already been hauling sand for 45 minutes—our hands raw and chafed with exhaustion just starting to creep in. Esther softly whispered, "It will be ok," to herself, then loudly told Bruno, "That's alright Bruno, next time. We failed you, we will get this higher." Her, Debbie, and I bolted for the water line, yet again.

Eventually producers stopped the challenge and gave us burlap sacks to fill with sand because the loose sand would not hold up to the weight of the people on it. This was after almost an hour of us killing ourselves. During that hour, tragedy nearly struck. I was bleeding from my hand, and knuckles, and my shins were cut and bleeding. Debbie was bleeding from both knees and Brody's elbows were sliced up badly too. Esther and I both had several yellowish marks on our arms from smaller collisions in the fray and the cursing from all of us was out of this world. I don't know if Esther accepted that we *had* to swear to get through this one but she didn't admonish us as she might've any other time. The Mormon is strong in that girl. Aggressions needed out and saying *fuck* is a wonderful remedy for that. At one-point Cynthia walked up to us and was struck nearly silent by the sight.

She stammered, "You guys look like an episode of the Sopranos. What the fuck did you do?" If looks could kill, she would have died like a mobster who crossed Tony in that moment. Really looking at her though, I realized her comment was made in horror. She was having reservations about what was being asked of the fatties today. Witnessing blood and crying will do that to you, I guess. Her comment might have done something to us, because it was then—with an inhuman bout of desperation and exhaustion—that Bruno made another jump for the flag and landed squarely on Brody's neck.

Brody was a snarky black gay man who spent a little too much time pointing out others personality flaws, including mine. I mean, he wasn't wrong, it just got old. He could be dramatic, was fond of name dropping and talked just a few decibels too loudly at all times. Often, he was pouty as fuck but had a good heart. He got a lot less attention from the crew and cameramen than most of the other contestants for some reason. This puzzled me because he was achieving in the gym at a faster rate than most of us and had called me a *cunt* during one minor spat over cheese of all things. I found him endlessly entertaining.

The noise from Brody's neck was horrible. You could hear a sickening thud. Brody couldn't move at first and finally over the murmured objections coming from crew, someone finally yelled for it to stop. Doc Malik rushed on set to Brody. It was surreally quiet. All four hundred pounds of Bruno landed on Brody's neck and head. I have no idea how it is that Brody didn't end up eating soup through a straw for the rest of his life. What is even crazier to me is that as soon as they found out he wasn't paralyzed, instead of stopping what could have obviously led to paralysis or at the very least some sort of permanent damage to someone, the production crew started the whole circus back up. Even more insane was the fact that all of us, including a discombobulated Brody, agreed to keep going.

"Alright Brody, you're right as rain," a producer said.

"I don't know," Doc Malik tried to interject. "He has had a pretty severe blow to the neck. I would prefer to look him over more thoroughly before continuing. He should probably not…"

He was cut off by Kit, a head PA or producer or something. I still haven't figured out exactly who she is. "I think Brody should decide that for himself. He seems fine. You are fine, aren't you Brody? If you aren't, and we take you to a doctor, you might not make it back to the Spa at all." That bitch. Brody could have an arrow through his head, and still they'd pull some emotional blackmail on him, and he'd agree with what's left of his coherence to stick around. Permanent damages to his neck be damned and if he isn't ever able to chew solid food again, he'll just have coffee and call it a diet.

"I'll be alright," Brody said, as he was helped to his feet. I know some of it was the desperation he saw on the faces of his team when they brought those care packages out earlier. A large part of this was for us. I felt a twinge of guilt. He managed a strained smile as Doc Malik walked off shaking his head for what must have been the zillionth time. How that guy didn't just quit his job daily, I will never know. The hope that perhaps someday he might actually get to help us was what kept him alive I think.

Bruno fell again, this time on me. I don't know how many people have had the experience of a giant man who has just jumped with all of his might been briefly suspended in midair and then plummeted with gathering speed land flat on you. It was something like what I imagine being hit by a freight train must be like. If that freight train was carrying lead and on fire.

Bruno was a cop and while he had a lot of extra weight on him, he also carried a lot of muscle and that was significantly less squishy when it hit you. I couldn't breathe for nearly a full thirty seconds after he hit me. For what was the first, and I hope last time in my life, I saw stars swirl around my head. I know how lucky I am that was all that happened. I am bloodied, bruised, crying, exhausted and missing my family, yet I know how lucky I am. I'm still here, in the game. The best thing that ever happened to me.

We *won* the challenge. I am nothing but tears and relief at getting to see what my family sent me. I've never needed something from familiar people that genuinely care about me more than I do right now. My joy was reduced when I looked to my right and saw the look of devastation on Farrell's face. It was the most unbearable thing I've ever seen. Right up until I saw Hunter behind him with tears streaming down his face too, just as bloodied and battered as we were, only with *nothing* to show for it. I couldn't stand the thought of them not getting what we had.

"Wait. So much happens off camera that no one ever sees, why can't Bravo Team have their care packages too?" I asked with a bit of hope of releasing that crushing guilt caught in my chest. These were people with children they hadn't been able to communicate with in weeks. I mean what's in my box, pictures from my ex-boyfriend, a letter from my parents asking me not to embarrass them on national TV? That feels frivolous compared to what they might be missing out on.

"She's right, everyone should be able to open their care packages. We won the challenge, none of us care if they get theirs too. You got your footage," Brody chimed in, carrying the full weight of a man who had literally risked paralysis to earn the box he was now holding in his bloodied sand covered hands. He was met with cries of consensus from the rest of the red team.

"Yes."

"Absolutely."

"We don't care, they miss home as much as we do!"

"No fucking way. Not a chance," Kit insisted. "There is no way that Alison is going to allow that."

"Just ask," Brody demanded.

"That's cool, we won't open ours at all if you don't let the Bravo Team open theirs too." I felt like a super assertive badass, only to be deflated moments later as the temperature on the beach dropped a few degrees. This could mean only one thing—Alison was here. She walked up to us, having heard the exchange and looked at us like we were aliens who had just made first contact by asking for a glass of warm milk.

"While it's um...admirable, I suppose that you all feel this way. The Bravo Team did not have the stamina or drive to win this round. If they had, they would be opening their packages right now, wouldn't they? I am not going to reward the sort of mediocrity that allowed you to get yourselves in this *condition* in the first place, am I?" She wasn't done. "That would be the opposite of helping you. If you continue to persist we will do away with *all* your care packages and manufacture another prize through editing."

I looked at Debbie in horror, tears streaming down my face now and Esther looked apoplectic with rage. Alison was being a bitch just for the sake of it and we all knew it but could do nothing about it. We wanted Bravo Team to have their packages but we wouldn't sacrifice our own to get it to them. Brody and I acquiesced regretfully and I looked over as Farrell, on Bravo Team, looking devastated turned toward the beach and walked back to the campsite after mouthing the words "Thank you anyway." I picked up my care package full of letters from friends and family, dusted the sand off and mentally prepared to open something so meaningful in front of strangers while overcome with guilt and sadness at my impotence.

When I think about this challenge, I think about how lucky I am. Two hours in the sand and water building a pile so that a giant man can jump over you for a flag fourteen feet in the air. I feel lucky that I'm not dead or injured and that Brody isn't paralyzed. Then, I return to the house and meet with Shea and my gratitude started to dissipate. I think she was back at the house doing something like shot gunning energy drinks and snorting pixie sticks while squatting any type of compact car she could get her hands on as we tried to kill ourselves in the sand today.

"O-M-G you guys I heard you won the challenge," she shrieked about an inch from Esther's face.

"Yes, we did," Kevin answered almost morosely.

"Why the long faces? You'd think somebody was dead! You're *winners*," The crazed enthusiasm was too much for the guys and making excuses, they hastily retreated upstairs to their rooms. "That's ok, we girls can spend a little time bonding. Let me see what you got."

After exchanging a look that communicated our lack of enthusiasm about sharing pretty special objects from home with this crazed cheerleader, Esther reluctantly opened her box.

"Oh goody," Shea actually fucking said *goody*. I thought I was going to sprain my eyeballs from rolling them at Debbie. Shea continued, "Did your hubby send you a flask? You know a little pick me up?" with an obnoxious stage wink as though they were in a 90's sitcom, "I know how you liked to go out partying and dancing before you got here." Esther looked at her bewildered. Shea had gotten Esther confused with me, or at least the *me* that casting had crafted, much like Debbie's blonde hair makeover I got a *possibly an alcoholic definitely dances on the bar and certainly strips for extra money at seedy clubs* persona makeover of my own.

"I don't know what you're talking about? I, I have a wife and I'm Mormon, Shea. I don't drink." Esther responded.

Shea laughed nervously and turned to me as though the previous conversation would be erased from existence if she just pretended hard enough.

"Well then, Tisa any pictures of your hot husband in your box?"

"Sure Shea, my parents sent me a drawing of the imaginary man they hope I land one day. I think my niece drew it. He has one arm and an oversized head but I'd probably still hit it. What do you think?" Red slowly began to creep up her neck.

"Fine, I get it. You don't want to share with me."

Yeah, that was totally it. Vintage Shea.

Chad would use the names of both Maria's or Farrell's children to motivate them during their workouts, while Shea still didn't even know the names of any of our team's children and thought I had a husband. She also persisted in calling Debbie, Esther and Esther, Debbie. It had been more than three weeks at this point and when she looked at our care packages she didn't know who did and didn't have children. She still hadn't connected with us about the things that were important in our lives.

She suddenly regrouped and in her signature style—of obnoxiousness she believed played as perkiness—had what she thought was a brilliant idea. "I know what will make this *amazing* day even better." This was an amazing day? If you were shot gunning red bulls and doing bicep curls in front of the mirror, like her, instead of reenacting the opening of Saving Private Ryan on the beach, I'm sure it was.

"We should totally harness all the leftover adrenaline you guys have from this total win with a gym workout. It'll be totes amazing," Again, she actually said the word *totes*. Uh, no. This smell coming from me isn't fucking adrenaline. It's sand, fear sweat, blood and possibly urine. I can't even tell anymore.

"Shea, I don't think..." Debbie started. But it was folly.

"Yes. That's the very thing that will be the icing on this fabulous cake." At this point the women of the Alpha Team were exchanging furtive glances and I was afraid that Shea had so much caffeine that she was floating somewhere in the stratosphere.

"Shea, it's eleven pm and we are still covered in sand and blood. I think running on a treadmill might be ill advised without at least cleaning off first. Chafing is a thing without the sand. I don't want to imagine *with* sand." One of us said.

Shea looked at us and it was like she just noticed us, like we just walked through the door. She wrinkled her nose. "Oh, uh, you guys are yucky aren't you? Is that smell you?"

"Yes, that smell is me, Shea and I am going to go take a shower. We will see you in the morning," I told her as I picked up my husband deficient care package and headed upstairs to wash this day, and hopefully a memory or two off me.

After fending off a bewildered Shea and showering in our room, Debbie came up with the bright idea of soaking in the hot tub which was one of the few legit luxuries we had on the Spa. Hot water on sore limbs sounded like heaven to me. We knocked on the guys' door and ended up a decent sized party of people hitting the hot tub. It didn't take long for the conversation to turn to our two favorite topics—food and sex. We were having neither so of course our minds circled around it like an adolescent school boy's.

"Do you even remember what sex feels like?" Chris inquired of the group, mostly just to torture people with the thought for fun. A few people sighed with nostalgia.

"At this point, I only remember having had sex, because I know I have kids. So, it must've happened," Debbie responded with a grin and several people chuckled.

"I'd give anything for orgasms and a breakfast burrito right about now," I said and like a few times before, the thought brought a flash image of Daniel to my head.

"Hell, I'd settle for the burrito," Bruno said. It was the kind of relief to us that Shea had thought working out would be—just chuckling and soaking in the hot water, trying to push away the memories of a rough emotional day.

"Perhaps you could ask Alison to bring you one." I quipped. "I'm sure she'd be happy to help you out. She is such a loving caretaker after all." Bruno smirked and we all fell silent as collective thoughts settled on the food and the hot sweaty sex we *weren't* having.

"Who here has ever had a threesome? I have," Maria chimed in. They were her first words of the conversation. Perhaps she was now caught up in the moment of sexual fantasies. The cricket from the earlier beach announcement started chirping before realizing this was also a lost cause and packed his shit to make a retreat in the uncomfortable silence. We looked at Maria bewildered and weren't quite sure whether we should cheer or pretend it didn't happen. She was a little too into this conversation, apparently.

"I've had three patties in my Big Mac once," Esther added trying to ease the awkwardness.

6/1/2015

Holy shit, there *were* some elevated temperatures in bed last night. Too heated, I think. Maria and Bruno apparently were not about to let the sex talk go to waste or maybe it was the food talk, either way it fucked up Brody's night. Brody confided in Debbie and I that he was sadly awake when Maria snuck into the room he shared with Bruno and had hit Bruno up for sex. It worked. They had full on awkward sex, under the covers, with cameras in the ceiling rolling and poor Brody trying his best to not move a muscle.

"I'd gone to bed and was under my cover not quite asleep when the door creaked open," Brody told us, shuddering slightly. "I was about to turn around and say hi, when I heard Maria whisper *which one is yours?* To Bruno. I froze up and thought for a second they were switching beds. I wish. They got under the covers, and immediately looked for the next train to Funky town."

"How much did you hear, Brody?" I asked fascinated and horrified but the look on Brody's face told me long before he could.

"*Everything.* So, there's that. It was weird," Brody acted shocked but I sensed his affinity for drama and theatrics looming just under his ruffled exterior. "They start getting into it, then Maria asks, as if it was a minor detail she just remembered, *don't you have a girlfriend at home?* And Bruno, stiffly answers *Well yes, but don't worry about that right now.* That was good enough for Maria"

"Classy as fuck," Debbie commented dryly, rolling her eyes.

Brody ignored her. "They start getting into it. A slight moan. Some rustling under those covers and it was over."

"It was over?" I said a little too loudly and surprised.

"Yes. Over. But get this, so it's over and there they are, just lying there, then Bruno asks Maria if she is on the pill."

I guffaw at this. "Really? That's the appropriate time to ask. Yup," Debbie was staring at Brody in disbelief.

"Yes *really*. And she says *Well yes and no. I am, but they took our medicine away when we got here, remember?* And Bruno just says *Oh*. That's literally everything. It just ended there"

"It just ended? Nothing else? What the fuck?" I was in awe.

"I know right? I guess they both figured it was better to just leave it at that. Maria without another word just got up and left."

"But…" Debbie stammered.

"I know, Tisa. If I hadn't been in shock, I would have laughed." Brody replied.

Fucking in the house was not an easy endeavor with cameras everywhere twenty-four hours a day. It's not specifically prohibited but we all know it *must be* frowned upon. Ironic, since it would be excellent as a form of exercise. I wonder if that was why Bruno and Maria went at it—trying to sneak in a little late-night cardio, maybe?

The producers *do* frown on fucking in the house. We all had to sign a piece of paper saying for the duration that we were on the Spa we would not engage in sexual congress with anyone. Not just each other. *Anyone*. Thanks a lot, Bruno and Maria. I think that's the first time in my life I have legally waived my right to have sex. Because I sure as shit didn't sign that abstinence contract circulated around my southern high school back in the day. I hope this one is the last I sign. Now I will have to turn down the scores of willing men that pamper me with sexual propositions every day on this Spa. Seriously though, as I signed all I could think about was if maybe Daniel—the hot PA guy—would make violating it worth it.

The camaraderie became too much for production to handle at the weigh in tonight because at one-point A.C. Moss took us all to task for cheering too much.

"Knock it off people, this is an intense competition. Not *the Family Feud*," Ha another show I don't watch. He was frustrated with the footage I guess, like when we screwed him out of perfectly good fatty drama at the beach. "I want to see no more cheering from you guys for the Bravo Team. It is ruining the weigh-ins for everyone." Everyone? Sure thing, A.C. We're all in the same boat here, right? Then I looked at his smug face, thought of my still missing *paycheck* and thought, *give me your fucking shoes or so help me, you...*

Production was always more than happy to cause strife, mess with your mind or push you into decisions if it added to the entertainment value of our struggle with our weight. They did not appreciate when people got along and were nice to each other. We still won the weigh-in, *too nice or not*, and Bravo Team will have to vote somebody off tomorrow.

6/2/2015

Shea and Chad came down and met with all of us today to discuss the results. The weigh-in had lasted until after midnight despite it being shorter with fewer of us left. Chad tried to soldier through the loss by telling his Bravo Team their weight loss was phenomenal.

"You guys did a really amazing job. I am proud of you," he said, while appearing to fight back tears. Honorable Chad, they might have believed you if you hadn't turned a few times to strategically be featured in profile for the camera.

"I know," Shannon chimed in. "I'm at twenty-four pounds lost after two weeks." I wanted to remind her of the fact it hasn't been two weeks. But the thing is, I can totally see how she might think it was. I have to concentrate sometimes to keep these things straight. Being cut off and told that you're basically not going to survive on your own gets to you after a while and you buy the company line.

"We will bounce back, Bravo Team," Chad went on, trying to pep his crew up to vote somebody off. A few halfhearted cheers and whoops were all Bravo Team could muster. I don't envy them, it was difficult for us to vote a person off the team and we don't even really like each other.

6/3/2015

They voted Maria off, which is both sad *and* funny. Mostly because she had just managed to cause us to sign the Anti-Intercourse Bill into effect. Perhaps she'll be home in time to get a morning after pill. The sad part is, Esther, Debbie and I overheard Bravo Team talk mad shit about her at the pool. How she took too many sausages at breakfast or how she was super annoying all the time. So much for camaraderie, Bravo Team. Fuck that. I guess there is nothing to be envious of, they're just as fucked as we are, all the kumbaya stuff was fake bullshit. Is nothing *real* here?

Chapter 5

As I stumbled down into the dining room to be mic'd up and start the day, I heard commotion coming from the little hallway on my left which led to the kitchen. This Spa has the most extravagant kitchen I have ever seen. There are all sorts of ovens, stove tops, exhaust vents, cupboards, drawers and something I believe is a griddle, all on a giant island. Is it obvious that I don't really have any idea exactly what most of them do because I live on coffee and protein shakes. Oh, and the occasional turkey burger I can overcook in the George Forman grill I asked for. That grill arrived with a lot of eye rolls, deep sighs and snarky remarks about how I should've learned to cook by now, and I would have, except I was busy perfecting my dancing skills instead. Grownups need that skill too. In fact, I'd say it was more important than cooking. If you can't dazzle with your dancing what good are you to modern society? You should see my jazz hands, you'll still be hungry but you'll be so dazzled it won't matter.

The commotion was Hunter and Shannon having a conversation—that sounded slightly distressed—next to the cabinets on the right as I entered.

"What's going on?" I asked, interrupting them. There was an awkward second of silence, then Hunter turned to me.

"You're not going to care. You already tried to get me to drink something that Chad wasn't about." Hunter answered.

"For the love of God Hunter, I wasn't playing the game or trying to sabotage you. It was for your stomach. It was obvious you weren't all right. You know what, whatever. Just tell me about whatever evil thing you're discussing I won't care about."

"There are directions from Doc Malik here that each of us are to take a tablespoon of this liquid in the mornings. Something is off in our electrolytes," Shannon interposed while Hunter was still acting like I snuck anthrax powder in his protein shakes on the regular.

I vaguely remembered certified nursing assistants coming to our rooms and waking us last week to take blood. Being woken up by a nurse with a syringe and a diabolical grin isn't an image you're liable to forget anytime soon. I had pushed it to the back of my mind in light of all the other drama going on. That has to be where the need for the mystery substance was established.

"Well, pass it here then, Doc Malik knows what he's doing," I said as I grabbed the container and a small paper cup off the table. But before I could finish measuring out a dose, Chad and Shea fly into the kitchen in a clamor with Shea half yelling, "Put that down!" I jumped so much I spilled it after getting just enough past my lips to know that whatever it was, it tasted salty.

"What the hell Shea?" I asked, looking at her angrily with mystery substance all over my hand and the floor.

"While I am sure that what you are taking will do whatever for your electrolytes, it's going to make you gain weight. You are going to hold on to water like a sponge if you take that and I will be damned if I am going to lose my shot...uh, your shot at winning this."

Chad chimed in as well, "Shannon, Hunter, as much as I hate to admit it, Shea is right. Don't take that." I like how they continued to passively aggressively fight even when in agreement. The message was clear. Doc Malik is trying to poison me with a vile Gatorade like substance. That pesky man. What does he know?

"You don't really need it, they're just being alarmist. Trust us, you want the best chance possible to stay here and save your lives," Shea said, adding strength to Chad's endorsement of tossing the bottle and moving on. I'm a little skeptical about the Bro-Science behind this but this is their party. I did show up here without a clue. Into the trash it goes and off to the gym I hustle to grind away towards this amazing vision of me I'm sure resides in Shea's head. It's not in mine, that's for sure. In my mind I finally get a nap.

Today's theme must be *ignore anyone not named Shea or Chad.* We got to take a Fat Camp Field Trip to the grocery store today with Dottie. Dottie is the registered dietician for the show who I had no idea even existed until they brought us all into the dining room to announce that we would be going to the store with her. This news was met with mixed reception. It's hard to get super psyched about going shopping with somebody you—until five minutes before— had no idea was alive. On the flip side it meant getting off the Spa for a bit and that was a very promising prospect indeed. I kind of hoped Daniel was going to drive us or be involved somehow. It had been a bit since I had talked to him. While our interactions had been relatively innocent so far, the connection to somebody who wasn't an outright asshole made me flutter.

Well Daniel wasn't there. What a bust. Dottie was there however, and her whole appearance could just as easily have been an elaborate prank played on us by Alison. I wouldn't put it past her. As usual, we were herded into those shitty white church vans, which scoffed at vehicular security.

It's still ninety plus here and there *still* isn't any A/C in these vans. Honestly, just take us for an eight hour drive every day for four months and we could probably lose as much weight as we did working our asses off in the gym. The challenge portion of the show could be to try not puking from the body odor alone. We drove for about an hour and fifteen minutes before we were at a supermarket that had presumably, been rented for an hour or more. Dottie greeted us as we were disembarking the van fleet, looking like a 1950's housewife welcoming her husband home from a hard day at the mill. She was wearing an apron. Is this real life? Nope. It's TV, friend, and everything is fucking *crazy.* We were led into the supermarket where Dottie had a little setup going with some pans and pots and cutting boards. First however, she gave us a tour of the grocery store with helpful tips and tricks to eating healthy. She took extra time around items of particular interest to us fat folk wanting to crash diet a smidge. All the time, a member of the production staff was hot on her heels. They made no effort to hide the fact that some of Dottie's suggestions would not be viewed lightly by Shea and Chad. Dottie motioned us back to her cooking island and started cooking a meal while going through procedures, calories and taste.

"So, in this recipe I use almonds instead of sugar," Dottie chirped. "It's unconventional but I've found that it works well and introduces some nice nutrients."

"Should we use almonds a lot, if we get the chance?" Bruno asked, as one of the few people who seemed genuinely interested.

"Yes exactly. Almonds have a lot of healthy fats and they taste good."

No sooner had she answered the question, before a production assistant cleared his throat.

"You need to follow your trainer's guidelines on what you eat. It's important that you adhere to their advice or you could lose and be forced to go home."

Every time one of us would ask a question, somebody from production would step in following Dottie's answer and tell us that we needed to follow our trainers' guidelines when it came to our eating. What the fuck? Why are we out here if everything she says—like Doc Malik's recommendations—are immediately dismissed. It's like being handed a book and told, *"Here are all the secrets to what you're trying to learn, but if you read it, they won't work for you."*

6/9/2015

We have this thing called *dark days*. They are usually devoid of a trainer and spent doing hours and hours of cardio on our own. We also spend the camera free day suspiciously evaluating what other people are doing and missing our families (who we still haven't heard from). Sometimes though, when we have a dark day our trainers come and take us to do something fun. Shea does anyway. Chad has more important things to do with his time than hang out with his team on the weekends lately. Maybe there's a tattoo conference or an audio book club he's attending. It's a weird change to have Shea being more attentive than Chad, as if they were running a popularity contest on the sly and she had been taking notes for weeks. She decided to take Alpha Team on what we have started calling Fat Camp Field Trips. The last one involved the frustrating trip to the supermarket where we only got to fill our mental shopping carts with non-information on nutrition. Still, ever the optimists— really at this Spa you have to be—we had high hopes for this one because it wouldn't involve cameras. They were proven unwarranted.

Shea's idea of fun was *not* my idea of fun. She took us to a place called Sand Dune Park, which actually and surprisingly contained a four-story high sand dune. Seriously, that was her idea of fun. She took the group of people who had bled and cried in the sand for days of filming and told her how it had almost broken their spirits, to a sand dune... *For fun*! What is it with this woman and sand? Does she own stock or something? There is nothing quite like flashing back to blood and tears while struggling to get your bulk up a four-story sand dune to make you think how fun life is. She however made one crucial mistake today—she let us run free for thirty minutes. As always, the magic trio, Debbie, Esther and I were together. We took the fuck off immediately under the premise that we were going to run stairs.

"Look," I told Debbie and Esther. "I don't know what you guys are going to do but I'm spending the next thirty minutes looking for a phone. I miss home. I have no idea what is going on there and the letters I've received were less than informative after being redacted by production."

"I'm down," Debbie exclaimed loudly then clamped her hands over her mouth and peered around furtively. "I'm down," she whispered, after she made sure Shea wasn't running toward us, arms stretched out, mouthing *noooooooooo*!

"All right. We have thirty minutes, let's haul ass." I reiterated.

Three days ago we had finally been allowed mail and it had already been opened. Opened and censored with a black marker, like we were receiving classified government intelligence instead of what mine really was... a letter from my mother detailing my father's gout symptoms and the weather. As you can imagine this was a less than satisfactory way to stay connected with people at home who loved me. If we didn't already feel like prisoners at the Spa, this put a dot over the proverbial *I*. They might as well stick bars on our windows and hand out orange jumpsuits. At least, if nothing else, the letters have led me to believe everyone in my family is still ok but only as certain as a redacted letter can make me. What if what was blacked out was so dramatic that I would choose to leave and that's exactly why production blacked it out? What if my dad had run off with the pool guy or my sister had decided to join the French Foreign Legion? I'd like to attend the farewell party if nothing else. There'd probably be an open bar.

"Oh, wow Tisa, yes yes yes," Esther said with thinly veiled excitement then mimicked my, "Let's haul ass." she hardly ever used swear words so I knew she was *about* this plan.

I am pretty sure that is the fastest I have run, in like ever. Which is ironic. The best way to make us work out would be to let us think we were running away. We spent the next thirty minutes running blocks away from the park trying to find a phone. Evidently, I'm so old I was born during the Great Depression and somehow believed California still had payphones on every corner. Do they even have payphones anywhere anymore? We thought we were sure to fail—with seven minutes left before we had to report in—when we spotted some poor dude in his car pulling out of his driveway.

"Sir! Sir!" I yelled, probably a little too enthusiastically as I ran toward his car, my arms flailing. "We are on a reality show that is really a fat prison camp from hell. Please, can we borrow your cell phone just to make like a two-minute call home?" I think I said all that in under a second and I'm surprised he even understood me. The guy looked terrified. I think he was afraid that these large sweaty women in matching red shirts were going to mug him. I swear he kept looking around for either a hidden camera that would tell him this was a joke or the Police. He acquiesced with a forced smile and we rushed to call. He got more anxious as the phone calls dragged on, perhaps because he had places to be? I mean, he was pulling out of his driveway. I didn't call home. Let's be honest, compared to Esther and Debbie, I really had no one to call anyway. I am single with a fish and if the fish answered the phone, I'd bail on this program and become rich travelling the Vaudeville Circuit with my amazing talking fish. My parents had been fine for decades before this show and they probably still are, so calling them would be a waste too.

Besides that, even if we only heard one side of Debbie's call we knew whatever her husband told her was super juicy. Both her and Esther cried after talking to their spouses and babies and I probably would have too, after screaming hello to my fish for five minutes, albeit for different reasons. While we walked briskly back to the sand dune and Shea's fun times, Debbie told us about her call.

"First of all, nobody has contacted our families and told them we were kept at the Spa. My husband had no idea where I was," she said, trying to hold her breathing steady enough to talk and walk at the same time.

"What the f…" I started but was so immediately outraged I couldn't even express the expletive. *Thanks a lot* producers. My fish will be out of his mind worried.

Esther, who was breathing hard from sobbing and trying not to lose pace, finished it for me. "Frick."

"But that's not all," Debbie continued, with a smug smile on her face, despite the exertion. "I hope you guys packed your captain's hats and your life jackets. We are going cruising."

She managed a chuckle at the look on both Esther and my faces. We were both about to ask what she knew but we walked through the gate to the Sand

Dune Extravaganza and had to be sneaky about not being seen by Shea until there was no way she could deduce we had left the park. Debbie swore she'd tell us later. We were greeted by Shea like a Labrador retriever. We ran the fucking four story high sand dune without tears or blood and Shea acted like she had once more brought joy and appeasement into our lives. Fuck.

We got a chance to talk in private today—which means we were talking in the bathroom since that is the only damn place cameras aren't allowed you don't get yelled at for disconnecting your microphone. Which you mostly don't do by the way, since it is a pain in the ass. Please imagine thirty audio guys listening to you take a shit daily and how any sense of propriety you may have had is now officially gone.

Esther and I were on Debbie like a pack of dehydrated contestants on a glass of water after a weigh in.

"Alright spill it," I demanded in what I'm sure might have been a voice that was normally reserved for interrogations.

"Yeah... Spill it," Esther followed. I had a brief visual of bullies in the school yard, shaking down weak kids for milk money. Except, we liked Debbie. We were just dying to know what she had heard.

"Alright. So, my husband told me that he had eventually been contacted and told he was to come on a cruise with us."

She must have realized from our completely vacant expressions that this information didn't in any way help us understand.

"They contacted all our loved ones and told them they were flying them out to board a cruise ship. We are going on a cruise and there will be a challenge. Spending time with loved ones will be the prize," she continued. We still had vacant expressions but this time from amazement at this piece of information and what it potentially meant for us.

"Are you telling us we might actually get to see family?" Esther asked incredulously. For her it meant a lot. "Like see them and talk to them?"

"It appears that way."

"And touch them?"

"Well... I guess, if you want to," Debbie chuckled then became pensive at the thought herself. I also thought of touching but my family wasn't in that thought at all and I didn't have to be on a cruise ship for it. I wonder if I could convince production that Daniel is family? *He's my only family that I desperately need about forty-five minutes alone with to fully appreciate, how about it guys?*

"Guys, we need to promise each other not to tell anyone," I said, snapping out of my own thoughts at the sudden realization that we'd be in trouble if production realized we had spoken to the dangerous outside world. I mean they were redacting our fucking letters.

"Yes, it's important nobody knows," Esther agreed.

"But" Debbie started, and I knew what was coming. "The others deserve to know too, don't they?" Her point was legit but it would complicate things. Besides, it wasn't like we were talking about withholding food or vital medicine. The show did that perfectly fine without our help.

"We have to agree not to tell anyone, Debbie," I implored. Esther nodded her consent. "Can we make a pact not to tell anybody about the cruise and family members?"

Debbie acquiesced and I considered the matter settled. I mean surely, I didn't have to make anybody pinky promise or make a blood pact.

6/11/2015

Debbie had a fucking attack of conscience. She told Bruno about our phone calls on fat camp field trip day because our family will be on the boat. That means his girlfriend will be there and Debbie was worried that he would get himself in trouble. He did actually fuck somebody else at the Spa and all, so I get her concern but that shit isn't my problem. Ok, whatever, this isn't that big of a deal. I need to quit with the paranoia. Except he *is* one more person knowing we found a fucking phone. One more person that might accidentally slip up and get us in trouble.

They *finally* did the big *surprise you're going on a cruise* announcement so Esther, Debbie and I acted accordingly. I sure am learning how to act here. Makes me wonder if they do daytime Emmys for reality TV participants. I should at least garner a nomination, maybe a SAG card, something. I mean, I practically had tears of joy at the announcement of something I knew full well and expected.

I'm pretty sure that's more than Gwyneth Paltrow did for her Oscar. The lack of surprise notwithstanding, we *are* going on a cruise which means more time away from this stupid Spa. As always, the cruise was announced in the manner in which I imagine Pharaohs in Ancient Egypt revealed the Pyramids to all the slaves who built them in the first place. Sure, it was fine to go places but it's not exactly as if the prior trips left us with unbeatable smiles on our faces. Plus, history has shown us the rewards for challenges had a way of hurting more than they did good. We were told to go pack a bag, which basically just meant throwing gym clothes and a toothbrush into a bag and that we'd head out early the next morning. The rest of the night was spent in limbo between eager anticipation of perhaps seeing family and trying to pretend it was just another night. We chit chatted in our room and as always, the talk turned to sex and food. My thoughts embarked on the same train as when we were hogging that poor scared guy's phone. When we finally went to bed, I was under my covers with a weird mix of excitement about the cruise and wondering if we would have private rooms there...and if *Daniel* would also be on the cruise.

6/12/2015

When we checked into the cruise, Esther being the evil genius she is, asked what room her wife was in when production wasn't paying attention so she could contact her. I didn't even think about seeing what room my mom might be in. I really do follow rules more than it may seem. I'll instigate the shit out of things—don't get me wrong—but I'm not getting laid or getting a rib eye steak for finding my mom, so I'll be ok waiting a bit to see her. They escorted me to my room and did the whole *lock me in* thing that they always do. It's truly awesome to hear that door slam and the following click as soon as you're inside a room. Doesn't make you feel like you're restricted *at all*. I unpacked what little I had, sat on my bed, and started looking at the wall. What else is there to do?

Remember when I was mildly excited about leaving the Spa because I wouldn't have to sit in a little room and feel like a prisoner? Remember how I was looking forward to the charm of the open sea? Yeah not so much. So far, cruising lacks the charm I had imagined—striped shirts, cabin boys, drinks, with umbrellas. *Instead* I have a shitty hotel room with a floor that sways, a shower that doubles as a toilet and no TV. I was straightening my gym shoes for the fifth time and evaluating what poor life choices led me here when something interesting finally happened. Somebody knocked on the door.

"Please God be a foreign prince with a pizza and huge trust fund in need of a wife," I said loud enough that whoever was out there would hear. I was sure instead someone had come to tell me it'd be another few hours of solitary waiting. When the door opened though, it wasn't some annoying PA or Shea telling me they had somehow gotten a mountain of sand onto the ship, and our next challenge would be to shovel it back into the ocean while avoiding the scorpions they had filled it with. It was Daniel, the absolutely not-annoying PA, who cracked a wide smile when he saw me.

"Hi Tisa. Did you miss me?"

I was momentarily struck dumb as I just looked at him, torn between jumping him or playing cool. I ended up somewhere in between as I made a weird half high-five half hug type gesture narrowly avoiding hitting him in the throat with an elbow. I also mumbled something that could best be described as the sound of a lawnmower being started violently.

"I have something for you," he said, with that same smile playing across his face, closing the door after him.

"Oh?" I asked, regaining my ability to form coherent fragments of sentences at least. My mind was racing. What did he have? Did it involve being naked? Oh *please* let it involve that. But was there time? Did they know he was here? I wasn't mic'd up was I? Was that what he came here for? Why isn't he telling me what it is? I'm not great with surprises and this was killing me.

"Here," he said as he handed me an iPod. I had not expected this at all and I stared at him as though a Popsicle had suddenly sprung from his forehead. I think he noticed the look of confusion on my face because he launched into an explanation straight away. "I've loaded music on it for you so you have something for when you work out. I co-host a show at my university radio and I dedicated a song to you on it. It's on the iPod too."

"Wow," I said. My look of confusion lingered as I realized the scope of the gesture. "That's so sweet, Daniel. Can I hear it?"

"Yes, it's right on there. Go ahead."

I put in the headset and scrolled through the tracks on the iPod. He had loaded a copious variety of music on there and the thought of having it for when

I did cardio was already melting my normally cold, black heart. I eventually found the radio track and listened to Daniel talk about a sweet girl he had recently met, how she was going through a hard program, and how he liked her and wanted to make her feel better. He ended the dedication with "To Tisa. When I see you, I forget what I am doing, and when I don't see you, what I am doing doesn't matter. Keep that smile on your face. It's hard to resist."

Daniel was watching me as I sat on my bed and listened. I looked up at him, and my eyes were nearly tearing up.

"I can't believe you did that you jerk, you made me tear up."

He laughed at my awkward reaction, "I think about you a lot. I wanted you to know that."

He stood there a little nervously and I felt a stronger than ever attraction. I moved toward him and hugged him tight. He hugged me back, just as tight, and only slacked his grip enough so I was held close in front of him. He leaned in and kissed me. After many weeks of wondering if it was ever going to happen, it was worth the wondering. As I kissed him back, and my insides were jumping with excitement. We stood, locked in time, as our lips connected hungrily. His hands were on my lower back and shoulder, pulling me close. I would not have minded if the entire trip at sea was just this but Daniel eventually let me go. I was almost dizzy with a plethora of thoughts and feelings—lust, affection and a new-found fondness for cruising.

"I have to go again. Production doesn't know I'm here and if they found out, it would be trouble for both of us," he said, as he touched my face. Even as I felt a rush of disappointment that he had to go, his touch jolted through me. "We will find time to continue where we left off," he continued in the playful tone I had fixated on when over-analyzing our every interaction. I was going to break records ruminating on this one.

"Good," I said as I shot him—what I sincerely hoped was—a telling look meant to convey what continuation it might just result in—and not my usual seductive face that involved both the weird eye twitch I get and my stress induced crooked smile that makes me look like I'm confused about where I am—sexy, I know. "Thank you again for the music, Daniel," I said with surprisingly heartfelt emotion.

"You're welcome Tisa."

"And thank you for thinking of me."

"Hardly something you need to thank me for, I can't help it at this point." He smiled a beguiling smile at me again as he opened the door. A moment later the door was closed and I was left alone, aching for more and trying to settle for what I got. I got on my bed, plugged in the earbuds again immersed myself in the music as my body and mind stopped racing. Then I played out every moment of our encounter over and over again in my head.

When I was finally released from my room by a PA whose name was something like *Not Daniel*, I spent an obscene amount of time bored out of my mind in that little cabin. Granted, my encounter with Daniel left my mind rather involved but even that dissipated by the time my door swung open. Instead, I was met with a dull and unfriendly face of some random production assistant telling me to get my shit together and get ready or something equally as charming.

I met up with Debbie and Esther at the buffet where cameras were already set up. We were going to film some scenes around food because it's best to keep us close to the one thing we should not under any circumstances touch. Production could teach the boys in Guantanamo Bay a few tricks. Being around food is harder for some contestants than it is for others. Both Esther and Debbie might have been fucked if it hadn't been for what happened at the buffet that took focus away from the food.

"Hi guys. Have a fun afternoon?" I asked with a mockingly chipper wave. I was very happy to be outside that room and talking to people again but still resentful in my endearing way. The Spa might be a shitty place but at least we got to talk to fellow contestants.

"Yes riveting," Debbie said drily but unable to suppress a smile. It was clear she was equally happy to be out. Esther smiled too but kept looking around as if she expected our family members to come running out at us with arms stretched, and balloons floating serenely from a big net in the ceiling.

"Did you talk to your wife?" I whispered.

"Nope. I saw her," Esther responded, giggling.

Debbie and I turned to her with eyes the size of saucers. "No way." we said in unison.

"Ha ha, yes. I got a hold of her on the ships phone and told her where I was. She snuck down to my cabin."

"Why Esther, don't tell me you got laid," I exclaimed with enough decibel to attract the attention of a nearby cameraman who glanced at us confused.

"Well…" she started.

"Yup. You totally got laid."

She blushed a deep crimson red. "All right, I got laid. As you put it with such class, Tisa," She clearly wasn't used to talking about such matters with people but on the other hand, she had sex and it made her jubilant. She did shoot me a disapproving look for good measure though.

"You lucky son of a…" I was simultaneously happy for, and envious of her.

We were almost high fiving as other contestants started to pour in around us and we had to act somewhat casual. We didn't want to arouse suspicion.

My envy evaporated as my well-honed slut-senses—they're like Spidey-senses only far more useful—kicked in and I realized Esther wasn't the only one to have gotten laid. I could be wrong, but married Blake and annoying Shannon weren't exactly subtle as I watched them play grab ass in the buffet line. What in the actual fuck?

6/13/2015

This boat is boring as fuck. Granted, I'm not much of a sailor but I've been on cruises before and they usually involve more drinking and sex and less sitting around in a cabin. On the plus side, I've befriended some dust bunnies under my bed. I think they've got a whole society going under there. We were picked up this morning and got to do some more standing around. Normally, this wouldn't bother me—I like my own company—but today there was potential drama. In lieu of absolutely nothing else to do, that drama seemed like something I didn't want to miss. If nothing else, being taken somewhere to stand around by production meant I got to actually talk to human beings instead of following the intricate lives of Mr. Dustbunny and his family. I met up with Debbie and Esther with production's blessing to do some more fascinating standing, both of whom were positively twinkling.

"Y'all bitches had more sex. I can sense it a mile away," I said, not without a twinge of remorse they hadn't brought my fish down to the boat so that I would at least have company if not sex. He'd feel right at home in the giant fish bowl I was currently living in. "Is everybody able to sneak out but me?" They both giggled as I realized I hadn't even really tried. Where would I sneak off to? I didn't know where Daniel was and if I did, I'd get him fired if I turned up in his room wearing nothing but a smile. I was almost at the point where I didn't care if he got in trouble or if I did. For now, I was just going to live through Debbie and Esther.

"Speaking of sex," Debbie suddenly interjected, "Guess who I saw being let into Shannon's room last night, as I was prowling the ship."

"Get the fuck out of here" I cried, in usual overly excited fashion. "He didn't?"

Esther looked puzzled for a moment then remembered the day before at the buffet, and Debbie's smile widened as Esther realized.

"Blake," we both said at the same time. Evidently everybody was getting laid but me.

"Yes, Blake," Debbie shot us both suggestive glances, as she waited for us to realize what she had already figured out.

I arrived at the conclusion first. "But, isn't his wife possibly on the ship now? For the challenge?" I asked, the full explosive potential of this situation became blatantly apparent.

Esther was shocked. "He's married for Pete's sake. And on a boat." I couldn't help but laugh at this. "It's not funny, Tisa."

"It is a little funny." I opposed with mock indignation. "He's sneaking around fucking Shannon and his wife is right here. *Right. Here.* It's shitty but I find it hilarious. Whatever, I'm a terrible person sometimes."

The smile Esther tried to suppress told me she secretly agreed.

"I wonder how that's going to go," Debbie mused out loud.

"Like most everything else around here. To shit."

"Should we tell him?" Esther seemed mildly concerned.

"I suppose. I don't know what we can do, I mean he fucked Shannon already didn't he?" I mused.

"That's true. But at least warn him that his wife is here, so he has time to prepare himself." Esther fretted.

"Prepare? For what?" I was genuinely confused. "He's not taking a pop quiz. He's about to face his wife after having fucked somebody else less than 24 hours before. There's hardly any preparing for that."

We remained silent a bit, pondering what we could do and if we even should. It was his own mess but still I suppose we could be good Samaritans and try to clear some of it a bit.

"We can't outright tell him. I'm sure the producers are just aching for a chance to bust us," I offered. I really didn't care enough about Blake's bullshit to get myself into trouble.

Debbie agreed. "We'll try to see if we can talk to him."

I don't know if I've ever been a particularly modest or shy person but today right before the challenge I was going pee and an audio dude opens the door in the middle of everything. There were around fifty people milling about behind him— all of whom seemed to look up at that exact moment. Some of them were holding cameras. Great job, dude. Way to start off this challenge shit. I collected myself and joined the other contestants in the waiting area before things kicked off.

Blake was talking to Bruno and I'm pretty sure I knew about what. You could tell from a mile away he was awfully pleased with himself. You had sex, bro. No atoms were split, cures for terminal diseases discovered or baby animals rescued from certain doom. *Calm down.* Debbie, Esther and I wandered closer and once in earshot, we realized we were right.

"I barely made it through the door, before she was all over me," he told a mildly interested Bruno. As he saw us approaching he trailed off, unsure if a bunch of women would appreciate his conquest as much as his bros. He still looked pretty pleased with himself, though.

"Perhaps you should sit this one out, Blake," Debbie tried, forsaking every pretense of subtlety. Blake stared at her, bewildered. He had not expected that.

"What? Why?" he responded befuddled.

"Well you know, uh, it's—" Debbie had clearly not thought that one through.

"You obviously had a rough night," I spoke up in a clear voice, which made a few people nearby look toward us.

Blake was momentarily thrown off by this and looked around sheepishly, as if we had walked in on him banging Shannon.

"You never know what comes next. Sometimes it's best to just take it easy," I continued. I had no idea where I was going with this, subtle isn't really in my skillset. But if he went on to compete, he would have the shock of his lifetime on national TV. Blake still didn't know why we were talking to him about sitting out but his face soon changed from stunned bemusement to the smugness he had sported earlier.

"Alright, girls," he said. "I think I'll be ok."

"But you could hang out at the finish line and cheer the rest on." I tried to convince him.

"You guys are just jealous."

We were all kinds of stunned by this statement. "What?" I asked, with what I'm sure was more stupefaction than was required.

"Obviously you know about me and Shannon."

"Look dude," I started, intending to tell him I was a lot of things and why jealous wasn't one but Debbie sensed the impending disaster and cut me off.

"It's not that," she tried, with mounting frustration. "Weren't you saying the other day your legs were hurting?"

Blake lost the arrogant look and replaced it with one of mild obfuscation. "Yes, but that's no big deal. Happens to us all. Stop trying to guarantee an Alpha Team win by talking me out of competing. It's pathetic."

"But if you sat today out, you'd get some rest and recover completely," Debbie went on. Noble of her really when his attitude was so shitty. I was ready to tell his smug face to eat a bag of dicks and enjoy his day.

Facing three women who seemed hell-bent on having him sit out was doing a number on Blake's head and he finally decided what our problem was. "You are afraid of losing," he said, and I had to stifle a laugh.

"No, really. We just have your wellbeing at heart," Esther said, not yet ready to give up.

"You are going to lose today and you want me out so you can win," He continued, ignoring her. He was certain we were trying to game him and he wasn't having it. His smug look returned, albeit for different reasons now, intensified. "You are scared."

Esther's face went ashen and the normally composed woman went full sass. "Alright, girls. Let him do it. Whatever," She walked off with the two of us in tow, leaving Blake looking perplexed again. Poor guy. Had no idea what was in store for him.

Well the challenge was interesting. Not least because it served as a platform for one of the most awkward and hilarious moments I've witnessed. Trust me when I say, I've witnessed and/or partaken in quite a few awkward moments thus far. Including an entire camera crew barging in on me peeing just today. Blake obviously wasn't convinced of anything but the fact that we were trying to throw him off his game or keep him from unleashing his crazy skills on our poor unsuspecting asses. Granted, he had no real way of knowing that we were trying to protect him but his self-important demeanor still annoyed the fuck out of me and I was short on empathy because of it.

We were all lined up in our teams at the start/finish line and stood there in restrained anticipation. Cameras were rolling and there was the usual drama for the audience bullshit buildup before the challenge was finally presented. It was a scavenger hunt. Other contestants were mildly surprised, but the kicker hadn't kicked in yet. Alison shot Debbie, Esther, and I a suspicious look at this point because we weren't kvelling in joy I suppose. It's like production is trained to spot any deviation from normal submissive brainwashed behavior. Perhaps I wasn't worthy of that SAG card I was certain some of our previous work entitled us to because I wasn't convincing enough in my shock and awe over the crazy creativity that was a reality TV scavenger hunt. I'm rolling my eyes so hard at the thought that I might need to see Doc Malik for a sprain injury.

Then they announced the *prizes* – our families. There was a member of our family waiting for us at each spot on the scavenger hunt. I raised my eyebrows, set my mouth agape and made eyes as large as teacups. Everything Paris Hilton—the ever-incandescent beacon of professional acting—would've done and more. I was genuinely happy to get a chance to see my mom but I had expected her. The same goes for Debbie and Esther seeing their spouses, both of which they had had sex with only the day before respectively. If they wanted genuine looks of amazement, they should've had cameras in those rooms two nights ago. I genuinely tried my best to look surprised but Alison was squinting at me, and I was pretty sure she would've come over and called my bluff, if it wasn't for Blake.

Blake had no idea what was going to happen. One second he was joking with the other guys that he totally fucked Shannon. The next he learned his actual wife—to whom he very likely swore eternal fidelity—was on this boat, mere feet from him. His face nearly made me pass out from suppressed laughter. He might've been in the middle of a sentence but whereas my expression had been faked, his was genuinely shocked and horrified. Blake's mouth was stuck on a guttural sound, he had glassy eyes, nostrils flaring furiously and arms kind of just hanging there. I can't imagine what was going on in that head of his but I'm pretty sure if we had a visual representation of it, it would be a looped video of Wile E. Coyote getting hit in the head with a giant hammer. There was no doubt that having just cheated on his wife, and then learning he would be facing said wife in mere moments did a number on Blake. His face clearly showed it. It was obvious to most people who would have cared to look. Blake was *anything* but happy to learn she was there. I only regret I have but one set of eyes or I would've been watching Shannon's reaction too. I'm certain I wouldn't have been able to hold back my laughter at that point.

When Alison saw Blake, she immediately forgot about anyone else's reactions. Other contestants were shooting Blake sideways glances and I fought a strong urge to ask him if he still thought we were trying to *throw him off his game* or whatever idea he had convinced himself was the case.

Soon after the game began. I volunteered to sit this one out because the other team had Chris sitting it out due to a nasty knee injury. It kicked off a 1930s slapstick comedy type session of people running around the ship looking for clues in a scavenger hunt with the right to spend time with your family as the prize. Each family member had a game piece and together they would make up the final location of the winning item. We were winning the challenge by a fairly large margin and again had to face the disappointed looks of mixed reproach and sadness from the Bravo Team.

"We should find a way to include them," I said during a brief moment with the rest of my team. "They lost the challenge on the beach too and still haven't gotten their care packages."

"They should've done better," Esther joked behind me. She flashed a smile when I faced her and we both knew what I was saying was the right thing to do. We all missed families and, in my case, goldfish.

"How can we make sure we both win?" asked Debbie. I was grateful my two friends were kind people.

"I don't know."

"Perhaps stumble deliberately or take more time with our pieces," Esther suggested. "If we make sure they catch up, we can finish at the same time."

That settled it. I went back to the finish line, we discussed it with the rest of the team and not being assholes themselves they agreed we should try to time the finish to be a tie. But because our track record was already blemished and my antics in particular seemed to draw the attention of the producers, they caught onto our game pretty fast. Alison, she of the ever vigilant to my possible bullshit shenanigans, came over to us, and it was pretty clear that production was having none of our shit.

"It won't work."

"Excuse me?" I asked, at first genuinely confused but deciding to play it dumb when I turned and saw who had addressed me. I felt like I was in a Scooby Doo episode. You know, the one. It's where those meddling kids foil the disguised man's sinister, yet simplistic plan. I think it was in season 4 or something.

"We know you're trying to make sure it's a tie. It won't work."

I decided it might be obvious or they just knew us better than we thought, so I played it straight. "We just want everybody to see their families," I said coolly. Like why the fuck did I even have to make that argument?

"I understand, but we need one team to win. This is a fucking TV show, not a playpen in your local nursery."

I was momentarily stunned by this sudden—and in my view—unwarranted harshness. "Excuse me?" I said, more befuddled than indignant.

"We'll make sure one team wins, or you can. I don't care." We all stood there, Bravo and Alpha Team together feeling kind of defeated and not really knowing what to think. We ended up winning the challenge but it felt hollow looking at the Bravo Team's faces. Another chance to reconnect with a home that seemed years and oceans away at this point, had slipped through their fingers. It was all a part of the game, but still it felt shitty to deprive them once more.

Silly me for thinking that winning the fucking challenge meant actually enjoying the prize we won. Instead of actually seeing my mother, I spent the entire fucking day filming me seeing her over and over again. Doing interviews about how awesome it was to see my mother again and watching her do interviews about how excited she was to see me. You know what the Bravo Team did today? They got to actually spend time with their family members without cameras or other assholes directing or holding them up. Nice. When I did get a few moments in my room with my mom, the way they treated her instantly pissed me off.

"Go there. Do this. No, not like that, like this. No, from another angle. Tisa, look up. Ok, talk. Cut. Ok, talk again." That was how most of my day went. Kubrick would have envied these production dick wads and their tenacity. They kept my mom and I discussing superficial shit. It wasn't until hours passed, that they left us for more than a moment.

"Finally. I thought winning this prize meant actually getting to talk to you for a moment and not just film sequences for them," I said, trying to calm my raging annoyance.

"Me too," My mom said. "They aren't very keen on sharing details about anything out here."

"Tell me about it. I understand keeping secrets from contestants because of the game, but this is ridiculous."

"Flying us out here was crazy too. Like we were nuclear scientists escorted to a secret testing facility. Couldn't tell anybody, couldn't do anything." She rolled her eyes.

"What did they have you do?"

"Sit in my room mostly. What is there to do really? It's not like my tennis partner is around."

I chuckled. What the fuck *was* there to do?

"Besides," she continued. "I was locked in the entire time."

It took me a few seconds to register. "You *what*?" I said, not sure I had registered it. Who the hell would think it okay to lock my sixty-year-old mother in her room with no idea what was going on? I guess I had forgotten I was on a show with people who didn't give a shit about others.

"Yes. They stuck me in a room and locked the door."

"That's bullshit. I had no idea they did this. Did they tell you why?"

"Something about keeping the game secret." She looked bemused for a second. "It wasn't really a big deal, but it still felt kind of weird."

"It is a fucking big deal. Who locks up… I'm livid they did this." I was. But, I knew I couldn't do a damn thing about it. I was pissed. I imagined my mom being black bagged on her way home from work one night, by a gang of excited production assistants, and tossed into the back of a van where A.C. Moss would cackle insanely for the entire duration of the drive. Then they would deposit her into a little room on a ship, while a guy with a voice modulator instructed her over the intercom. Man, fuck these people.

In typical Shea fashion, she managed to fuck up something as simple as a celebration, the one thing we had that didn't involve unabashed shaming or feeling like death was hovering above our heads. The Alpha Team got together with our families on the deck next to the pool, to introduce them to Shea. It was actually a really nice set up. We were happy to be with our families and there was even a bottle of champagne. How cosmopolitan. I mean that shit was purely for the cameras. There was no way we were going to be drinking a glass but it still lent the scene a certain air of genuine festivity and joy. Then Shea opened her mouth and every illusion of a close and intimate bond forged in joyful but hard-earned tears between us and her was derailed.

"George, I just want to let you know what a fighter Esther is. Her tenacity and spirit are amazing." she said through, what I almost thought was a theatrical lump in her throat. We all looked around a little bewildered. George was *Debbie's* husband. Shea was singing Esther's praises to *Debbie's* husband. Brody, who had figured out what was going on faster than the rest of us, tried to catch Shea's attention to clue her in. Ever oblivious to anything except the cameras, Shea instead continued to prattle on, this time turning to Esther's wife, "Debbie is also an amazing team player who—"

At this point I was dying. How long had we been here and this woman still didn't have our names right? Say what you will about Chad but I have a feeling he wouldn't have done this. So much for that deep emotional bond between the trainers and their teams. Esther and Debbie didn't seem too upset by the whole mix up. Just another day at the fat camp honestly. All three of us caught each other's eyes at that moment though, and between us an idea was born.

I've never seen a human being freak out so much from water. I'm still laughing so hard I cannot catch my breath hours after. Like the A-Team at the end of each episode, Debbie, Esther and I, without a word, managed to coordinate a plan without a word. We threw Shea into the pool. You know, to *celebrate*. And as payback for not knowing a damn thing about us. Mostly to celebrate though. You would've thought we had thrown her into a vat of acid.

"Oh my God," she spluttered as she quickly resurfaced and hastily made her way toward the ladder. Most people were chuckling because there was a sort of post-game locker room throw a barrel of Gatorade at Coach thing going but a few were already furrowing concerned brows. Shea couldn't really spout obscenities like a sailor, as she was hyper aware of the cameras on her but she was definitely freaking out. "My hair! My makeup! She shrieked, emerging from the pool looking not unlike a penguin. She was clawing at her hair—half trying to cover it, half trying to straighten it—all while she desperately fought to maintain a facade for the cameras. She forced a smile and mumbled—perhaps more to herself than to the producers—that she hoped they wouldn't use this. I hope they *will*. I'm still laughing.

6/14/2015

The cruise gym isn't terrible and there is a track on the deck to run on too. I was allowed to take my mother to the gym for my workout this morning and the Bravo Team was already there. Poor Chris is still beat to shit and limping. He was using a machine I had never seen before, which allowed him to sit while pedaling with his arms. It seemed to do the trick as he was working up a sweat.

I was fascinated by the fact that Shannon and her friend were working out next to Blake and his wife on treadmills because Shannon had insisted they move closer so she could talk to his wife. It was like watching two trains on the same track hurdling towards each other. I can't even imagine the level of anxiety Blake must have felt standing between his wife, and the woman he had just cheated on her with. I had filled in my mother about the fun dynamics there and she was equally as icked out as I was.

We got on the treadmills behind this whole debacle and marveled at the awkward games that played out in front of us.

"I just *love* your hair," Shannon told Blake's wife over Blake's head as they were all lumbering along. She smiled a sweet honey dripping smile that would've had even Winnie the Pooh needing insulin.

"Thank you, Shannon," she replied merrily. "I do it myself," She flashed a proud smile to Shannon, whose overly sweet smile left her face as soon as Blake's wife wasn't looking at her anymore. They worked out in silence a little. Then Shannon reached over and touched Blake's hip. She made sure it was out of his wife's sight. Blake looked over, confused and Shannon shot him daggers with her eyes—pure jealousy and anger. Blake slowly glanced at his wife to check if she had noticed. It was so awkward to watch. My meddling over inflated sense of justice had me nearly shouting out, *"Shannon is banging your husband!"*

"Are you enjoying your time on the boat?" Shannon went on, not content to let anybody off this carnival ride from hell just yet.

"Yes, we're having a good time," Blake interjected, trying to defuse the situation inconspicuously.

"I asked your wife," Shannon said, just sharply enough for Blake to pick up while still leaving his wife in the dark.

"Yes, absolutely. A nice ship," she said. "Very luxurious."

"I'm sure you would think so," Shannon replied. Her smile razor sharp with warning for Blake to let her continue. The wife didn't look at her this time but Blake shot furtive glances Shannon's way. I wasn't sure if he was pleading with her to stop the madness or trying to tell her he was as upset by all this as she was. She touched his shoulder again and Blake did his little sideways glance move once more. After a few minutes of extremely thick silence, Shannon and her friend—who had otherwise remained silent through this whole show—bid people a good bye and left the gym. About the same time that train wreck ended, I got distracted by the circus sideshow that was Chad entering the gym and bee lining for my mother and me. He went on to tell my mom—with me sitting right there—that I could win this whole show. My mom didn't really know what to say but was obviously delighted to hear such accolades from one of the trainers. It's hard to say what motivated him. Perhaps he really did believe it? I trust Chad about as much as I would trust a vending machine egg salad sandwich, so we will have to see.

6/15/2015

The cruise is over. Not because the cruise was actually over but because production *told* us it was. We were herded off the ship and into our old friends, the white church vans. I'm pretty sure these vans were at some point used in an industrial bakery, for their ability to hold immense heat. To add insult to the injury of riding in the vans, we had to tell our families goodbye in the parking lot with a nice audio backdrop of humming engines looming over us. There were tears. Almost universally. Blake's goodbye was monitored like the NSA by Shannon, who didn't miss a single crocodile tear or awkward hug from across the lot. I got the feeling her fingers were idly fiddling with a shiv in her pocket, and at moment's notice, she could launch across the parking lot and stab Blake's wife in the jugular amidst confusion and war cries. I was caught up in saying goodbye to my mom, making her promise to put a picture of me up next to my fish tank at home. Fish get lonely too, I'm sure of it. It was weird to say goodbye to her though, after such a short time and knowing I'd have to go back to that damn Spa.

The bus ride back was hell on wheels. The aforementioned heat notwithstanding, everybody was sad, pissy, and puffy-eyed from tears. Well nearly everybody. Two people were damn near partying. Blake and Shannon were sitting together, cuddling, laughing and holding hands. Hell, I'm pretty sure Shannon would have straddled Blake right then and there to mark him and remove his wife's scent, if it hadn't been for prying eyes. My spirits were bolstered by the death stares they were receiving from my fellow contestants though. At least I wasn't the only one disgusted by a level of duplicity that would've made Harvey Dent quit politics.

6/16/2015

Back at the Spa. It's drab and dull and honestly, I miss my family. Seeing my mom was nice but also threw into sharp contrast just how miserable I am in this God forsaken shithole. To top off the misery, Bravo Team won the weigh in. *Shit*.

6/17/2015

Feeling a little better today and motivated by the weigh in loss yesterday, I was back with Esther and Debbie in the gym. We're all just off the treadmills when Kevin comes slinking up to us, looking like he has a master plan and is recruiting for a bank heist. I was briefly reminded of one of those bank robbing Disney characters in the eye masks and had to stop myself from chuckling. He didn't say anything at first, just sort of hovered next to us like he was getting ready to work out but nothing happened.

"You alright, Kevin?" Esther asked. He looked at us like he just noticed us—physically impossible since there wasn't anybody else in there, and we are three women who take up space. Also, we aren't exactly the silent types.

"Yes, sure," he said noncommittally, then entered our little circle. This felt like a setup. Like a staged routine. "So, who are you guys going to vote off?" Yup. Something was up.

"I don't know, Kevin," I started. "I'm getting sick of Debbie and Esther, so I might petition the show to have them both sent home." I'm hilarious. Kevin joined Debbie and Esther with an awkward chuckle.

"Who are you going to vote for, Kevin?" Debbie asked. Probably what he wanted to be asked so he didn't have to segue his suggestion into the conversation. I imagined him saying *Glad you asked, Debbie. Let me present my plan*, with a top hat, monocle and Power Point presentation. Reality sadly, was less entertaining.

"Well…" he began. He glanced around at each of us briefly like he was about to give us the password to his secret club. "I thought we should vote Brody home," He skipped a beat here and sensed reluctance. He immediately launched into a weird tirade that downplayed the severity of suggesting an alliance. "He's been having a hard time lately and I think the family thing on the boat really hit him hard. He might not want to admit it but I think he really misses home. He's just not doing everything he can, and it might hurt us all."

I eyed Kevin briefly. This was rehearsed and thought through. His execution sucked but he was definitely trying to play the game. He was about as opaque as a pane of glass. Can't blame him, I guess. It *is* a game and even if most of us haven't given much thought to end game, I suppose there is a time where it'll be pertinent to consider who you'd want to keep around. But I wasn't prepared for this bullshit. Not right now.

"I think Brody is doing alright so far. It was rough for all of us in that parking lot. Has he said anything?" Debbie asked.

"Oh, nothing specific, you know. Just little things," Kevin wasn't stammering but he might as well have been. "Little things," he repeated as if to emphasize the importance of how little these things were. So little only the trained eye would pick them up, apparently.

"Well we'll see, Kevin. I'm not sure Brody is doing that bad," Esther said in what felt like a closing statement.

"Perhaps not," Kevin was fiddling with the treadmill again. His escape pod. He got up and pushed buttons and the conversation was kind of over. We loafed off with a quick wave and left Kevin to brood and scheme by himself.

Kevin's a bastard. I could throat punch him. The vote off tonight was a shit storm. There was bawling—snot running, red faced—ugly faced bawling.

Esther, Debbie and I had talked about the encounter with Kevin after we left the gym and considered his weird behavior and suggestion. We didn't really want to vote off Brody in particular but there wasn't any real alternative to us at this point. Since Kevin seemed to have some sort of master plan going, we thought perhaps it would become apparent. Brody *did* seem to miss his home a lot and the guys on the team thought he wasn't pulling his weight, for whatever that was worth. Kevin might have insights we did not. We weren't delusional enough to convince ourselves we were doing Brody a solid but overall, perhaps he was the best contender for a one-way ticket home.

The vote séance shit starts as always with a one on one with the camera in a little room, where you spill the beans on why you're voting the way you do. A good way to get people to talk shit about each other, I'm sure. You sit in a chair that looks super comfy but feels like bus station waiting room seating and smells exactly like what it is—a small chair sweaty people are interrogated in. *How does production manage to make even something as simple as a chair feel that horrible?* You are then asked leading questions to fret out possible controversies they can exploit. After that, we have to march repeatedly down the hall carrying these ridiculous silver trays. The march feels like we are this weird fat butler parade. The parade ends in an oddly shaped room decorated with fake refrigerators bearing our names and us all sitting in a row, so they can frame us and catch reactions. We go through the motions of mindless bullshit small talk before getting down to brass tacks. *Sure Cynthia, I learned a buffet is my arch nemesis on that luxury cruise where I was locked in my room and lost a lot of water weight in that six-hour van ride back to the Spa with the broken A/C. Come to think of it, I think it was the best week ever.* I had written Brody down on my card and tried to justify my choice in the interrogation room feeling kind of fake doing it. Now we each take our turn revealing who we voted for and explain it to the poor asshole. It's stupid.

We have deliberately been placed in order at the table, Esther, Debbie, Me, Kevin, Bruno and then Brody for dramatic effect. Esther and Debbie predictably vote *Brody* and I follow suit. Next comes the backstabbing fuckery magic. Kevin votes for Debbie and in what I'm sure is my classiest moment ever, I blurt out, "You Bastard" forgetting the thirty million people including my mom that'll view that shit later. Note to self, remember to prep Mom for that shining moment if I ever make it out of here alive.

The moment steadily gets worse as the other two guys reveal that they have also voted for Debbie. As I sit there stunned they start bringing in the Bravo Team looking self-righteous as fuck. I don't remember much else. Blind rage at Kevin kind of overshadowed other events. Followed by broken hearted sobbing because the Bravo Team was given the choice of who to send home and, for reasons as of yet unknown, they chose Bruno. They chose sweet hearted, crazy tall, strong, universally adored Bruno. Fuck this game.

Chapter 6

Shea, in her infinite wisdom, suggested we go for a run this morning. This dumb bitch really thinks that the way to get over our heart break at Bruno being sent home is to go for a run? *A run.* There is nothing more a bunch of exhausted, emotionally beat down, physically injured unconditioned fat people want to do to self soothe, than to run up and down a hill in 100-degree weather. The only thing propelling me down that stupid hill I know I'll be slogging back up again in a minute, is the blind rage exploding just behind my eyes every time I think of Shea's annoying blonde face or Shannon's equally annoying blonde face.

As we left the elimination room snotty faced last night and still crying, we encountered Shannon, Blake and Chris sitting casually in our path gloating. At least it seemed that way from behind all of our tears. Because I am pretty sure that Shannon is a mean-spirited two-faced succubus and Blake just an empty vapid shell. I chose to address the only other human in the room, Chris, and asked him why in the world they would get rid of somebody, perhaps the only actual person, that was universally loved. Bruno was everybody's favorite He was someone who seemingly effortlessly got along with all of us and literally risked his physical safety for the team during all the challenges. Chris explained calmly and patiently that Bruno was the biggest threat. Coming in as heavy as he was, he had the biggest potential to lose the most weight and thus win the entire game. To the three of us—Esther, Debbie, and I—this show being an actual game wasn't really something we had explored in any real depth yet. I mean, we decided that we liked one another and formed sort of a tentative alliance but mostly it was just a friendship. Not unlike something I would have formed any other day, without cameras or crazy producers telling us what to do. It had now smacked us in the face that, *surprise*, everyone else was already playing the game more than we had realized. It stung both to feel so naive and to have to learn we were still that naive with Shannon's dull bovine eyes staring at us from her self-satisfied face. She kicked it over the top for me when she mumbled, "However are you going to get your ass over a wall now Tisa, with Bruno gone? So much for the Alpha Team winning all the challenges huh?" Chris saw the look of rage instantly blooming on my ugly cry induced, swollen snot covered face, and not being an insufferable douchebag, knew to get her out of the room immediately. Lest there be an incident where I let my crazy show on national TV more than I already had.

Back on our stupid fucking run in temperatures I'm sure they'd cast envious glances at from Venus, I managed to exhaust myself and am crying. The cheerleader from hell, Shea, was next to me in yet another of an apparently in exhaustive supply of pink camo baby shirts telling me about how she won't let me quit like I have quit everything else in my life. What in the actual fuck is this bobble head talking about? I'm not even sure she knows how to spell my four-letter name much less knows if I have quit anything in my life. If extensive background checks on us existed for the show as she claimed and she studied them, it puzzles me that she still has trouble with our names. Surely in background checks, names are the first thing they look into and document? It dawned on me she means because I am fat, I must have obviously given up on everything in my life and that's why I can't run this hill. It's certainly not because I have been working three jobs, getting two bachelor degrees and completely neglecting myself. Absolutely has to be because you know, I'm a quitter. The absurdity of all of this bullshit hits me just as hard as the metaphorical wall I hit from over exertion and I lost it. Losing it here for me looks like walking and laughing hysterically. I look over as I'm walking back up this ridiculous hill. Crazed spandex and bedazzle clad Shea is right behind me screaming "Run!" so hard there is spittle forming at the corner of her lips. I give zero fucks about her no matter how loud she yells. And I see Kevin who has literally just sat down. Head in hands, tears formed at the point just before hulking sobbing breaks free.

Because like me, like all of us, it's not that we cannot or do not want to run a hill this morning, it's that we want to be allowed to feel. We want to feel our grief at Bruno, someone we had bonded with, leaving us. We didn't want to eat the feelings away and we didn't want to run them away. We just wanted a moment to feel and this crazed fitness automaton was not understanding. To her we were just lazy fatties, not actual humans. I mean we had overheard her telling crew that Hans—her weightlifting competitor fiancé—told her to strip and shower as soon as she got home from filming at night to *get rid of the fat sweaty people smell* she emitted from training us all day. Surely forming bonds with other people was out of the scope of our capabilities, right?

"Shea. Shea, stop yelling. Stop. I'm not running another step," I said between breaths. She looked at me surprised. Probably because someone my shade of red going blue from a run doesn't usually have enough air to speak. It appears she actually listened. "Shea we are hurting, we are sad and this was an awful blow to our morale as a team."

"Oh. I didn't...Oh, alright Tisa," she said, like she had just now realized fat people had emotions "Maybe we need to sit as a team and discuss this," She turns to where Kevin is sitting and the rest of the team are slowly coming up the massive hill at the front of the property, "Get it in gear Alpha Team," she barked. "I want a team meeting on the stairs at the top of the hill."

When everybody made their way to the top of the hill, the guys were pulled away by production for interviews. The women still desperately trying to catch their breath by the stairs, waited as Shea trotted up and delivered an epically tone-deaf rant in this amazingly chirpy cheerleader voice. I'm in awe of her cluelessness. "Sit down. Sit down here right now and listen to me. Now, I understand that you guys are super upset about Bruno going home but I am not gonna let you spend another day of your life quitting. I don't know if anyone has ever told you guys this honestly but the whole reason you guys are fat is because you spent your whole life quitting. I understand you don't want to hear that but honestly what got you here to this Spa in the first place is that you've given up on yourselves. You've obviously given up on having a wonderful life and you've accepted this idea of mediocrity. You have embraced laziness as a lifestyle and have totally given up on positivity. I'm not gonna tolerate it anymore because I understand what you have been through, why you just don't like yourselves enough to do something about how you look...uh, I mean your health. I am gonna be that person, that shining light and that beacon of hope to save you so that you know that you don't have to quit anymore."

If I could breathe after that run I would laugh so hard I couldn't breathe all over again. What the hell is she talking about? I'm fat because I'm lazy? Last I checked before I came to this Spa—the land of bullshit and make-believe—I worked three jobs while finishing my last year of college with a double major. On top of that I'm waiting to start law school where I earned a full fucking scholarship, after killing myself studying for the LSAT. And Esther over here to my left? Esther's got a kid under the age of five, runs her own company, helps run her sisters clothing business and volunteers multiple nights a week at her church. Then there is Debbie, a mother of two kids only 10 months apart, who takes care of them, works forty-eight hours a week as a dispatcher on top of playing sports like softball almost nightly. I'm not sure on what planet anyone of us would be considered fucking lazy. Fat? Yes. Lazy? No. Thank fuck production just called us for a challenge.

Because it makes total sense to force people who are trying to lose weight to eat food to stay on the Spa that is helping us lose weight, we had another challenge today. What this one consisted of was food, along with the calories in the food laid out on tables, then a ring where we stacked the plates after we ate the food. While we did this there was a timer going and when it stopped the plate on top won immunity. Because I am not completely stupid, I realized that if Debbie, Esther and I all worked together agreeing to share the immunity pass and use it for the first person who needed it we could win this challenge and told them so.

"Guys, let's make sure that one of us is always the last plate on this stack and then agree to use the pass for any of the three of us that need it."

"Done." "Absolutely." They agreed.

I'm so grateful that I'm not working alone but also, why the fuck am I standing out here in the sun eating food I'm not hungry for and announcing how many calories are in everything I eat. The dumbest thing about all of this is that the Bravo Team is self-assuredly watching us eat this food like somehow it's hilariously guaranteed to make us gain weight. I am in a fat camp in the middle of nowhere being told I am so fat I could die at any moment and contaminate other people with fatness while doing it and we are competing to stay here by *eating*. *Makes sense*. Nothing like a timed binge eating competition at fat camp.

I won. I'm the best at strategically timed binge eating contests. I won myself a free pass. Awesome.

You know what Shea and production taught us next? We learned how to feed our feelings with pudding. How convenient and awesome is it that not only does a pudding company sponsor the show but we fat people love silencing feelings with food. It was a commercial. We stood around looking awkward, stuffing pudding into our mouths as cameras were rolling and some guy was barking directions. Binge eating and then shooting a pudding commercial. What a day. When the cameras cut we spit that shit out so fast it should've been the immunity challenge.

"Shea, I think maybe you need to get to know us more. I don't think you have a grasp on what our lives are like at all or why we might be upset right now," I almost regretted it the moment I said it. But it just flew out because what the fuck was she *talking* about?

"You think I don't know Tisa but I do know," I could almost hear the violins cue up as she started a spiel that would make the writers of Full House cream their pants. "You have this idea that just because I haven't been fat that I can't relate to why you might be fat and how bad you're obviously hurting inside and it's reflected in your fatness."

So, my weight now means I'm lazy *and* sad? This is amazing. I'm almost in awe waiting to see what my new health guru is going to tell me about myself without even knowing my full name. If she had squeezed out a solitary tear, I would've known she was pulling our legs. But no tear appeared, even if I'm sure she wished one would. To her this was a genuinely touching moment of intimate bonding between her and all these fat people she didn't really care about. Like Kevin Costner in every movie ever, she was about to share that piece of personal info that would make the team rally behind her and totally win everything.

"You see guys, I understand your hurt and pain because like you, I encountered obstacles when I was younger," Oh boy. Did you step on a Lego too? "I was bullied. Especially when I was, a teenager. You know how cruel kids can be. I was a military brat and I moved around so much and I got picked on so much. You wouldn't believe how mean and awful the other girls could be to me when I got to a new school. It was so painful," Shea heaved this world-weary sigh to convey the emotion of what she was about to reveal. And then came the kicker. "The girls" she covered half her nose and mouth with a hand like she was struggling to hold back tears. "They picked on me because...I was *too* pretty."

Oh, okay, yeah that is totally the same thing as literally facing oppression from society as a whole because of your body shape. I'm going to go out on a limb here and guess that maybe meeting friends for Shea was difficult because she says stupid shit to people like, *I get what you are going through* and follows it up with the most oblivious anecdote ever. Just a thought.

What reality am I living in right now? Shea sat in front of me crying about her body image issues and her *fat days*. How in the world am I supposed to feel a connection with a person who is crying about how awful she feels on days that she thinks she *might* be mistaken for someone with my body? Get the fuck out of here! Good thing I had those snacks at the binge eating challenge today cause, lord knows I need the strength to get through this without head butting Shea straight to purgatory.

Nobody said anything for a few seconds because people were stunned into incoherent thought. Debbie had a confused look on her face, as if Shea were speaking Russian. When the silence was so thick you could've sliced it with a butter knife, she continued. "I totally understand where you guys are coming from when you are judged for the way that you look."

I think I blacked out after that comment. I'm not religious but Jesus help me with the ocean of bullshit I am swimming in right now. Great talk. See you out there guys. If internally rolling my eyes burned calories, I'd be Kate fucking Moss.

When she finished this heartfelt confession, she bounced off somewhere to film her own interview. She left the three of us in a stunned silence. Then I broke. I laughed so hard I lost my breath. I looked at Esther and Debbie through tears of laughter, immensely grateful that there are people here who actually *do* understand.

On the bonus side of today we spent hours in a van waiting to do the challenge. While this doesn't sound like a bonus, Daniel was working. For once, I didn't mind the sweltering heat in those church vans. I crawled in the back, thinking it would be another usual bullshit drive to another bullshit event. Which would've been true but while other people were filing into this and other vans, Daniel scuttled up and told the driver he'd be riding with us. He shot me a glance as he leaned in through the passenger side window and my chest kind of fluttered. When he crawled into the back seat with me, I thanked any deity listening, that it was a two-seater in the back, so we'd be by ourselves. The rest of the van filled, as they do, and just sat there as always. Like we were waiting for some unspecified event to occur before we could get moving.

"Hi," Daniel simply said as he landed in the seat next to me. I'm sure he saw my face light up as he did.

"Hi," I responded bubbly. He leaned in closer to me, and his scent twirled around my head, making me dizzy.

"You are a threat, Tisa," he said, frowning in a way that made me want to eat all of his face right up.

"You don't look that scared," I said with a smile. All right, sometimes my flirting wasn't amazing but I was in a church van waiting for a bizarre reality TV challenge, smelling like cattle and occasionally daydreaming about cheese. I had limited options available to me.

He chuckled and even if my line wasn't Shakespeare, I could tell it landed right. He smirked, then lowered his voice. "You have immunity on the show now. You are a threat to everyone."

I was slightly disappointed he didn't say I was a threat to his decency or something cheesy but I bounced back. He wanted to talk shop and seemed to have my best interest at heart. I lowered my voice too. Kevin was sitting in front of us had headphones on and Brody sitting next to him appeared to be sleeping but still I didn't want to take any chances. "What do you mean?" I said while feigning innocence. I knew what he meant but I liked hearing him talk and I felt like he might have to leave unless I kept him engaged in conversation. I didn't want that to happen.

"Your immunity puts a target on your back," He leaned in closer. Even in the sweltering heat, I could feel the hotness of his breath inches from my face. My heart beat so fast, I wasn't sure if the whole van could hear it. "They might all collaborate to get you out of the show next opportunity they have," He looked into my eyes and I forgot what he had just said or why I should care for a moment. Then his eyes moved down my body and I'm sure he could see my chest twitch with a thumping heart.

"I will keep it in mind," I lied. My mind was nearly incapable of sustaining any information at that point. It only focused on his face, his eyes and what was happening in my chest.

"Good. I don't want to alarm you but just thought you should know," He hesitated a second, then put a hand on my thigh. "I'd like you to stay here a while longer," I nearly yelped when his hand touched my thigh, both in surprise and at the release of tension between us. I wanted him right then and there. Logistically this might be complicated because these church vans aren't exactly known for their spacious interior. Also, other people were there. And even if I hadn't cared at this point, I'm sure somebody would frown on Daniel boffing a contestant in the back of a transport vehicle full of people.

"I'd like to see more of you," he continued. I knew he was probably indicating he wanted me to stay on the show but I hoped he *also* meant me in less clothing.

"I'd like to see more of you too," I said, finally able to manage actual words.

"Yeah?" His hand moved up an inch, as if my words had been what he was waiting for to proceed.

"Oh yes. I'd like to see what that belt holds," Nobody ever accused me of being subtle. His hand grabbed my thigh through the fabric of my sweats. I secretly wished I wore a dress or something less ugly than sweats. I also wished that I didn't smell like livestock and wasn't in the middle of the fat camp from hell. I also wished we were in his car somewhere remote and had champagne and strawberries or something equally as cheesy. But my life was awkward and messy, not a Nicholas Sparks novel so I resigned myself to what I could get. He chuckled. His face was close enough to mine, so that I could've leaned forward a bit and our lips would've met. My breathing was shallow now. Right then that fucking van was my favorite place to be.

"Oh damn," I whispered. There was definitely something between us.

"Fuck," he whispered back as the vans came to a halt. It wasn't the cute turned on wanting more, kind of fuck. It was an exasperated *I had plans that have been thwarted* kind of fuck. Brody in the seat in front of us jerked awake. Daniel pulled his hand off my thigh. I moved my leg away from him and straightened up. People were walking toward the vans and any second now the door would open and we would be carted off to new adventures. I cursed the show again.

The crew member who poked her head through as she opened the door started barking orders at us. She needed just one look at my flushed cheeks to know I was up to something. She surveyed Daniel, who did his best to appear indifferent and occupied with something on a clipboard. I mourned the tragic loss of what would've no doubt been a mind-blowing orgasm right in the church van, with people around us. Perhaps it was for the best because I don't know if I could've stopped myself from being obnoxiously loud. It would've been awkward. I mean, I guess it would've been *more* awkward because hooking up like a teenager in the back of a full church van is pretty damn awkward. Worth it, *possibly*. But awkward.

"We'll finish up later, Tisa," Daniel said noncommittally but I saw the brief flash of mischief in his eyes before he climbed out the doors. As I climbed out, the crew woman shot me a filthy look. Don't hate, lady. You weren't the one just cheated of an orgasm.

It took hours of waiting but the mechanical issues with the escalators for our challenge were addressed and we got our happy asses on them at two a.m. The goal of this challenge was to walk up a down escalator, basically going against the monitions of countless mothers and the recommendations of health and safety inspectors everywhere. They had each team placed in the center of two escalators and you had to keep going until everyone else dropped dead. Kidding, sort of. You had to keep going until you couldn't or you fell so far back you hit a flag posted near the bottom. The winning team gets to choose what opposite team member sits out of the weigh in. Last man standing gets ten grand. Poor Chris was injured and got straight fucked at even a shot at the money because he couldn't participate. I would've pitied him but I had just been fucked out of an orgasm so, that's life bro. My favorite machine at the gym was the Stairmaster so I was heavily favored to win—see what I did there? *Fat jokes*, ugh.

I *didn't* win. Who knew money wasn't enough for me to go until my heart exploded? Also, even if it had been hours, I was still recovering from the van encounter. My mind wasn't in this. Blake's dumb ass tried to play mind games to make Debbie think he was giving up and psyched himself right on out of that competition. Congratulations, dipshit, you played yourself. Debbie won. I mean her heart rate was over 195. Production panicked when she couldn't catch her breath, fell off the escalator at the bottom and passed the fuck out. Seems *totally* healthy right? But she won ten grand so who cares about a potentially lethal heart rate? I'm rolling my eyes again. Ten more calories burned. I need an orgasm and then to go the fuck to sleep.

6/19/2015

Shea bounced into the room like an aggressively blonde version of Tigger this afternoon to see how the challenge went. Either she is personally sponsored by a baby gap half-tee company, or she bought one out years back, because she has an endless supply. Brody's face when she came in, in yet another outfit like that made my life. He has an expression that says snark silently and I intend to try and master that skill because in both this show and real life it seems like a skill that would come in way handy. She did her little cheerleader bounce and gave her obligatory inspirational quote stolen from a poster with a kitten and a waterfall on it then we moved on to the myth that is the *Last Workout*. I am not sure I'll ever get used to the pretending that I am doing my *last* workout before a weigh in when actual weigh in days are nothing like this spectacle. But the show must go on, or something like that, right?

Super excited about my hours of cardio and some showing off for the camera, followed by an evening filled with repeated slow walking to the fake gym stage like we are the cast of Armageddon heading towards doom or glory. Only instead of a space suit and Ben Affleck, I'm in a sports bra freezing my ass off for hours with Shea looking like she is surveying cattle she despises for merely existing.

6/20/2015

I like how I stand through those damn weigh-ins with my arms crossed the entire time like I'm perpetually pissed when in actuality I'm hiding nipples hard from the cold. I could cut fucking diamonds and it offends the sensibility of producers that I have autonomous bodily functions. They told us they will be providing us with pasties to help with that, not an actual shirt or anything to help with the cold, just pasties to disguise my indecorous response to said cold. This also explains my perpetual resting bitch face during the weigh-in. Nothing quite like freezing, standing for hours cheering for people killing ourselves to make our bodies less disgusting for public consumption. Added bonus tonight I get to look forward to peeling sticky band aid type things off my boobs later in the wee hours of the night.

After hours of stepping on and off that giant fake scale and feigning surprise over and over again, like Shelley Long in a Kubrick film, we were a little disheartened to see that we had chosen to make Blake sit out the weigh in for the other team. While waiting for the production to be ready for me again, I sat down, and Blake walked over sitting a little too close to me.

"Hey Tisa?" he opened and my heart sank. There was no possible positive outcome of a conversation with Blake. He was both dumb and an asshole.

"Yeah, Blake, what's up?"

"So, I'm just wondering. I see that you have a tramp stamp," He paused like I needed time to consider this groundbreaking piece of information. I didn't respond immediately thinking he would go on but he just looked at me sideways in weird anticipation.

"Yeah, I have a few tattoos."

"Well, I was wondering if you could clear something up for me." Clearly a rhetorical question shoddily disguised as an attempt at being witty. "I'll bet you totally do anal don't you," I wasn't sure I heard him correctly. Even for him, this was outlandish and I'm a pretty outlandish human being. By all means, I applaud it. But where the fuck did he come off thinking he and I were anywhere near the level of close for this to be anything but super creepy? "I mean, not to be rude but girls like you, with tattoos and your attitude are totally into anal aren't you."

"Well Blake," I started, my voice cold enough to freeze his nuts off, "there are so many things I would do in bed, except you know, fuck you." I heard the audio guys lose their shit laughing across the soundstage after that one. Classy guy Shannon is fucking with, that Blake. Who would've guessed a dude cheating on his wife during a reality show would be such a pig? I stared dead eyes at Blake and he didn't seem to have more to add to the conversation. I walked as far away as possible without being bitched at by production for not being where I was needed.

Next, I got to watch the death knells of Gretchen's time on the Spa sound across the faces of the Bravo Team when she stepped on that scale and lost *only* two pounds. If they lost this weigh in it was obvious from that moment onward, she was packing her bags to go home. I just kept thinking about her reaction to our *inspirational quote* tee shirts that production had handed out to us that week. Predictably they said things like, *For My Kids* or *To Make Myself Proud* or *Because*

Society Is Fucked And Says I'm Not Worthy Fat. All right, maybe not that last one but you get the point. Gretchen's said something like *To Have Kids* and I thought I was going to piss myself when she looked at that shit and asked in her beautiful calm southern accented voice, "Excuse me, what is this shit? Am I too fat to have children? Is there something I don't know about that means fat people are no longer allowed to reproduce?" I mean, I'm sure I added that swear word in my head but her voice was laced with it and it was a thing of sheer beauty watching production stutter a reply "Uh, uh, uh...it just means it's a goal." Like that train wreck garment needed more speed on the tracks.

Debbie, Esther, and I made it perfectly clear that if we lost, Brody would be packing his bags and heading home. It wasn't personal, we were slowly learning this wasn't about weight loss but about winning and he was weighing the team down. Luckily for Brody, the Bravo Team lost the weigh in. Kevin pulled in a ten-pound weight loss making our total loss the highest. It was nice knowing you Gretchen. You are probably the lucky one.

6/21/2015

Not gonna lie, it is pretty nice to tell Shea when we win a weigh in. It's awfully cute when she does her little bounce clap routine. I'm assuming she mastered it when learning self-defense from all the people attacking her for being so beautiful in middle school. Ok, I'm being a bitch, it was *high school*. No, really, it was cool to tell her we won, though. I could be facing Chad's wrath this morning instead, enduring a speech about how much I've learned and that it's really okay to be going home with my new dehydration techniques to get me healthy. I would also have had to face that elimination torture ritual tonight. So, I am grateful for the little things.

As predicted, Gretchen was toast. As not predicted, Shannon and Blake have become more brazen with their extra marital affair. I'm pretty sure I could still see the tail lights on the van driving Gretchen away as Blake was unpacking his shit to move into the room she used to share with Shannon. That's cozy. I hope to Blake's disappointment Shannon has a tramp stamp and doesn't do anal.

Chapter 7

This stupid bullshit. The gym is *closed* for the week. We came down to a big closed sign hanging on the door to the gym, like a scene out of a Looney Tunes short. At first, we all actually believed that the gym was closed, so we did what any normal fat person on a reality TV show about losing weight would do—we broke in. You may take away our gym but you won't take away our producer given right to work our bodies to shit for the pleasure of the viewing masses. Then they cued the trainers to walk in and stop us. What this move really meant was a day filled with bullshit filming of scenes where Shea and Chad prove their skill at torturing fat people outside of the gym. This meant incessant pep talks, tough love speeches, and cheerful hand slapping of the trainers. In all probability these two actually hated each other, because their friendly competition was really a fierce competition for ratings and a new contract. It also meant seeing Chad call out names from his team with uplifting messages, while Shea more than once called out the wrong name to somebody… again. It's only been like a *month*. Seven people are a lot of names to keep track of, I get it. My favorite moment of today would be overhearing Chad telling Shannon to stay in the game she needed to *play like a man*. What the fuck does that even mean? There are several men in the show too. Does she need to play like them? Because they aren't necessarily doing better than she is. I'm not sure Chad even really knew what he meant and he probably didn't care. He wasn't invested as a person in any of these people. As long as the camera was on, Chad was on. How does a *man* even play in weight loss reality TV? Is there a separate set of skills here I'm unaware of? Does it involve Hooters wings and the color blue? Stupid.

Actually, maybe my favorite part was filming our *Last Workout* today—days before our weigh in is even going to happen. I wonder sometimes how they decide when to film these things. The *Last* workout, obviously, is the ultimate workout you feverishly churn out with the fear of the impending weigh in painted on your desperate sweat soaked face and, having to fake it was a weird thing. I could do sweat soaked face no questions asked. Frantically working out because time is running out, when you have days to go, was just weird. However, it added to the funhouse quality of seeing Chad make his team move furniture for a workout.

Unsurprisingly, the gym was open again right after we filmed. Weird how that works.

I don't know if it's part of the shtick of the people working on this show but all the conversations with other people about how my body looks now after time spent beating it mercilessly here are super fun. If I have to keep hearing about how *totally different* I look, I am going to lose it. Is it part of some psychological torture or do the production people genuinely think this is what we want to hear? I didn't hate how I looked when I got here in the first place. That was never my sole motivation for doing this. I really just wanted an adventure and a cool story to tell. I have been conflicted about this from the start, and while I get that it'll make life easier in the world to have a smaller body, I don't seem to have the depth of self-loathing everyone around me has or believes I should have. It's fucking with my brain.

Production thought it would cement this new *motivational* technique by having us try on smaller clothes. I guess it was some weird *look, progress,* thing, but I'm also sure it was meant to illicit an emotional response, because nothing sells better than a fat girl crying with joy at being less fat. Debbie, Esther, and I were in our room when a PA popped her head in and said they were going to give us some clothes to try on, and they were our *goal clothes.* Before we could process this, a guy brought them in and left. Like wild animals approaching a foreign object unsure of what it is, we started looking at what they had brought us. It was pretty unspectacular, but at least it was different from gym clothes.

"Well it's something new I guess," Esther said, surveying the clothes with guarded interest. Debbie picked a dress from the stand and looked at it like a professor reviewing newly found data.

"I like this one," she announced and held it up in front of her. I looked at her, and it did look good on her. I looked back at the rack of clothes and felt weirdly like I was back before the show—trying out clothes before going out dancing—only now it was on national television. There were more options to try than a couch colored dress with flowers on it.

"Try it on," I said, enthusiastically. I riffled through the clothes, trying to find something that, in my head, I would get to see Daniel in.

"I might actually be able to fit this," Esther said, the excitement was evident in her voice. She started taking her sweats off and put on the dress. It did fit. "I never would have thought," she said, trepidation turned to mirthful surprise as she twirled in front of the only mirror in the room. Debbie paused, mid getting her dress on, and marveled at Esther.

"Well shit," I said, half in disbelief. I felt a strong urge to put everything on but picked out a piece I liked with Daniel in mind. I undressed too and put the dress on. It slipped over my ass snugly and internally I sighed reluctantly. It felt weird. The dress felt good. It fit. But putting it on felt peculiar. "Well shit," I said again, staring at myself in the mirror.

"You look good, Tisa," Esther said. Debbie nodded vigorously and I concurred. I looked amazing. But without sounding self-obsessed, I had thought I did before, too. Now I was smaller in size and I was given clothes like a dress up doll. Like me being able to fit in a dress and look better was what this was all about. I guess it was. I hated and loved what I saw in the mirror at the same time. Debbie noticed the conflict on my face—have I mentioned how every emotion plays on my face as soon as they occur to me?

"Are you ok, Tisa?" she asked.

"Yes. But doesn't this feel a little weird?"

"The dress?" Debbie wasn't quite there yet.

"No, the dress is fine. But this whole situation? Us now."

"How so?" Esther was confused too.

"Well I like what I see in this mirror," I said, running a hand over the dress. "But I feel like I'm being, I don't know, like my hand is being forced? Does that make sense?" I could see in their faces that it *did* make sense but they still weren't quite getting my point.

"I liked myself before this, even if I sometimes couldn't find clothes I liked that fit me. Now I'm smaller and they give us these dresses and I think I look amazing in it. But I don't know if I like myself more now, than I did before. And I feel like they, or everyone thinks I should."

"Yes. Like we are better people now that we aren't as big," Debbie said. She surprised me because she wasn't the one most vocal about these thoughts. "I keep getting that vibe off production and crew now too. I'm not a better person now."

"And you weren't a worse person then," Esther put a hand on Debbie's shoulder and we fell silent, lost in a rare emotional moment. I was never all that comfortable in those, so I broke it up.

"We do look hot as fuck though."

Because the Universe acts in that weird way it does, Farrell said something today that made me think more about how absurd all this focus is on what we look like. "We are big people so there are things I had never thought I could do," he said. Like, that's a thing. Why the fuck are we all talking about our body shapes when I am a fat woman who has just learned, that I can actually run. No one is celebrating that. No one has even shown me before in my life, that someone who looks like I do right now—and not at some nebulous even smaller size—*can* run. That feels important to me this week, that I haven't seen anyone who looks like me doing the things I can do and am doing. All anyone wants to talk about is how my ass looks smaller in these jeans. What if that's not what is important though? What if what is important is learning I can move my body and lift heavy things looking exactly as I do now. I'm outrunning a camera girl who smokes like it's her career and is the size of my thigh and no one says anything to her about her health or her habits. Maybe I need more sleep, or food, or sex because my emotions are fucked and it's weird I'm getting pissed that all people want to talk about is how much smaller I am. I mean, that is the only reason why I am here. To get smaller to save my life, right? I'm feeling so fucking confused. I might just need to get my head in the game instead of over analyzing everything as is my Motus Operandi.

6/23/2015

They took us on another *fat people field trip*—as we sort of affectionately call them—to a Mexican fast food restaurant. Like so many other of these hilarious little outings, this was basically a commercial. Or a way to monetize us by having us do advertisements for sponsors of the show. Today we learned how to special order and micromanage everything on a menu—something that will surely make us super popular with all restaurant staff at home. On the plus side, we will probably end up getting an extra side of spit for free. However, the ad shit doesn't even really bother me much anymore. It's a break from the monotonous working out and even if I feel the pull of the gym, any time I'm not in there, getting out and seeing people other than the usual suspects helps combat the weird isolation of this place. Also, every outing since the Daniel church van incident has me hoping of a rerun. Today the fat people field trip showed some of us just why we were on this show to begin with, and why being around other people has ups and downs. We arrived in the church vans, as usual, in the parking lot of the Mexican restaurant where we'd be shooting. A small crowd of people were gathered for reasons I never deduced. Perhaps they had picked up on the fact that a TV production was going to shoot there. Like flies to shit, they buzzed in to crane their necks and get a few minutes of fame. I'm sure the sight of a bunch of fat people exiting vans was hilarious because some of them started pointing at us, like they were at the Zoo.

"How many fat people can you fit in a van?" a tall blond dude asked, just loud enough so his voice carried to everyone. There was laughter and when we walked past him, it was clear he was pretty proud of that moment.

"I hope he drowns in guacamole," I muttered to Esther and Debbie as we strolled past him, outwardly pretending he didn't exist. Normally they'd chuckle but it only drew a smile from Esther. Debbie was looking crestfallen and it hurt my heart that some random douchebag would so eloquently illustrate why being a fat person in society was less than awesome most of the time. Adding insult to injury, we had to wait just outside the entrance because of whatever production bullshit had to be set up inside.

"They need to knock down a wall for you guys," another dude yelled. His voice was half drowned out by a truck being started but it carried to us just fine. I flipped him off, which I'm sure made him think he was all the more hilarious. Debbie looked like she had been punched in the gut. Fuckers.

We were finally let inside, where we would have the privilege of pretending to eat special homemade Mexican meals that were really just fast food with all the delicious things like cheese, omitted. Not that it matters as we didn't really eat. We did the standard filming trick where we just put food in our mouths and smiled for the cameras, then spit it out as soon as they yelled cut. Which, as I understand it, isn't really that different from actual movie and TV show productions. I wonder if they are getting that SAG application form to me soon. I could be up for an Emmy at this point. We hung around while the trainers shot some little intro clips, so production could string together a coherent ad. I overheard Shea say, in her best overly dramatic movie trailer voice "On the cruise, they were scared to be in the real world." Bitch, we were locked in our rooms on that damn boat. Like we had a choice about being in any world, real *or* make believe.

Our trip from the restaurant to the vans was less eventful than hours earlier. It was almost night fall and there were only a few really persistent stragglers present in the parking lot. None of them made comments as we entered the vans. No Daniel today. I could really have used him close. He had become a face of freedom for me or at least a kind of sanctuary. When he was around, I felt less pressure from this huge production. Even if he was part of it, he seemed like he also cared about my personal well-being. Not something I encountered a lot in these circumstances.

6/24/2015

I sat in a van in 100 degree heat today waiting for the challenge—only without the added fun and stimulation of a hot PA next to me. My reward for this endeavor was to end up with an ass literally made of bruises and to experience one of the most awkward love messages in my life. It was a thing of beauty.

Production took us to the stadium where the 1984 Olympics were held and we were allowed to watch videos from home on the giant big screen while we all stood in the middle of the field. Kind of awesome actually. We all miss family so much and it had been weeks before we were finally allowed to get censored letters from home. It was weeks after that before we were allowed to speak to anybody on the phone and that was merely for five minutes at a time with a chaperone hovering over our shoulders. Production was worried we would give away show secrets. As though I was going to spend my five allotted minutes detailing what everyone weighed or who was going to get voted off to my mother I hadn't seen in forever.

"Hey Tisa, how are you holding up? We really miss you and we hope..."

"Yeah mom, shut up and take notes. Brody lost eighty-five pounds and Kevin wants to vote off Shannon." Just ridiculous.

So, the videos were actually a really beautiful feel good moment for us. I got to see everyone else's children and cried happy tears at seeing the greetings from everyone. I got to see my niece, nephews and my ridiculous parents on a giant fake moose outside of the local ice cream shop where they live. It was wonderful and gave me a little respite.

Then Blake's greeting popped up on the big screen effectively replacing any remnants of a feel-good moment with drama. Blake's wife appeared larger than life on that Jumbo Tron screen, and through gasps of shock from most of us, Shannon promptly took his hand, bracing him for what was to come.

"Hi honey. I miss you so much and your parents miss you so much," Blake's wife's disembodied head proclaimed gingerly from the screen. "While you've been gone, I have been working so hard too at the gym," Her smiling earnest face as she tells Blake how much she loves him is almost too much for me to take, as I watch Shannon hold his hand and rub his back like he's just been told he has cancer. Then comes the kicker, and I nearly choked. The camera pulls back to show that his wife is in the baby section of a local store.

"And when you get back, honey, its baby making time." At this point the tension on the field is so thick it weighs more than all of us combined. Conveniently Blake's message is the last one and after his wife's smiling blissfully unaware face leaves us, an awkward silence settles—with people unsure of where to look and what to do. Like the silence after Grandpa cracks that racist joke at Christmas Dinner. *You want to throat punch an old man but also you promised your mom you'd just ignore him and everyone knows you won't* kind of silence. That kind of silence. Shannon was still rubbing Blake's back but at this point it was probably more for her own sake than his.

"Well that was nice," somebody said in an effort to either break the tension or to joke about how awkward this was.

"Yes, actually it was," Shannon weirdly shot back, finally coming out of her back-rubbing trance. Was that sarcasm, or just awkward grasping for words? Blake had let her hand go sometime during the video. I don't know if he did so out of guilt or shame, or some weird sense of respect for his wife. She grabbed it again.

"All right," Hunter responded, non-committedly. He looked at them both incredulously. I almost laughed at the whole situation. Having your own shit thrown up on a massive screen in front of everybody can't be fun. It made me wonder if production knew about the affair and if this was some twisted humor from them at Blake's and Shannon's expense. I can't say I blame them.

"It's what happens," Blake finally snapped out of his silence. Several heads turned at the statement and I felt some strong words float towards the surface with gathering speed. I was cut off before I could make a move by Esther, of all people.

"Are you fucking kidding me with this? It's what happens? What kind of coward are you, dude? Yes, it's what happens but even with this show keeping us locked up, you've had several chances to tell your wife. But you *didn't*. You just let her go on thinking everything is peachy keen." She was uncharacteristically pissed off, and I got why. There was enough bullshit going on with us being whisked away for months without proper contact with our families to have this shit added on top. I didn't have a spouse and kids I was kept away from but I'm sure my goldfish missed me terribly though I also knew he wouldn't suffer deep emotional trauma at my absence. Blake's wife thought they were a sure thing and wanted to have kids when he was home. She was working her ass off on the outside. Esther had a wife and kids that she missed, so this affected her deeply.

"Esther, calm down," Shannon tried, but Esther wasn't having it.

"You stay out of this, Shannon," she said without removing her eyes from Blake. He looked like he would be ok with being voted out of the show right then and there. "Unbelievable."

"It's been so long. What does she expect me to do?" Blake said, and I'm sure he regretted it right away.

"What does she expect? How about a little decency? Loyalty? Humanity? Or just honesty?" Esther was practically screaming at this point and I had to admire her a little for going all out. It was clear this had touched a nerve for her. "Instead you pull something like this on national television. Shameful."

Blake seemed to consider a response but was saved by production who came up and told us we needed to split into our teams. Esther walked away with us while shooting Blake and Shannon dirty looks as they went the other way.

After we all recovered from the bullshit that was the *Blake and Shannon Shit Show*, the challenge was explained to us. We get to run the stairs in this stadium and then do the wave all the way across, run back down the field and cross the finish line. Sounds easy right? Fuck no. You do five hundred squats in one-hundred-degree weather and get back to me. I'll wait. On top of that, they brought in the trainers to cheer us on, which I think was code for *get in the fucking way.*

There were several rough parts involved in this challenge. First and foremost, my ass. Despite what everybody seemed obsessed with telling me, it still wasn't small enough to comfortably sit in a stadium seat. What this meant was that every time I plunk down into a seat, I banged the shit out of my ass and thighs. It didn't take long for it to be bruised. And it didn't take long after that for it to be numb. *Like steel toe boot to the ass and I wouldn't have batted an eye* levels of numb. Add to that running up and down stairs in this heat and it's a recipe for disaster. Half way through I started pondering if I would be the first one to crumble. My ass was straight purple and I felt like I could puke at any moment. But Kevin beat me to it. I don't think I've ever seen a grown man cry like I did Kevin today. Not long after I thought something's gotta give, Kevin took a dive. Just legs giving up and him tumbling to the ground, then he broke the fuck down. He quit. Straight up calling it quits. "Naw, man, I'm done." Debbie, was having none of it though. With most of us watching in stunned silence, Debbie went off on Kevin. Debbie, who might very well have been the embodiment of Wholesome American Warm Apple Pie—and who likely won every Corn Husking Barn Yard Dance Queen in addition to Miss Congeniality at her home town state fairs—turned into a raging beast. Like losing this challenge *would dishonor her ancestors or cause her family to be executed* raging beast. It was the strangest thing watching the prom queen threaten to rip a grown man's arms off and beat him to death with the bloody stumps.

"Kevin, what are you doing? Get up. We aren't done," she screamed as she faced Kevin's nearly lifeless frame splayed on the ground. Kevin didn't react. She stepped closer. "Don't even try to pull this now. We need this."

"What?" Kevin stammered from the ground between coughs that sounded like his lungs were exiting his body. "I can't do this anymore. It'll kill me."

"Then let it kill you but do it somewhere else," Debbie pointed off the field and nudged Kevin with her shoe—a little too aggressively. Shea—probably jerked out of memories of how awful being too pretty was for her—noticed something was going on and rushed in.

"Are you guys ok?" she said in a chipper tone. Obviously, a guy on the ground and somebody gesticulating angrily while screaming was about as far from ok as you can get.

"No, I can't do this anymore," Kevin started but Debbie cut him off.

"Kevin wants to quit, which is fine. We can do this without him. We will take the penalty and can still win. But he needs to get out of our way then." The other team was still working their challenge while our team had come to a halt because of all this.

"Come on, guys. We're a team. Remember? Kevin, you've got a little more in you, I know it," Shea dug deep within her soul and channeled all the merry togetherness she felt we had as a team. None of us felt that from her but whatever.

"I can't. It's too hard," Kevin was nearly crying now and Debbie looked at him like he was hot garbage.

"Precisely. So, get off the field and let those of us with balls finish this."

"Debbie, we should try and lift Kevin up and get him back in the game," Shea squawked. But it wasn't helping.

"No. He knows what's up. He wants to quit, let him quit. We'll handle this on our own. I'm sick of lifting people up."

Shea looked dumbfounded. She looked uneasily at Kevin then turned to production. Debbie was getting more and more annoyed.

"Look, Shea, it's increasingly simple. Kevin says he wants to quit. So, he should quit and we can get on with this," Debbie looked like she was just about to hoist Shea's body over her head and beat Kevin with it.

"I just can't do it anymore," Kevin said, mostly to himself at this point because neither Debbie nor Shea were listening.

Shea ran off to consult with higher ups, what the procedure was for this. Kevin stood firm on his choice though and when she came back a little later, she indicated for Kevin to get up and follow her out of the stands. When he was finally out of the equation, we got back to the challenge at hand but it was too late. The other team hadn't spent fifteen minutes fighting each other and a coach, so we were helplessly behind.

We lost but it was a spectacular show.

"Oh my gosh, you guys," Shannon squealed, her bland *Becky face* with a stupid grin plastered across it. The Bravo Team was huddling up in post victory cheer. Hunter seemed to be leading them in a weirdly coordinated yet obviously impromptu victory cheer.

"Who ran the fastest today?" he screamed, fist raised to the sky like he was Freddie Mercury.

"Bravo Team," everybody else responded.

"Who had the best wave?"

"Bravo Team."

"Who beat the Alpha team?"

"Bravo Team." He whipped the little crowd into a frenzy at this point. Everybody must be on edge today. I looked over at Debbie, whose look of disgust could probably kill. Esther was standing a little behind her. Kevin was sitting on the ground again of course. Chris had taken over the Bravo Team celebration with a little dance routine. One after one they all fell in. It was like they had won the actual 1984 Olympics in the *Making a Wave* category. I half hoped Debbie would charge in and knock them all down like bowling pins but she gave up her anger so we left the field dejectedly and pondering if we'd see Kevin alive again.

We spent hours in the sun today. We ran around a stadium and did five hundred squats and when we were done all we asked for was water. We were obviously covered in sweat, all of us are out of shape and it was a really hard challenge in that heat. Objectively the hardest challenge yet. When they brought in bottles of water, we rejoiced—thinking it would be a small reward for all that time spent. But obviously things aren't always simple as that here. They brought us bottles of water that we had packed ourselves earlier in the day, which had been sitting in the white church hotbox vans all damn day. And like that wasn't enough, serving ninety-degree water to people who were burning up in the heat. They broke out actual coolers for the trainers, the cameramen, the audio people and for the host. They stood there in front of us with water so cold it had ice chunks. Even Bravo Team—who had gotten over their annoying victory rush when they realized there'd be refreshments—looked incredulous at this. Hunter stood with the cap in one hand, water bottle full of hot water halfway to his mouth in the other, frozen in time. His eyes followed the motion of a cameraman's bottle literally dripping with ice chips, its contents slightly opaque from the condensation fogging up the cold plastic. The camera man put the bottle to his lips, took a drink, and noticed several of us looking at him like puppies in a butcher shop. He almost spit it out, which would've been even worse and he walked off looking pretty uncomfortable. Farrell lost his shit at this point. I had never heard a Jersey guy scream and lose his shit until now. It was, WOW!

"Are you guys serious with this? You give us damn near boiling water to drink after running around all day, while you guys get chilled water for doing nothing?" he shouted at nobody in particular but pointed enough so that it was for anybody who could hear it. "Why are you treating us like animals? We are not animals."

I had a quick flashback to John Hurt as the Elephant man screaming he was a human being. I nearly chuckled but I was actually outraged too. Why *are* we being treated this way?

"This is insane. Why do we have to drink hot truck water? It's been in the sun all day and you think it's ok to give us this? What the hell?" Farrell punctuated this outburst by hurling his bottle of water at the stadium wall and it exploded everywhere.

At this point Chad realized he might have a problem and intervened. I don't think Chad truly realized what assholes production were being in this moment or how it felt to be treated as less than human after being run like circus acts. But he led Farrell away from the crowd a little and quieted him down. He gently reminded him that he was lucky to be there and that his life was being saved almost daily by them allowing him to be on the show. Farrell quieted down and rejoined the group without saying anything but I could tell he was still furious. We drank our hot water, then got back into the vans like nothing happened—because, we were lucky to be here after all.

6/25/2015

They brought in big wigs from production today. Evidently, my hair sucks.

"Uh, Tisa, why don't you spike your hair up anymore?" inquired random bigwig production person I've never met before.

"I've been here for months now with no access to the outside world. You realize hair grows right? I don't own enough hair product to make this stand up."

I was stared at by several people who didn't see me but saw my potential for advertisers and viewers at home. I was losing some of the persona they had cast me for and they needed to spruce that image up again.

"We'll get a hairdresser in for you."

"For me? I don't know if I need one," I said, only *half* kidding.

"We'll get a hairdresser in for you." the rando reiterated. Ignoring me because why would my opinion really matter anyway. "And you should try applying some makeup." So that was that, I guess. New hair and they want me to wear makeup, in the desert, in sweltering heat, while I work out. Makes sense. Tomorrow is going to be so much fun.

6/26/2015

Yet again the endless walking up and down that fucking hill to the weigh in, this time with spikey hair and the added 18 pounds of makeup. Good thing the scale is fucking fake. The haircut is the weirdest thing though. They kept shouting at the hairdresser to make it less noticeable that my hair had been cut. Because apparently showing the viewers how we could lose twenty pounds in a week was fine and totally believable. But us getting haircuts during the show would somehow stretch the bounds of believability? At least the Bravo Team lost the weigh in. I don't envy their elimination room moment or having to tell Chad.

6/27/2015

So, I lost my shit. Blake and Shannon went traipsing by holding hands. I turned to the guys on the Bravo Team, Hunter, Chris and Farrell, all lined up on ellipticals in the gym with me.

"You are all incredibly devoted, happily married men who respect your spouses. How the fuck can you stomach watching that shit?"

Chris and Hunter just laughed "Tisa, what makes you think we can? Everything we think doesn't come out of our mouths or show on our faces like it does yours, you'll see." Okay, Yoda, whatever. I was so annoyed I left the gym and went for a run. Don't get me wrong, I'm not the morality police or anything, I get that shit happens but damn, you're going to be on national TV. Give the person you married a heads up about what they're going to witness or stop that shit until you are done with the show if you're crazy about each other. I'm completely aware that I'm getting upset over shit that isn't my business. Let's be honest, I also need to get laid and it's making me salty. Where is Daniel? I haven't seen him on set lately, he provides such a nice distraction.

The Bravo Team guys were serious when they said they weren't cool with Blake and Shannon. During the afternoon, Farrell, Hunter and Chris rounded up Debbie, Esther, and I so they could make their intentions clear.

"We're going to vote Shannon home," Farrell stated.

"Oh wow," I exclaimed, before I had processed the thought completely.

"Yeah. We're sick of her hooking up with Blake," Chris said. I fixed him with a quick stare.

"You're voting her off because she's banging Blake? Why not vote Blake off?" I felt annoyance rise in me. They're going to vote *Shannon* home. Blake and Shannon are both being super shitty and inconsiderate to people in their lives at home who will witness this shit but let's be real here, Blake is the only one of the two with a spouse.

"Well," Farrell began, looking suddenly uncomfortable. This had backfired on him with me and he realized it. "She's making him lose focus."

"I don't know if Blake has a lot of focus on his own," Esther chimed in. I mentally high fived her.

"Well that's true," Hunter said.

"She is pretty fucking annoying, I'll give you that," I said. I didn't like Shannon, I didn't like Blake either and I would've preferred he was sent home but either of them not being around anymore felt like a win.

"She is," Chris said, then rushed to add "They both are." Compromise. Whatever. I can't wait to see her face when she figures out she is going in the elimination.

Holy shit, Shannon hasn't figured it out. She has no idea she is going home. The three of us Alpha Team women were in our room, waiting for night to fall upon us. Actually, I am pretty sure we were doing the cheer from the Buffy the Vampire Slayer movie in our underwear, but I digress, mostly we were sitting on our asses prepared to be quarantined to our rooms like we always were during the other team's eliminations. The evenings before elimination and during were always weirdly full of hushed excitement on part of the team that didn't have to eliminate anybody and diffident anticipation on the part of the team that did. We were talking about whatever people talk about when they aren't really talking, when Shannon showed up at our door.

"Hi guys," she said it with a little wave, like she was our good friend, even if it was obvious she was in enemy territory. I felt a pang of sympathy for her. She was the only woman left on their team and I think she might feel the weight of that.

"Hey Shannon," Esther responded, always relentlessly nice, you know, when she wasn't going the fuck off on Blake. "What's up?"

Shannon glanced at the three of us and it seemed like internally she made up her mind she should probably latch on to Esther, if she wanted to be heard. "I actually came to ask you if I could borrow a shirt from you, for tonight. I wanted to wear something I hadn't before, production wants me in blue and I am out of blue clothes."

"Oh, uh, sure I guess," Esther said.

"Just for the elimination. You'll get it back after," Sensing the hesitation, she hastily added, "I'll have it washed obviously."

"All right, Shannon," Esther gave in. We knew Shannon wasn't long for this reality TV world and we also knew when she was voted off, she'd leave immediately and Esther could kiss her garment goodbye. Esther handed her a blue shirt from her drawer and smiled. Shannon took it and thanked her. A beat passed and nobody started up a new conversation with her. Everybody just sort of stood silently in their places. Shannon turned around and marched out without another word. As soon as the door closed and we knew she was well on her way, we all cracked up.

"Yeah, you won't see that shirt again," I said.

"Not unless they do an at home segment for her later on where you guest star asking for your shirt back," Debbie cried.

"It was my favorite too," Esther feigned shock. We all melted into laughter again then got back to the serious business at hand of perfecting our Buffy cheer while waiting for the Bravo Team elimination to end so we could leave our room.

When we had been allowed to leave our rooms again, like us roaming the hallways on the prowl for trouble or a rumble during elimination was somehow a thing. So, leaving was forbidden. The three of us decided to hit the gym for some late night working out. We had chuckles more than once about the blue shirt and mused on how crazy Shannon's face must have looked when her name was announced as the one who'd have to leave. We imagined she'd look at Blake—who'd look back at her—shocked and confused. Perhaps she'd be dragged away kicking and screaming, while Blake was held back by the other guys. We were giggling in the hallway when we ran into Farrell, Chris and Hunter. I immediately questioned them about the incident.

"It wasn't quite as dramatic as that," Hunter started, "but she hadn't seen it coming, that's for sure. I guess she figured by dating one of the guys, she'd have a free pass from all of us or something. Thing is, Blake isn't tight with any of us, so I don't know how she arrived at that conclusion."

"Her face though? How was it?" I asked in all my pettiness.

"I hate to say it, but it was pretty hilarious. You guys know as well as I do elimination isn't a fun moment but I could've laughed at this one."

"And how's Blake?" I continued with my petty schadenfreude.

"Oh, he's in their uh, his room crying now. Like sobbing into his pillow," Hunter said, waving his hand in the general direction of Blake's room.

I secretly smirked a little, even if the thought of somebody else being miserable and crying wasn't inherently a pleasant situation. I'm trifling like that sometimes. Blake is a dick. Shannon was so fucking haughty. I was pleased. Judge me, I don't care.

"The reason we came looking for you guys though, is something else," Chris said, and we all fell silent. It was like this was the Potsdam Convention and we were about to split Post-WW2 Europe between the superpowers. "The thing is, we figured it'd be cool if the six of us worked together until we had eliminated the rest."

"And then?" I asked him.

"Then it's every man for himself."

"Well, how is that going to look this week?" I asked, with I'm sure, suspicion emanating from every pore of my body. "I mean, I get that the goal is the six of us as the final six but you still have Blake and we have Kevin and Brody."

"That's the thing, you guys *have* to get rid of one of them," Chris said, completely serious.

"Are you asking us to lose the next weigh in?" Debbie looked incredulous but I could see the light in Esther's eyes brightening appreciatively as she slowly started nodding her head.

Chris started in, "Hear us out." He was gearing up for a whole sales pitch, with the surreal seriousness of negotiating with the Devil for his soul.

"We don't need to," Esther interrupted, "Debbie, Tisa, it makes sense even if we weren't working with them. Kevin and Brody are our primary competition and it's getting down to the wire. They need to go either way and if we can seal this alliance right now as we get rid of them, I say we are in."

Honestly? At this point I gave two shits. There is still that immunity in play that we have. Besides I just spotted Daniel standing outside by the fireplace—

down the steps from my room—and by the look in his eyes he sees me too. I would agree to anything to extract myself from this conversation and get some private time with Daniel. Luckily, what I am agreeing to is actually a good plan. The guys were now eyeing Esther with suspicion—this had gone a lot easier than they had expected. But it was basically their own plan and we are all in agreement. There wasn't much else to say.

"Uh, sure, yeah guys. I'm in," I said distractedly and I left to get to Daniel.

I exited the corridor like a cat sneaking in through a crack in the window, before either Esther or Debbie had a chance to ask why I was skipping out on our workout. I didn't want to explain all this Daniel stuff yet. I barely had any time with him and having people bring it up all the time wouldn't help. He was sitting on the stairs when I got out to him and I sunk down next to him. The sun was setting over the hills, chased by the dark night sky that under other circumstances would've been super romantic. You know, circumstances where I wasn't in ugly sweats and he wasn't working for a TV show I was on. Someplace where we both had drinks, fancy clothes, fine dining and a bed. But under these circumstances, the sun setting and him next to me was like balm on my soul after a rough day.

"Hi," he said with his usual air of nonchalance—like we had scheduled the meeting months in advance.

"Hi," I said back. I hadn't seen him since the church van incident and I wondered if he felt it was awkward. I didn't but I wasn't the kind of person often susceptible to awkwardness. People with a high level of shame surrounding their life choices don't usually go on reality TV. He smelled nice. I wondered how I smelled. Probably like sweat, drama, conspiracy, and longing for him. He didn't move so I assumed I was ok. "You are not going to believe the day I've had."

"Actually I am. I saw the prelims," He chuckled. Prelims are preliminary footage. He'd been looking at the shit show at the stadium today. *Of course* he had. "Debbie wasn't happy, was she?"

"No. No she wasn't. It was crazy out there. I could have used you on the ride home," I smirked, even if he wasn't looking directly at me. "Or on the ride there. Or when I got home." He laughed.

"I'm sure you could," He put his hand on my leg and I had the familiar feeling of wanting more rush over me.

"We could always take a dip in the pool?" I suggested, throwing caution to the wind. I had wants and I'm sure he did too. "Or if you know where they keep the keys to the church vans, I'm not adverse to that either," I said, and laughed.

"I can't, Tisa," he said.

"Is production keeping you on a tight leash?"

"No. Well yes, they are, but that's not why just now."

"What then?" I asked, feeling like he was super far away all of a sudden. Was I being dumped without even having had the fun of a relationship of any kind?

"Well," he started, and hesitated slightly, "I'm kind of on my way out of a relationship," he admitted

I was flabbergasted, then annoyed. I guess we weren't really anything to each other but flirts. Still, I felt like this should perhaps have been mentioned earlier. You know, maybe *before* I knew what his erection felt like. "You're in a relationship?" I asked in disbelief, repeating his statement in my disbelief.

"It's complicated. We're breaking up. I'm here all the time and she's busy with school. We don't spend a lot of time together. It's been a long time coming."

"Complicated," I repeated. I was starting to sound like a parrot. I was torn between being annoyed by this surprise and wanting to believe that his relationship really meant as little as he presented. I just wanted to walk away from this conversation still being very fond of Daniel and wanting to move it forward.

"I didn't expect to meet a *you* here, Tisa. And it's sped up the process of breaking up because I want to move on this. But I don't want to while things are complicated. I wanted to do it without a lot of bullshit." Daniel explained.

I hadn't heard him swear before and it sounded velvety when he did. His hand was still on my thigh and it still felt good—even if I also felt like pushing it away. I was frustrated, but also attracted and he *did* make sense. "You're breaking up with her?" I asked.

"Yes. We've got a lot to sort out between us and I'll deal with all that. But yes, that is my plan. And when I do, if you want the pool or a church van sounds like a date."

"I'll think about it," I said, deciding on aloofness. I did feel a little gutted but I reminded myself that we'd really only had brief encounters. I stood up and the hand he had rested on my thigh grabbed my hand as he looked up at me.

"I really like you, Tisa. I didn't expect somebody like you to turn up here," He kissed my hand and I could feel the warmth of his lips, even in this heat. "I hope I get to see you around still."

I watched him back away as he smiled at me and through my frustration at how this night turned out, I still felt the urge to find those fucking church vans. I went up to my room instead and sulked.

Chapter 8

I did not know a human being could make the wailing sounds I heard coming from Blake's room last night. I woke up during the night and thought somebody was testing out our next challenge where we'd have to slaughter pigs. It sounded otherworldly. I get it. He is in love and she had to leave him for months. But still, wailing like he was four years old exasperated me. I covered my head and fell asleep again.

At four a.m. I woke up again and started getting ready for the gym. I threw on my standard sweat attire and took off for the gym. I ran into Daniel on the way and despite aggravation still roaming my brain, it was the familiar notion of joy at seeing him that was predominant.

"Hi," he opened, as per his usual standard.

"Hi. Do you always work?" I asked. It was rhetorical, because there seemed to be plenty of days where he wasn't here.

"Pretty much," He indicated a cup in his hand. "Would you like tea?"

"Uhm, sure, yes thanks," I said, then took the cup. I was impressed with the beverage since there was basically only one brand of sugar free peach tea I was *allowed* here and it was pretty much the only thing that kept me sane. I cannot believe he noticed that and apparently had either gone to pick some up in the middle of the night after work, or in the wee hours before he arrived this morning. I felt a great and renewed appreciation for Daniel.

"It's sweet and fruity. Reminded me of you," He smiled ahead of himself.

"Ha. Of course it did," I said. He was corny. It was kind of cute. We walked along a little bit, before he spoke again. I took a sip of the tea. It really was sweet and fruity. The little things mean a lot here.

"I'm sorry about how all this happened. Like I said, you kind of took me by surprise, and I got carried away."

"I know. It's all good." It wasn't really, but what can you do?

"It's hard to stop thinking about you."

"You should probably try. But not too hard," I played it detached, hoping he'd be both encouraged and a little discouraged at the same time. Because of the *complications*. I mean, if that's how we are referring to significant others now. I didn't feel I was on the same level of Blake shittiness but I wasn't thrilled with my new-found hypocrisy in this situation.

"How are you doing out here, Tisa?" he asked, changing subjects. We walked down the last hill before the gym and I suddenly wished the path were longer.

"I'm good. I'm doing well," I said, before realizing that it might have been rattled off a little too hastily. I got by but I wanted Daniel to think I was on top of things. "You know, hanging in there."

"You will let me know if there is anything bothering you. Or that I can do for you?"

"Are you allowed to do these things?" I figured hooking up with contestants in church vans was frowned upon at best but I only now thought about all the little things he did for me. If they were all right. Bringing me tea, music and private talks. I didn't want the others to know about Daniel because I didn't really know about Daniel myself yet. I figured I should keep it to myself so I didn't get him in trouble.

"Naw," he said casually, "I don't think they care too much about little things like this. But go quietly with it just the same, ok?"

"I figured I should," I said. We were almost at the gym door. "Thank you for the tea, Daniel. And thank you for the talk."

"It is my pleasure," he replied. He paused, took my hand and gave it a squeeze. "Have a good day."

"You too." I looked him in the eyes, they twinkled and he smiled at me. It made it harder to maintain my irritation with him.

We had to do the endless walk down to a challenge again this morning. Today's funstravaganza was a calorie counting challenge where we had to look at food and determine how many calories were in them. I am pretty sure a fat person didn't come up with this challenge. You know how I know that? Because I've been counting calories since I was in the fourth grade. That was the first time my parents put me on Weight Watchers. I couldn't add grocery prices in my head or convert currency while traveling but calories I could count like a pro. I can tell you the calorie content in damn near every food across every group on the planet. For extra bonus points I can probably tell you the macros in each food item too. Need to estimate the number of carbs in your meals to achieve world domination? I'll be your sidekick. You need a calorie count on your last four meals based on dish names to arm a nuclear device? I'm your Huckleberry. Oddly enough, despite this amazing skill, I'm still fat. Today my calorie counting superpowers were used for good not evil though. Winning this challenge means we get to decide which members of the opposite team have to do things like, not have their beloved trainer for seventy-two hours or eat all their meals outside the Spa. Seems like legit things to do to people who are struggling with their eating and exercise habits. Fuck it, it's a game right?

They busted out a plate of fried chicken and I knew right then and there we were going to win. And lo and behold I was right, we won. We decided to assign eating out to Chris and Blake—and took Chad as a trainer away from Hunter and Farrell. Viciously playing the game, right?

Predictably, Chad took the news poorly. Also predictably, the winners assigning the losing team restrictions meant *nothing*. Hunter and Farrell still trained with Chad when the cameras weren't around—like they hadn't just lost a challenge barring it. Eating out didn't mean shit either, as both Chris and Blake ate just like they had all along. The only redeeming factor though, was that *eating out* involved pretending to order take out on phones with no one on the other end of the line and a stack of menus. I hope, at the very least, they felt foolish doing that. Oh, land of bullshit and make believe you never fail to amaze.

We filmed another *deep* moment with Shea today and I'm actually feeling a bit thrown for a loop. Don't worry, it's not like I'm about to sob all over the pages but my breakthrough moment in this discussion was supposed to be about how I am angry all the time, or how the emotion I am most comfortable with is my anger. The thing is, I wouldn't say I'm an angry person. I mean, I called it anger I guess but when I sit and think on it, what I really believe is, that I'm a *confrontational* person. I suppose that could be seen as a personal failing I need to work on or a strength I possess. I'll analyze that shit later, right now let's focus on my *anger*. I address shit that happens in my life, point blank, as I see it, when I see it. There are so many things that feel like bullshit to the core of me that I can't not speak on it. That looks like anger to a lot of people because they are uncomfortable when the social trope of smiling and nodding isn't maintained. It's especially jarring when a fat woman refuses to act jolly. I'm not a *good* fatty. Debbie said she did the exact opposite with her emotions. She feels this obligation to always be cheerful and to always be smiling. I've done that too. Be the person who, if I am just pleasant enough, show you I am eating enough vegetables or turning down the pizza you offered me maybe no one will notice I am fat. If I just *behave* maybe no one will make a comment on my body. If you don't give anyone a target then maybe they'll leave you alone. It seems like a strategy I've attempted to employ my entire life and its failed. I mean, it obviously doesn't work - both because I cannot do fake for very long, and also because no matter how *good* I am, or how agreeable I appear it doesn't matter. Even if I eat endless fucking salads when out to dinner with friends or order that plain vodka on the rocks while my friends ordered mixed drinks and burgers. No matter how many "You're so *good* Tisa" reassurances I got for demonstrating what a good fatty I was from people who have never fluctuated a pound in their life and order bottomless cheese fries. No matter how hard I devote myself to being one of those fatties who works so damn hard to fit in, to not be fat, or to desperately be noticed for more than just being fat, I still stick out. I was still fat, and apparently that mattered more than anything else about me. I was still that same girl who—when dancing with a guy at a bar—was told I was *thick* so that was a good thing but he could never *date a fat girl*. When I asked him what a fat girl was he answered by telling me anyone who weighed over an arbitrary number I had passed a long time ago. I laughed at him and he seemed genuinely confused because apparently, he didn't realize he was desperately hitting on a girl well past the number he thought was a deal breaker. He should check his definition of thick again. And this shit is everywhere, these fucking arbitrary numbers assigned to measure my worth. What's worse is now I do it to myself constantly here at this Spa. It reminds me of my teens where I got it in my head that beige was a super grown up professional color to wear. So, I overhauled my entire wardrobe to nothing but beige tones. I lasted for six months. I wasn't beige. *I am fat.*

In classic Shea fashion her deep insights on psychology and society at large meant telling us, "It's so much easier to be angry and say *I don't care that I'm overweight* and not do anything about it." Um, no. That doesn't feel right either. I want to know on what fucking planet Shea lives where being fat is easy? If being fat and living in my body were easy, I wouldn't be here. There wouldn't be millions of people watching me desperately trying to not be fat anymore. I wouldn't be reminded by production daily about how lucky I am because two hundred thousand other fat people wanted my spot.

This afternoon Esther, Debbie, and I were tasked with filming a bit for processed turkey lunch meat. Making an advertisement for a show that exploits us for money seems like a good tradeoff for being allowed to starve myself to death on TV. Production found us making lunch and asked us to make our food with the flavored turkey, and it was absolutely horrible. We worked it into different things and everything tasted like wet paper.

"All right. I'll add this sun-dried tomato flavored turkey to a sandwich," Debbie said. She carefully laid slices of the deceptively normal looking turkey on bread with lettuce, as if she were defusing a bomb. Esther and I were both considering what flavor we'd try.

"I think I'll go for Applewood smoked," Esther exclaimed, leaving me as the only participant still undecided. She tore the package open and grabbed a few slices. Debbie had completed the crafting part of her sandwich as I picked up a package of Cajun style sliced turkey. I was looking for something to stick this turkey into, when I felt it had gotten weirdly quiet in the room. This was unusual with the three of us, so I looked up at Esther and realized she had frozen in mid-action, looking at Debbie. My eyes panned to Debbie, whose eyes were as large as teacups. She held her sandwich in both hands—a few inches from her mouth—with a big almost cartoon like bite out of it. I'm pretty sure I could see a perfect print of her teeth in that sandwich. She wasn't chewing, though. Just standing there.

"Debbie, are you ok?" Esther asked. Debbie nodded slowly.

"What are you doing?" This was killing me.

She resumed chewing. "Just savoring the flavor." I had no idea what was up with her. Esther had assembled her sandwich now and started to take a bite. Debbie's eyes followed her every movement closely with tense anticipation. Esther took a bite and started chewing but Debbie stopped again.

"Wha…" I started, then Esther stopped chewing, with her mouth agape making a weird harking sound. Debbie broke down in hysterical laughter and shortly after, Esther chimed in.

"This. Is. Horrible," Debbie said between guffaws. "Oh wow."

"Terrible," Esther agreed.

I tore the package open, tossed slices of turkey between some bread and bit in. It took mere moments for my taste buds to be assaulted by the atrocity that was this turkey. Both Esther and Debbie were looking at me and then I broke down. I cried laughing. "What the fuck is this?"

Esther and Debbie had tears streaming down their cheeks. It tasted like a group of dogs had played in a warm pool all day. Kind of like when you're at dinner at Aunt Beryl's—who stopped using salt during the war because it was too expensive—and never picked up the habit again.

"This turkey – if your dinner is just too tasty," Esther said, holding up a torn package of the meat, to roars of laughter.

"Because your taste buds deserve less," Debbie carried on.

"This turkey, the food equivalent of bad sex." I chimed in.

Somebody poked their head in to see what the hell was going on with us. We all silenced, looked at each other and cracked up again. Whoever had looked in on us shook their head and left us alone. We'd have to pull Emmy deserving performances out of our asses for this one. Sigh.

6/29/2015

Oh goody, a challenge involving heights. I am terrified of heights so today was obviously fun. I think it's intertwined with my not wanting anyone to realize how much I weigh. I freak even when someone tries to pick me up. As if they'd drop me like a hot potato the minute they realized I'm not a feather. Today's ridiculous spectacle involved strapping one of us fatties into a harness and pulling the lucky chosen one into the air. While that person was up in the air, the other team members would run to grab flags, that they would bring back. Running back then lowered the strapped in person to the ground again, where they would be handed a flag to take on their next trip up. The goal was to do this until all the flags were flying high in the air and to do it faster than the other team. Complicated? Yes. Just imagine being in an uncomfortable harness flying up and down, hoping people didn't trip or miscalculate. I was only about one kind of thing strapped to me, and it definitely wasn't ok for national television.

Luckily Esther volunteered to be in the harness. Also, she was the lightest of all of us all, so pulling her up and down didn't seem as daunting as if it had been someone else. We started off strong. Brody was cheering us on from the sidelines since he was injured and we had to have someone sit the challenge out on account of the other team being one person down. Apparently, things had to be equal. Go figure. Brody had managed to turn his ankle on a moonlight run with Blake last night. Since Shannon was history, Blake had desperately looked for solace in somebody who didn't yet think he was a piece of shit, and Brody delivered. The two of them had gotten really close and spent most of their down time off camera together.

The first flag went without incident. We were coordinated, surprisingly nimble, while running to get the flag, then back to Esther without missing a step. But the aesthetics ended there. And the cluster-fuck began as we got dirty and gritty like Seals during hell week.

"Hold, hold, hold, guys," Esther yelled, trying desperately to get us to hold her steady as she was attempting to Velcro the flag to the pole thirty feet in the air. In our feverish excitement we heard *Go, go, go!* so the three of us turned around and stampeded back toward her suspended in midair without having had the chance to attach the flag to the pole. As we ran toward her it lowered her away from the top and any possibility of attaching it. "Guys guys. I didn't get it," she screamed, waving the flag around signaling her frustration. We got our shit together and hoisted Esther up so she could attach the flag. We still had a chance to win with our recovery but eternal glory wasn't quite ours yet. In a classic case of crossed intentions, Kevin believed that Debbie grabbed our last flag to bring to Esther and Debbie believed Kevin grabbed it. In actuality it was still sitting sadly on the ground at the starting point—looking as pitiful and defeated as we felt. I'm not going to lie, I'm mostly glad my ass wasn't the one who dropped that flag. I've seen Debbie lose her shit over challenges already and I'm not emotionally prepared to take a verbal ass whipping. We lost, fair and square. Obviously, the Bravo Team decided we got the intense pool workout while they got the meal at the hotel, our prize options for today's challenge.

Not that it should come as a surprise to anyone but in true reality TV style, our *intense pool workout* consisted almost exclusively of fucking off in the pool while making a scene for the cameras. What we actually did was harass the shit out of the Bravo Team as they ate their meal. We looked like the kids from Oliver asking *May I have some more, sir?* at the edge of the pool. We stared at Bravo Team as though they were a circus act (which is not too far from the truth) that consisted of eating filet mignon and shrimp cocktail while wearing matching sweat suits. I think Debbie might've identified too much with Oliver. I am pretty sure I saw her shed a solitary tear at the sight of beef.

After the inevitable workout the entire Bravo Team had with their trainer— because obviously they still had their trainer despite losing that right only shortly before. Chad left to go home to whatever Hollywood mansion mercilessly beating fat people for a living while shilling crash diet books allows one to procure leaving Debbie, Esther, and I in the gym with Hunter, Farrell, Chris and Blake. It was scheming time.

Like tittering children in the school yard, we sidled up to the treadmills Chris, Hunter, and Farrell were running on. Blake was at the other end of the room, and he was wearing earbuds.

"So…" I started. When it came to scheming, I had apparently been elected de facto spokesperson for the three women, which was kind of weird, because scheming is not my strong suit. But I suppose playing the game had to be a thing eventually, even for me. We wanted Kevin the fuck out of this show. Chris, the de facto leader of those three dudes, slowed his treadmill to a full stop and the other two followed suit. It felt like we were the Kardashian sisters, meeting up to settle yet another controversy or Photoshop scandal.

"Yes?" Chris asked when he stepped off the treadmill. Like he didn't know what we were all doing.

"Are we playing the game or are we playing the game?" Debbie inquired, more abrasively than intended. Suddenly five sets of eyes were on her. She blushed.

"Well. What Debbie means," I picked up the torch. "We want Kevin gone," I felt like Michael Corleone ordering the kiss of death for Fredo. You know, if Michael had been wearing a red ill-fitting sweat suit and stuck in fat camp while giving the order.

"It would even things out," Hunter said with his usual panache for stating the obvious.

"He's dragging behind and I honestly think he wants to go." I wasn't making that last part up even if it felt like justification for getting rid of him. Not only wasn't he thriving. Hell, none of us really were. But most of us were dealing with it better than he was. The whole stadium quitting incident illustrated quite clearly that Kevin wasn't going to go the distance.

"I suppose Blake could do with a win too," Farrell said and shot a sideways glance at Blake, who was on the floor in the other end of the gym. "He's been a ghost since Shannon was sent home and I think he knows he's toast. It'd be nice if he would contribute a little more. Or at least stop being annoying."

"That's a pretty tall order," Esther said with a chuckle. The guys smirked. Blake really *was* annoying.

"So, what do you propose?" one of the Bravo Team rejoined, bluntly getting to the point.

I pondered it for a moment. "If you have a way to sweat extra this time, we'll make sure to sweat less. Like we won't dehydrate as brutally." It had been an off the cuff remark, but all six of us had little light bulbs go off over our heads simultaneously.

"We could put trash bags under our sweats for the last workout," Chris postulated, half joking.

"That's it. We'll do that and send Kevin home next weigh in," Farrell chiming in as he hadn't said anything too committed yet, and didn't want to be left out completely.

"And we'll do what we suggested, stop dehydrating as much. We can't go completely off it because Shea would shriek loud enough to wake the Terracotta Army back to life," I scoffed at the thought. "But we'll make sure we don't go all out."

"Deal."

"Deal."

Great, we were all in agreement. I fought the urge to pinky swear.

6/30/2015

We saw the doctor for the first time today since we were evaluated way back at the beginning of this circus. Despite not having seen a proper physician all this time, we were told to discuss how he had been monitoring us closely the whole time we had been there. If *monitoring closely* now means we hadn't seen his face in weeks and production kept any advice he had for us to themselves? Yep, the dude was *totally* monitoring us closely. Our labs apparently showed positive progress, which is fantastic. Who doesn't like positive progress? But I'm left wondering just how important my blood pressure is when I'm literally bleeding through my shoes and I cry all the time. I'm trying to stay focused and remember even if I feel awful, I'm saving my own life. And if I ever forget that I am saving my life and getting better even if it feels awful, production and crew tell me all the time how much better I'm getting. I'm pretty sure some of us are off medications for high cholesterol or high blood pressure while on this show. I don't have a medical degree but I feel as if these things are important and like they should be able to co-exist peacefully with an exercise and diet regimen. I mean, a regimen that doesn't involve crazy starvation, dehydration and beating the shit out of myself in the gym? Right? But again, I'm not an MD. So, Spa tactics it is.

More advertisement fun happened while chatting with the doc. This time it was Blake's turn to realize his inner acting dream and for a product that was actually relevant to us—pain relievers. I wish they would tap me for pain relievers instead of tasteless turkey. I could pop pills and smile for the cam without breaking a sweat.

Blake was brought into the kitchen, because the kitchen in this mansion was huge and for some reason always looked spotless. Probably because we lived on a diet consisting entirely of fake cheese and low-calorie wet dreams with little to no need for actual cooking. Some of us were standing in the doorway, looking in, watching this weird spectacle unfold. Blake was asked to pretend that someone in his family was taking pain relievers. That's it. That's the whole thing. Not Shakespeare but then Blake was no thespian. He was looking at papers with, presumably, the dialog he had been given, and his face clearly reflected what most of us would have probably thought—*this is bullshit*. There was a hint of desperation in his face too that I contributed to having to shoot ads for products you didn't give two fucks about, for no money. But when his monolog started, I had to clasp my hands over my mouth to stop from laughing out loud.

"Hi, I'm Blake and when my wife has a headache it hurts the rest of the family too," he stated as he strolled weirdly sideways through that huge kitchen, putting on his best worried smiling face—no doubt considering what his wife and Shannon respectively would think—when they saw this ad on their TVs at home. "It's harder for her to deal with cleaning and have enough energy to run the household as efficiently as she wants to." My hands were clasped over my mouth again but this time in anger because this ad was bullshit lies about Blake's life *and* clearly anachronistically sexist. *What the fuck.* Blake strolled his way to a bottle of pills perched precariously on top of the counter. He picked it up without looking at it; the label clearly facing the camera. Expert work, I had to admit. Perhaps he was a thespian after all. "That's why she takes these. To help relieve her pain so she has time to live the life she really wants and I am here learning to live the life I want." I nearly snorted in laughter at the truth in that last part. Shannon seemed to be the life that Blake wanted. That was that. They did the routine a few times with slight variations in position and minor alterations to the dialog but apparently this was all it took. I assume they added animations of silhouetted humans with red pain markers jumping out at the viewer and blurry sequences of a family playing in the grass after Blake told us which pain reliever works best. I retreated to my room and recounted the events to Debbie and Esther, and we all shook our collective heads at this shit show.

I guess fresh off his new acting gig, Blake was feeling a mix between empowered and lonely. Fame is a fickle mistress, isn't that what somebody once said? I digress. Blake missed Shannon—and his wife perhaps? Probably not—and knew he was kind of unpopular among the remaining contestants. Brody made up for some of it but he still slinked around by himself most of the time, if Brody was otherwise occupied. Still it came as a surprise when Blake appeared before me, asking me if I had time to talk. Since I was on my way back from working out, I acquiesced. I could do with a swim in the pool anyway and that's where he was headed. I changed to a swimsuit and went down to the pool area. Blake was already in the water. I sat on the edge—getting my feet wet—not too far from him. It was quiet for a beat as my skin acclimated to the cooler temperature of the water.

"How are you doing here?" Blake asked, breaking the silence. I was momentarily thrown by the harmless nature of the question. I didn't mistake it for genuine interest because it was clearly rhetorical. My answer was in kind.

"Oh, you know. Getting by," I was fluff so far. I didn't ask him to talk, and while I had nothing else to do, I still felt like singing into my hairbrush in front of the bathroom mirror would be time better spent. "What's up?"

"I miss Shannon and it gets lonely here, so I thought it would be nice to chat with somebody for a change." It did get lonely but more so if you were kind of a dick and spent your time moping around instead of engaging people in actual conversations so my sympathy wasn't that deep here. I didn't mention this. I did wonder why he picked me to discuss this with. We hadn't been openly antagonistic with each other but I don't think anybody thought we were close friends.

"Yes, that's true. It can get lonely here, which is ironic considering there are people around all the time. The cameras kind of kill any real intimacy," I realized my statement was probably outside the scope of this conversation. What can I say? I do care about connections, selectively of course.

"Mm. It does." Blake replied, sort of smirking to himself. I wasn't sure he heard me, or understood what I meant. Perhaps he just didn't care. "I think I'm in love with her."

"Well that's great, Blake," It was. But I wasn't sure why he was telling me. I slid into the water and the familiar feeling of being carried by invisible forces that enclosed your entire body washed over me. If only it would wash me away from this weirdly personal conversation I had stumbled into. I looked at Blake who was at the point in the pool where standing, his head and shoulders just barely poked above water. The sun was setting and it was growing dark enough for the lights in the pool to be on. Under different circumstances, with a human instead of the walking douche-canoe that is Blake it would be romantic. For a brief second, my mind wandered to the thought of getting Daniel in the pool with me one night. Perhaps with a couple of glasses of chilled Chardonnay. I dismissed the thought because I am sure someone would shriek in horror if a bottle of wine was found at the Spa. Also, the last thing I wanted was to daydream about Daniel fifteen feet from Blake. Blake's body was ghostly pale and weirdly distorted by the surface tension of the water when I looked over at him again as he spoke.

"I know you probably don't like me because of this whole situation with Shannon."

"I nothing you, Blake." I said, and with what I hoped was sincerity, I added, "I'm not trying to be shitty here. I neither dislike or like you. I find you to be a minor walk-on character in my life that I give very little thought to. It's your life. Would I have acted differently? Yes, I'd like to think so. But things happen and it doesn't really matter what I think. If you're in love with Shannon, then more power to you."

"I am," he said. I think he lightened up a bit at what he figured was—if nothing else—an acceptance. "We both felt it right away when we met here and could speak with one another. The attraction was there right away during the audition process at the hotel, but connecting here solidified it"

"All Right," I responded, without genuine interest but I couldn't really say nothing then get out of the pool.

"Yes. I think it was love at first sight pretty much," He obviously did based on how chuffed saying it out loud made him look. "Instant attraction."

"Those things happen and when they do, it's usually awesome." I didn't know what my part in this conversation was. Maybe he needed to tell me he loved Shannon in some attempt at justifying to me that he was cheating on his wife on national television? Tell *her*, not me. I don't care.

"Yes," He paused a beat and then with a brief glance at me, he continued. "We went at it like bunnies too."

"Oh? That's cool. New love and all that," I kept it deliberately vague looking for a way to gracefully exit the pool and this conversation. Since we didn't eat and had very little going on in our lives, sex and food were practically all everybody talked about at the Spa. But it was still a leap from bullshitting with several people, to hearing Blake give me an exclusive insight into his sex life. But again, what could I really do? Also, I can't deny I *was* a little curious. By curious I mean that I'm nosy as fuck. It's a flaw. I'll add it to the list.

"We had sex all kinds of places at the Spa. In the bathrooms, in our own room, once I moved into Shannon's room."

"Quite the stallion, Blake." I said drily. He missed my disinterest and continued.

"We even had sex on the crafting table."

Now horrified at the thought, I responded "Uh. The one in the tent reserved for the crew? Like the table they all eat meals on?"

"Yes. That's the one," He looked self-satisfied and was clearly proud of this endeavor. A small part of me was impressed the other part of me was grossed out about *Shannon and Blake sex* near people's food. They did however manage to sneak into a tent that was normally off limits to contestants, just to have sex. I fought the urge to high five him for that and stifled my laughter.

"Isn't that where they keep their snacks during the day too?" I knew it was, but I felt like Blake needed that question, and by all means he was having a moment here. Who am I to deny that?

"It is," He replied.

"That seems um, difficult to coordinate so as not to get caught and super unhygienic," It actually seemed hilarious.

"We knew there would be no cameras or mics there, we also found a spot on the hiking path behind the house, up the trails, behind one of the big boulders."

"Oh, wow, that was...innovative," I said sort of mockingly. I mean, I'm a huge fan of get it where you can and no stranger to sex outdoors. There was this one time on the hood of my car in a snowstorm in Alaska. But I didn't share because, well, Blake didn't give a shit and who was he to me really to share that awesome story? I realized what Blake really wanted was to brag about fucking Shannon, an accomplishment I wasn't super impressed *or* concerned with. I was pretty clear I wasn't invested in this convo but I think just the exchange was enough for him. I still wasn't quite sure why I was the lucky winner of this particular lottery but it was no skin off my nose.

"One of the crew guys loaned me his phone and I called her you know?" he said, not making eye contact. Ah, now I understood, he was feeling guilty. "I know Debbie and Esther really miss their families and if you hit up Tim, the guy who helps in audio, he might let them use the phone too. Don't tell him I told you."

"Got, it, Tim. Okay, thanks," I dipped my head under water and slicked my hair back, before I moved to the edge of the pool and hoisted myself out. "Time for bed, I think."

"Yes, you're probably right," He moved to the stairs out of the pool, and I walked away without another word spoken. What a weird encounter. And the bar for weird in this place is pretty high.

7/1/2015

Last Workout always makes me laugh because of the absurdity of the filming schedule and today was no exception. Shea talking about how desperately we needed to win this while we knew we were trying to throw it also made it a wee bit uncomfortable. But then again, so were most interactions with Shea. She was the kind of person, where almost 100% of the time she opened her mouth, you knew some awkward fluff, devoid of any self-awareness, would come out. I had done a long cardio session with Shea sporadically trying to encourage me, with no real effect. Sweat was pouring down and I had gone to grab a towel by the door, when I passed Kevin. He was on a recumbent bike, largely ignored by Shea, because he had positioned himself away from the rest of us. Shea was usually where there were the most contestants because that is also where the camera would be.

"What's up, Kevin?" I asked, as I picked up a towel.

"Not much," he said, looking bemused. "Just trying to get by."

"You had a rough time with that challenge the other day," I don't know why I said it. *Obviously* he knew, he was there. But still, it flew out.

"Yeah. I just wanted to go home. I didn't think I could go on."

"I could tell, you barely pulled through. Debbie was laying into you."

He looked at me and said with a sad voice "I miss home. It's taking my energy."

"Well perhaps you will get to see them sooner than you think," I said, and I knew why my comment just before had flown out. It needed to be said.

He looked startled. "What do you mean?"

"Well Kevin," I fixed him with a steady gaze. Michael Corleone the fat sweaty female version hard at work again. "We are going to send you home, if we lose the weigh in."

"You *are?*" He nearly fell off the bike as he tried to get off. His voice was a mix of genuine surprise and acceptance. He didn't want to leave but he did want to go home.

"You aren't pulling your weight in here. I hate to say it, you're dragging us down with this sad puppy bullshit." Fuck it. Time to just go all out. He needed to hear it like it was.

"I've tried, but I don't seem to do as well as the rest of you with challenges. My weight loss numbers are great though," he began, throwing his hands up in a half confused half defensive measure.

"Kevin, it doesn't matter to us why or how. This is a game. It's not personal. The weight loss numbers are a liability along with the lack of trying at challenges. It's really not personal." It kind of was. But also, he wasn't actually doing well. "It's probably the best for you too."

"I guess," He knew all those things were true and he didn't want to fight it too much.

"At least this way you know ahead of time. So, you don't feel stabbed in the back any more than you have to." I'm the good Samaritan, aren't I? I was right though. He looked dejected but I'm pretty sure I also detected a flash of relief sneak its way across his eyes but let's be honest it was probably me assuaging my guilt. Being honest about doing something shitty still means you're doing something shitty. I left him with those words, as he went back to pedaling.

As I returned to the treadmill area—and a Shea ceaselessly edging Esther and Debbie and Brody on—I noticed a PA enter, with a dude that looked like somebody who wouldn't be caught dead in the gym when the contestants were working out in there (remember, no A/C, scorching heat and a bunch of people sweating like farm animals). He walked towards us with a firm and determined gait. I didn't immediately connect the dots but obviously it was about me. If it was trouble it was about me.

"Tisa, do you have a minute?" the PA asked. It was clear I had plenty of minutes to spare for them. I followed the guy to a different part of the gym with the PA trailing behind. As we reached the wall—and literally couldn't be further away from everybody else—the Agent Smith looking dude turned around and fixed me with a stern, authoritarian gaze. I steadied myself, preparing for the worst.

"You know, telling other contestants that you are planning to send them home ruins the game for everybody," He said it without blinking. I wasn't sure he had ever blinked in his life. He looked like he had his eyeballs medically moistened every evening before retiring to his cryogenic chamber for a good night's sleep.

"I was just giving it to him straight. Everything here is so much bullshit, I don't want to be bullshit all the time too."

The PA tried to mitigate things. "It's not fair to Kevin."

"It's exactly fair to Kevin. He knows what's happening now," I felt a rising irritation.

"It doesn't matter what's fair," the dude said. It was clear his opinion outranked the PA, who stepped back again. "Telling other contestants that you are trying to send them home ruins the game for everybody." This is what I get for forgetting there are cameras everywhere. Where was Blake's sneak-fucker stealth advice in avoiding them when I needed it?

"Doesn't ruin it for me." I said, probably overstepping my mandate. He looked at me, and I looked right back, looking for some kind of emotion to pass over his face. None. Nothing.

"Don't do it again. We can send you home any time too. But we'd like to help you here. This isn't helping us help you."

"We just want to help you, Tisa," The PA was back on the front lines again. "You are lucky to be here, and so is Kevin."

"Alright, but…" I began, but he cut me off.

"Just don't do it anymore." And with that he walked away. The PA looked at me with thinly veiled contempt. I ruined her lunch or made her look bad, I guess. I didn't care. But I did feel the familiar sting of letting people down poke into my sides. I was lucky to be here. *Maybe.*

The weigh in went predictably with the Bravo Team choosing to have Kevin sit out. He gave a speech for the cameras where he randomly gave himself some nickname like *the x man* but said Bravo Team had assigned it to him...um, ok. Either way he lost a good amount of weight that didn't count for our team. I guess his superpower tonight was being a waste. Oh fucking well. The Bravo Team acting all worried about the results for the cameras was pretty amusing knowing they had worked out in trash bags to lose extra weight and we hadn't dehydrated as much as we usually did. When I pulled the number I did on the scale, it was considerably more weight lost than I had anticipated. My concern that we had won the weigh in inadvertently showed all over my face. It's amazing how you have no idea what your body is going to do with weight loss. It really looked like we were going to accidentally win this weigh-in. What a shit fest that would've been. Luckily for all of us, and our plotting, Farrell managed to lose so much weight this week that he pulled off the win we were all hoping would happen. I almost cheered when they won but managed to stop myself before I was too obvious. Chris and I did look at each other though and smiled. Kevin managed to be surprised by the loss. Probably because despite knowing we wanted to send him home, he wasn't actually sure we would until it happened.

7/2/2015

There was no way that any of us women were voting for one another. And the idea that I would use the free pass to save anyone when I had immunity this week was just ridiculous. Just as I had honestly said to him, Kevin was sent home. To his credit, Kevin took it well.

Because there was this aura of being trapped all the time, things kicked into overdrive for us every now and then. I mean, I know it's a beautiful Spa with a house that's nicer than anything I've ever lived in. But a beautiful prison is still a prison. Sometimes like tonight, we sort of regress like unruly teenagers. I went from living on my own for almost a decade, to not being allowed to buy my own groceries, go for a walk without permission, or have privacy in my bedroom. Often you can't even go to the bathroom without a mic on—thirty lucky audio guys get to hear me poop. Tonight, some poor unsuspecting production assistant left a golf cart with the keys in it. Oops. Debbie, Esther, and I joyrode the shit out of that thing. It didn't take long for some of the crew to become savvy to the fact that three insanely giggling contestants were riding an unsanctioned golf cart about the premises. In true Benny Hill fashion, a few of them chased after us and it wasn't until they managed to coordinate their efforts using walkie-talkies and movie military vernacular, that they got us cornered. It sounds more dramatic than it was but they did have to physically block exits so we'd have to commit hit and runs to move further. I'm all for having fun but I'm not sure committing a felony in the name of fun is what I'm about. We ended up giving up the cart, and stern and judgmental faces told us the usual about us being *blessed* and how this beautiful life on the Spa could be over in a heartbeat if we didn't dance to their tunes. And in true fashion, we felt like shit for wanting a little change in our daily routines and apologized for misbehaving. It was like I was six again and my dad was pissed because I had been running around the house instead of walking in an orderly fashion. Esther, Debbie, and I extracted ourselves from the scene without being taken out back and beat up or forced to eat bugs by an angry production assistant. But we all felt the rush in our bodies from joyriding the golf cart and like that itch you can't quite reach, we needed something else.

"We should go swim," Esther said. "In the pool," she added—as if we could trek the miles to the ocean anyway.

"The pool is off limits at this hour," Debbie said, then stopped herself as she realized she sounded too much like a voice of reason. "We should go."

"Deal," I said, as we quickened our step. We then went to our room and changed into bathing suits before we clambered down the stairs in the direction of the pool. We barely reached it, when we became aware of several people standing around the pool house. It wasn't immediately visible from our room, which is why we hadn't realized until we were actually there. They were production crew and they were having beers and shooting the shit. I indicated to Esther and Debbie that they should be quiet as we snuck closer—like the detective at a villain's lair in some old movie. The mood was suddenly tense among us three. The production crew were discussing the show.

"I didn't shoot that part, though," one guy said and a few around him laughed. It was obviously the end of a funny anecdote about filming.

"Maybe one day, my son. Maybe one day," another dude said and patted the first one on the head in a paternal fashion. People chuckled again.

"Fuck off, dude," the first guy pushed his arm away. What a grand old time these guys were having but I was starting to get bored as shit since the PA of my eye was elsewhere and not hanging with this part of the crew.

"You'll sing a different tune when you hear what I'm shooting next."

"What will you shoot?" a third guy inquired.

"The next challenge. The prize will get us some hilarious takes, I'm sure."

"The prize?" the first guy asked with a bewildered look on his face. He must've been new. I snuck a little closer and felt like I was about to crack a case wide open. Debbie and Esther had stopped breathing behind me. Or so it felt. I thought I could hear their hearts.

"Yes. The prize is a video call home to their families. Imagine the looks on their faces when they hear that. And I'll be right there for it," He mimed shooting film with a camera and people around him laughed. Ostensibly, that was a big task for him. I signaled to Esther and Debbie to retreat. Mission complete. Despite the excitement kicking around our bodies, we weren't about to go swimming in the pool with 20 crew members looking at us. Plus, this had given us food for thought. All three of us thought about those calls already as we walked up the stairs to our room. Debbie about talking to her kids. Esther about talking to her wife. And me about seeing if my goldfish was belly up yet, or if he was excited to see my face on a screen.

Chapter 9

7/3/2015

ou know how as soon as you get a win, you feel like you're ahead of the game? The old universe finds time in its no doubt busy schedule, to take you down a peg or two. Just when I was self-satisfied as fuck and didn't think I could be surprised anymore, *today* happened. They marched us down to the weigh in gym early in the day, and there was this peculiar anticipation in the air that unnerved me right away. I *hate* surprises. To add to the fun of this no doubt whopper of a surprise, I feel like shit. This is the first time I've been sick since I got to the Spa and all I want is sinus medication and to be left alone. Head hurting like a motherfucker. My nose is alternating between being clogged completely with a single thin drop still somehow managing to make its way to a permanent position right at the tip of my nose then suddenly allowing all air to pass through unobstructed. With all this going on I nearly burst a lung with oxygen when I inhale expecting blockage. I know I should be paying better attention to what's going on but honestly, I just want some Sudafed and a fucking nap. We make it to the weigh in gym and the remaining contestants are rubbing their eyes while standing around in fight or flight positions. At this point we've been conditioned to feel like waiting around is the silence before a storm. Unless of course, you're lucky enough to have a PA who wants nothing more than to tear your clothes off in the back of a van. Then waiting isn't the worst. There is a lot of hushed chitchat among the crew and people running around like we're on the eve of a large battle. Finally someone steps up to the proverbial plate and makes the announcement.

"Henceforth the teams are split up. One person from the Alpha Team will be paired with one person from the Bravo Team and so on. And for the first time in the show's history two people will be sent home at once." A dead quiet falls upon us and people start to look around at each other, both silently lamenting the fact that we may be torn from those we know best and the fact that we'll have to work together with somebody we don't know that well. She continues, "The pairs will be decided via one person who wins the next challenge." Debbie and Esther look horror stricken and I know I should probably be more worried that we will now be sending home two people and that I will be paired with somebody from Bravo Team. But I can't get worked up about it. Can I go back to bed now?

Miraculously, production let me take a nap. I took a nap. Here in the fat camp from hell, I actually got thirty minutes of sleep. I'll take it. When they did wake me up, it was because it was challenge time once again. I'm utterly shocked and surprised that this challenge also involves eating more food. *Imagine that.* If I could lose weight via sarcasm, not only would I win this warped game show in a day, I would also go on to make millions. I'm not super worried about whomever I get paired up with since I have that magic immunity pass still sitting comfortably in my back pocket.

We each had to choose a covered window that contained either a food item in it that we then had to eat, or the power to assign pairs. Brody got lucky and won the challenge and now has all the power to make the pairs. I *won* a hot dog. Awesome. When I woke up this morning, I do remember thinking there would be nothing better than eating a hot dog that had been sitting in the sun all day as part of a challenge. And low and behold, Lady Fortuna smiled upon me. If she hasn't retired perhaps she'll grant me enough luck that this hotdog will give me the shits too.

Brody was supposed to spend the day in isolation deeply contemplating the burden that rests upon his shoulders when making these new pairs. Unless you count hanging out with Blake as isolation—and I'm sure Blake's wife might—he did. He also made a decision. I feel for the guy, this isn't a decision I would want. I feel enough bullshit suspicion from the others because I have that free pass. There's a weird obligation and pressure that comes with having that kind of thing and knowing that you're a target *because* of it. Brody did a pretty solid job in pairing people up, especially for not having any idea that Farrell, Hunter, and Chris were working with Debbie, Esther, and I. The pairs ended up being Hunter and Esther, Debbie and Chris, Farrell and I, followed by Blake and himself. Poor Debbie broke my heart crying because she was worried that she was going to sabotage Chris accidentally. There is so much desperation to stay in this game. I'm pretty pleased with my partner myself. I feel like he will solidly work hard and we will be a good team. On the other hand, at this point you could have paired me with Sarah Palin and I would've said anything as long as I could get sinus meds and something for my fever.

The best part of this whole pairing up thing was Chad's reaction. The dude looked like someone had swapped out his protein powder for straight powdered sugar when we told him that two people were going home this week. I'm not sure why he didn't already know. Or perhaps he did and this was a masterful performance. On the other hand, it was cringe worthy watching Shea try to commiserate with him and getting completely ignored. Their rivalry in this show was amusing to me. He obviously wasn't about her. At least as a competitor. And it felt kind of like it spilled over into real life. Not liking Shea? Imagine that?

"Are you f… serious?" he screamed, when we told him. "You can't be serious."

"No, it's real, Chad. It's what they told us," Chris was running point on this one.

"Unbelievable," Chad looked like he was about to powerlift Chris and slam him into the floor. Shea stood a few feet away looking desolate. This was apparently a major upset to them both. You'd think we, the contestants, would be the ones taking this the hardest but Chad and Shea were not coping well with this. "One of my boys will be going home," Chad said, mostly to himself, I think. His anger was replaced with a weird sort of paternal instinct and he just stood there surveying the guys like they were sons he was about to send off to war. Shea, not wanting to be left out, walked over to him and tried putting her arm around him. But Chad didn't notice. I almost felt sorry for Shea. *Almost.* This was the weirdest moment for a good while. And there have been plenty of contenders thus far.

Chad managed to suppress the anger, but only long enough so he could take that anger out on Brody in the gym. I don't envy that shit at all. He beat the crap out of Brody on workouts. Watching Shea and Chad argue over training styles sort of made my day though. It marks the first time I've seen Shea make any real sense. Why was he beating the shit out of people in the gym? I mean, it looks good but who wants to go to the gym if you're falling out on the floor every time you're there? Shea, against my expectations, realized this and tried talking Chad out of going harder on Brody. Team collaboration doesn't look like a thing for Shea and Chad. It's funny how much the competition isn't just between all of us but between the trainers too.

The scenes we filmed in the kitchen today were hilarious because I may be a great many things, but a chef I am *not*. Every bit of advice we gave for the camera is the polar opposite of how we actually eat here. Despite us smiling like some deranged Stepford Wives in the kitchen, dishing out eating healthy tips like we were paid by the sentence, it was all bullshit. We don't eat what we told the cameras to eat. At all. If this was really reality, we should be filming coffee ads and segments advising people on what energy drinks were the best for killing your appetite. Our actual diet here is a joke. Our trainers have taught us to live on sugar free gelatin, fake cheese, processed meat, crackers that resemble press board, orange roughy, protein shakes, egg whites, and butter spray. And we've had lots of it. Sugar free gelatin is a fan favorite. It's not a fabulous diet over all, but okay, it's livable if maybe you were eating it in quantities substantial enough to balance the hours of excessive exercising. Spoiler alert—we *weren't*.

We were doing the whole milk ad thing. Cameras set up, and the kitchen was again spotless and looking like it was ready for another day at a busy Michelin starred restaurant. We were set up and put on our best smiles with glasses of milk in our hands. Then we listened to Shea's canned speech about the benefits of drinking milk. She then prompted us to *make a milk mustache*. This went on for a while and it was grueling. My cheeks hurt from plastering that big fake smile on there for so long. We never actually drank the milk. Shea practically shrieked *spit the milk out* (like somehow just holding it in my mouth was going to make me fatter) as soon as the cameras stopped rolling.

It was time for the first duo challenge. Because this is already a fucking circus, it involved holding a metal stick that was on fire in a gas ring without touching the ring. You know, shit Steve-O would love to do while people pelted him with oranges. We had to hold the poles over our heads with one arm. I was fucked. Farrell is around eight feet tall—there was no way I could hold a pole at the same height as him. Good thing I didn't have my heart set on that video call home to my goldfish. I would have to catch him up when I saw him next.

The real joy of this challenge was watching Blake and Brody make it to the very end with everyone knowing that Blake was shitting his pants at the prospect of having to video call his wife on national television after banging Shannon for weeks before she left. The whole business was awkward enough for a lifetime. For everybody. After we all dropped like flies one by one it was down to Chris and Debbie up against Brody and Blake. The pain reliever gig had equipped Blake with De Niroesque acting skills because he did some remarkable pretending with that whole, *oh no, I can't hold it Brody,* routine and I had to stifle my laughter. Especially because not moments before, he talked Brody into slowly letting go of the pole *just to see* if he could hold it on his own. Sure as shit, he couldn't. Gee, who would've guessed? I hope Brody wasn't looking forward to seeing his family either. I'm glad Debbie gets to see her babies though.

I had seen Daniel mill about during the afternoon, so I knew he was around the set today. Debbie had already passed out on her face and Esther was in the bathroom. I showered and felt kind of frisky, so I decided to sneak out and see if I could *run* into him. Despite this being glorified fat camp, we, or at least I, had become surprisingly nimble from all the sneaking around. Not that I did that much, but any time you wanted anything done and didn't feel like millions of people needed to know about it, you had to sneak around. I walked down the stairs and heard voices that I steered toward. I tried to make it in the general direction of the gym, so if somebody saw me, I could just say that was what I was up to. At this point in the game eyebrows would only be raised to half-mast at the thought of contestants sneaking out to get a little late-night workout. I wouldn't have minded a different kind of workout, but I knew even if I *did* find Daniel, that probably wasn't going to happen. I could be sent home and he could lose his job. But just seeing him would be a thing.

"Hi," a voice I immediately recognized, said behind me. I spun around.

"How do you do that?" I said, genuinely curious. He seemed to have secret passages that enabled him to be right behind me if I was looking for him. I wonder if the Spa had secret passages. That would be kind of cool.

"I invented teleportation years ago. Been keeping my cards pretty close to my chest," he quipped. My goodness he was charming—annoyingly so.

"You'd rather work as a production assistant on Fat Camp USA?"

"With teleportation I could see the wonders of the world but I'd still rather use it to get to you." Check and mate.

"Flattery will get you everywhere," I said, and I kind of meant it.

"Good," He pulled me into his embrace and kissed me. It surprised me enough I nearly screamed but his warm mouth caught me in time. I put my arms around his neck and pushed myself into him. It wasn't sex but it will do. We both ended the kiss, which left me mildly out of breath.

"Tomorrow," he said enigmatically.

"Tomorrow?" I asked confused.

"I can't promise anything. But I'm going to see if I can find an excuse to take you out somewhere."

"You can *do* that?" I could barely contain the anticipation in my voice. The prospect of several hours alone with him. Not just barely out of sight or in the vicinity of a camera or microphone. Legitimately *away*.

"I don't know but I'll shop the idea around and see what comes up. If not, I might just kidnap you. I'm sure a high-speed chase is your idea of a perfect date."

"It's definitely top five."

"I'll find you tomorrow."

"I'll look forward to it." I would. He took my hand in his and kissed it. A cute gesture I hadn't experienced before but I liked it. We said good night and as I strolled back to my room, I gave my mind free reign to imagine just what we would do the next day. Thankfully both Esther and Debbie were asleep when I got back, so I didn't have to answer any prying questions.

7/4/2015

The Last workout—inane and as fake, as it was chronologically—was brutal. If it wasn't for Debbie, I'm pretty sure I would've dropped dead. Or at the very least puked all over the place. I still haven't quite figured out how to regulate my breathing when I run and I end up doing a weird hyperventilating thing. My heart tells my brain that my lungs have decided we are going to die now. It made me sad to realize that with the weigh-in tonight, my core group of support, Esther and Debbie, may no longer be here. I've come to love those two kooky women.

That motherfucker. Farrell. He threw that fucking weigh-in. I can't stop crying. I'm crying because I feel like I am the naivest bitch on the planet because I didn't see this coming. I was *still* so damn blind I didn't realize he threw the thing until Daniel pulled me aside and told me. I mean *of course* he threw it. How else would you gain weight here? I am so gullible. His fucking smirk on that scale, though, pisses me off the most.

Before I realized *why* he smirked, I felt sorry for him. He stepped on the scale and had gained weight. I thought it was devastating to him. I must have looked genuinely bewildered because right after we were done, and people were dispersing, Daniel strolled out among us, all casual like, and whispered to me, that Farrell had thrown the weigh-in. I must have looked shocked, because he repeated it.

"He threw this. Deliberately."

"What? He did? How do you know?"

"He had to."

"How?" I asked, more just as a rhetorical question because I was in disbelief about the whole thing.

"Didn't work as hard or he water loaded. I don't know. But he did. I gotta go." He strolled out again before too many prying eyes caught him.

Mostly, I am pissed that Farrell didn't give me the heads up that he was going to do this this week. Had I known I wouldn't have killed myself in the gym trying to put up a good number so I wouldn't disappoint him. That motherfucker. Next weigh-in I am going to be screwed because I lost so much this week. I can't do it again for next week. I am so mad that I'm considering using that stupid free pass for someone else, so we'd be sent home, just to burn him for playing the game without giving me a heads up. What a bold dick-hole move. I wish it hadn't taken Daniel to point out that he did it on purpose because it would've made a spectacular scene if I had realized it while Farrell was still on that scale. Absolutely I'm using that damn pass on us. I'd love to see him sent home but I'm not ready for me to be sent home with him. To top it off, I got to be near Daniel and I couldn't even appreciate it. I was so pissed off I missed the moment. Thanks a lot Farrell you, duplicitous sack of shit.

It was elimination time, and I dreaded it. We were four pairs left. Two of them had people in them I really didn't want to lose. One pair was Brody and Blake. I didn't *not* care about Brody but let's face it, he was no Esther or Debbie. Farrell and I lost the weigh- in along with Chris and Debbie, because of Farrell's bullshit. So sending Brody and Blake home wasn't even in the realm of possibilities. I was going to use the immunity pass for me and by proxy Farrell, and he knew it. That meant that Debbie would be sent home. The mood in the elimination room was less than awesome. We had to sit in the pairs we were assigned and I wanted to grab my free pass and ram it down Farrell's throat. I played nice though. I'm sure the ensuing brouhaha would end up robbing potential viewers of their belief in humanity. I couldn't bear to look at Farrell's stupid fucking face when I used the immunity pass to save us because he had played me. So, we were immune and next up were Debbie and Chris. Who were eliminated. I felt like I had done it. I had thrown Debbie under the bus to save myself. But it was a reality. We all got up and I felt the familiar lump in my throat. I had known Debbie for mere weeks but it felt like forever because this place is fucked. Without those little hints of friendship, it would've been insanity. She looked at me, then at Esther, we had teary embraces. It sucked. I was going to miss Debbie. Chris high-fived Hunter and Farrell, then they were led away to pack their shit and leave the Spa. That was that. At least it's every man for himself now.

Farrell, that fucking dipshit, forced me to use that free pass and we are still in pairs. The host told us to sit down again after saying goodbye to Debbie and Chris to share the good news. Fun times. Not only are we still in fucking pairs, we are competing against a pair from home now. Yes, they just marched in six people—three men and three women—who had apparently been playing along from home. Well, I guess I have a new direction for my anger then. Farrell is still a fuck-face, don't get me wrong but learning we had been competing against everyone at home this whole time, when we were explicitly told they were not competing against us is bullshit. This means more people to eliminate and more time at this fucking Spa.

Apparently these six people from home have had a registered dietician doing their nutrition and they looked small. Like, kick our asses' small. Which doesn't bode well for us as the entire time this same dietician tried to teach us, if we asked a question, a production member would step in after she answered and redirect us to our trainers. We listened to our trainers, unlike these small strangers who obviously were doing something right without trainers. Your trainer is larger than life. They are this omniscient and omnipotent TV personality superhero that is all controlling and they have as much at stake as you do. So, you listen to production when they tell you that is the person to rely on for your diet and you shun everybody else trying to tell you differently. When you hear repeatedly that your trainer is the one who will save your life, the one who keeps you at the Spa, you listen. I'm looking at these six people who don't look anywhere near as beat to shit as I am, are smaller than I am and I'm starting to wonder just in how high regard production actually held my health. Maybe I *shouldn't* have listened.

There was the most awkward mixer between us and the new contestants. My junior high dances were less awkward. It was at that point I realized, these women were going to have to sleep somewhere. I'd be damned if that was going to be *my* room. Not while Esther and I are still aching from the loss of Debbie. Her bed wasn't even cold yet. Fuck that. I didn't start this show out ready to play the game here. I'm about ready to play now though.

Chapter 10

7/5/2015

You have got to be fucking kidding me. I'm sure these are nice people but I have no desire to prolong my time here competing against them. I'm sure no one expects us to trade friendship bracelets or braid each other's hair but the level of animosity from this show is off the charts. I had no idea how petty I was until last night. Ok, maybe I suspected I had a petty streak, but it's definitely been thrown into sharp relief here. No one that has been isolated at this Spa cares one damn bit about anything except getting these newcomers the hell out of our house. If the show attempted to create a fun new dynamic, they failed *miserably*. Obviously, that wasn't the goal—happy people make for good TV about as much as watching grass grow—but I'm an eternal optimist about other people's motivations, sort of. Don't get me wrong. As people, I'm sure they're as good as any other human being. But I am tired, I am beat to shit and just fuck these people. I'm petty. I'll work on that with a therapist later. But right then? I didn't want to deal with the self-assured bitch from whatever random state who casually mentioned that she thought my ass would be smaller by now. Hand me a blade and I'll show you a smaller ass. Get the fuck out with that.

I was not about to share my bedroom that had been my home with Debbie and Esther for months, with these strangers.

Esther and I—still kind of shocked at Debbie not completing our trifecta—went to our room and sat down in shared disbelief.

"This is bullshit," I said, never one to mince words. Esther looked up. She didn't use swear words but I felt as if this could be the one time she might compromise her principles. She *didn't* however.

"I'm gonna miss Debbie," she simply said. A moment passed and we both looked at Debbie's now empty bed. We remembered simultaneously that they would probably move the new women in with us at least for the night until their weigh-in dictated which of them would be staying at the Spa.

"Holy shit," I lamented, and Esther covered her mouth. "They are going to have them in here with us."

"Debbie is barely off the Spa property by now." Esther looked legitimately offended at the thought of a stranger in Debbie's bed. I wasn't about the thought of having anybody but Esther and I in this room for the night. I don't know what exactly I thought should happen. We needed a period of mourning before we could meet new people and forge new relationships. Or perhaps I just wanted a moment of peace from this shit-show. One night where we got to have our way without weird stuff thrown in our faces.

"That isn't going to happen," I said as I got up and walked to Debbie's vacant bed. Esther followed me, her eyes widened. I grabbed the frame of the bed. "Here, help me."

Esther got up and grabbed the other end of the bed. We started flipping the bed up and blankets and pillows we hadn't moved first fell everywhere. The blanket covered Esther's face and she flailed her arms to remove it and not drop the bed. Her loss of balance caused me to almost trip as I side stepped to compensate, and the mattress started falling out of the frame and over me so I was nearly knocked against the wall. Esther had gotten free of the blanket and was pulling the opposite way on the surprisingly uncooperative bed frame.

"Tisa, pull… *pull* the other way," Esther yelled with no small amount of desperation in her voice. Neither of us were spatially aware. I complied and we managed to get it somewhat steady. As we dragged it to the door, it quickly became apparent that we would not under any circumstances be able to fit it through. It had been assembled or built in that room and it was going to stay. We struggled, unsuccessfully, for a while, during which Esther hurt her toe and I nearly sprained a wrist. It was like the Three Stooges sans a Stooge trying to move a house. We managed to get the frame back to the ground and each sat on our respective beds, out of breath. We would've laughed our asses off, I'm sure, if we weren't pissed off at, well, *everything*. Sheets, blankets and pillows were littered everywhere. Only moments after we had given up, the three women arrived in our doorway, with confused looks on their faces. They each looked from Esther, to the mess on the floor, to me and back to Esther, with puzzled expressions that did nothing to soothe my resentment. How fucking baffling was this to them? They were clearly entering an already established dynamic and we had just lost somebody. I wasn't trying to be a bitch about it but I didn't want strangers in my space. Moments of dense silence followed. Then Esther said something, which kind of broke it.

"You just missed the pillow fight," She commented.

The girls chuckled and stepped into the room. Dawn grabbed the bed frame, and with help from Barbara, they put it back to where it had been. Seth picked up the bedclothes and put them on the bed before she sat next to Barbara. Dawn was still standing and I could see she was half-way inspecting the room like a lifelong Elvis fan at Graceland. Her eyes glided over every detail as she was taking it in but settled on my headboard. I was about to ask what the fuck she was doing, when she spoke.

"Look at the face on that hottie," I was confused. *What* hottie? I turned around. She was talking about a picture of Daniel and I, which was taped to my headboard. It was a picture from a photo booth on one of the fat camp field trips we had taken. Daniel pulled me into the booth and slipped the print out to me like somebody in prison would slip packs of cigarettes to a fellow inmate. I cherished it as my only window to a life I missed from before the show. One where I was a human who did human things like date and eat. Daniel wasn't a part of that life really, but he came to represent it for me in a big way here and I was territorial about him. "I've been *about* that guy since he was the PA that helped at my hotel before filming!" Dawn continued, giggling.

This did not bode well for a friendship between Dawn and me. It was no doubt supposed to be playful and attempt at bonding. Perhaps Dawn was just completely void of situational awareness and couldn't read my vibe. My vibe screamed petty bitch. All her commentary did was intensify my dislike of the situation and direct it all at her. I hate her face.

After that I decided that Dawn—if she should end up staying—was my mortal enemy. Smothering my animosity for the moment in an effort to be friendly, Esther and I managed to chat a bit with the three of them and learned that Dottie—the dietician we had been told to disregard at every turn—had been giving nutritional advice and made diet plans for the thirty-six contestants at home during the whole show. Yeah. That seems about right.

7/6/2015

Fresh from the fun events of the night before, we were all in the gym going at it in usual fashion today. Esther and I stood together and we took weird solace in the fact, that Farrell and Hunter didn't immediately mingle with the new guys either. Brody and Blake were also by themselves. The gym was sweltering hot but at least there was enough room for 4 distinct factions to work out without having to trip over each other. Dawn, Seth, and Barbara—still flying high on their proper diets and normal work-out regimens from home—had not yet grasped or experienced what working out here meant. For starters, it meant having a ridiculously chipper Shea shouting at you. That takes a little getting used to. It also meant working out in suffocating heat. It meant being scrutinized by others every time you weren't actively working out. At this point in the game being thrown onto the Spa with contestants who more closely resembled a pack of scheming coyotes, also meant you couldn't really feel safe. I learned that the hard way from Farrell. Dawn did the same thing she had in our room yesterday, where she walked around, touching everything so as to assert that it's actually real. It was major crazy and I couldn't help asking Seth and Barbara if this was normal.

"Hell if we know," Barbara said. She was a curly haired lady from Wyoming who had been a legal clerk for thirty years and had decided something had to be done about her weight. Apparently that *something* was a TV show. "We only interacted with her when we were all at the Spa months ago with you guys and via conference calls until the day before yesterday."

"Ah, of course," I said, wondering why this hadn't occurred to me before. They didn't really know each other. They had been at home, after all. This pleased me to know that they didn't have an alliance already. Perhaps, if we tried to include these two, we could give them the scale manipulating tips we learned so one of them would stay instead of Dawn. Petty? Yes. I never claimed I wasn't. This was a game and I was finally playing to win.

"Well I guess we might as well officially welcome you to the Spa then," I said in my most pleasant voice. My ability to fake it astounded even me at times. "I'd say don't try anything you see here at home but it seems I'm too late for that."

"Oh yes. We've already tried it at home. It worked well enough so they brought us here," she quipped back. Well played lady.

"Have you met Shea yet?" Esther was on another treadmill but joined in the conversation anyway. You learned to talk and run at the same time, or you wouldn't get to utter many words during the day.

"Yes," Barbara answered. She paused, considering her words carefully.

"It was interesting, wasn't it?" I asked, before she could form a coherent sentence. Her face broke into a grin.

"Yes," she said. It was clear she was scared and felt foolish for not immediately bonding with a trainer.

"She's an acquired taste," I looked over at Shea, who was talking to a crew member by the door. No doubt making sure the cameras were set up to maximize her screen time.

"We work out a lot. So get used to that," Esther had her maternal voice on now. "And I don't know how and what you ate at home? But in here, the only dietary advice comes from that lady over there," She indicated Shea. We all looked in her direction just in time to catch her looking at her own reflection.

"I don't know what you've seen on TV from home of previous seasons. But chances are good it's a lot different in real life. I would prefer my new housemates be as chill as possible about all of this." I felt like Deep Throat dishing out information on Watergate on the down low. They saw me look at Dawn who was on a bike pedaling away. In my head she looked up, cheery faced and waved like a 1950s Pleasantville housewife when the neighbors drove by. There was a lot of waving in the 50s. She didn't wave. Didn't even look up, but my point was made. Dawn gave off a crazy sort of brain washed vibe.

This weigh-in was bullshit. How stupid of me not to realize that of course they had already weighed-in on a cattle scale like we had and this was fake bullshit like our weigh-ins. All of our *tips* for the two women who weren't Dawn were all for naught. Their weights had been documented the day before in some nondescript hotel room before coming to the Spa. Feeling incredibly stupid, I spent an hour watching people weigh-in. People who had spent the last months at home, surrounded by family, talking to an actual doctor, having the guidance of a registered dietician, sleeping next to people who loved them, and getting laid on the regular. The final insult? They had *all* lost more weight than us. *What in the actual fuck.* This triggered a long rant from me, mostly for the benefit of Esther, Farrell, and Hunter, who were standing next to me. But through the magic of technology and mics, the sound guys got an earful too.

"What the actual fuck is with this bullshit. I've been working my fingers to the bone on something like six calories a day for fucking months. All while they have been at home getting laid and sleeping in their own fluffy beds. Pack my bags. I know you production assholes are listening. Pack my bags and send me home to sleep, sex, and food. When these goobers got up in the morning, they didn't have some Fitness cover model screaming bloody murder at them, telling them that going an extra three hours on the treadmill is all that is needed to solve all life's problems all while admiring herself in the mirror. No, no, no not these fuckers. They could get up, have their morning dietician sanctioned breakfast, probably a quickie with the wifey or whoever before working out for, *wait for it*, a total of *two and a half hours* a day. And if they felt like they wanted some water, they had some fucking water. If they wanted a break, they had a fucking break. If I wanted a break? I'd be personally offending somebody. This fucking Spa is bullshit. And you Farrell. Congratulations, motherfucker, you played yourself. So much for only competing against this group. Now we have these new assholes to compete with and guess what, they've got us beat at this point. No immunity. Nothing, because you had to game the system. Look at them. No bruises, no bags under their eyes. Cocky and well rested pieces of shit. I know you hear me people in the control room, I'm fucking leaving. Pack my bags, guys, I'm out on the first jet."

I was on a roll. I could see the audio dudes crying from laughter in the back. Farrell didn't know whether he should laugh or cry. Esther blushed from all the swearing. But I knew she agreed. This was complete fucking bullshit.

I've been starving and working out for hours on end every day, interrupted by doing ridiculous challenges that resemble some bullshit found in a sideshow act to get my ass whooped by these people who say they were eating three meals and working out for two hours a day. *Two. Hours. A. Day.* That's like a rest day here.

Every one of the men and women from home had lost more weight than we had. *Every. One.* Not only had they lost more weight than those of us who have been beaten to shit by the training and nutritional advice—if you want to label coffee, and dehydration nutritional advice here—they are also without injury and they are not functioning in such a state of paranoia that they cannot think beyond *the game*. The final results of this demoralizing farce of a weigh-in sent four of the six returned contestants home. We are now stuck with Dawn—oh fucking goody, she of the desperate fandom, snarky comments about my ass, and eyes for Daniel—and Greg, a dude I literally forgot the moment our handshake ended. A man so boring that if he were a color he'd be beige. I've never even been to whatever state he's from.

Having Dawn as a part of our *team* makes me miss Debbie so much more. Shea and Chad were predictably and understandably pissed at the new contestants and their weight loss numbers. I mean, it does sort of make a trainer look superfluous when the people you've been beating to shit were so roundly tromped by people who worked out by themselves at home. *Awkward.* I'm sure I'd find it hilarious if I wasn't also kind of pissed off by it.

Before we were mixed with the new people for good, Shea and Chad had a little talk with us. An inspirational talk, I guess you could call it.

"They are nice people and they have worked very hard to get here with you guys," Shea started, obviously trying to play nice. Chad? Not so much.

"They are going to buckle under the pressure in here," He cut her off. He almost stood next to us facing her, like we were totally in this together now and were just trying to peer pressure Shea into joining the gang. "They aren't going to last five minutes with this program I've made for them."

"You guys were the originals," Shea said to us. "You already know what it's like in here and you know what it takes to go the distance."

"They'll never want to leave their states again, once I'm through with them." Chad said. He was pretty worked up about this.

"We'll handle their work outs. It's up to you to just keep focusing on yours."

"You focus on dropping that weight and you can beat them. Easily," Chad's confidence was kind of contagious. Or perhaps it was the rage at being outdone by a bunch of newcomers. It was clear that we should hunker down and get them out of here.

Shea tried to have a meeting with Dawn to get a feeling for why she had such better weight loss numbers than us. The only thing I learned from this is that Dawn is young and prior to the show lived almost exclusively on booze and cheese. In addition, I learned that she is a fan girl nutter. I'm jealous of the former and a little frightened by the latter.

We were in our room—after making it clear that Dawn's room was the empty one down the hall—with Dawn on a bed and Esther and I on our beds. The meeting with Shea earlier had been a weird kind of third degree interview, where Shea had failed to conceal her professional interest in Dawn's weight loss.

"I am sooo excited to finally get to totally bond with you guys." Dawn started. I wasn't sure if she was about to try and make my nightmares of friendship bracelets and hair braiding come true or if she was about to murder us. Instead, she pulled out a notebook. A stack of notebooks in fact, from her bag. Did she want us to journal together? No. It was much worse. She opened one of the books and motioned for us to join her. Esther got up and I reluctantly followed suit. This was way weird. The book contained statistics, incidents and cut outs of contestants from all of the previous seasons of the TV show. A scrapbook of every bit of information she could gather. She flicked through the pages with an occasional comment when a particularly curious page turned up. She put the book down and picked up another one. It was for this season. As she flipped pages, there we all were with cut out pictures and guestimates on weight loss based on how long we had been there. I glanced at Esther and her raised eyebrows told me that I wasn't the only one who found this disconcerting. I briefly considered if I dared fall asleep tonight. I didn't want to wake up to Dawn removing my face so she could wear it.

Dawn's first workout with our team was a hot mess. She told production she was letting us win in sprints so she didn't come off too cocky, which seemed kind of oxymoronic, and then she proceeded to argue with Shea that the workout wasn't hard enough.

"This is nothing like I do at home," Dawn whined. I could almost feel several assholes pucker up. Shea turned to her.

"What *do* you do at home?" she inquired. It was clear she wasn't super interested in what Dawn did at home.

"Well, I usually go a lot faster and switch back and forth between the treadmill and the bike," Dawn was treading on dangerous ground. She turned to the rest of us. "I don't get why you don't just go faster. You've been here a while?"

"Well they don't *go faster*," Shea started, and her look could've drawn blood, "because they have been here a lot longer than you, they work very hard every day and they give everything they've got every day. You just got here. They haven't seen their families or friends in months." She was not having this insolence and I actually felt a flash of respect for her. Sure, her professional integrity was also on the line but she didn't make it about *her* for once. That was kind of cool. Dawn slinked a little, then started running. Shea didn't stare her down, which was also to her credit. Dawn was a part of her team now, whether she liked it or not. I felt a host of 80s movies flash before my eyes, where the outsider comes in and is universally hated but one little situation turns her into the hero. In the end, everybody rallies behind the unlikely coach to clinch the victory. I wondered what epiphany Dawn would have rallying us to her cause.

Meanwhile, elsewhere in the gym, Chad deliberately beat the shit out of Greg. Ouch.

7/7/2015

Whoo Hoo! Fat camp field trip day to Target. The trendy people's Wal-Mart. How exciting. I was well rested when I woke and feeling a smite less annoyed with this whole situation. I had a plan so cunning, you could stick a tail on it and call it a weasel. Last night after hours of working out, I got to chatting with Greg. I managed to remember him beyond just knowing he was a person that exists and come to find out he wasn't actually a douche. Weird how that works sometimes when you talk to people. He and I went for a walk and he let me in on a little secret. He had brought a burner phone. Why the hell did I not think of that? When I had gotten to our room, I told Esther and she was as excited as I was. For her. Because let's be honest. Unless Mr. Goldfish had developed lungs and was hanging out by the phone waiting for it to ring, who was I going to call? There was a phone jack in our bathroom—for reasons unknown—and getting a cheap landline phone wouldn't set us back much so a burner phone wasn't even necessary. Esther talked eagerly about calling her family all the way to the church vans. I had to calm her down a little bit so we wouldn't reveal our plans to the general public. We kept up our game faces when we got to the vans. If our acting careers don't take off immediately after this show, perhaps a career in international spy work is in the cards for us. I've gotten almost *too* good at doing shit on the down low here. The church vans were their usual suffocating stuffy heat, and we all managed the usual chit chat about sex and food—that was a staple for people who got neither. We arrived at Target and as usual, we got to sit in the vans in blistering heat while the crew made arrangements. A few people stopped with puzzled looks on their faces, at the vans just sitting right in front of the entrance. A PA stuck her head into our van and explained, that the reason we were at Target today, was to buy ourselves new clothes. We were no longer fat enough to fit our old clothes. I was now impressed that they hadn't just taken us to Wal-Mart but had opted for the fashion mecca that was Target instead. No matter. It wasn't like I was on national television in anything I could find that fit at this point, right? I dismissed the thought when I saw Esther's thinly veiled excitement at the prospect of getting to call her family. That was our mission today.

We were finally given the go ahead. We poured out of those damn vans single file to the astonishment of at least a few stragglers hanging around still looking puzzled. Inside Target, the A/C was a blessing and I could've stayed there for hours, just for that. We strolled around the clothes area, picking up hangers at random. Some of the stuff I could actually get used to. We do our thing to keep suspicion down, try on some pieces, acting either overly excited or overly critical. If it wasn't for the practically hovering PAs, the changing rooms would've actually afforded us a bit of privacy. My mind drifted to Daniel real fast, half wishing he was working on our field trip today, half glad he wasn't because if so, the chaperones could've really pissed me off. When Esther and I had both chosen some clothing to purchase, we were allowed to wander off a bit while the others still shopped. This was our chance to sneak off and find a phone. While skulking around the electronics department we ran into Brody, who flashed a guilty grin. Evidently, he had gotten the same idea.

"Blake was borrowing a PA's phone for a while to call Shannon," he said, casually. For a brief moment I was annoyed at Daniel because he hadn't offered me that but then I figured he was probably *already* risking a lot.

It didn't take us long to procure a ten-dollar phone. It was small, relatively inconspicuous and it would get the job done. We picked up a few other random items—to pad a shopping bag so it wasn't obvious that we also had a phone. I got the, if I do say so myself, rather brilliant idea of buying a cheap new pillow, so I could stuff the phone in there. I'm pretty sure I could've won the Cold War single handedly, had they only deployed my cunning.

Back in our room later, Esther nearly tore the pillow into shreds to get at the phone. Who knew having loved ones was this intense? She plugged the phone into the jack in the bathroom and we both looked at it sitting there, almost too scared by the possibilities. She finally picked up the receiver and slowly put it to her ear. The fireworks going off in her eyes told me there was a dial tone. She punched the number and it actually rang. I went back into our room wanting to give her privacy, and even with the door closed, her shrieks of joy were unmistakable. I also put some music on in case her voice carried. I considered calling my parents briefly and while I was homesick, it wasn't really for them. It was more just to be in my own space without people wanting me to do stuff all the time or having to get up and drive places. Or just to sit outside my house in the morning, having a cup of coffee while enjoying the sky growing steadily bluer. Or sleeping on a Sunday, knowing I had nothing I needed to do. Or being able to get laid when I felt like the time was right for getting laid—without having to sneak around or secretly flirt while the eyes in the back of my head were ever vigilant. I missed those things but I couldn't really call anybody that represented them. Hearing how happy Esther was from talking to her wife again made it worth it.

The guys had to film a gelatin commercial. More work for free because we are just here to dance and sing for the entertainment of the masses. I was happy I wasn't in it. Fucking gelatin. It was basically all we ate here, so I suppose if anybody were to be spokespeople for it, it would be us. I didn't envy the dudes having to go through the filming though. I went for a swim later where Hunter came out and told me about it. They had to act like a bunch of bros casually standing around the kitchen, shooting the shit and, for some godforsaken reason, decide to bro it up over cups of gelatin. Sugar free fraternity. Because that's *so* fashionable. My mind cut to images of a bunch of dusty septuagenarians on the cusp of retirement brainstorming ideas for this ad.

"*I know!*" *one would exclaim raising a gnarled but perfectly manicured fist into the air. "Young guys in a fraternity are joking about women or sports or cars or some such, and they share a cup of gelatin.*"

"*Yes, Murray, by Jove, you've got it!*" *another would cry. "This is what young scallywags do these days, I have seen it on the moving picture box!*"

7/8/2015

This challenge was a joke. Also, we all behaved like the pettiest assholes on the planet. I can own that. We were in our now designated two-person teams and each duo had to move a literal ton of something. There was a ton of water jugs, tires, bricks and a ton of various weights. To decide which pair was going to move what, there was a calorie counting challenge. I'm usually pretty on top of the calorie counting game but Brody was not taking prisoners that morning, so Blake and Brody won it, giving them the privilege of picking who moved what. Dawn and Greg were screwed unless they won the calorie counting challenge, and sure as shit they didn't because they spent their time at home following actual dietician ordered diets and training regiments, and *not* perfecting their calorie counting or dehydrating skills like the rest of us. Enjoy those bricks we all knew you would get. Blake and Brody chose the water jugs for themselves. Nobody was surprised at that one. Esther and Hunter got the weights and Farrell and I had the tires. I had no illusions of winning this challenge or the prize of a big screen TV and Netflix for a year that came with it—and by the way, what the hell kind of prize is that for people who acknowledge their difficulty staying active—but Farrell was pissed.

"I swear this show!" he went off after we'd moved perhaps half the tires and Brody and Blake finished their water jugs without breaking too much of a sweat. "Who comes up with these challenges? I want to meet whoever comes up with them and ask why not a ton of feathers? Or why not a ton of marshmallows? Why are tires so special? It's ridiculous. This is a ridiculous challenge. What the hell is the point of it?" He flailed his arms around in abject frustration, then took to pointing at random crew members like he was calling them out. A few of the people behind the cameras were looking around confused, unsure if they were being singled out or what was happening. The sound guys were, true to form, laughing their asses off and I was laughing to tears myself from the absurdity of this and Farrell's amazing and unreasonably angry rant. I think this might be one of the few times in my life I actually peed a little laughing. There was no way he and I were going to win this challenge but we finished anyway. Not for any noble *never quit* philosophy or anything like that but because we knew there was no way in hell Dawn and Greg were going to waste time moving all those damn bricks and we just wanted to make them look like quitters. Yup. My petty knows no bounds. If I had any class or gave a shit, I would've gone over and helped them move their bricks. But I don't. It'll be one more thing to make note of to work on when I care about being a better human being and I am not so tired, bruised and hungry. Oh, well.

Greg and Dawn obviously didn't end up moving their entire ton of bricks. I mean, it *was* a literal ton of bricks. We had just arrived back at the Spa, when we were greeted by Chad, who looked surly. Chad often did but there was *tough love* surly Chad and there was *you done fucked up* surly Chad. This look was the latter version. It was clear Chad knew about the bricks and we were about to get a speech.

"Guys," he started, as all of us had filed into the lobby of the Spa. Chad was standing on the second step up the stairs like a pastor speaking to his congregation. We were all looking up at him, weary and just wanting to get this over with. "We do a lot to prep you all for the challenges. They are an important part of the game. And we are here to help you in this game, to become better people and win. Don't you want to win?"

"Yes," some people murmured in unison. Obviously a rhetorical question.

"Yes," Chad repeated, "of course you do. So, it is kind of a kick in the shin, when you don't take it that seriously. Dawn and Greg, you didn't even finish this challenge today. That isn't how winners play this game. That is how quitters play this game. And with all the time we invest in you, to help you win this game and excel, quitting isn't an option. It just *isn't*. I want to see more winning attitudes from now on. Especially from you two. You need to learn to finish what you start."

He fixed Greg and Dawn with a stern gaze and it was clear this whole scene was orchestrated just to make them feel shitty about not moving their ton of bricks. Kind of a dick move but that was Chad. Being something of a petty connoisseur myself I respected it. He stood in our way a few seconds longer until he figured his point was made, then he stepped aside letting us go up to our rooms.

Despite our lacking enthusiasm, the challenge was pretty rough and we all felt beat to shit. But that obviously didn't mean we wouldn't be hitting the gym later on. A shower made up for a lot of lost energy, if nothing else than to make you feel kind of like a human again. I had showered, put on my sweats, and was walking toward the gym, when I heard a familiar *hi* behind me. Daniel was at my side before I had a chance to turn around. His hand brushed mine and I fought the urge to quickly grab it in mine.

"Hi," I said, perhaps slightly more enthusiastic than I had anticipated. I wasn't having a day rougher than usual really but the challenges always did drag things down a bit. Daniel's appearance significantly improved it for me.

"It's good to see you," Daniel said, looking sideways at me. "You look fine."

"Ha-ha. You liar," I said, unable to quite conceal my joy at the compliment, despite deflecting it with a joke. He smirked. As always, my mind raced ahead of me, looking at every possible nook or cranny on the route towards the gym where I could potentially drag Daniel and, if nothing else, have a nice make out session for a bit. As always, my mind came up blank. Damn Spa. Damn people milling about. Damn route to gym with no niches to be felt up a little and kissed.

"Tisa, I may or may not have a surprise for you soon," he said. When I looked at him with anticipation, his eyes met mine and I thought I saw excitement in his too. Maybe he was taking me away from here? Could he really take me away? It might not be white knight shit but even a few hours away from all this in his company would be all kinds of amazing. I didn't say anything because it was obvious he couldn't say more. I felt like asking too much could scare the moment away, like the cusp of a dream you are chasing right before you wake. Good Lord, I get sappier the longer I stay here. "I'll find you later. I just wanted to see you. And tell you." He put his hand on my shoulder, and I got chills. We didn't physically kiss but with the way the air felt around us, we might as well have. He winked a cute wink, then veered off my path again as quickly as he had entered it. I felt the little butterflies in my chest flap their big slow wings and as a kid before Christmas, I just wanted to go to bed so it could be morning already. As I was entrenched in thoughts of what he and I could get up to later, I was interrupted by a male voice that I, for a brief moment, thought was Daniel's again. It turned out to be Greg, who must've walked not far behind Daniel and I, and who had, apparently, heard everything.

"Tisa," he simply said. I spun around, and I'm sure he saw the brief flash of joy leave my eyes as soon as I realized it was him and not Daniel, because he added, "It's me, Greg." pretty fast.

"Oh, hi," I said, trying not to sound like he had just stabbed me in the kidneys. I turned back around when he was by my side, and we strolled on.

"Is he a PA?" Greg asked. He had clearly seen and heard everything, so there wasn't a point in trying to make anything up to distract him.

"Yes," I said, as casually as I could, while the butterflies were quickly folding up their wings. We walked for a minute, while I wondered what he was going to say.

"He looked like a nice guy," he said. I was surprised. I thought I'd have to hear incessant teasing or judgment.

"He is actually pretty nice. He's helped me out with some music for my work outs."

"Are you guys dating?" Greg asked, sounding much like I imagine a brother would sound like if I had one, deliberately not looking at me. I didn't look at him either when I answered because I felt the need to be weirdly evasive.

"I don't know." I realized I actually *didn't*. I wanted to, and I thought he did too, but things were, to use a cliché, *complicated*. Obviously. "Things are complicated."

"They are," he agreed, then paused. "With somebody working on a show like this, it might always be. You know, complicated. He seems like a nice guy but this industry is, well, *complicated*." He reiterated. It felt a little awkward, like he wanted to say something outright but didn't want to overstep. It felt sweet rather than intrusive actually. Like a big brother telling you, to watch out for yourself, without revealing the brotherly love too much. It was kind of early on for a friendship with Greg, if we could even use a word like that, for any connections made with someone competing against you. I was really touched at how sincere it was and I appreciate that authenticity even more since being here. But that's me. And perhaps that's Greg.

"Thank you," I merely said and I meant it genuinely. It was nice of him to look out for me.

"I just know how it is with these things," he continued, still looking ahead trying to time his longer stride to my shorter one. I looked at him for the first time since he caught up to me and my quizzical look made him chuckle. "Honestly, I don't. I don't have a clue how it is with these things. But coming from the outside and seeing how upside-down emotions and things are here, I have perspective you might not. Losing weight is an emotional thing in a culture where some bodies are valued more than others, even more so when you're isolated from the real world. People will treat you differently and it is a lot to take in."

We strolled on a little, getting closer to the gym. He drew breath, like he was about to say something but then changed his mind and exhaled. I could almost feel the resolve in him as he drew breath one more time.

"I don't know who he is, and I don't know how the show feels about this sort of thing. I'd just want to make sure I didn't put myself on the line by saying something to you about it. If that makes sense?"

"It does," I said. And it did. We didn't need to say anything else. We both knew I probably wasn't going to change much of my behavior with Daniel based on Greg's opinion and that wasn't his intention anyway. He just wanted to let me know he looked out for me and I found that kind. I mean, I still wanted to send Greg the fuck home but at least he was actually a legit dude.

7/9/2015

Chad was still in a mood, we hadn't been up and working out for long before he was at Greg's throat again. The *At-homers* had had food journals designed by a doctor, that they tried to adhere too at the Spa too. It consisted of actual food and not just dehydration, pain killers, tears of despair in the shower and personal anguish. Greg was at the gym updating his, when Chad came by and stood next to him, hands on hips.

"Can I take a look at that journal?" he asked in more of a demanding tone. Greg handed him the journal and the rest of us on treadmills and bikes were all staring while trying not to look like we were. Whenever Chad decided to single somebody out with a rant or some other bullshit, it was both embarrassing and amusing to watch. Greg looked unmoved by the situation. Chad flipped through it in the manner of somebody who already knows the answer but is deliberately making a scene for emphasis. "This journal is no good. It's all wrong."

"How is it wrong?" Greg asked, not missing a beat. Esther, who was about to step onto the treadmill, came to a halt with one foot up. Chad looked at him in disbelief.

"How is it wrong? How is it right? You can't eat all this and expect to keep up with these people in here," Chad waved his hand in our general direction, missing us by several yards and causing Brody and Farrell to look confused at the mostly empty space Chad had indicated.

"But it's designed by a doctor and registered dietician," Greg replied. Chad scoffed.

"Doctors aren't experts at *everything*," Chad was technically right, doctors aren't experts at everything. But it was obvious that Chad thought *he* was. "I put together the dietary plans of the contestants in here and if you try to follow this plan, you will lose this game."

"Then I guess they'll beat me fair and square," Greg retorted. In that moment I hoped he didn't get too jaded from his time in here, because that was awesome.

"Don't you *want* to win? Don't you want to get thinner?" Chad's priority for those two things said a lot.

"Well sure," Greg replied with stoic calm, "and I think the doctor's plan is a good step in that direction. It's worked well *so far*, and I think I'll keep following it."

"Greg, I can't accept this journal. It's wrong and it doesn't work with my program," Chad said. He had his hands on his hips again and I think I even saw him flex his muscles, trying to pull some alpha power. "If you can't adhere to it, I don't see how we can continue to work together on this." A collective sharp breath was drawn by the audience. That was usually the death blow the trainers or any of the crew had to deliver to us contestants for us to click our heels, salute the flag and obey. The fear of being sent home or losing this amazing chance to be the beautiful societally acceptable human beings that we can under all this fat, is so great, a threat is enough. But not for Greg. Either he was an amazing dude who didn't give a damn, or he hadn't yet been conditioned enough by this Spa to feel like us. He took the journal from Chad and opened it up. Chad looked like he had just walked in on his own parents having sex, horrorstruck and partly unable to comprehend if this was a twisted joke his subconscious was playing on him.

"Well perhaps I should work with Shea instead then," Greg said as he started back on his journal updating business. Chad stood for a while longer and then just walked off mumbling *fine*. Most of us were silently looking at Greg, who didn't look up, mouths agape. We were so brainwashed that the mere thought of saying no to a trainer was enough to cause sleepless nights. Only Blake was by himself way in the corner, having missed the show.

We all went about our working out, slightly stunned. But apparently drama never walks alone because not an hour had passed, before Dawn broke down with Shea.

"I can't do it your way," she exclaimed, probably louder than she had intended.

"I'm trying to help you, Dawn." Shea replied sharply. She was clearly annoyed.

"I know, but you aren't helping me. I have my routine from home and it works for me," Dawn's words came out stilted because she was choking back tears. "All your workouts are based around the Alpha team."

"Exactly. And look at them. It works," Shea was defensive.

"It works for them, but *not* for me. They can't keep up with me." It wasn't untrue. She wasn't beat to shit and tired and injured. *Of course* we couldn't keep up. Shea did not take this well.

"It *does* work," she said indignantly. "You're gonna have to suck it up, because it's *all* or *nothing*." Making ultimatums wasn't often heard from Shea but she clearly felt her professionalism was brought into question here by a fat girl no less. That had to gall Shea further. Dawn looked like Shea had just shown her photos of kittens bound and gagged about to be thrown into a river.

"I'll go at it alone then." Dawn said, trying to collect herself and failing. Tears were streaming down her face. Her dreams of what the show was, a place where magic happens daily, were shattered again. If Shea had had water in her mouth, I'm sure she would've done a spit take. Dawn got up and looked from Shea to the rest of us. Her lip was quivering and I thought Shea might actually reach out and grab her arm to console her. Instead, Dawn stormed off in the direction of our rooms before she could. Esther and I were done working out not long after and headed to our room. We found Dawn still crying in her bed under the covers. She didn't turn around when we walked past her room and we didn't talk to her. Crying wasn't anything new to us. We just knew to do it in the shower, where they couldn't film us. Welcome to the club, bitch. Tears for dinner.

7/10/2015

All anyone wanted on this weigh-in was the ability to vote Greg and Dawn home. Nothing personal, just go. As per usual, we did the hours long walk to the weigh in. Welcome to that tedious shit, newbies. I was counting on Farrell rocking my fucking socks off with his weight loss since he played me so damn dirty last time. I wasn't disappointed. Still think he could've warned me before that stunt but I'll take the twenty-pound loss he threw up and dedicated to me because he knew his sorry ass owed me.

On the bright side this was the first weigh-in where the women were allowed to wear tank tops. I guess my nipples protruding from the cold that is nighttime in the damn desert was no longer an issue, as no one handed out the band aids this week. The normal fat girl attire of sports bras and spandex shorts were magically replaced with an actual shirt. I had been freezing my ass, and nipples off for weeks while the guys got normal exercise clothes. If life were fair they should've at least been stripped to speedos, socks and pasties. I guess I've reached that magic weight where I'm required to wear a tank top so as not to induce lustful thoughts in viewers at home with my new body shape. Sometimes you just can't win. At least I'm warmer.

Esther and Hunter lost, just as planned. Hunter is done. Losing Chris as his support system and bringing in two new team members just reminded him of how much he really wants to be with his family. Honestly, I don't blame him. If I had more than a goldfish to go home to, after seeing the results these people accomplished in their homes, *without* the misery of some camera happy harpy screaming at them? I would want to be around people that loved me too instead of playing this game. I feel worse for Chad than I do Hunter. He truly doesn't seem to see how badly Hunter wants to go home to his family. Instead Chad is taking it personally. What weird fragile egos these trainers have. They are thin and trim, exactly what we are all killing ourselves to achieve here. You'd think that would make them happy.

7/11/2015

The elimination was emotionally grueling despite knowing what would come. We really did all have this idea it would be the six of us until the bitter end. Chris, Hunter, Farrell, Debbie, Esther, and me. When we lost Debbie and Chris the fight sort of went out of us—like the hero of a movie when he thinks the romantic interest has died and he has nothing left to fight for. Only nobody has any romantic interests here, and we all know no one is going to fucking swing in and save us. Now it is every person for themselves. No more pairs. On top of that change, sending Hunter home –even knowing that he really wants to go to be with his family and his heart isn't in it here—feels like another painful loss. I am super fucking tired of painful losses.

Chapter 11

Esther plays this game with strategy and deviousness I had only previously seen in family games of Mario Kart. She is genuinely one of the kindest people I have ever met but she is *also* an evil genius, the likes of which would make even James Bond wet his pants. We are on our own now. Individuals. Competing against one another. But I watched that woman drink salt water this week, in an attempt to retain more water for the weigh-in to keep me here and send Hunter home like she wanted. She put a lot of trust in the fact that Hunter, Farrell and I weren't lying to her and going to secretly vote her off after gaining weight. Not to mention the unpleasant laxative effects hours later after the weigh-in that salt water does to you. I don't know what is going to happen with the rest of us left here but if I was only half assed playing before now, shit just got real. For me and poor Esther in our bathroom, again. And again.

Chad is pissed. This isn't out of the ordinary. Chad seems like he's been pissed a lot recently. But he really was not about Hunter leaving. There was never a doubt

Hunter was Chad's favorite. Plus, let's be honest, winning this is just as important to Chad as is to any of us. I wonder if the trainers get a bonus if one of their contestants wins, because they certainly *behave* like they do. Chad has turned into that mean girl at your junior high, who will do anything to be homecoming queen, president of the class or steal your lunch money. The Bravo Team is practically in exile now. Farrell and Blake are *definitely* not allowed to sit with us anymore.

Our team on the other hand has welcomed Greg and Dawn with *sort of* open arms after Dawn and Shea had their little come to Jesus meeting and we got over wanting to call special elimination just to vote them the fuck home. Unfortunately, Dawn not being used to the culture of the Spa, (a culture born of a complete lack of shame being observed doing things like squatting to pee behind production on a regular basis) is having meltdowns about every thirty minutes because she is worried about looking fat or stupid on national tv. I'm not sure how the number one fan of this show hasn't realized we are supposed to look both fat and stupid all the time. I guess she didn't have a section in her notebooks dedicated to this.

"*Argh*," Dawn screamed in frustration. She was doing squats under Shea's careful supervision. With each squat, Dawn was getting redder in the face and Shea was trying to egg her on even fiercer.

"They are just squats, Dawn. You can do this," Shea encouraged.

"No," Dawn protested.

"Yes," Shea was trying her hardest to stay positive and not scream at Dawn. Dawn tried another few squats, then stood up straight.

"I look stupid. I'm flubbing all over the place in these clothes," She tugged at her shorts demonstrably—like a kid who doesn't understand why mommy is making her wear a jacket. "At home I can wear what I want but here I have to have this tank top with tiny shorts on and I look stupid."

"You don't look stupid. It doesn't matter," Shea tried, to no avail. There were tears in Dawn's eyes now.

"It *does* matter. It's on TV. I feel horrible. I don't feel horrible at home," She stomped her feet when she said the last words. "I don't want to do this anymore. I just want to go."

"Dawn, you don't look stupid," Shea was frustrated, but tried her best to keep reassuring Dawn. They had just worked out an agreement and already things were rocky again. "You *can't* quit. You are doing so well."

"But I'm flubbing around on TV," Dawn wouldn't let this go. She was crying now and Shea looked exasperated. She told Dawn to take a break but it was probably more a break for Shea. I wonder if she hit the bottle on the down low to get through this. I know we probably would if production would let us. Dawn calmed down a bit when Shea wasn't hanging over her like a hawk. She was just sobbing now. It was painful to watch and I feel like a bitch because for most of us here, feeling like our bodies are a punch line is just another day at the office. I mostly want her to shut up so I can power through this and be done today. But honestly, Dawn is right. What is so wrong with wanting to feel good now? Or take a little pride and comfort in looking nice. Why are we all so impatient with her for pointing out how awful this place makes her feel? There is something deep here I can feel but know that I am missing its depth. I feel like Alice Through the Looking Glass here. I find myself siding with production, sighing at Dawn and rolling my eyes while wanting her to be quiet. I want her to just accept that this is how things are and if she just shuts up about it, her, and more importantly, my time here will be easier. I know this isn't right, but God, I am so tired. I have accepted the way things are here, why can't she?

Shea didn't hit the bottle on her break. Instead she came back with a Shea Style Pep Talk to help Dawn through her hardships.

"I know you feel bad about your body but your legs are so great that I guarantee the other girls in that house are looking at your legs and wishing they looked like that in shorts." Why to feel better about herself couldn't Dawn just be allowed to wear pants? Instead the made-up envy of other women is why she should love her body. Cool, pitting us against each other to *motivate* Dawn. Shea has now put us all in a beauty competition we never asked for. Fuck this place.

I feel Dawn's pain, even as I want her to shut up about it. I understand feeling like I am never good enough and I am so tired of hearing that I feel that way because I am a *fat girl* in my head. I want to rally to her side, I want to scream that she is right and that if we felt good enough we wouldn't be here. We would be home, wearing whatever we liked and moving our bodies to love them and not to punish them. But I didn't scream. And I didn't rally to her cause. Because I am a coward. A tired bruised coward and all I want is for her to shut the fuck up so I can get over another day here.

This afternoon production came in to the great room where we were sitting waiting on audio to mic us up and a PA informed Chad and Shea that they had a promotional photo shoot that had been last minute rescheduled to this afternoon. The look of sheer unadulterated horror on their faces made my day. They both had meltdowns at the news. They were enraged because they didn't have enough time to dehydrate. Shea actually wept. Whoa.

In what has to be the biggest mind-fuck day ever, even after hours spent contemplating my body image, and being pitted against other women based on my appearance in a weird attempt to help Dawn with her body image. Then watching my supposed role models of health break the fuck down over bodies that are supposed to be the type of bodies that cure all our problems. The big surprise of this morning is, that we are being taken to a Beverly Hills salon for make overs. Followed by a photo shoot for a magazine. Where the hell is that therapist who is supposed to be associated with this show? There is so much shit to wrap my head around here, and all I can manage to come up with is, "Please don't make me blonde. I hate how I look blonde."

This was the weirdest salon visit I had ever experienced in my entire life. I am not a salon type person anyway. I enjoy being pampered as much as the next person, don't get me wrong, but my college budget was more that of a Netflix and a box of hamburger helper without hamburger because I can't afford meat type lifestyle than an all-day mani/pedi massage type deal. We walked into the salon and the hotshot big name owners were also there. It was kind of a parade onto the premises with all the crew and cameras. The owners apparently flew in from their other location in NYC just to film today's makeovers. I wasn't impressed. If they had hamburger helper perhaps, we could talk. I did feel bad for poor Brody as he's bald. By the look of the all-day scowl on his face, he also felt badly for himself. He was just sitting there while the rest of us were coiffed. They couldn't even throw in a head massage at least? Boo.

One of the two owners decided to cut my hair and she approached me like she had just pardoned me moments before the guillotine. I thought I could be a stuck-up pretentious bitch sometimes but this woman put me to shame. Just as she was about to cut my newly dyed—you guessed it, fucking blonde hair she looked at one of the camera men and with the seriousness of a dusty old professor of four decades, said

"You're going to want to film this. Move in closer. It's going to be spectacular and I move really fast."

I locked eyes with Neil, the cameraman, and we both rolled our eyes at one another. He still moved in close to film it, because whatever. I had never known until that moment that a haircut could actually hurt. That woman beat my head with those shears, like she had been trained as an information extractor for the CIA. You would've thought she was sculpting the fucking Venus de Milo with the ferocity with which she beat my scalp. She was so proud of my finished look it was like she had invented Post It notes. I looked like 1987 Rod Stewart. At least that was *my* generous assessment of my look. As we were leaving the salon to head to the photoshoot, one of the producers sidled up next to me and called me *Ponyboy* and told me to *stay golden*. Fucking comedians up in here. If I didn't like how I looked before, making me a blonde when I specifically asked for anything but, was *sure* to make me feel comfortable with my appearance. Thanks a lot. Even more exasperatingly a part of me was suddenly scared that Daniel would see me and not be able to see past the Rod fucking Stewart look I had going on.

The women who ran the magazine photoshoot were so kind and loving I cried. I'm not kidding. I think I had forgotten what it is like to have someone remember that I am a person. Not only that but for a few hours I felt like a *valuable* person. They listened when I confided my fears about trying on a dress because I had always done my best to hide my curves instead of accentuate them. They celebrated what we looked and felt like right now. They also didn't pretend that my weird coppery colored hair looked good on me. That honesty and validation made the sincere celebration of my body and myself that much more authentic. It also hardened my resolve to get my hair dyed dark again, to take back a small bit of who I am.

"Try this one," Esther cried enthusiastically as she held out a dress for me in the changing room at the photoshoot. "It might distract from your hair a bit." She was wearing a cool red dress herself, which really looked good on her, something I had not minced words in relaying. She appeared genuinely happy, and it was kind of an amazing thing. I took the dress from her, stripped the one I had been wearing, and put it on. It fit me perfectly. It did distract from the blonde 90s Pamela Anderson hair pretty well too. I looked at myself in the mirror and my smile widened.

"That looks really good on you," a voice from behind us said. We both spun around, like a show down in a saloon was about to happen. It was Dawn. She had on her sweats still, and looked wistfully at Esther and I.

"Thank you Dawn," I said. And I genuinely appreciated it. The body competition thing Shea had stuffed down her throat still lingered in the back of my head. I wanted to make up for feeling cowardly. "We need to find you something awesome too."

"No, I don't know," she started but Esther was on board immediately.

"Yes!" she shouted as she disappeared into a clothes rack, only to reappear moments later with a purple dress. "This one!"

"You think so?" Dawn asked. She was unsure but Esther's enthusiasm was contagious. Both of our smiles were wide enough, that Dawn felt like it wasn't just bullshit. We really were in the same boat. She started to pull down her sweatpants but paused a second, suddenly self-conscious. She cast a fleeting look at us but we were both mostly self-involved fiddling with our own dresses and she decided it was safe. The dress did look really good on her. We stood behind her as she glanced in the mirror, and her face cracked into a smile. Esther giggled, while Dawn laughed in relief. More dresses were torn off racks and tried on. Some amazing, others laugh inducing bad. We felt proud of ourselves and our bodies. For a fleeting moment I felt like a Tim Robbins character breaking out of Shawshank Prison by crawling through 500 yards of shit. The feel of freedom making it all worth it.

7/13/2015

In today's edition of *Tisa finds out shit by chance*, I learned what fresh horror awaited me at the next challenge. After spending the usual hours waiting in the church van with my fellow contestants, talking about sex, I had to pee. Apparently being excused from the white church vans—even when the call of nature is strong—requires begging. But production eventually relented and allowed me to go and use the bathroom. A PA blindfolded me and walked me to the restroom. How about that. While standing in line I innocently started chatting up the others waiting because I hadn't seen them before, and because that's what I do. I chat with everyone. It helps distract from the fact that I am in fat camp hell.

"I haven't seen you before, are you just production for the challenges, or like wardrobe or audio?" I asked.

"No, I am just here for today. I'm a crane operator."

Did this guy just tell me he was a *crane operator*? What the hell was a crane operator doing for our challenge? I urinated as quickly as possible, called for a PA to come blindfold me and walk me back to the van so I could tell the others I had just met a crane operator. I wanted to see if they had any theories on what the hell we were in for today.

"Guys," I said, as soon as I was back within the confines of one scorching hot church van. "You won't guess what I just did."

"If it's just peeing, then it's nothing new, Tisa. We all do it," Brody said, with his usual snark. Esther chuckled.

"No, Brody, it's not. Also shut up, because this will impact you too," I shot back. Brody wasn't impressed but at least he was paying attention.

"I just spoke to a crane operator," I said, then paused for effect. Not a muscle moved in anybody's face. I don't know what I expected. "For today's challenge, guys," I added. This elicited the effect I wanted.

"A crane operator?" Dawn exclaimed in abject horror.

"Yes," I looked at her. Then Esther and Greg. "Any theories?"

"Uh," Greg started, trying to come up with something. "We will be in the air somehow?"

"You think?" Brody asked, back in the game. "Obviously, if he is operating a crane." Greg looked part annoyed part sheepish.

"What do you think, Brody?" Esther asked.

"That we will be in the air somehow," Brody said and made a face at Greg.

"Anyway," I said preempting a snark war from breaking out. "I am scared of heights, and being in the air," I shot Greg a look, "is kind of a scary fucking concept."

"Perhaps something else is in the air and not us," Dawn said, trying to mitigate my fear. "And we just have to build something to get it."

"That doesn't make it better," I said. It would still mean me being above the ground in some capacity. Dawn looked crestfallen.

"No. As much as Tisa hates it, we'll probably be in the air somehow," Greg said, with the seriousness of an adult trying to reason with a bunch of unruly children. "It only makes sense."

"Urgh. I am terrified of heights," I repeat, more to myself, than anyone in specific.

"I'm not a big fan either, honestly," Dawn said, and Brody, despite being a smartass, had to concur. Heights weren't our friend.

So, yep, there were cranes. Not just cranes but spin bikes attached to clear Plexiglas platforms hanging from cranes thirty feet in the air. It is as if production had scanned my brain for the worst-case scenario and somehow made it into a challenge on this show. This is the thing my nightmares are made of. It only lacks me being naked and heckled by a large group of jeering people. Luckily for me there was a booze cruise happening on the harbor directly adjacent to this erected monstrosity. So, I got the heckling part. *Fun.* As we climbed onto these bikes to be raised thirty feet in the air, a bunch of drunk people on the boat began to scream at us.

"Hey air biker. You left your jackets at home," some dude screamed, to general applause from his drunk friends. We looked at each other, like what the fuck does that even mean. Jackets? We ignored them. I was distracted from it as Brody went to sit on his bike and it broke. The seat came undone and he fell a few inches shaking his entire platform. Roars of laughter from the drunk brigade ensued.

"Looks like you need to get a handle on those bars," somebody yelled. How hilarious.

"Maybe try a lower gear."

Brody flipped them off which was obviously a mistake. Gales of laughter. I could practically hear the booze numb their little minds. Meanwhile I am going *"Um, nope, nope, nope,"* in my head. I am about to trust my life to a bike duct taped to a platform hanging thirty feet in the air and that sucker just broke on Brody before we even left the ground. I spent the next ten minutes running through every bad decision I had made in my life leading me to this point. By the time somebody called my name, I hadn't even made it past high school.

The challenge involved bicycling as fast as possible and for each two miles you pedaled you were allowed to choose another player to move ten feet down. Once you were moved three times, you were on the ground and out of the game. The prize for this medieval torture? Immunity.

It occurred to Dawn that she and Greg did not have a snowball's chance in hell of winning this challenge even if my cry baby ass didn't get on my bike. Although we were all nice enough to them, the undercurrent that they were outsiders was still going strong. The resulting fireworks from her realization were spectacular. I've never seen anyone yell at the host of a reality TV show that way before. If I hadn't been completely engrossed in my own fear I would've reveled in its gloriousness. Dawn stomped away, and Cynthia shouted after her, hoping that reason might work.

"Dawn, what's the matter?" Cynthia opened, like she's trying to convince a petulant child to come back to the Christmas tree after she got a pair of socks.

"It's not fair. I don't want to play unless they make it fair," Dawn replied. It's hard not to hope they just throw her ass out at this point.

"What isn't fair?"

"The game. It's five against two."

"What five against two? What do you mean?" Cynthia might've played dumb here, I don't know. It was obvious what Dawn meant.

"It's those five," She indicated Farrell, Esther, Brody, Blake, and myself. "And they are going to gang up on us. I'm tired of being ganged up on." She pointed to herself and looked around for Greg, who stood awkwardly between her and us. A pretty decent metaphor for where he was on this issue. He looked like he'd prefer to not be mentioned.

"Come on, honey. Nobody is ganging up on you," Cynthia tried in her sweetest voice. "Just come back and we'll have fun with this challenge."

"It won't be fun. I'm pissed off. They are gunning for the new people and I don't want to play. As long as there is voting it won't be fair. I'm gonna look stupid. You might as well send me home," Dawn was crying now, and it was a whole fucking spectacle to behold.

"Honey, nobody wants you to be sent home."

"Yes they do. I need the immunity and I know they won't give me a chance. It's not even worth going up there to try." Dawn stormed off, tears running down her face. What a shit show. I couldn't decide if I felt sorry for her or if I didn't care. It was kind of true. But also, we were all pretty much in it for ourselves at this point. Cynthia looked at Greg like this is your responsibility, bro. Greg looked torn for a second, then he ran after Dawn.

"Dawn, I know how you feel," Greg said when he caught up to her. "But we are here, and we might as well try our best. These people aren't ganging up on us." I felt momentarily shitty. Because *of course* we were.

"You know they are, Greg," she replied. "You know this isn't fair."

"Perhaps. But we knew it wouldn't be easy. We are here now and we should try to do this," Dawn was drying her eyes. I can't believe this platitude turned things around for her. But then again, what option did she really have.

"I guess. But it isn't fair."

"No, it isn't. But it is still calories you get to burn. And they can't take that away from you," Mr. fucking motivational speaker to the rescue. I don't know if the thought of burning calories was enough, or if he slipped her a twenty on the down low but she was apparently ready to continue the challenge. With Brody's bike being fixed, we were all ready to put our lives on the line thirty feet in the air with raucous laughter from the drunken cruisers as our backdrop. Good times.

After sufficiently humiliating myself with a steady stream of tears and foul language, I won. There were points during that challenge where I swore so much while pedaling that they turned off my mic. I think I made a few of the booze cruisers weep frightened tears. My mom will be so proud. I actually came from behind to win. I managed to get over my paralyzing fear of heights to pedal the bike like Lance Armstrong had coached me for years, sans drugs of course. It was worse than it sounds because as I would pedal it would shake the whole platform that was hanging in the air thirty feet above the dock. I was pretty sure the chains would snap at any moment and I was going to plummet to my death. I have spent my whole life believing I was too fat to safely ride that amusement park ride that goes up in the air and spins you around on swings and now my brain was telling me that this was going to be the way that I died. I avoided that ride for years. I avoided letting my partner's pick me up during sex and this, on this shitty spin bike duct taped together thirty feet in the air, I was certain, I was going to go to my death instead of in any of the aforementioned fun activities.

The first person to hit two miles was Greg, who immediately sent Esther ten feet down. I hit two miles next and sent Dawn down because even locked in fear I am a petty bitch. I convinced myself I was doing her a favor—she might feel sad if her whole tirade before this challenge wasn't rewarded. Brody hit two miles next and sent Greg down ten feet, which actually bummed me out because Greg had been pep talking me through my tears this entire time. Farrell hit two miles and moved Greg yet another ten feet down. Dawn, in a move that surprised me chose to move Brody down ten feet when she hit her first two miles. I was terrified his bike would break again when it moved. Esther—who was brazen in her lack of fear of heights— was dancing and singing on her bike and sent Greg down his final ten feet to take him out of the game. Blake hit his two miles and sent Dawn down again. I hit mile four and opted to move Dawn right on out of the game. Brody then moved Esther down ten feet, followed by Farrell moving her and taking her out of the game.

All that was left was Blake, Brody, Farrell and my sobbing ass. Blake hit four miles and promptly decided to move me. The only thing more terrifying than riding a bike hanging thirty feet in the air was riding that bike on a platform being lowered by a crane operator that I met in line for the bathroom. I kept ruminating on how he had looked like he didn't know what day it was much less how not to drop me to my death. I uttered a few choice words as the tears flowed and placed a curse on Blake's entire family for lowering me. I hope his dick falls off. Jokes on that guy though, I hit six miles right after that and sent Blake down ten feet.

Brody hit six miles next and brought Farrell down to twenty feet with the rest of us. Farrell returned in kind and sent Brody down. I hit eight miles and moved Blake again, because really, fuck that dude. Blake hit six miles and surprising everyone, he moved Farrell down ten feet. Brody hit eight miles and moved me down. Cue more crying. Farrell made it to eight miles and took Brody out of the game. I reached mile ten and took Blake out of the game.

At this point Farrell is at nine miles and only needs to hit ten to take me out of the game. I have just reached ten miles and have to hit twelve to take him out of the game and win immunity.

I fucking won. I am the baddest bitch alive. If bad bitches cry so hard in terror that snot runs down their face that is.

Who knew sheer terror could make you move so fast? I chafed a hole in my thigh. A gaping bleeding hole. But hey, I have immunity, and I didn't die. That's two for me.

7/14/2015

I pity the two guys left on Chad's team. He was beating them to shit and doing all these things that looked brutal. I mean, when is the last time you saw a professional trainer in your gym actually stand on their client? Chad was forever doing things like standing on the guy's legs while they did wall sits or having them hang upside down from treadmill handles while standing on their chest. I'm curious as to what muscle group that works. Mostly I am just glad I'm not them.

I felt no guilt telling Shea to back the fuck off at this *last* workout filming. I have immunity. I am not going anywhere this week. What I am going to do is change my damn hair if I have to kill someone to do it. I went to a PA and told her that if they didn't send me somewhere off this Spa to change my hair, I was going to break out, buy a bottle of box dye and do it myself. At this point that was entirely possible too, because Blake and Brody found a hiking route that took you up this one hill, then if you shimmied around a giant water tank and climbed through the chain link fence you could get off property and go into the little town nearby then come back with no one the wiser. I knew this because those two had managed to come back with Starbucks twice now after *hikes*.

Production, luckily for me, dug my new Ponyboy hairdo about as much as I did and agreed to let me off the Spa with a PA to return to the salon to have it fixed. I had intentions of being gone for hours, even if it meant ditching whatever PA was with me. I had immunity, so everybody can suck it. I went back to my room, showered and prepared for the struggle that would be riding in the church van with somebody who was forced to interact with me for hours. Preparing for the heat, I dressed in a tank top and a skirt. Since I didn't have to do a challenge or some other bullshit where I was going, I felt it was ok to dress a little fancy. Plus, I am from Alaska and this place is hotter than the face of the sun. Oh well. At least I would get some of my old self back when they dyed my hair again.

Oh boy. The PA assigned to take me to the salon was Daniel. I had entertained the thought very briefly as I showered but dismissed it because would I really be that lucky? I guess I am, because when I came down to the common room, I saw him walking toward me. For a second, I looked around like I wasn't sure he was coming for me. But he was. The little butterflies were starting to kick up some dust inside me and it didn't subside when he smiled at me.

"Hi."

"Hi?" I wasn't still certain what was happening. Was he just saying hi or was there more?

"I hear you're going with a PA to the salon today?"

"Yes?" Still confused.

"Guess who that PA is?," He looked at me and his eyes twinkled.

"You're kidding," I said too loud as always, before I clasped my hands over my mouth. He smirked. He wasn't.

"Nope. And we'll be driving my car. Not the van." I got both him and I didn't have to sweat in those fucking vans? I made a mental note to check a calendar later on, to see if I had Rip Van Winkled my way to my birthday.

"Not too shabby," I said, trying to act aloof. The salacious look in my eyes probably gave me away. It struck me that I didn't actually know what car he drove. If his car was a black church van, I would laugh and cry at the same time. Who was I kidding? Just getting off property for the day was a bonus. Spending it with him, with nobody else around, was icing on an already decent cake.

"Just wait right here and I'll go and make the final arrangements," he said, and indicated a chair.

"Yes, sir," I responded, then chuckled at his fleeting confused look. My insides were going haywire at the prospect of today. He came back some fifteen minutes later, during which both Greg and Dawn had passed me, shooting me baffled looks that I returned with a non-committal smile. That's right, bitches. I'm being rescued by a white knight on a trusty possibly black church van steed.

"Alright, Tisa. Let's head out."

I followed him outside to a staff parking lot. We came to a halt by a black Jeep Wrangler. He walked over and opened the passenger door for me.

"Nice ride," I said. I was impressed and exceedingly happy it wasn't a church van. Of any color.

He closed the door, strolled around the vehicle and got in. The inside of the Jeep was well maintained. The only debris cluttering the interior was a book on Chaos Theory and an empty coffee cup. Who *was* this guy? He turned the key, the engine kicked on, and the A/C started cranking. Thank God. He looked at me and smiled. I flashed a smile back, and I think possibly the light in my eyes might've blinded him. The feeling I had entertained briefly in the shower that morning was back, being in this car with him, *alone*. And we were going places, for me, all day. It almost made the months of bullshit at the Spa worth it for just this one day. He looked over his shoulder as he backed out of the parking spot and his profile made me giddy.

We hit the road and were soon on the highway. Daniel struck up a conversation and we were shooting the shit about this, that and the other. It was laid back and pleasant. Talking to somebody about something other than food or the show was liberating. Even with Daniel being associated with the show, it was chill and we didn't talk about it at all. He told me a bit about what else he had been doing and I told him about myself, family and what I had done for school. It turned out he had also double majored for his undergrad. English and creative writing. It was how he'd gotten into the business. Hoping to write and create shows. He admitted this PA thing wasn't quite what he had hoped but at least it was a foot in the business doors. He cracked several jokes that made me laugh, and that too was liberating. Wit and good looks. My, oh my. The dull desert landscape littered with random enclaves of strip malls and fast food restaurants whizzed past us outside the car. During a brief moment while I was looking out the window Daniel placed his hand on my thigh. Just resting, a very light pressure from his fingers. It gave me pleasant goosebumps. I slowly turned toward him and caught him peeking at me too. I thought about telling him to skip the hair appointment and just find a hotel. But I also desperately wanted my hair fixed.

The drive to L.A. took a bit, even with him making the speed limit and then some. The landscape wasn't amazing but just seeing it move by fast and steady, taking me away from the Spa was a weight off. We headed to the salon right away and walked in with me determined to fight for a change of my hair. As it turned out, no fight was needed. The employees there were just as appalled by their hot shot boss's work as I was. They obviously couldn't contradict her in front of the cameras and had to stand idly by while she butchered my hair. Their professional integrity, if nothing else, was happy to see me walk through that door again. A very nice apprentice hairstylist took my hair under her care. I got a dark red dye job and some strategic scissoring done. It came out more along the lines of what I had imagined in my head. And it *wasn't* blonde.

Daniel had nipped outside during this to take a few phone calls. He was still technically at work, even if it also kind of felt like a date. I asked the hairstylist if it was possible to also wax my eyebrows and she happily obliged. I felt like a new person after having them fixed. My face was the thing about me I was always really happy about. Having it fixed up a little —after not having the ability to do much for months—was amazing. It's probably the years of back handed *you have such a pretty face* compliments rearing their head in my subconscious. I was looking at myself in the mirror when Daniel walked back in, putting his phone away. He looked up and caught sight of me in the mirror. His eyes were as big as saucers and his mouth froze, mid-word. He collected himself and walked to me.

"You looked amazing before, but that hair," he said, as he touched it. "Really wow. *Wow.*"

"Wow, huh?" I said, coyly. It felt good inside.

"Wow indeed."

We strolled outside to his car again and the sun was shining. My hair wasn't in the 80s anymore, my eyebrows were fixed and I was kind of on a date. I smiled at Daniel and he smiled back—his smile made me want to mess up my hair with him.

Next stop for us was lunch.

"How does a hot dog sound?" he asked me as we pulled away from the hair dresser, his hand on my thigh again. It actually sounded good.

"It sounds pretty good. Are you taking me out for a hotdog?"

"I know just the place," He smirked at me. It was nice to have somebody local to show me places. We made a few turns, as I looked out the window, and commented on a few things I saw. I didn't want to appear like a complete tourist but I was in L.A. after all, and I had always enjoyed people watching. Daniel took me to Pink's Hot Dogs. It was packed, which I guess is the usual. I looked over their menu as Daniel ordered for himself. I suddenly felt weird—like I was cheating by eating food outside the Spa. I ordered a turkey dog—with no toppings—which made the guy behind the counter ask if he got that right. Not a usual order, I guessed. We sat down, and I delicately removed the turkey from the bun and ate just that. Daniel didn't acknowledge it and I appreciated that. We talked about the restaurant and about my life in Alaska. He talked about his DJ'ing and playing music on his college radio station. Just random things. As we talked, I made sure my legs were touching his under the table. It didn't take long before his hand was holding mine. Talking without cameras was liberating, and his smile made me want to do terrible things to him. I had finished my one turkey hot dog—and feeling a little guilty about it if I am being honest—and he had devoured his. We got up to leave, me not wanting this day to end. Fortuitously it didn't have to because Daniel brought up the surprise he had mentioned the other day, before Greg had given me his *big brother* speech.

"There's a place I've wanted to take you for a while," he said as we got into the car.

"Oh?"

"Yes. I won't reveal *too* much but it's one of my favorite places. I wanted to share it with you." I halfway hoped his favorite place was a hotel with a masseuse but alas not all minds were as debauched as mine. We drove off, his hand back in place on my thigh and my mind trying to focus on things happening outside the car so as to not get carried away. He took a lot of turns this way and that. We didn't really travel far but my navigation skills are lacking so I could've been in another state for all I knew. Daniel led me to the entrance of a retro-y feeling building with *Amoeba* emblazoned across the front. We stepped into an old school record store. An unrecognizable but pleasant tune was playing in the overhead speakers and a few people milled around either putting records up on the shelves or taking them down to study them closer. It had a vibe both historical and touristy that I totally dug.

"This is my favorite record store," Daniel simply said. I had to give it to him, it was very lovely.

"I like it," I said. "A lot." I moved around the different genres and letters indexing vinyl albums, taking in the ambience of the place. It felt like we had been submerged into a cooler time. Very chill. The music added to the vibe of the place and I felt relaxed, *truly relaxed*, for the first time in what I felt was months. I sank into a chair and leaned back. Daniel grabbed an album and sat down on the edge of my chair, avidly talking about it. He was enthusiastic and it was kind of adorable. I leaned forward again and looked at the album. It was by somebody I didn't know. I looked up at Daniel, who was still talking, and hoped he would look at me. He did when he noticed I wasn't really listening. He looked at me and I at him, he moved his face closer to mine and our lips met. He nearly dropped the album. He put one hand behind my neck and pulled me closer. I wanted to just stay here. Live in this store, perhaps. Not go back to the Spa. But it was late afternoon by now, and as much as production had been okay with me going off to fix my hair, I didn't think they'd be okay with me staying out all night. The kiss broke off and we both caught our breath.

"I'd like to stay here and do that more," I said.

"I would like that too," he responded. He paused a moment. "You know we can't. But I really wanted to show you this place."

"I'm very happy you did. I love it," I said. I did, and the kiss didn't hurt my opinion of it. He got up and stood in front of me. I got up as he put the album back with the delicate hands of somebody handing a baby off to somebody else. Then he took my hand, and we walked to the car, leaving the hipster vibe behind us. In the car, he started maneuvering us toward the highway. His hand wasn't on my leg like earlier and I wasn't sure why but reasoned that he'd probably need more focus to extricate us from the mesh of traffic. I looked out the window at the now darkened L.A. and the lights flying by. As we moved toward the Spa, the number of cars thinned considerably.

"You could put your hand on my thigh again, if you want," I said.

"Yes. Of course," he said, then put his hand on my thigh almost mechanically. "I didn't want to," he began, but trailed off.

"Oh? Does it help to know I wanted you to?" I asked, hoping that's what he meant. He relaxed a little and his fingers flexed around my thigh, making me turn a bit in my seat so he would have an easier time reaching me. It was almost pitch-black outside, the sun cast the last burgundy rays minutes ago. I could see the outline of Daniel from the lights of the dash board. He cast glances at me as his hand massaged my thigh. His palm felt smooth on my skin and I turned even more toward him. I fleetingly glanced the speedometer as the jeep closed in on 100 mph. He moved his hand further up my thigh and started touching me in a way that made it impossible to catch my breath. He passed 100 mph and I passed the point of no return. It nearly knocked me out. He was breathing heavily too and when my head cleared a little, I felt him pull away leaving me content and emitting a small sigh of satisfaction. I would've wanted more but I saw the lights of the Spa in the distance. He was silent and I could feel his lack of release in the air of the jeep. I reached over and ran my hand up his thigh and he practically groaned from all that was left unfinished for us.

"One of these days," I said, and I would've winked at him, if it hadn't been dark.

"One of these days," He repeated back with a satisfaction and longing filled sigh. "I would like that," he said, and I giggled. It was pretty clear we both would. The Spa drew closer. 100 mph makes quick business of distances. He pulled up in front and leaned over toward me. He gave me a surreptitious kiss, both of us keenly aware of the repercussions of our actions in this environment.

"Brave," I said. It did feel brave of him to risk it "I'll see you around."

"I hope so."

"You will. And next time, you'll get to see more of me," I said doing my typical awkward flirting while closing the door on his anticipatory sigh. I flashed a smile though the window and went up the stairs. He drove off toward the parking lot or home or wherever. I got to my room and Esther was already fast asleep. I quietly went to the bathroom and cleaned up. No crying in the shower tonight MoFos. I slept better than I had since getting here.

7/15/2015

I woke up feeling pretty happy. Orgasms and good sleep will do that. Another reason I am unbearably chipper is, today is another *dark day*, which means no cameras are at the Spa—like yesterday when I was allowed to leave with Daniel. I'm floating on a Daniel infused *I have immunity* cloud and don't really care what the hell we do today. It turns out that after working out for two hours in the morning we were granted another of what we had affectionately come to call *fat camp field trips*. Today we were getting to go to the movies. The best part about these trips is that they are an emotional, as well physical break. They are the one time you know everyone is taking a break because you can see them sitting there with you. We had all become so obsessed with losing weight every minute of the day, we started to develop paranoia. If you didn't know where someone was, you always assumed they were doing more than you and felt guilty for it. Yesterday was kind of a tough one for me because I only worked out in the morning. Thankfully I hadn't eaten much, and also—orgasm which is supposed to burn some calories, right? The bad part of fat camp field trips were those damn church vans. But I had gotten to escape in a jeep last night, so I suppose I shouldn't complain.

On this particular field trip to the movie theater, however, somebody still managed to ruin things. Dawn was, once again, the culprit. Midway through the movie I got up to use the restroom and I look behind me as I stand up and there she is, in the back of the theater doing squats. I don't think I have ever wanted to kill someone until that moment. Ok, maybe a few. But I hadn't wanted to kill anybody in a while. I would have stoned her to death with boxes of Reese's Pieces had I only been allowed to purchase theater candy. We were watching the cinematic masterpiece Ghost Rider 2: The Spirit of Vengeance, and still she managed to make that movie more unbearable than Nick Cage ever could. So much for taking a break.

7/16/2015

I had the easiest weigh in ever since it didn't matter what I weighed. Farrell managed to lose enough weight to stay safe and so now we will be voting for either Blake or Brody to go home. This is a no brainer for me. Bye, Blake.

7/17/2015

Today made me realize that I understand absolutely nothing going on with this game. Chad came to Esther and me at the gym today.

"Guys. I'm gonna need you to vote for Brody today," He looked us both square in the eyes.

"Excuse me?" I said. For a second I was about to be unreasonably offended that he mistook us for his protégés, Farrell and Blake. Esther looked like she was in a dream and knew everything she saw was bullshit.

"I need you to vote for Brody," He was serious. "I've only got two guys left and you are still five people on your team. I need this."

"You want us to vote off somebody from our own team?" Esther asked, still looking like it was all just a joke she expected to wake up from.

"You realize this is wrong," I said. Chad looked at me like I was stating the obvious, and I immediately felt that I was the naivest player in this game. "You do," I simply stated as realization dawned on me.

"I'm running out of contestants here, guys," Chad was almost pleading. I considered asking him to get on his knees and beg but I thought perhaps that was letting my mouth write checks my ass couldn't cash. He was still a trainer.

"Is your team in on this?" Esther asked, finally feeling like she was sure it was reality.

"They'll vote for Brody of course. But there is just the two of them. I'm losing to Shea here, guys. A brand-new trainer. This is my career, my life." And there we had it. It was a dick measuring contest for these two and Chad was losing.

"All right," Esther said in a matter of fact manner. "I'll do it."

"Thank you," Chad said. I thought he was going to high five us both. He didn't. Perhaps he realized it would've been a little too shitty. He turned and left.

"You'll vote for Brody?" I asked Esther, once Chad was out of earshot. "Why? What? Why?"

"He lost nothing this week, Tisa," She was right. He *hadn't*. "And that means he'll lose a lot next week. We've seen that before," Again, she was right.

"That's true."

"If we vote him off now, even if Dawn and Greg don't, we'll nip that in the bud." I didn't like it but she had a point. Also, I owed her, so I'd vote however she wanted. I had immunity so I knew it wouldn't be my ass whether I stabbed people in the back or not. Still, I felt a little iffy.

Feeling kind of guilty, I kept running on the treadmill. When Esther said she was done, I told her I wanted a little more. She waved a cheery goodbye and left. I stuck around for another ten minutes, before I walked out towards the house. I saw Farrell on the way and veered off in his direction.

"So, your trainer came to me asking me to vote a specific way," I said, keeping it kind of vague.

"The Brody situation? Yes, I'm aware of it."

"Ah good. Esther and I agreed to it. But I feel a little bad. I gotta be honest with you, I would've voted for Blake," I blurted out. I am an over sharer by nature.

"Don't worry about the Blake issue. I've got that covered," Farrell said, then flashed a pretty weird confident shady smile at me. "Just trust me."

"All right," I said. Usually when people say to *just trust them*, I do the opposite. But what choice did I have? I was barely aware of there being an actual Blake issue, outside of me finding him annoying and obnoxious. Perhaps Chad and Farrell had some weird plan. Why would Chad stoop to asking the opposing team for help? I was so confused as I made my way back to the house.

Well, that was a bloodbath. Farrell wasn't lying when he said he would handle the Blake issue. He plays the game like Esther and decided that Blake was not just his biggest competition but that he was stealing Chad's time away from him and he wanted to win. I felt terrible voting for Brody when I saw his face as we lifted the covers of our plates revealing his name. Greg and Dawn voted for Blake, so we were tied at two versus two. Then it was Farrell—conveniently placed as the last contestant to reveal his tie breaking vote. With that same fucking smirk he had on his face when he fucked me over weeks before, he lifted his cover revealing Blake's name. Brody was saved but no thanks to half his team. Blake was gone thanks to the only other person on his team. Knives in people's backs left and right. Esther tried to convince Brody after, that it was all a ruse and that she knew Blake was going home the whole time but we had been asked to add to the drama of the moment. I'm pretty sure that wasn't true, and she was again playing the game at a mastery level I had yet to reach. I voted based on promises I made to two people—Esther and Chad. Team workouts with Brody are going to be super awkward now after he removes that knife we put in his back and Chad is down to one contestant. I can't imagine he will be too pleased about that. At least I won't be on the receiving end of his rage.

Chapter 12

The only one that seems to really miss Blake, is Brody. I don't blame him. Who else is he going to trust? The long-standing members of his team? Who literally just showed him, in no uncertain terms, that they were ready to throw him out on his ass? Not a super fun thought to go to sleep with, I'm sure. Chad lost his shit when he found out Farrell voted Blake off. I don't envy whatever brutality is being inflicted on that guy right now. I would be witnessing it except Chad has taken his isolation routine one step further and Farrell isn't allowed to spend non-filming days with us anymore. Total seclusion now. As Chad was taking Farrell away I could hear him talking to Farrell.

"I have only you to focus on, just you, and you're going to get all of it. This is what you wanted. This is your dream."

"This is not my dream, stop telling me what my dreams are, stop it," Farrell managed to reply before he was practically black bagged. That dude is screwed. I wonder if Chad will actually kill him or if it's just going to be intense torture.

Besides contestants being put in isolation, this place is a mad house. Greg slept in front of the gym door last night to make sure that no one was getting past him to work out while he was sleeping. Just on the ground, with a pillow and a blanket. We are almost afraid to stop moving or sleep for fear of not doing enough. The pressure to do more is pretty heavy.

7/19/2015

We spent a big chunk of today filming what I am assuming is another commercial. I say assuming, because there weren't specific instructions for us. We were told to get in the kitchen and then it was all of us *preparing* a holiday meal—which was only a *little weird* in the middle of summer. We messed around with foods you might see at a holiday dinner for a while and tried to look like we were both having fun and that this was totally natural, with blazing sunshine on a scorched desert outside our windows. I'll just add it to all the other weird shit here I've pretended to do. It was supposed to be all of the contestants and our trainers laughing it up over eggnog, mashed potatoes and turkey but Farrell was still not allowed to sit with us. So, it was Esther, Greg, Brody, Dawn, and I with Shea supervising. It cracked me up to hear Shea giving an interview talking about how the holidays are the time of year when people are supposed to be enjoying the food they eat. It was particularly amusing because she had made us spit out that turkey as soon as filming was done because it was precooked turkey and I guess the sodium levels were the things of her nightmares. But lucky for us, there was enough fake spray butter for everyone.

Even my exhilarating car ride with Daniel wasn't quite enough to power through the brutality that was this last elimination. But that didn't mean I hadn't thought about that little adventure, often. I hoped something like it would come about again soon. I felt more desolate now in the show with all the crazy going on, and like I wasn't good enough or doing enough. I could really use somebody to just touch me. So, when Daniel came up to me on my way from the gym, I was ready to jump into his arms and be taken away. It didn't quite go that way.

"Hi."

"Hi Daniel. It's good to see you," I was enthusiastic at a level normally reserved for high school cheerleaders and sort of regretted it immediately. But surely he was as excited as I was, only less awkward a human being than I.

"How are you doing?" he asked as he touched my shoulder with what felt like more intimacy than ever. It felt good, and I felt myself moving towards his touch.

"Ok, I guess. Things are crazy," It was an understatement, but I didn't want him to be too worried.

"I know. And they aren't getting better," He fixed me with a compassionate look. I felt alarmed.

"They aren't?" I felt like things were already crazy enough.

"The next challenge," he started, "is going to be rough. I don't know all of it, but it involves a horse race track."

"A race track?" I was confused.

"Yes. I know it isn't much to go on, but be prepared to run." I imagined whatever torture they could use horses for during a challenge and internally shuddered "The prize for the run, however, is to see a loved one," he said, and looked at me with a weird gaze I wasn't sure what that was about at first.

"Not that important to me, then," I said. "I wouldn't know who they'd bring anyway." This seemed to relax him and I guess he thought I had some long-lost love I hoped they would bring in, if I won? Nah, dude. Just the goldfish of my dreams.

"No, of course not."

"Well thank you for the info," I said. I was about to turn around and walk away, when he grabbed me, whirled me around quickly then kissed me. It was unexpected, but pleasant. I guess I did leave him wanting more the other day. We separated again, and he squeezed my hand before disappearing through a door. I went back to my room with my heart beating a little faster and added worry about the challenge. I talked to Esther about it but with so little actual information to go on, it was hard to really prepare for anything. She was a little envious at the chance to bring in a loved one, because she'd be about seeing her wife. Probably partly for the same reasons I'd like some more alone time with Daniel. She wasn't doing the challenge though because the pain in her knees and right calf muscle was murder. She had finally convinced Shea—who tried her best to make Esther feel like she was just being a whiner—that the pain was actually debilitating. Without Esther in this, I felt even more on my own.

7/20/2015

I don't have a lot of shame. In general I mean, people who apply to go on reality TV probably don't—at least not until they are subjected to the bullshit of reality TV—but I don't embarrass easily. Even when I probably *should be* embarrassed. Today was some humiliating bullshit though. What group of thin people thought up this challenge? It would have to be a pretty fat phobic bunch of assholes.

"Guys, these fat people just won't quit. It's like they just don't get how little we think of them," one exec would say to a room full of people who eat flaming hot

Cheetos covered in melted cheese dipped in ranch dressing while drinking a beer and smoking a cigarette for every meal without ever gaining an ounce so couldn't possibly understand why fat people can't just be **healthier.**

"I know. We make up so many bullshit competitions for them, and for some reason, they just keep on powering through. It's almost as if they thought their lives depended on it?"

"Well said. It's like they just don't get it. Also, I'm making a note to tell them their lives depend on it."

"I know. It's because they aren't ashamed enough of themselves. Being ashamed of myself works for me," says the one not genetically blessed exec who lives on kale smoothies and hasn't seen their family or slept in fifteen years to keep up their workout schedule.

"Yes. What can we do to really humiliate them?"

"I've got it, fellow thin people. We will make them carry the weight they have lost."

"But... is it enough? Will this humiliate them enough?"

"No, you're right. We need more. It needs to really hit home."

"Guys, get this. We put them in stalls on a racetrack and call the race like they are livestock racing after something they won't ever catch."

"My goodness, Johnson, you've got it! You should be promoted to head of diet promotions immediately."

I balked as that scenario played out in my head. When I realized what was supposed to happen, I said no. Nope. I refused to run. Like the giant hypocrite I am, I had mocked Dawn when she protested the unfairness of the bike challenge, but today, I get it. I started to walk away from the stalls, lest I'd be fighting a PA while she was trying to push me into it. A PA caught up to me.

"Tisa, you should do this. It's part of the game," she said, trying to look like she was both on my side, and like I was a huge nuisance to her.

"Have you seen what they are doing?" I asked. "Stalls."

"I know. But it's part of the game. It's a challenge," She was explaining it to me like I had no idea what was going on.

"That's obvious but it's humiliating and dehumanizing. How would you like to be put in a horse stall?" I don't know why I bothered. She didn't give a shit.

"It's part of the game," she said again. As if repeating it enough would magically convince me.

"Well." I started, but she cut me off.

"If you don't play it, they may just send you home. It's why you are here. They chose you over hundreds of thousands of others, not to mention those at home who didn't even make it this far. You were granted a spot here. To help you. If you don't want that help, then why are you here at all?" This was the kicker. Like a sucker, I lost my train of thought and didn't really know what to say.

"I guess," I said, and had slowed to a halt. "But this isn't ok. It's a horse stall. It's humiliating."

"I know it's not ok," she replied, trying to soften her voice to make me feel like she was still on my side. "But it's part of the game." The fucking game. I walked back to the challenge area with her nearly dragging me, pretending she was supporting me. They hooked weight plates up to me with carabiners and opened the stall door for me. I waddled in with weights hanging everywhere and my pride under my shoes. This made me feel awful. I didn't think it was possible to feel so shitty about myself as I did getting in that horse stall and waiting for that bell to ring. I'm pretty sure I could hear weeping from one of the neighboring stalls. I was certain it was Dawn. How the fuck is this *okay*? I let myself be coerced into this challenge but I refused to play by their rules. So, when the bell finally rang and the doors opened for us to storm out like wild beasts whipped into a forward pushing frenzy by the thought of letting people who don't give an actual shit about us down, I refused to run. My lame ass way of protesting was walking the whole race to the end until Farrell asked me to run the last few feet with him. What did I have to lose anyway, really? It's not like I was desperate to see a romantic partner like other people were. If they told me I would've gotten a two day all expenses paid trip to some hotel with Daniel, I might've pushed personal pride aside. But right now, I just wanted to be done. Some disembodied voice was calling the race out on the speaker system as though we were horses to bet on and had a few jokes at my expense, as I walked around, losing plates of weight along the way. Farrell and I crossed the finish line together. After how I felt from this challenge, that at least was really a surprisingly nice moment. For how crazy Farrell is about playing the game, it was cool of him to not be a dick. Esther talked to me a bit afterward and told me how glad she was that she didn't have to do it both because it was bullshit and she was injured. I'm really concerned about her legs.

7/21/2015

I am so glad Greg won that awful challenge. His wife Abby was flown in to visit the Spa and she is amazing. It hasn't been more than a few weeks since they last saw each other but their reunion was still kind of moving. She was allowed to join us for various activities during her stay at the house. One of them was the fake *last* workout. Which she noted wasn't the last workout at all. It must be so weird for somebody outside to come in and see how much of this is fake. We alternated burpees and step ups onto a bench. I was beat, bruised, tired and emotionally exhausted from the challenge. Shea was screaming at us and I just needed to catch my breath. I stopped for a moment and put my hands on my thighs and my head between my knees. Abby defied Shea's yelling, asking if I was okay.

"Get moving, Tisa," Shea screamed. "You've got this." I clearly did *not*.

"I can't yet. I am light headed," I pleaded. It should've been obvious but it wasn't.

"Of course you can. Get up and get going. You are a fighter," Shea wasn't letting up. Abby stopped doing what she was doing, and walked towards me. "Abby. Back to work," At least Shea knew her name right away. I'm pretty sure that was because Abby wasn't fat and therefore registered as a *real* human being to Shea.

"Tisa, are you all right?" Abby asked, ignoring Shea. She put her hand on my arm.

"I just need a break," I said through gasps.

"Then have one," she said. "This isn't your last chance after all," She chuckled. It wasn't. I knew it wasn't. But I still worked like it was. I felt horrible about not powering through but she made it a little better.

"Thank you," I said. Shea was yelling in the background but at somebody else. I ignored it.

"I don't like leaving people behind," Abby said, smiling at me again. "I'm a runner. We have a run group and everyone looks out for one another. I sort of thought it would be like that here for Greg." I appreciated that a lot. It's how I thought of myself—when I wasn't ridiculously warped by this show. Loyal. I stood up, caught my breath and got back to my bench.

"I'm good again," I said, reassuringly. Abby made sure I was actually good before she returned to her own spot.

"I knew you could do it," Shea yelled at me like nothing had happened. That I *hadn't* just nearly passed out on the floor.

After the workout, while we were drying off and catching our breath again, Abby came over and asked if I was still doing all right.

"I'm good," I said, wiping my arms with a towel. It was in vain because the lack of A/C in the gym and us being in a desert, meant we'd be soaked in sweat whether we dried off or not.

"Good. It's crazy hot in here," she mentioned, and laughed. "Why is it this hot in here?"

"Because we'll sweat more and lose more weight," I replied, off hand, before realizing how crazy that might actually sound to an outsider. She looked like I imagined she would upon hearing that. Shock and outrage.

"Are you *serious?*"

"I'm afraid I am," I said, then flashed her an apologetic smile. I don't know why. Not like I made the calls around here.

"You guys don't even notice it anymore, do you?" She was suddenly serious, and I almost felt like I was ratting out the show. Like I owed them my allegiance.

"No. We don't."

"Greg is obsessed too," She shot a look in the direction of the others, some feet away. Greg was lifting a dumbbell for Shea. "He doesn't realize how much, I don't think," She looked back at me. Not accusatorily, and not with pity, just compassion. I didn't say anything. "I hate that he is here. I hate what it is doing to him," She seemed almost sad now. I didn't know what to do.

"He'll be home again soon," I said, and realized that could sound like a threat. "I mean, whether he stays or is voted home," I added hastily. She laughed.

"Oh, I know. I wouldn't mind if you guys would just vote him home today," She winked and chuckled more. She was kidding. *Half* kidding at least. She didn't want to rob Greg of the chance to win but she also didn't like him being subjected to all this bullshit. I don't know if she knew about the challenge that got her to the Spa to begin with... she would probably be aghast.

We all gathered in the common room to hang out with Abby before she had to go home. Well everybody but Farrell—who wasn't allowed to leave Chad's cold grasp. The rest of us laughed, hung out and talked. It was pretty good to talk to somebody from the outside. Besides Daniel, which didn't really happen much. And truth be told, Daniel wasn't really from the outside. He just had more access to it. But talking to Abby was also a little scary. After being here for so long you have no idea how warped things are until someone from the outside tells you.

"It's not healthy for you here," she said to all of us, with a suddenly serious voice.

"Honey, it's not *that* bad," Greg started, immediately reassuring her.

"Oh, it is, Greg," she replied. "You haven't even been here that long and you're obsessed. I can't imagine how it is for the rest of these guys." There was no malice in her voice or judgment. Just concern, legitimate concern. It was a weird concept all of a sudden, after only experiencing concern for the story line or marketability of your choices from others for months.

"We just try to get through it," Esther said.

"I know you are, and I admire it," Abby said, looking at Esther. "I hope it doesn't skew you too much. Because things are crazy here," She looked around at us. We knew deep down things were crazy here, even if we were kind of balking at the idea of somebody from the outside telling us how things were. She was amicable about it, so nobody flipped their shit. But it did cut kind of deep. We steered off the topic until it was time to retire for the night. Under normal circumstances, at our respective homes, this could've probably been a lovely evening with some wine, friends and good food. Instead it was a weird wakeup call from despair. Abby said her goodbyes, since she had to leave before the weigh-in the next day. It was kind of a sad goodbye. Obviously for Greg, but for the rest of us too. For me, she was a breath of fresh air. Even if it had poked holes in the security I found in the routines here, it felt like she lifted the veil a little on what we were going through and legitimizing how I felt at that challenge. I'm not prepared to really see it yet.

7/22/2015

Esther was granted a trip to the doctor today, on account of the continuing pain in her knees and calf not magically going away. Who would've guessed injuries didn't work that way when you never rest? Shea was not pleased but a PA came to tell Esther that they would be taking her off the property to see a nurse practitioner. I guess the doctor was busy. Esther asked if it was all right to bring me along, and the PA shrugged like she couldn't care less. I tagged along.

The nurse practitioner spent considerable time handling Esther's legs. Bending them, listening, checking reflexes and pushing on her calf—causing what looked like considerable discomfort for Esther. She consulted notes and looked at papers. Finally, she had a verdict.

"Esther, you have bursitis," She paused, looking at Esther with critical eyes. "Yes. In both knees," she followed, as Esther was looking incredulous and was about to say something.

"Oh my goodness," Esther said. She looked at me as if I could magically fix it.

"You also have a torn calf muscle. It's why you're in so much pain."

"Torn?" Esther responded, raising a hand to her mouth in disbelief.

"Ideally, you should rest. These things will get better but not if you keep putting strain on them," The nurse practitioner was trying to appeal to Esther's sense of preservation. She knew what she was up against.

"I can't do that," Esther looked dejected and said it as much to herself as to the nurse practitioner.

"What?" She obviously wasn't used to people flat out refusing her medical advice.

"I can't. Can't you just give me something for the pain?" Esther was pleading, and tears were forming at her eyes.

"Esther, if you keep this up, you could permanently damage your knees. And your calf. And who knows what else."

"I know. But it's just two more weigh-ins, then I'm done. I just need to get through those."

I looked from Esther to the nurse practitioner and wanted to say something but I didn't really know what. "Just two more weigh-ins, and it's over," I repeated, like somehow two people saying it would convince somebody with years of medical expertise that it wasn't a problem.

"I just need to manage the pain. I have to keep going. The show is almost done and I *have* to do this. I need to be treated so I can get through this. Can you please help me with that?" Esther said, tears now streaming down her face.

"All right. A steroid injection will reduce the inflammation and can help with the pain but you should rest as much as possible even with the injection," the nurse practitioner said, looking at both of us with maternal concern. "You guys are really starting to identify with your captors, you know that *right*?" I had my undergrad psych degree and knew exactly what she was referring to. It didn't feel awesome to hear it though. She was administering the shots to Esther, who sat tearing up. What a fucking predicament. Two more weigh-ins. I was ready to go home.

After that sobering trip to the doctor with Esther, I immediately spotted Daniel standing in the driveway upon our arrival back at the Spa. He looked like he was helping the crew set up but caught my eye when I got out of the van and subtly motioned to meet him around the back of the house. My mind immediately jumped to sex. Sweet, I'm about a quickie hook up. It turned out not to be a quickie hook up. I knew that.

Behind the house, Daniel caught up to me and motioned for me to disconnect my mic. I was confused at first—my mind still focused on what having my hands on him right now would be like. He motioned again and it was like we were in a spy movie where the hotel room is bugged. I was alarmed as I fumbled with the mic. I finally got it unhooked and looked at Daniel with scared eyes.

"They know about us," he said, deliberately not touching me. "They had a talk with me yesterday."

"Oh," I exclaimed. I didn't know what that meant in terms of consequences but he seemed to be stirred by it and so I was by proxy. Also selfishly, I was alarmed at the thought of not having the little oasis of interactions with him as a means to escape even if only briefly.

"They have threatened me with terminating my job here and a lawsuit," he simply said. I was almost brought to tears.

"They've accused me of interfering with reality."

I nearly laughed out loud. *Interfering with reality.* On this TV show where literally nothing was real? That's got to be a joke.

"Do you want us to stop...well, whatever it is we are doing?" I asked, fearing the worst. I started creating escape scenarios with him in my head. They involved a convertible and endless supply of money and a tropical locale. I'm sure my goldfish would eventually recover from the devastating blow of abandonment. Daniel didn't grab me and ask me to run away with him though.

"No. I don't want to stop talking with you. I'll do what I can to stay here until you go." It was sweet really. It made me happy but also concerned. What if I got him fired?

"Will we be able to see each other?" I asked, kind of catching myself for just being about me again.

"I don't know how but I'll try to see you when I know it's safe."

"I'd like it but don't take crazy chances. There is always after the show," I said. After a brief pause, I looked at his concerned face, and said "Right?"

"Yes," he replied. "There is always after the show."

He indicated that I should plug the mic back in, which I did, and without touching me, he waved goodbye, and retreated around the house. It was a weird conclusion to the interaction. I didn't expect him to embrace me lovingly, right outside the house but it was almost like he couldn't get away from me fast enough.

With less people left the predictable endless walks down to the weigh in are significantly shorter so that was a plus. The rest of tonight's weigh-in wasn't predictable at all. I was happy for Brody after how awful he felt last week that he was really pleased with his result this week. He was all smiles. When Dawn stepped on the scale and saw her number though, all hell broke loose.

"No way. No way," she shouted from the scale, "I worked harder than anyone here this week. I know I did." The host tried to reassure her that she was doing great, "This is the number I always get stuck at on the scale. When I dieted and exercised to exhaustion in high school this is the smallest I ever got no matter how little I ate and everyone kept telling me I was just meant to be a chunky person." We all chimed in with platitudes that were now ingrained in us during weigh-ins. It didn't work. "I don't believe it. We aren't allowed to see the actual scale and I don't believe this is what I really weigh."

"What do you mean, Dawn?" Cynthia asked no longer with a reassuring voice and looking like she wanted to tackle Dawn. "The scale is right there."

"It's fake," Dawn nearly screamed. She was crying now and things were going to hell in a handbasket at an alarming pace. I imagined the editors working overtime.

"Dawn, step off the scale," production squawked, chiming in as a disembodied voice over speakers, for the first time ever during a weigh in. "You need to let the rest of the contestants weigh-in."

"But it's unfair. I know it's unfair," Dawn was sobbing but started moving off the scale. I felt a pang of sympathy for her.

Farrell stepped on the scale and I guess Chad had done well with isolation, because Farrell's loss pushed Esther into contention with Dawn to be sent home. They'd have to duke it out at the elimination ceremony. Dawn was crying, Brody was smiling, Esther was in pain, Farrell was whisked away and I didn't know what the fuck to think.

7/23/2015

Chad was pure joy at learning Farrell was safe from elimination. I thought he might break his arm from jerking himself off so hard taking credit for Farrell's weight loss. Shea heard the amount of weight that Dawn lost and grimaced. It didn't occur to me until that moment we were all killing ourselves to lose weight and here we are upset that someone had actually lost weight. Only one more weigh-in to go. I need to leave this place.

7/24/2015

Second to last walk down that damn hall past all those horrible photos of us looking sad while carrying a tray with a name on it and I am ready to not do it anymore. There was no doubt Dawn was going to be voted off tonight. I mean, there may have been a little doubt if Brody was harboring a grudge for Esther's vote for him and Greg did a surprise switch in loyalty. But I never doubted that it was going to be Dawn who packed her bags. I honestly think she's better off. She'd lose too much weight in tears alone if she didn't get out of here.

Chapter 13

The pressure to stay this week has driven most of us to insanity in my completely untrained psychological opinion. I feel the worst for Esther. After the trip to see the doctor and hearing from the nurse practitioner just how injured Esther is—, plus having shots in her legs to mitigate the pain—I don't blame her one bit for telling production that they can stuff it up their ass when they tell her she needs to run, possibly further damaging her body to get *a good shot*. I am more blown away by Shea, she of zero medical experience, trying to badger Esther into working out in ways that could permanently injure her for the sake of good TV. Tempers are running high here now.

"You went to the doctor and you're still here. It must be alright then," Shea said, surveying Esther with the closest you can get to disdain without actually being able to call it.

"She was a nurse practitioner and she actually wanted me to rest," Esther shot back. Not to mention Doc Malik telling her the same thing repeatedly. She was torn between wanting to win or at least stay, and not wanting to ruin the rest of her life just because Shea needed to look good on TV.

"You got a good night's sleep, didn't you? Just like everybody else," Shea was laying it on thick.

"More than a night, Shea. My calf muscle is torn. It's pretty serious."

"Isn't winning this *also* serious? You are so close, now. You are losing so much weight," Of course that was an argument to Shea. Losing weight meant you were doing A-Okay.

"It *is* serious. But this is my health. Everyone who has looked at it has said it is pretty bad," Esther said, refusing to budge.

"So what? I'm your trainer. You are acting like a slacker because winning isn't important to you. It is to me. You are important to me. Don't be a quitter. Make your health important," It was insane to hear Shea dismiss medical advice without batting an eye, as long as it was for somebody else. Esther looked like she wanted to wrap her hands around Shea's throat. She decided against it, which was fortunate, because I might've been an accessory to murder if she had. Instead she dismissed Shea with a wave of her hand and walked away. Shea looked like she wanted to run after her but it was just a play for the cameras.

For the love of God, why do people keep choosing me to have heart to hearts with? I'm not friendly. I'm not particularly warm and fuzzy, yet people in this mad house continually come to me to share their emotional issues. After berating Esther, Shea needed some sisterly advice I guess, and sought me out in the house as her go to friend to confide in. Can't she talk to Chad or something? I mean if he weren't somewhere as hidden as a nuclear fallout shelter for the President beating the shit out of Farrell.

"Tisa, I believe in you," she said, with the air of somebody telling me they were adding me in their will as the sole benefactor to their rather large estate.

"Thank you, Shea," I responded, with the air of somebody being added to the will of an uncle they had never heard of, and who looked destitute.

"You can win this. You have worked harder than anybody." I appreciated the words but wasn't sure I believed them. I didn't appreciate the added pressure though.

"I don't know, Shea. I have worked hard but I don't know if I'm good enough to win. I'm pretty beat. The last few weeks have been rough," I wouldn't normally come to Shea with thoughts about the show and Spa but since she seemed to need this heart to heart, I figured I'd share too.

"Exactly. You can totally win this, Tisa. I have a lot of pressure too. It's my first year as a trainer and Chad is working extra hard to beat me," She hadn't heard anything I said. Great. A heart to heart where only one heart was actually important and of course it wasn't the contestant's. "You've lost a lot of weight now. You must feel so lucky."

"Yes, I certainly do," I said, even if I wasn't sure it was really true. For Shea, being thin was the epitome of a good life. For me? I wasn't so sure anymore. Obviously, it *had* been a thing. I did sign up for this show. But I also remember my life before the show as being pretty good too and I wasn't in pain or hungry all the time then.

"You have changed your life completely. I'm so proud to have been a part of that journey," Shea was not above patting herself on the back. This wasn't really a friend talk as much as it was a way for her to boast for the cameras and save face after being dismissed by Esther. I hadn't really changed my life. I haven't even been participating in my actual life for months. What I had done was lose a lot of weight. Losing weight doesn't change the bills I'll be going back to when I leave here. It doesn't change how smart I am. It doesn't change who I am. It just makes me less fat. We chit chatted a little more as we walked around the grounds but thankfully the big gestures from Shea were toned down while I spent the duration of the walk contemplating what going home was going to really look like for me.

7/27/2015

Today's challenge was interesting for a couple of reasons. While I was loitering around after being freed from a church van, I heard there was going to be a prize for this challenge. Oddly though when Cynthia actually announced the details of the challenge, the prize I had heard rumor of was missing. Instead of anything tangible we were now competing for *a sense of pride in ourselves*. Had the challenge been an eye roll competition it would've been over after that moment with my undisputed victory. Pride in ourselves, what was this fuckery? The actual challenge was a sprint triathlon. We all had to swim a tiny reservoir, bike five miles then run one and a half miles. I'm not even sure those distances are a sprint triathlon? I'm pretty sure it's like a kid's triathlon. I was still intimidated as fuck. My track record on a bicycle wasn't stellar. I had visions of me making it out of the water, getting on my bike, slipping on the pedal, and face planting on the asphalt. It could be glorious television.

Since there wasn't an actual prize at stake, I was really impressed with how we all pulled together and did sort of turn this into a celebration of what we could do. Both independently, and together as human beings. Brody really struggled with the swim portion, I struggled with the bike and Esther needed to walk the run portion because of her injuries but we all stuck together. I'm cynical and dismissive of a lot of things but it was really lovely to feel like we did not leave anyone behind. Even Shea and Chad were allowed to somewhat participate—I mean, not the swim of course, that would mess their hair up— and cheered us on while accompanying us on the course. This was the first team effort and cohesive group since the very first month we were here—*before* insanity and competitiveness set in. It was ideal.

We all finished together and had a disgustingly amazing sweaty group hug. It felt genuine and amazing, especially when we ambushed Cynthia with a hug. This is the most authentic moment I have had in months. Then I remembered that I had overheard that they originally planned to offer immunity to the winner of this challenge but changed their minds when they realized that Greg—a man who had been completing athletic events like this at home already—was going to beat all of us hands down. The thought stole some of my joy. There was no way they could let a contestant from home win immunity and remain in the final four. It would undermine the entire concept of the show. Why would people need a magical fat camp when the guy who did it at home beat everyone?

7/29/2015

As usual the last workout *wasn't* our last workout. Our real last workout happened this morning sans trainers and looked like most all of the last workouts at this Spa before we were weighed in the morning, only even more pathetic. I got up, put on my usual outfit consisting of sports bra, tank top, t shirt, hoodie, spandex shorts, sweat pants and a ball cap to head down to the un-air conditioned workout. Yesterday, about twenty-four hours prior we all stopped drinking water to attempt to cut water weight and we wouldn't be drinking any during this morning's workout before we stepped on the scale either. Standard weigh-in day routine.

I got to the gym and the guys had beaten me there, closing all the windows and doors to make it as hot as possible in the gym while we all did cardio in our multiple layers to sweat as much as possible. The guys would regularly swish water around in their mouths and spit it out but I couldn't even let water touch my lips or I knew I would drink it.

We were all lined up on side by side ellipticals and I finally broke. Months of this same routine and I had just had enough. Tears welled up in my eyes and started flowing down my cheeks. Greg caught me out of the corner of his eye.

"Tisa, are you alright?" he asked with concern.

"I am." I said, sobbing. "It's just this place and all this time. It's almost over. I'm so hungry. I'm so tired." Esther, herself pretty beat up, immediately broke down crying too.

"Me too. It hurts. I miss my home," she sobbed. I cried harder. Brody had tears down his face too. He didn't say anything but I could hear him sniffing.

"I really miss home too. I can't wait to go," Farrell said, desperately trying to remain composed. He failed. "It's been so long since I've seen home, and my kids."

"My wife made me miss home too," Greg said. He was a silent crier. Just tears. "And it hasn't even been that long for me. You guys must be so homesick."

"We are," Esther and I said together through snotty tears.

"It's like being at the world's worst wrestling camp with all the training and dehydrating but never actually getting to wrestle," Farrell noted. A few of us chuckled through hiccups and sobs.

All five of us fell silent as we were still working out, with tears running freely, and sniffing and wiping of cheeks. It was a sad sight.

"At least all these tears mean we are losing more water weight," I noted. Everybody lit up a little with laughs. It felt kind of like series closers on the TV shows from the 80s where the actors were actually live performing in the studio. When the show ended, there was bowing and clapping and thanking before the main actor demonstrably turned off the scene light, casting the familiar set into darkness. We wrapped up the workout, got our shit together and left the gym for the final time. It wasn't a sad farewell but it was kind of a weird mood. The amount of times I've wished I could get the hell out of there, were now replaced with a nostalgic feeling of *just a little more.*

I was a little shocked at tonight's weigh-in, just because I had never fallen into the position where I could be voted off before. Fortunately? Greg fell into that same dangerous territory with me. The weighing was pretty unceremonious. Nobody cried foul or tried to break the set apart to see if things were real. Greg and I had taken to going on these nightly walks together where he gave me brotherly wisdom that I actually valued.

"Tisa," he said on the last of them before this weigh-in, "I'm probably going to get voted off after the next weigh-in."

"What?" I was genuinely upset, even if this had been on my mind all along and I was pretty certain he would too. "Don't say that."

"It's true though. We both know it. Dawn had a point when she freaked out about things being rigged." It was true. She had a point. It annoyed me a little that she did.

"I guess you're right," I conceded.

"It has been a pleasure meeting you, Tisa. Even if it took a little to get over your adversarial barrier," He shot me a sideways glance. I smirked.

"You aren't over it yet." See? Deflecting sincerity with jokes. He knew I knew what he meant.

"I know I'm pretty much just a perfect stranger to you, despite weeks of this show together, but I want you to know, that you are a remarkable person," He didn't shoot me any sideways glances this time and I didn't smirk. I didn't say anything in fact. "I hope you remember that when you get out of this Spa. That you don't sell yourself short. You shouldn't," It was really very moving. I hadn't enunciated the thought but I thought highly of Greg too.

"I really appreciate that." I simply said. I did. We walked on in silence for a while, until we had returned to the Spa again. "Good luck tonight."

"I don't need it. But thanks. The same to you." We hugged. Awkwardly. I halfway wished it wasn't the last time. I realized he was a lucky man when I met his wife and I understood the reason for the *luck* even more now.

When we saw the results at the weigh in tonight, I looked at Greg and he winked at me. We both knew the deal. He was going to be voted off in the elimination.

I was right. They voted Greg off the show. Can I go home now please?

I'm burnt out, home sick, sick-sick, horny as fuck, hungry, hurt and unhappy. I do not give a *shit* anymore about this show and yet the producers have me sitting around until midnight, jumping out of my skin, while they set up our final scene interview. Right before it was my turn to go in, A.C. pulled me aside. This scene must be a big deal if he was skulking around the set.

"Tisa, please be emotional," he whispered. "Try to bond with Shea. If you can cry, that would be awesome. We aren't getting any of the responses we need from the contestants with Shea tonight."

Ok, that shouldn't be too hard. I'd cried so much over the last six months it could be turned into a drinking game, *Take a Shot Every Time Tisa Cries*. Pep talk noted, I thought I was ready for this but as I walked in for my interview, I burst out laughing. Propped up in the middle of the room was a giant cutout of my before photo. It was like a Flat Stanley, only this was Fat Tisa. I sat with Shea and Fat Tisa. All two-dimensional glory of her in a sports bra and ill-fitting shorts.

"I'm *so proud* of you, I want you to keep going," Shea's earnest eyes burned a hole through me and I could tell she was expecting or hoping I'd break down. I am so delirious from starvation and exhaustion, I can't stop giggling. Someone else might have been so overwhelmed by this ambush *they* ended up crying but it wasn't gonna be me.

"Y-y-yes Shea, I won't give up," I managed to choke out without directly snorting laughter into her face.

"Look," Shea said exasperated, jabbing her finger toward Fat Tisa.

I didn't want to look at Fat Tisa. Why did I need to look at Fat Tisa? I know what I look like. I was reminded by the producers daily that I was an abomination to the eyesight of average people, even if I hadn't realized it before now. Besides, I was too busy checking out Shea's bad-ass jeans—which were bedazzled and had a heart stitched on the back pockets. Hmm, maybe I could get small enough to wear those at the finale?

The finale. Four months away. The producers were throwing four of us — me, Farrell, Brody, and Esther —back out into the wild, with the expectation that we would lose as much as humanly possible just short of cutting off a limb. Viewers would possibly notice that and production didn't want to spend money manufacturing a plausible backstory. I'd already lost a considerable amount but my weight was still way too high to become the first woman to win this show. Even though I was over the experience of beating my body mercilessly, I realized I still wanted to win badly. I desperately wanted to show people I didn't take this gift for granted. Otherwise, what would all this blood, sweat and tears be for anyway? The idea of being ungrateful or letting down the two hundred thousand other desperate people producers told me ad nauseum applied for the show but weren't fortunate enough to get picked sounded like the worst thing ever to me. I finished the ridiculous interview without outright laughing at Shea but I'm sure it wasn't the heartfelt moment people were clamoring for. I'm an acting fail this evening.

Finally, out of that damn Spa. Our first willpower test came as soon as we left the property in one of those church vans. The last ride in the church vans. Daniel was our driver. I'm not sure how he was able to finagle that, or if it was purely by coincidence, but it pleased me. That way I could catch his eyes in the rear view mirror a few times. I didn't know if he could read my eyes but if he could, he'd know I wanted to be alone with him. I announced that we were starving, because for the umpteenth time, nobody had bothered to feed the fatties while we waited to shoot the last scenes. After much grumbling —the stomach and complaining kind —Daniel pulled into a fast food drive-thru, the only thing open this late. We were a little stunned and a lot nervous. All of us had been talking incessantly about fast food for the last six months, like a soldier wistfully reminiscing about his girl back home. Now here she finally was, smack dab in front of our faces and we weren't sure we were in love anymore. Panicked but profoundly hungry, we all ordered plain burgers wrapped in lettuce, protein-style—God forbid a motherfucking bun should come anywhere near our person, carbs are evil apparently. Then, as we placed the juicy, grease-drenched, all-beef patties in our mouths, the van became dead silent, until we each let out a small moan and pretty much simultaneously orgasmed. Because food finally!

A millisecond later though, the self-doubt, self-loathing and brainwashing took over again.

"Should we be eating this?" Farrell, the frontrunner, said.

"I don't know," I cried. None of us knew because we were sent home with no instructions, advice or guidance. Except in how to dehydrate or spit food out before even a single carb reached the point of no return on our tongues. We discarded the food because eating it was too scary to us. Money wasted. Daniel drove on, and we finally pulled into the hotel for the night. I was descending into this crisis of conscience as we were disembarking and Daniel pulled me aside.

"Tisa, I know it's weird suddenly being out of the Spa again. But it's ok to eat. Your trainers aren't here. You look amazing."

"Thanks, I guess," I said. It was nice to hear I was attractive but I wasn't sure if he really understood. The food had been denied for so long. I knew we had a responsibility to keep up what we had been doing. This was a gift. So we could lose more weight.

"You have more to go through for the show, interviews and pictures. I've made sure yours are done first so we can see each other later," he told me, cutting my train of thought short. It was immediately replaced with thoughts of less clothes and closer proximity. He squeezed my hand like he did so often, then turned around to the rest of the crowd.

"That goes for the rest of you too. You still have interviews and photos to do, before you can sleep and flights home in the morning," he announced to them, making them think that was all he had just told me. I groaned internally at the thought of jumping through more hoops for this production. It was already way past my bedtime. Thoughts of a hotel room with no cameras and microphones but one Daniel later made me feel like I could do it.

The photoshoot was rough. Not only because it was way late, but because we said our goodbyes during and after it to the great annoyance of production. We kept crying and they had to scramble to cover it up with makeup and lighting. My interview was whatever. I sat and talked about how rough it was leaving the Spa now, and about winning and wanting to do my best at home. I think I even threw in some bullshit about how honored I am to be one of the final four and how I don't want to let Shea down. I was starved for everything at this point, I would've told a camera I was the reincarnation of George Washington if somebody asked the right question. There were tears. Nothing new. Esther and I hugged many times. We'd see each other again in a few months but it still felt weirdly like an end to an era. Farrell and Brody shook hands, then we group hugged. I would've passed out, if it weren't for thoughts of potential sex keeping me somehow coherent enough to have pictures taken. I just wanted to get the hell out.

Well sex happened. But at a price. I had finally been let go from the photoshoot in the conference room part of our hotel. I went to my room and found a note from Daniel with his room number on it. It said to come up as soon as I could. Butterflies were going nuts all of a sudden. It was like I was finally going to succeed in this endeavor and it excited me. I shed my clothes and jumped in the shower. I went back out and lamented the fact that I didn't have something special to throw on. But fuck it, right. It was coming off soon after anyway. I put on some clean sweat pants and a t-shirt then rushed out the door. In the elevator I felt myself getting more and more agitated. Some of that was the worry that I might run into a member of production and ruin everything. I almost ran to his room and knocked on the door. I heard quick shuffling inside as Daniel sprang to open it for me. He pulled me in, nearly slammed the door behind me and our lips were together almost immediately. It was like things couldn't move fast enough. His hands were under my shirt straightaway, and my knees nearly buckled. My hands, in turn, were under his shirt feeling his torso. He was pulling me in close to him, his hands on my ass, and I felt him against me. I pushed him away, pulled my shirt off over my head and wriggled out of my sweatpants. I stood in front of him, completely naked. It was the first time anybody had seen me naked in an intimate way in months and the first time after all this weight loss. His eyes consumed me, I laid back on the bed while he pulled his shirt off. He unbuttoned his pants and I involuntarily bit my lip in anticipation. I was more than ready for this. So was he. He finished stripping and I couldn't take my eyes from him.

"Do you have protection?" I asked, because I'm not a complete moron who wants an STD or to get knocked up in the middle of a weight loss competition. He did. I was kind of impressed that he'd planned ahead. I held my breath in anticipation. I barely knew up from down as he moved with me rhythmically. I knew I was ramping up for a magnificent climax. I lost track of his movements and sounds. Losing all control because I hadn't felt this amazing in forever and wanted more. More of him, more of this. I wrapped my thighs tightly around him, thrust my hips to the right and flipped us over so that I could control my orgasm. I was straight up gluttonous about it too. There was no gentleness. Any embarrassment I felt at exposing my changed body had vanished. He forced his hips upward and I was gone. When I returned to the real world, he was breathing hard and I was almost near collapse. "Holy shit," I said with a laugh. "I needed that."

"So did I," he said with a new huskiness to his voice I hadn't heard before. I rolled over to one side and took in a deep breath. My body was still rocking with waves of pleasure.

"I can go home happy now," I said. An idea came to my head. "What are you going to be doing the next three months? Maybe you could visit? We could reprise this performance."

"Oh, maybe I could. I've got a few things I need to sort out here but I could take some time off to come, I'm sure." His voice sounded weird.

"Things to sort out?" I asked.

"Well, just some stuff for the college radio I DJ'ed at, and I gotta arrange the moving out too."

"Moving out?" I was suddenly confused. "Moving out of where?"

"Well my, uh, the girl and I are still living together," he admitted, the huskiness in his voice replaced with a disconcerting cautious tone.

"You *are?*" I asked as I got out of bed. "Are you *kidding* me? I thought that was handled a long time ago?"

"No. It isn't. It's a work in progress. It's getting handled," he replied as he stood from the bed.

"It's been a month, Daniel. How long of a process is this? Because the only thing getting handled right now from where I'm standing is your libido. Are you still together?" I knew the answer before I asked.

"No, we are breaking up."

"You are breaking up? So that's a yes, really. You still live together? When does she get to find out you're breaking up? What the fuck are you doing with me then?" I was hurt and angry. I quickly put on my pants and looked for my shirt. I felt exposed all of a sudden.

"I am breaking up. I mean she and I *are* breaking up because I want to be with you. It's just complicated," he said, as he began putting his clothes back on.

"You are breaking up to be with me," I repeated. "That's ridiculous, Daniel. I'm pretty sure she isn't aware that she isn't with you and you have no right to be here with me now. I don't know what is going on here but I don't think I want to be a part of it."

"But *I love you,*" Daniel blurted out, stunning me to silence. I thought I hadn't heard it right. Then I laughed really hard. Like a Disney villain laugh.

"No you don't. You barely know me. Go back to your girlfriend. Now you don't have to break up with her. I just made it uncomplicated for you, you're welcome." I put on my shirt and left his room with the door slamming behind me.

I felt shitty and the juxtaposition with how good I had been feeling only moments before, just made it worse. I fought back tears in the elevator. Fuck that dude. He didn't deserve tears. Plus, winners cry in the shower *not* the elevator. I got to my room and realized I had left my key in my room earlier, in my rush to get out. Argh. A walk of shame to the front desk at four a.m. for a new key—cheeks still burning from a mix of post-orgasmic bliss and pure rage. They were nice about it because I obviously didn't have any ID to prove who I was and I was terrified they would call production. I got my key, went to my room, and prepared to get the fuck out of this town post haste. Fuck this show. I'm going home.

Chapter 14

*L*eaving the Spa and the show is kind of a mind fuck. I have managed to keep a somewhat coherent journal through my stay in CA but being back in the real world is so much different than I had expected after almost six months in the Californian desert, I don't know if I will be keeping this up as well. You know how you imagine something for a long while, wishing it, dreaming about it and shaping this idea of what it is in your head? Then when you actually achieve it, you are like a kid in a candy shop. Only this time all the candy turns out to be made of glass.

A PA knocked on my door at six this morning. I was already up. I showered not long before, to rinse myself of Daniel yet again. The knock on my door was a welcome sound, and I tore it open almost before the PA's knuckles had ceased to connect with it.

The first thing I learned when I woke up in my hotel room, after fucking and then being fucked over by, Daniel was that I wasn't allowed to go to my real home in Alaska. Because my only family in Alaska consisted of one, possibly deceased goldfish, the producers insisted I throw my *I'm Not Fat Anymore/Jaws Drop to the Floor* party in Maine.

"Good morning, Tisa," she said with a weary smile. I was pretty sure she hadn't slept much either. At least she probably hadn't dumped somebody while she could still feel the remnants of him inside her like I had. I assume so anyway.

Maybe Daniel fucked her too. I said nothing. I wasn't in the mood to be super friendly. She hesitated a second, unsure if I'd say anything or invite her in. I wasn't. Either of them. "I have your ticket for Maine here."

"Maine?" I looked at her like she had offered me a round trip to Mars. "What?" I stopped myself before I swore in her face. Not that I really cared, but I was super confused.

"Yes. We feel it is better if we shoot your homecoming in Maine where most of your family is," She looked at me like she expected me to punch her. I wouldn't but it's nice to know my reputation preceded me. A reputation designed for the show.

"But I'm from *Alaska*. I thought I was going *home?*" I stutter, still in shock.

"You don't have any family currently in Alaska," she said. "Your parents are in Maine and they have been informed and will welcome you there later. We have a crew with them already."

"*Maine,*" I repeated, looking sheepishly at the ticket she was still holding in her extended hand.

"Yes. Your plane leaves at ten a.m. and we'll have somebody pick you up shortly," She looked around the room, checking how big of a mess I had managed to make. I had been in the room about an hour altogether, so it was pretty limited. She seemed to approve of this. I'm sure she had to deal with annoying contestants doing annoying bullshit a lot and finally one of us got it right. I took the ticket from her hand and thanked her. I was tired and exhausted emotionally and the fact that I was going to Maine instead of Alaska was slowly starting to process. At least Maine means leaving LA, which is really a big step. I am sick of the Spa, cameras, interviews and all the bullshit. I do want to get back to working out this time in my own environment. I mean, I get to see my parents, so hooray for that I suppose. I hadn't been homesick for them really, so it felt weirdly out of place. I had been homesick for, well, *home*. Alaska. My place. My neighborhood. My usual hangouts and, by all means, my goldfish. Now it had to be postponed even further. I really wanted to get back to Alaska not attend an impromptu family reunion. I've been away from the place that makes me feel like *me* for too long. It sounds stupid but I want to put my feet on the ground there, and breathe the air because I don't know who I am. I know, that sounds insane- who doesn't know who they are? But everything is changing so fast. I look completely different, I feel completely confused and to be honest- I'm not sure I like myself anymore. I know how weird that is to say, but I've never looked at myself in the mirror and hated what I saw as much as I have the past six months and I feel like going home will stop it, or at least slow it down. I don't know. I can't even explain what I don't like, I weigh a lot less and that was the goal. I just want to be in the last place I felt like *me*.

I closed the door—perhaps a little too fast—on her and retreated to my bed. The cover was still on it. I leaned back and closed my eyes. I hadn't had a drink, yet everything felt like it was spinning. I really wanted to go outside and run but I didn't know just when somebody would show. I had showered and it felt like a hassle. I wouldn't have been able to sleep if somebody had paid me to, so I opened my eyes and sat up again. My room really was kind of ready to go. I kicked the last few items into my suitcase and zipped it up. I missed the Spa and it annoyed me. I hated that place but it felt like safety right now, as opposed to this. Going someplace I wasn't sure of. We were kept in the dark at the Spa a lot, in terms of what was happening. That trend seemed to be continuing but out here it felt more alone. I didn't have Esther with me. She was somewhere else in the hotel or had flown home already. I wondered if production told her she needed to fly to Hawaii because her second cousin twice removed had insisted on throwing her a big party.

The knock on my door finally came about forty-five minutes later. I had been sitting in the chair in my room, reading whatever I could get my hands on. Which wasn't much. I wanted to listen to music but the only music I had was from Daniel, and it pissed me off. As somebody who had experienced many long waits on the show, the past forty-five minutes still felt like a grueling long time. I opened the door to a guy wearing an outfit that had *driver* written all over it. He immediately looked for a suitcase he could grab, which only gave him away further. I stood aside and let him grab my suitcase, before I followed him out of room and down the corridor. We rode down in silence and went through the lobby without encountering anybody. The times of miracles are not yet over, it seems. By the car was yet another PA I hadn't seen before. From what I can only assume is an unending stream of people ready to jump in at moment's notice.

"I'll be flying to Maine with you. Did they give you your ticket?" Oh great. A babysitter for the plane ride. They really weren't about me being alone and getting weird ideas like, oh say, flying to my fucking home state instead of Maine? Or to Costa Rica. Or Australia. Anywhere else really. I held up my ticket and nodded. Conversation was tedious at this point. I just wanted to leave. "All right then," she said in an ironically chipper voice. Good lord, we were going to have a fun day together.

The ride to the shit show that is LAX was long and tedious. Like the universe was clawing and fighting to keep me there. I spent the whole ride in the back of the car with this PA next to me, in silence. Just staring out the window. The driver shot us occasional looks in the mirror and I'm sure he had an internal laugh at the sour mood that resided in the back seat. It was like we were two five-year olds who had just been told to quit fighting, or so help me I'll turn this car around. Traffic outside was dragging on and I felt internal anger build in me. It manifested in the almost irresistible urge to flip off people in the other cars. I kept my cool though. I wondered if my nanny felt the same way. Perhaps we could bond over mutual hatred of other commuters.

We finally arrived by the curb at LAX. The driver pulled my suitcase out of the trunk and put it next to me.

"Let me just go and check us in," the PA said, while she grabbed my suitcase. She didn't have a bag, and I wondered if the reason she was annoyed was, that she had been ordered out for an impromptu trip to Maine and hadn't packed shit. I followed her into the lobby area and was suddenly appreciative of her when I saw the amount of people and the size of the lines. She walked right to the desk and started conversing with the agent there. I imagined people in line being tired and pissy seeing it, and blowing gaskets left and right. She came back shortly after and handed me a boarding pass. She didn't say anything but it was clear we were heading straight to security. I don't know what I would've been doing anyway. Getting a stiff drink would've been an option months ago but now the thought of alcohol with all its calories was freaking me out. We cleared security and headed to our gate with ninety minutes yet to go, before boarding started. At least I could get a book now, so I'd have something to read.

"I'm gonna get a soda," my PA announced while scanning the nearest news stand. "Do you need anything?"

"Actually," I started, and she spun to face me. I realized this was the first time we had actually spoken in our nearly two-hour *friendship*. It had just occurred to me I was parched, having not had anything hours before and after interviews, photoshoots and sex. "I'd like a water. And I think I'll buy a book. For the flight."

"All right. We can do that," she replied, looking a little happier with everything now that we were actually communicating. We went to the stand and I picked out a random cop novel from the paperback section, while she grabbed our drinks. "I'll pick it up," she said when I started rummaging through my handbag for money.

"Thank you," I said. The show had balked repeatedly at every single shitty expense for months. Dragged their feet on getting us our three hundred dollar a week pay checks, refusing to get clothes that fit but wow, they were OK with buying me a book. I wondered if she paid out of her own pocket, just to get me to shut up all the way to Maine. I'm pretty sure she did. I couldn't blame her. I probably would've done the same thing. We got back to the gate with my bottle of water in my hands. I opened it and felt a weird resistance to drinking some. I thought of how much weight I might've lost in the past twelve hours from not drinking and wondered if I would ruin it now. I had an urge to go back to the gate and step on the luggage scale to see if I had lost or gained weight since leaving the Spa. After settling in, I was about to extract my book from my handbag again but the PA stopped me.

"I should probably tell you a bit about what will happen when we get to Maine."

"I'm surprised you know anything. Usually we're all kept in the dark until it's happening," I said, not without a certain amount of disdain in my voice. She ignored it. Good call on her part. I was being an insufferable bitch and knew it but couldn't seem to help myself.

"Your parents know you're coming, obviously. They are very excited to see you." I doubted this was really the case. Well, perhaps my mom was. I don't think my dad has ever been excited to see me. I distinctly remember him being perpetually annoyed by the mere sight of me, *especially* when I was a teenager. There is a reason I live in Alaska and they live in Maine. "We're going to film you coming home to them and their reactions to your new look," She ended the last sentence with the intonation indicating that my new look was an exciting thing to everybody. I didn't quite agree.

"That's exciting," I said, with zero excitement in my voice.

"We'll put you up at a hotel for the night since we are arriving so late," she said, positively cheery like she was telling me Prince would be playing just for me at baggage claim when I arrived. I nodded my consent and she left me alone after that. I gave it a few minutes of grace period before I picked up my book and tried to forget everything—her, Daniel, the Spa, being home-ish, losing weight and working out. *All* of it.

After an uneventful landing—which I suppose is really an ideal landing—the PA and I were whisked into a car by a new driver. For a moment my mind did jump to scenes of grandeur with me, the prodigal star ordering cars and drivers and lavish receptions left and right. However, that notion was thoroughly dispelled when we arrived at the hotel. Calling it nondescript was doing it a huge favor. It was almost literally in the middle of nowhere Maine and took us two hours of boring silence to get to. While I waited for the PA to check me in, I noticed a large group of people were holding a ten-year class reunion in the conference room. It smelled like desperation and bud light. I figured they were my kind of people but I needed to get some sleep before the hours of filming with family I barely know welcoming me home scheduled for tomorrow morning. I opted out of crashing the party, getting hammered on cheap beer and hooking up with the first guy who hadn't puked in the last hour. My family are great people, don't get me wrong. But I literally hadn't seen any of them except my parents in years and reuniting with them all while pretending we were in a state completely across the country was a little strange and I needed sleep to prep for the impending weirdness.

I got to my room and the PA told me she'd be down the hall, and that I shouldn't go anywhere. Like where the fuck would I even go? We were in *Maine*—literally hours from anything resembling a city I knew. I told her not to worry. As soon as she told me she'd pick me up the next morning—conveniently not arranging anything in terms of food for me—and she had shut the door, I unpacked my running shoes, donned them and my trusty sweating outfit, and went outside. It was still warm and humid, despite the sun slowly sinking below the horizon. I started running.

8/3/2015

Everything was pretty rushed this morning. A camera crew was waiting in the car, stylists and all the usual production bullshit were there too as soon as the PA got me up out of bed. I was already awake because I had basically gone to sleep at a respectable 9:30 PM the night before after a long run. I felt like doing more but the hotel didn't have a gym—which was really typical of this production. If I didn't work out, they would tell me I was lazy and didn't deserve my spot in the finale. Yet, they put me in a hotel *without* the means to work out. Luckily, I had learned how to beat the shit out of myself in and *outside* of a gym. I went through the motions preparing for camera work. It had been a nice twenty-four hours, give or take, without a lens in front of me, *or* every word I said scrutinized by a crew of guys with their hats on backwards and t-shirts with coffee stains. Even with tons of people running around, there is still a lot of waiting and now that I'm alone, without Esther or Debbie or even Dawn, it's lonelier. I finished my book, so I resigned myself to sitting in a chair waiting until time to head out. I was picked up and driven to the party in what I assume is a 1972 limo borrowed from the local funeral home. I guess you could argue they tried to go for old school class but really it was likely just about saving money. In their defense, I'm not sure where they could've acquired a limo in Bum-fuck, Maine, but still. A regular car like my Civic at home would've felt less douchey. Family I haven't seen in years at a party I am sure they were told they had to throw in my honor and I roll up in a limo? Ugh.

The drive over involved looking out the window at passing highway roadside shops and signs like I was finally home and pretending to recognize everything. The truth was, I *wasn't* home and I hadn't actually seen any of these stores and locations passing me by, ever. I didn't grow up here. I had barely even visited here. My parents retired to Maine after I moved out a hundred years ago. I sure hope the Screen Actors Guild card is in the mail because I performed the role of returning daughter beautifully. Especially when I exited the vehicle outside the venue that had been booked and my entire family was there. True to their character, the producers asked my mom and dad to fly in my sisters and their kids for the party. They had also told them to book the fanciest place they could, because all of this was what *I* wanted. So my sisters were there. And their kids. And my parents. And cousins—some of whom I'm certain must have been hired actors for the occasion because I don't remember half of them. I smiled at everybody and acted like I was super happy to see them. Truth be told, I would've preferred a fist-bump hello at the airport and straight home for a nap. But that doesn't make for good TV. After my family obligingly did the whole *omg Tisa you are so thin* bullshit for the camera then went to a fancy restaurant (where everybody ordered delicious foods except me, who ordered water) production casually pulls me aside and tells me that I am responsible for the $400 tab and my dad needed to pay the venue rental fee. They brought me to a different state, then left me with the bill. Fantastic. All I could think about—as I begrudgingly paid that bill—was producers telling me on the show, "It's not about the money, Tisa." while wearing $800 shoes. Those cheap exploitive fucksticks.

I did take some small measure of joy watching my uncle school production about the footage they were taking though.

"You do realize all these trees you are filming are indigenous to Maine, right? These aren't in Alaska," The PA he was addressing looked at him and snickered.

"You do realize that viewers believe these people are losing ten to twenty pounds in just a week, right? No one is going to notice that these trees don't belong in Alaska," My uncle turned toward me and shook his head at the ridiculousness I'd allowed myself to participate in with this spectacle.

I was permitted to drive home with my parents and the drive in my parent's' car was the first time I had felt any kind of real freedom in a while. No PA at the destination. No cameras. Nobody controlling where I went. This is amazing. When we arrived at their house, my dad took my suitcase out of the back of the car. I walked up to the house, leaving the suitcase behind. I was so used to not being allowed to do anything on my own, I had forgotten that this was my family not people hired to carry it for me so I didn't abscond from the set with all my belongings. My dad wasn't about that, though.

"You're gonna have to carry your own suitcase here, princess. Nobody else is going to do it for you."

I carried my own suitcase.

My family was blown away by my dramatic weight loss. It made for excellent TV, I'm sure. Was I blown away? No, because when I finally got to my parents' house and stepped on a scale my weight had magically shot up again. I was freaked out.

My body might look great on the outside (bullshit number on the scale not withstanding) but on the inside, I am a train wreck. I know I am malnourished and I have so many aches and pains, I have been popping Aleve like Pez since the Spa. I was so numb you could stab me in the face with a fork and I wouldn't have felt it. Stepping off the scale was the final weight in the emotional load of it all. My exhausted ass stumbled to the guest room and passed out. Finally, I slept. For sixteen hours.

8/4/2015

Production has relinquished their grasp on me a little. They diverted attention elsewhere. Not that it mattered much. I just stayed at my parents' home and obsessed about getting my workouts in. I only leave the house to run and come back to sleep. Rinse, Repeat. It's not the two days at home I had imagined or hoped for but it's still pleasant to be without a camera in my face.

8/6/2015

After too little time with people who loved me, it's once again time to fly back to LA. A PA called me yesterday, and informed me a ticket would be waiting for me at the airport. No driver and no personal assistant this time. Just get myself to the airport. She also said, I was returning to LA and not going home because we would be shooting a workout DVD with contestants from the last two seasons and our trainers. It had been mere days since I had seen Chad and Shea but the spell of power they had over me didn't feel as strong after being out in the real world again, thank god. I wasn't so worried about doing everything they told me to do or losing my chance at *saving my life*. Maybe this trip back to LA will feel different around them, since I feel different after leaving. I feel like I get along pretty well with Chad anyway, because whatever he was, at least he was honest about it. My fondness of Chad is because I too played *his* game. Honesty. Chad is open about wanting to win and behind the scenes, he had plotted and bartered with members of my team. I respect the blatant deviousness and lack of fake friendship. He basically radiated, *do this my way or I'll run you over*. I can respect that shit. No fakeness, no BS and straight up about what he wanted. He and I aren't going to be getting matching tattoos or anything, I don't *like* him, but I respect his approach.

Being on set again, it's obvious that now that the possibility of being voted off is over, Shea and I feel no compulsion to be nice to each other. There isn't even the veneer of needing to pretend we are about one another. Today when she couldn't get the exercise moves down during filming, I got outwardly impatient. By outwardly impatient, I might mean I was mean as fuck and asked how it was that a national fitness pro couldn't seem to figure out her left foot from her right. I overheard the choreographer call me a cunt while soothing Shea's bruised ego and add, "I can understand why it's so difficult to work with these girls." She was right, poor Shea. It *must* be hard to do simple exercise moves while well-rested and on a full stomach. I was hangry and took months of frustration out on Shea today. But she is seriously so fucking annoying. Like vapid and fake pleasantries. If the phrase *Bless Your Heart* were a person, it would be Shea. I took a beat so I wouldn't head butt her in frustration and thought back to a moment when Chad had my back when dealing with similar shit earlier in filming. "It's not a thing, Tisa," he chuckled. "You used to fuck up bitches like this in high school all the time, didn't you?"

I actually didn't, I avoided them like the plague, but producers had decided that my *character* would be the bitchy party-girl and Chad decided that's who I was. Actually, *everyone* decided that's who I was. After a while I didn't have the energy to correct them anymore. I wasn't the first, last or only person to be typecast on a reality show, and how much was it going to affect my real life anyway? I can't avoid Shea but maybe I can check out mentally for the rest of this hot mess.

As Shea tried to learn how to count out loud while doing lunges –a task as difficult as walking and chewing gum at the same time basically—I focused on how I was going to be flying home, to my *real* home, after this. The DVD is only two days of me being holed up in the same hotel I had been in back before I was even cast. I can make the best of this. I can't say I have fond memories of the last time I was here, but this will at least be a shorter stay. Truth be told, I barely have any memories at all of this hotel. Only that they kept losing my panties. At least this time I am allowed to have a key to my room and have no reason to send my clothes out to the hotel laundry.

8/11/2015

Home. I am finally home. I get to leave the plane to a warm August day with weather clear enough to see the mountains. I stopped a second and heaved a deep breath. Not L.A. air, that's for sure. No matter where I travel, when I arrive back in Alaska I always feel as though I haven't really been breathing until that moment I am home again. I had almost lost myself to the moment, when somebody tore me out of it with a tap on my shoulder. It was a producer hustling me along. Producers had come with me because actual footage of Alaska was necessary. Who knew, right?

Anyway, as far as I can tell the plan is to stage scenes that will play up my party-girl persona the show had assigned me. Because fuck just being me for a moment. They had asked for and gotten the names of a few of my girlfriends and had arranged for us to go out to a bar right away tonight before I even landed. We went straight to the hotel room, after some random producer told me to find a way to get my makeup done. I didn't even bat an eye at the absurdity of it all. Of course, production wants to film footage of me getting off the airplane looking like I just woke up from a ten-year coma followed by a shot of me arriving at a bar looking like it was red carpet time at the Oscars all within a fifteen-minute timespan. Sure, let's do that.

Makeup done to the best of my ability and I am already significantly more excited about getting to this shoot because I finally get to see people I really want to see. Don't get me wrong. Seeing my family was awesome and feeling the love was good for me. But this is Alaska. This is home. These are my people. Luckily for me, production has even rented a car this time and I'm allowed to leave the shoot at the club with my friends instead of having to beg transport off production or call a cab. I get to be home, and alone with my chosen family after this. *Finally.*

I have always been used to adapting to new places, and having *home* move every few years. But Alaska is the one place I have lived the longest consecutively and it's where I spent most of my adult life so far. It's also where I was born. I can feel myself smiling on the drive to the club as I recognize places I used to frequent. It's only been six months but I had fantasized about all these places so many times in my head at the Spa, that seeing them again was like being in a familiar dream. We finally pulled up to a local bar—the *same* bar I had been at the previous New Year's Eve and come to the realization I should try out for the show. I immediately saw familiar faces waiting outside the door for me. As the door opened, I burst into tears of joy. I tried to hug all of my friends at once, and predictably, we all cried *and* laughed. I'm sure people walking by think we are filming a murder at the number of tears and screeching going on. After the initial elation leveled—and on the stern behest of production—we decided to actually go inside the bar. Doing shots for the camera, which were really just 7-Up and Diet Coke was first on tap. Total party girl downing that fake alcohol.

We filmed for a while, laughing, joking and shooting the shit. Production was satisfied and the cameras finally left. My friends and I celebrated my being home. *Really* celebrated. It was chiller without a PA standing around with a clipboard ordering me to drink, smile, laugh or look interested. My friends took it in stride but I'm sure it felt super weird to them both watching me take orders, something I'm not prone to doing and seeing the ugly machinations of *reality* TV in all its glory. It's nice to cut loose with people I know. Granted, I drank water, while they drank water and vodka. But it doesn't matter. I laughed. Genuinely laughed, and for some time, I almost forgot what I had just been through and was still going through with this whole weight loss reality TV weirdness.

I was left with Britta—who was the reason I got into this whole thing to begin with—and her boyfriend, Sanjay. We settled in a seat and just talked. Well, she and I talked, while he drank beer. Mostly, though, in the back of my mind, I was a woman on a mission. I needed to get laid. Badly. While others on my season had found a way to fuck each other multiple times, I unfortunately hadn't been fucked as much as I had been fucked over. I was in the mood to remedy that situation.

As Britta prattled on, I spotted a gorgeous woman in glasses, who looked oddly familiar. Whatever. Anchorage is a small city. Probably because I had been imagining sex with a partner for months when I wasn't fixated on Daniel. You know how it is, no food, no sleep, no sex, LOTS of daydreaming. Glasses are my catnip. If you don't live in your mom's basement and are wearing a pair, I'm probably going to be about fucking you. If you DO live in your mom's basement, it'll probably take a little convincing but it's still not impossible. She was sitting with some buddies, and I managed to finagle my way into their circle with Britta and Sanjay. I had every intention of having sex with this woman, but there was one problem. She was *really* drunk. Like in my excitement I mistook sheer shitfaced drunk for her being mysterious and deep. She had her hand on my thigh, and I ached for more to happen, but she was pretty honest with me; the amount of alcohol in her blood would likely hinder any kind of activity other than passing out at this point. So instead of hooking up, I scooped her up along with Britta and Sanjay when the bar closed and we left to have breakfast. Actually, they had breakfast. I had water and a side order of sexual frustration.

"When you completely sober up this can happen if you still want, call me." I told her, matter of factly when I dropped her off later. I hoped she would take me up on my blunt offer because she was cute and I felt a comfortable connection with her. When we talked while she sobered up over eggs and bacon I found myself forgetting there were other people in the room. She promised me she would. I went home with Britta and wondered where the hell my suitcase was. Still at the hotel probably. Thanks a lot production assholes, way to drop the ball on that. I'd have to get that later in the day and hope production left it when they checked out. Right then, I just wanted bed, a blanket and my own familiar surroundings.

8/12/2015

I woke up before noon, despite the late bedtime. First thing I thought when I opened my eyes was, *where the hell was I?* But it came back to me fast. Months at the Spa, various hotel rooms and some time zone bullshit had me kind of discombobulated. I strolled around, just taking it in again. The sun was out and the light just flowed through my window. I cursed production making me go get my suitcase as I got showered and dressed.

Driving for the first time in six months was interesting. I have never considered myself an amazing driver but I made it to the hotel without casualties or grievous bodily harm, so I'll chalk it up as a win. They had my suitcase stored and I was chuffed production hadn't fucked that up somehow. Not that there was a lot of stuff in there I had a close relationship with but I had gotten used to working out in clothes from the Spa. It would feel weird not to, since I was still on the show, technically. Not having cameras on me all the time was going to take some getting used to as well. So far it was sort of amazing. I've always been someone who likes being surrounded by people so this new version of me that relished the idea of being completely alone was sort of throwing me for a loop. Nothing sounded better than being left completely alone right now, with no one wanting something from me.

I threw the suitcase in the back of my Civic and took to driving around a little to get the feel of the place again. I considered stopping somewhere for lunch. I think my last meal was before I left Maine, but I know I had a few bites of Britta's eggs at breakfast last night so getting a meal when I failed to stick to just drinking water after the bar is a bad idea. I need a workout, that should help me gain my willpower again. I went home and unpacked my sweat suit so I could go for a run.

When I came home, and showered, I had run so long that it was already the afternoon. I noticed a missed call on my phone. I was pondering who the hell would be calling me from a number I didn't recognize when the phone rang. I picked it up.

"Yes?"

"Hi it's Jane," said a voice on the other end.

"Who?" I said, irritated because I had no idea what this was about and I don't care about switching my cell company right now.

"Uhm, Jane. From last night" She sounded unsure all of a sudden, like perhaps she had dialed the wrong number.

"Oh, shit sorry." I giggled. "Hi Jane. I remember. I was wondering if you would be alive today or not."

"I'll have to plead the fifth on that." she said. Her voice was deep from the slight hangover and just the perfect amount of gruff and smooth. "I am not doing well, truth be told. But when I came to, the first thing on my mind was you, and I wanted to call you as soon as my tongue wasn't 2 inches thick."

"Is that a bad thing?" I said, and kind of shot myself a look in the mirror. I guess classy is just my resting mode. She didn't say anything for half a second, and I managed to convince myself that she was going to hang up on me for that terrible joke. She didn't hang up. Instead she chuckled.

"Only when I want to talk." she hit back, with just the perfect amount of slyness in her voice. I felt the mission from yesterday stir in me again. "How are you doing?"

"Oh, I'm fine. I didn't drink, so I slept like a baby and just went for a run." I sounded like the least fun person on Earth all of a sudden. I should've followed it up with "And I had kale for breakfast!" just to completely bore her to death. I hoped she remembered fun me from yesterday, and that I hadn't gotten lost in the mists of alcohol.

"The reason I'm calling is, because I'd like to see you." I guess she had retained enough of our encounter to warrant seeing me again. My heart jumped a little at this. I tried to calm it down. This was really a hookup. That's what I wanted. Nothing else. I had enough on my plate as it was. Still, despite not getting laid last night, and despite her being mysterious and deep, mainly being alcohol imbued, there had been something I connected to. That familiar quality I couldn't quite put my finger on.

"Sure. What did you have in mind?"

"How about a coffee later, and perhaps a movie?" she said. "I can't guarantee I'm worth a lot more than that today, because I was pretty drunk. But I would really like to see you when I'm somewhat sober." I smiled. She had felt the mission I was on too, and didn't want to let that go. You and me both, babe.

"That sounds good. When?"

"How about now?"

"Now?" I looked at my watch, without really seeing the time. It was a kneejerk reaction, because honestly, I didn't have anything else going on. She was about to say something, and I thought perhaps she would retract, so I cut her off. "Now sounds good. I'm ready when you are."

"Great. I'll text you the place, and see you there in twenty?" she said, and when I agreed, we hung up. I was more excited about this than I should be. It was just a random girl, and I wasn't even sure it would amount to anything. I checked myself in the mirror, and threw on an old hoodie I had around and my jeans. It felt really good to be back in my old clothes again. I got the text from Jane. It read "Meet me here. I'm looking forward to seeing you." with the address and name of the coffee shop attached. I had butterflies floating around me as I drove. Silly. I had them before too, and the guy turned out to be a jerk. But I couldn't stop it. Classic me. Infatuated with somebody who fucked me over, and soon after I'm school girl giddy for literally the first person off the plane. I pushed the thought out of my head. Fuck it. I was leaving again soon, to start law school, and get serious with this working out for the finale. It was OK to have some fun.

When I got to the coffee place, Jane was already there, sitting at a table. I hadn't been drunk when I saw her, so she looked as good now as she did yesterday, but still it felt like I was seeing her in a new light. Granted, she also wasn't drunk out of her mind today, so it was kind of like a new her. She was looking the other way when I came in, and noticed me after I had looked at her a little. She smiled, and I kind of liked that smile. She waved me over and got up as I approached the table to hold the chair out for me. It was cheesy and at first I thought she was removing it, because I had forgotten what manners looked like. When I realized she was doing it for me, that cold defensive shard of ice inside my heart melted for a second. I composed myself, but I felt the heat from it melting for just a second spread out into my veins. She pushed the chair in under me, and sat down on the opposite side again. She took up the menu and signaled the waitress over, as she asked me if I was hungry. I was starving, but I didn't want to eat, and I wasn't about to let her see the crazy that was me just yet. I told her I was good, and just wanted black coffee. She got one too, from the waitress who smiled an awful lot at her. I couldn't blame her, but I also wanted to stab her, can't you see I'm in my best jeans and a hoodie? This is a date lady, move along. Thankfully she had a job to do.

"Thank you for coming out with me on short notice," she said, when the waitress had left us alone. "I'm happy you remembered me."

"Remembered you? It's been less than 12 hours. I may be crazy, but I'm not that crazy," I said.

"You seemed to have forgotten me yesterday," she said, and smiled a sly smile I ate up.

"I did? When? I'm confused." I wasn't sure what she was talking about. Was she still drunk?

"You don't remember me," she cried triumphantly. "I wasn't sure, I was too drunk yesterday, but as soon as you walked into that bar I knew it was you. A face as beautiful as yours sticks in my mind."

"Remember me. From what?" I asked. My mind was racing. The show wasn't airing, as far as I knew so she couldn't have seen me on TV. Had she been in production somehow? Or did she stalk me? I thought about getting up, but her demeanor was pleasant and not threatening. She thought my bewilderment was amusing, and her eyes shone with warmth and good humor.

"New Years. We met that night. We went home together. We, well, you know." She fixed me with a look of anticipation, a smile skirting the corners of her mouth. It took me a second to realize what she had said, and then it hit me. I knew there was a reason she felt familiar. She should. And there is a reason I was drawn to her last night. The odds of this happening knocked the air out of me.

"Oh shit." I exclaimed in my usual loud manner, before I clasped hands over my mouth. I looked at her in equal parts shock and amazement.

"Yes!" she said just as loud as me, and laughed. A hearty guffaw. I couldn't help but crack up with her. "Apparently it was a more memorable New Year's for me than it was you." She smirked.

"No, that's not it, I've just been really busy, like, my life got sort of crazy and…"
I realized how lame that sounded and made eye contact with her, grateful she looked
amused and not hurt. We both laughed at the awkwardness of the whole thing, well,
at my awkwardness. Actually she seemed pretty chill about it all.

We were still laughing when the waitress came back with our coffees. She
looked annoyed at me, like she had plans I had ruined or something. Back off
lady, I've already marked this one. She left in a huff. Jane stirred a sugar into her
coffee, smiling. I caught myself smiling too, at her and in general.

"That is so weird." I said. She looked up at me and smiled that sly smile again.

"It's how the universe works. Of all the bars in all the towns in all of the
world, you walk into mine. Twice." she said. I gasped. She just half ass quoted
Casablanca at me. (Kind of the best movie of all time, fuck you *Citizen Kane*,
yeah, I said it, *Casablanca* is better.) Was this real life? I didn't know if she was
joking, but I did believe that was how the universe worked. We sat in silence for a
little, sipping our coffees. It was a comfortable silence. It felt easy being near her.

"So, what have you been up to since that fateful night?" she finally said,
breaking the moment with a little harmless snark in her voice. She looked at me
with genuine curiosity.

"Well, I've been down in California." I started, not really knowing how or if
I should broach this whole thing. It felt unreal now, to tell this girl I kind of
liked, that I had been filming a TV show. Jane was an outsider, and as weird as
that sounded to say, it meant she had no idea what I had just been through and
was still participating in. She seemed to not even notice the change in my
weight. It scared me a little. And attracted me to her a lot. Here was someone
completely untouched by that drama.

"Working?" she asked, sipping her coffee and pushing up her glasses in a
way I already really enjoyed.

"Well yes and no." I replied, and figured I might as well live up to my
reputation as being upfront and frank about everything. "I was actually shooting
a TV show. Reality TV. Weight loss TV. I don't know if you noticed, but I'm
different than I was at New Year's." I didn't have it in me yet to explain that the
difference was more than just how I looked. It felt weird to say even that much.

"I noticed, but honestly? I mostly remember your eyes from New Year's and
those look exactly as I remember. They remind me of times when I was a kid at
our house in the countryside, the sun setting after a warm day, before the fireflies
came out, and we'd tell stories around the fire." She looked intently at me when
she said this, and I visualized those nights in my head, and it threw me off.

"They do?" I said, completely forgetting what I had just said. "Why?" I wasn't sure what answer I expected. I'm not the best at taking compliments, really. Especially ones phrased like poetry. She sipped her coffee and smiled at me.

"Because they are beautiful." she simply said.

"Oh." I'm seldomly stunned into silence, but I didn't know what to say other than that.

"Look it." she said, putting her cup down and looking suddenly serious. "Here's the thing. I really dig you. I know we've only met twice, both times with at least one of us starting the night under the influence of alcohol. That said, you were brilliant and hilarious, and you had a big impact on me. I know you walking into the bar yesterday with me there is probably just a coincidence, but I enjoyed our time together in January, and I enjoyed last night too. What I remember of it. I didn't want to lose out on talking to you when completely sober, since the last time I sobered up with you we didn't spend the time talking. I mostly wanted the opportunity to catch one more look into your eyes. That's why I asked you out."

"Oh." I said again, processing her words. I felt bad for not remembering her. I mean I did now that she mentioned it, but not knowing when I saw her. I feel like my making her into a conquest and not a person was something I should probably look at about myself, not right now because there is this gorgeous human sitting across from me drinking coffee, I just feel bad I didn't see her the last time we were together. Like see her, see her. I dug her too, and I wanted to remember every detail. I realized she had just been incredibly open and genuine with me, and I was just sitting there. I reached out and grabbed her hand that was on the table, gave it a small squeeze. "I'm glad you did." I meant that.

"Good. For a second I thought you would get up and politely run screaming out of here." She smiled at me. Her hand was warm in mine. Calloused (oh that Crossfit) and strong, but still soft. I wanted to intertwine my fingers in hers.

"For a second I thought I would too. But only because I was scared of how much I wanted to stay and hear more." I smirked at her. "Honestly though, you felt familiar to me last night. It's why I was instantly drawn to you, I think. Well that, and your good looks." I flashed a crooked smile. "But seriously, that familiar feeling. Almost like you were a memory."

"I was."

"You were. But not a conscious one, if you know what I mean." She did. She turned her hand palm up under mine, and touched my wrist. It sent sparks up my nervous system.

"Would you like to go to the movies with me?" she asked. I was still caught up in her hands on my wrist.

"At the theater?" I asked, absentmindedly.

"That's where they are usually played." Her voice curled at the end of sentences when she was being coy. I loved that I knew that about her already.

"Alright, hotshot. You should take me to a movie."

"Cool. Hope Springs is playing. Meryl Streep and Tommy Lee Jones. Unless you're into hard hitting action, in which case we've got Expendables 2 just out." she rattled off. I eyed her suspiciously.

"You just happen to know this?"

"I had hoped it might be a thing. I did some homework." She smiled sheepishly.

"I haven't seen a movie in 7 months. Alright, that's not true. I have attended several movies in the last seven months but my head wasn't really with it. I understand how weird that sounds, but it's true. I don't care which movie we see. As long as I get to spend more time with you, I'll be good."

She halted her movement in midair to look at me with eyes that suddenly felt vulnerable and intimate. Then she smiled a sweet smile that kind of made my knees go soft. God, how many smiles did this woman have in her arsenal? "It makes me happy that you think so. I feel that way too."

As we got up, and ready to go, she dropped money for the coffee and doubled it for a tip. I was impressed. I would've tipped that waitress a punch in the throat, but only because she was looking at me funny, and I'm unreasonable in my constant state of hunger. I liked that she was a good tipper. I don't know why all this jumped out at me all of a sudden. It was like a lot of puzzle pieces in a puzzle I had struggled with for ages, were finally looking like they had potential to fit. When we reached the exit, she held the door open for me, and I laughed.

"Nobody holds doors for women around here usually."

"Chivalry isn't quite dead yet." she responded, and I hoped she was right. "Do you want to follow me there, or will you ride with me? I'll take you back to your car after, obviously."

"I'd like to ride with you." I did. I felt completely at ease with this woman, despite having just re-met her yesterday. I had thought Daniel was a good guy and he wasn't really. I had felt fine around him, but he was still production and I hadn't really gotten that close to him. Perhaps that was him, I don't know. But with Jane I was closer in less than 48 hours, than I had been with, well, anybody before. It wasn't because we had been intimate like that really, but there was just a feel to her. An unforced intimacy. I was acutely aware that this could be a mirage born of carb deprivation, but I had spent my whole life being skeptical. I trusted nothing around me right now with all the TV show make believe and this woman hadn't done anything except give me an orgasm and leave without so much as stealing a t-shirt the last time we were together. So, I was going to go with it. I got in her car, and buckled up. It was comfortable, and smelled weirdly nice.

"Sorry for the mess." she said, as she got in. I looked around.

"What mess?"

"Oh, isn't there one? How lucky."

I laughed. She smiled her smug smile. It was perfect, and fast becoming my favorite thing. She pulled out of the parking lot, and headed toward the theater. I looked out of the window, and felt a peace I hadn't felt in months. Like I was finally somewhere I was supposed to be. Like I was in the process of making a right choice. For once in my life. I mean, Expendables 2, c'mon, of course I was making the right choice.

It was a short drive. Anchorage isn't that big really. She parked, and we got out. It wasn't terribly crowded, and she bought us two tickets to Hope Springs.

"It's more of a proper date movie." she said. Good thing she was in charge of getting the tickets.

"So, we are on a date?" I asked. It was rhetorical, I suppose, but I kind of wanted to hear her say it.

"Absolutely." Perfect. "Would you like anything from the concession?"

"Uhm." I began, and felt a strong urge to share popcorn with her in the theater, but then felt shitty for considering eating popcorn. "Just a bottle of water, I think."

"Extravagant. I like it." she said, and shot me a deadpan glance that made me chuckle out loud. It cracked her up. "I like your laugh."

"I like you." I said before I thought it was perhaps too forward. Then again, we had actually slept together so it was probably ok to throw caution to the wind. I was always direct, if nothing else. She didn't respond, but her face and eyes told me it wasn't too forward at all. We headed into the half empty theater, after she got me a bottle of water, where the previews were already playing, and found some decent seats. The movie was not bad. I didn't honestly keep my focus on the movie a lot, so it was pretty much like every movie I had seen in the last months. About ten minutes in, my elbow on the armrest touched hers, and I felt like I was back in high school again. Middle school even, thinking "I hope she likes me. Did she feel us touching?" It was the weirdest thing. I had slept with her already, and now here I was nervous about touching her elbow. I looked at her hands resting on her thighs. We had touched yesterday, but she had been drunk. And today in the coffeeshop, but that was different. Now we were in a theater. On a date. It was pretty cliché, and I kind of loved that. It was a classic setup. And this time, with no Dawn doing squats in the back to fuck it up. I tried focusing on the movie again. It was a sweet middle aged romcom. I hadn't ever been to the movies with a date who not only was ok with, but suggested a romantic comedy. Usually it was a fight. Not that I don't enjoy big loud action movies. They are fun. But I was a sucker for cheesy romantic comedies. The ones Lifetime or Hallmark produce two of a day, with nondescript actors you vaguely remember seeing in something else are a staple for me at Christmas, like eggnog. And it was usually a solitary endeavor for me watching those. My mind kept drifting to her. I thought about pulling the old yawn and stretch move, but she was taller than me, and it would've been awkward. Plus, did anyone actually do that in real life? I didn't have to wait too long though, before she put her hand on mine. She took my hand in hers and I felt her fingers run along mine slowly like they weren't sure of their ground. I felt my heart beat a little faster, and when I spread my fingers and let hers slide between mine, and we locked them together, it felt like a bond was forged. One I didn't really understand, but also one I didn't have to understand. It felt instinctively right. The rest of the movie floated by in a haze of contentment. She whispered a few hilarious comments to me underway, and I quipped back. We giggled like kids, and not once during the movie did her hand leave mine. When the credits rolled, we both sat for a while, not wanting to break the connection. She moved first, with a sort of apologetic shrug of her shoulders. We walked out with her arm around my shoulder, my body pressed against hers. I could almost hear her heartbeat, and I wasn't sure I ever wanted to stop listening. We got in her car and drove towards the coffee shop. I wanted to talk. To talk about **all** the things. But I didn't want to break things either. This is fucking surreal. I want to look around for cameras because this shit does **not** happen in real life. What alternate universe am I living in that I ended up on reality TV six months ago and now my life looks like a fucking rom com? I don't want an answer to that. I understand this is unbelievable, but it was fucking happening and I wanted it to go on. She pulled in and parked, and we both got out of the car, and stood between her and my car for a second. I looked up at her. Her smile turned to concern, and when she was about to say something, I let it pour.

"Jane. I don't know exactly what is happening here. You and I, I mean. Or anything really. My whole life. Wait, give me a second to regroup. I know I sound insane. I decided six months ago I would move to New Hampshire after I finished the part of the show that happens in California, because I have a scholarship to law school there. My plan is that I'd work there while I worked out and lost more weight before I have to go back to the show in December. I'm leaving in two days. I didn't expect I'd run into a- well, a **you**. I mean, I meant to meet someone, and just sort of hook up. That sounds terrible-I know but it's true and then you. You and this whole meet-cute thing that really happened and this shit isn't supposed to really happen outside of Meg Ryan movies or whatever. I just, I really feel bowled over by this here now. I want to explore it because this doesn't happen to *real* people. I want to see what it is, but I'm also scared that if I do, I'll get distracted. I don't know what to do, all I know is I don't want this to end yet. I feel like there is something here, but I don't know if that's fair to you. I'm scared that by saying this, you will disappear and I am not sure what I'd do if that happened. Also, I may be crazy and I haven't had a refined carbohydrate in months so I'm a little worried I'm hallucinating all of this."

"Tisa." she said, as she pushed some of my hair behind my ear and took my hand in hers. "I don't want this to end either. Things may not be ideal with you going away, but I am not prepared to let you completely out of my life again, I wanted to call after New Year's but you hustled me out without your number and I took the hint. This feels like I've gotten a second chance. I want to explore this too."

"Yes?" my heart was racing, and I wanted to crawl into a little hole and escape my own anxiety that I was scaring this woman away.

"Yes." She stepped closer to me, and looked into my eyes. I couldn't have looked away if I tried. My heels left the ground without me realizing it, and I was on my toes leaning into her. Her one hand was around my back, and her other hand was touching the side of my neck just behind my ear. It sent shivers of delight down my spine. Her fingers brushed against my jawbone, and I felt her hand on my back tighten a little. Both my hands were on her stomach, and I could feel her pulse beat through her shirt. "Absolutely." And then our mouths met, and I don't know how long passed. I disappeared into the softness of her lips, and the incandescence of her eyes. Her tongue very carefully circled mine, with a reluctant passion, that increased the longer we kissed. I closed my eyes, and lost track of who did what. Her mouth was so warm on mine, and her hands so firm in touching me. If the world had ended just then, I would've died happy.

The world didn't end. The kiss did, however, with me drawing breath, and her straightening up again. I felt dizzy, and was happy she was standing so close, so I had something to lean on. What felt like minutes passed, before either of us spoke. I was the one who broke the silence.

"Please don't let this be the last time we do that."

"It won't be." She smiled at me, and I trusted that she meant it. "I have some plans tomorrow. I would like you to be a part of it. If you want to."

"Plans?" I asked, not sure what she meant.

"Yes. Let me rephrase that. I am making plans for tomorrow, and I would very much like you to be a part of them." She looked at me inquisitively.

"Yes!" I said loudly. "Yes. I would like that very much."

"Good. Then I will text you details." she said, with a determined smirk on her face. "I look forward to seeing you tomorrow."

"That is mutual." I said, as I took a step towards my car.

"Sleep well, Tisa." she said, and winked at me. "And thank you for a perfect first date." With those words, she entered her car, and started it up. I walked around my car and got in, as she was pulling out. After she had left, I sat in my car for a few minutes, closed my eyes, and relived that kiss again a few times. I could still feel the buzz on my lips from hers, and how her hand had held my face. I was going to sleep well tonight for sure. The faster it would be next morning, the better. But until then? I needed to get my ass to the gym.

8/13/2015

Like I told Jane, I had toyed with the idea of moving to New Hampshire for the remaining months before the finale, so I'd be closer to where I had been accepted to law school, while I further whittled away my body. When I was in Maine doing my grand homecoming bullshit, I discussed it with my dad and solidified the plan. After I did the coming home to my proper state thing, he would fly up to help me pack a car, then drive to New Hampshire. I didn't have any responsibilities keeping me in Alaska when I knew I had to leave for law school, other than my goldfish. And my goldfish had died. It made more sense to be somewhere closer to school.

Dad arrived at ten. I had already spent two hours running at the gym before I showered and picked him up at the airport. I was mildly annoyed at having to break my workout to pick him up. As we drove into town, he gave me the old dad routine.

"Don't blow this, Tisa," It was hard to interpret exactly what he meant, so I just nodded without moving my eyes from the road. It was a statement. One that didn't require an immediate answer. As soon as we arrived at my place, he got started on packing things up. Before I left for the show, I had sold off or given away a lot of my stuff. It's a thing I do when big changes come along. I clean out. The idea of moving for school had been around since before the show, so it made sense. We got things stuffed into a few boxes and suitcases, then took it all to the car. I was putting a suitcase into the backseat, when my dad picked up the sort of conversation from earlier—as if we hadn't just spent an hour and a half doing something else.

"I'm serious, Tisa. Don't blow this."

"Blow what? How am I blowing it? I'm working out hours daily."

"Just don't blow it. It's a huge chance for you," great, now my dad and the show were reminding me how lucky I was to be selected and I had a responsibility not to waste this chance.

"I'm not." Thanks for the pressure, dad. What the hell? "I'm doing everything I can," I pushed a blue IKEA bag filled with clothes into the back seat.

"Good. I expect you to take this all the way," What the fuck was he talking about? I didn't have the energy to figure this Dad speak bullshit out. I haven't lived with my parents for years; I am pretty sure their advice is optional at this point. He put a box into the back of the car and surveyed the work. He seemed satisfied. "What are we eating today?"

"I've actually got plans, dad," I said.

"Plans? We leave early in the morning, you know," He looked gruff. Not because I had ditched him for other plans, he didn't care about that. But because he was practical and he'd pull me out of bed at five a.m. to get on the road, no matter what time I'd gotten into bed.

"I know. It's just dinner." I didn't actually know what it would be but I assumed dinner, because people usually eat dinner during evenings. Normal people do, at least.

"Dinner?" He fixed me with a scrutinizing look. I could see the little cogs turning in his head. "Don't you bl..." he started.

"I won't," I cut him off. Enough about messing things up. I worry about that enough for the both of us. I won't let anyone down, being ungrateful or disappointing anyone is my worst fear. How does my Dad not know this?

As we went inside again, I got a text from Jane, asking if she could pick me up. I went to take a shower and went to put on clothes that didn't make me look like I had just stepped out of a 1980s boxing movie montage. Jane arrived 20 minutes later. I wasn't quite prepared to have my dad meet her and especially not prepared to have her meet my dad, so I just grabbed my phone and wallet and told my dad I'd be back later. I didn't feel bad about leaving him. He had my car if he needed to go anywhere, and he had lived in Anchorage for years himself.

He knew what was going on. I rushed to Jane's car, and got in. The day felt significantly better already.

"Hello," she said cheerily, as I buckled up. "How's your day?"

"Meh," I said. "My dad's, well, my dad. We communicate, but I'm not sure either of us really know what the other is saying. I got my shit packed up though. So, there's that." I sighed.

"Still going, huh?" she asked, with a smile.

"Yes. It's the smart thing to do." We both sat for a second in silence. I wished I didn't have to leave AK now, even if I knew I should.

"Thank you for yesterday," she said, breaking my train of thought and throwing it to our kiss. "I had a really good time."

"Me too," I said, genuinely enthused by the thought. "The kind of night I wouldn't mind a reprisal of."

"Well you're in luck," she said, smirking.

"Oh?" I looked at her. God she was a beautiful woman. I patted myself on the back for having good taste, even through a New Year's Eve vodka induced haze.

"Well since yesterday was sort of impromptu, I thought perhaps I should arrange a proper classic date." she said, as we turned toward downtown. "So, I've booked a table for us at a nice Italian restaurant. Not too fancy, but I read reviews of it, and it looks cozy."

"You read reviews?" I forgot to feel anxious about the idea of going to a restaurant and not eating. My crazy shining through and her running away screaming because of it and was instead amazed at someone taking this sort of initiative. Though I'm wondering how I disguise the fact that I am only pushing my food around on my plate?

"Yes? How else am I supposed to know if it's worth taking you to?"

"Well, I guess," I started, but I didn't really know where to go with it. "That's true. I'm just not used to that sort of thing. Someone doing that before we go out, that attention to detail."

"Well I'm not used to someone like you. You make me feel like doing special things." She flashed a look at me that made me feel like I could jump into her arms and live there forever. I didn't have an answer to that. I couldn't even smile. Just stare. We made more turns, as she maneuvered the city. Finally, we parked in an area of Anchorage I wasn't even sure I had ever been in before. It was nice. She led me to a small restaurant with classic red and white checkered table cloths, and crispy bread sticks on the table, along with olive oil. There were black and white pictures of Italian cityscapes and countryside's on the walls, and I think Gypsy Kings were playing from small speakers above. It smelled of rich newly baked bread. Despite it being 6pm, there weren't a lot of people here.

"One of the reasons I picked it, was because it seemed like an undiscovered diamond in the rough." Jane said, as I gazed around the place, feeling like it was the most amazing little place I had ever been. She put her hands on my shoulders, and I automatically leant back towards her touch, as my heart skipped a beat. A waiter came up to us and led us to our table. It was casual and still I felt woefully underdressed. Jane was wearing jeans and a t-shirt, so it wasn't like I was standing out. It just felt so date-y, that it kind of brought my mind to movies of the old days, where dates always involved skirts or dresses, and had their hair done, as they nibbled a little cheese from a Rome sidewalk cafe, and chit chatted with every passerby. Jane took a menu and handed it to me, and I was brought back into the reality I had kind of dreaded. Food selection. I was so hungry, but I hadn't worked out as much today as I had wanted to, and if I ate some of this food, I might go above my calorie count for the day. Granted I hadn't eaten anything but a little processed meat, and this was a date after all.

"Anything take your fancy?" Jane asked me, after I had stared blankly at the menu for a good two minutes. I looked up and met her gaze, and I think she might've recognized my anxiety. "It's ok if you aren't too hungry. As long as it's okay that I am." she said with a smile that conveyed sincerity. No judgment or condemnation. No opinion or wagging fingers. Just a wish for me to have a pleasant evening. I smiled back.

"I think a salad would be amazing." I said. "All of this looks really amazing." It did.

"You can always have some of mine, if you feel like it." she said. She shared food? She shared food. My smile widened. The waiter came over with water, and we ordered food right away. Jane had a glass of wine too. It was so nice at this little place, and I felt relaxed again soon. Even when our food came, it felt like everything was going to be fine. And it was delicious. We talked and laughed and I almost forgot, that I was leaving in the morning. I had a sip of her wine, and my cheeks blushed up. I was a lightweight. She chuckled, and I felt like she was laughing with me and not at me, and it made me chuckle too. I took her hand on the table and the date felt even better than those stupid ladies in their stupid sidewalk cafes. I'd much rather be in an Italian restaurant in Anchorage with this woman.

She settled up, and we headed to the car.

"Thank you for dinner. That was really amazing." I said.

"Of course. I have more planned, if you want." I looked at her with surprise.

"There's more? Food?" I half wanted to hit the gym and work through this salad. I dismissed the thought.

"No." she laughed. "Not food. Well food for the soul perhaps. I booked a room at a hotel, and thought you might the spend the night with me?"

"Yes!" I exclaimed, without thinking. She looked briefly surprised, then laughed. I smiled. "I thought you'd never ask." I clicked my tongue and winked at her. She smirked. We got in the car, and she pulled out onto the street. Her hand found my thigh and my blood felt like it was heated up a few degrees by her touch alone. I wanted her to break the sound barrier getting to that hotel. And she nearly did. We parked and went inside, but instead of heading to reception, we went straight to the elevators. When I looked at her quizzically, she merely smirked.

"I had banked on you agreeing and handled this earlier today." I whistled approvingly.

In the elevator, she put her hand on my shoulder, and I turned towards her and pulled her close. We kissed as both her hands almost engulfed my face close to hers. I couldn't get enough of her kiss, and when the bell dinged on the 20th floor, I wasn't aware if we had stopped or others had entered and left the elevator. She pulled me down the corridor to the room, inserted the key, pushed the door open and rushed us inside. I didn't notice anything. There was only her and I right then. Her lips found mine, and my hands grabbed her back. Her muscle and the curve of her shoulders drove me wild. I felt lust rush through me, and by the feel of the heat coming from her, it was mutual. Her hands were all over me, expertly caressing and grabbing me in a way I hadn't been touched for a long while. I wanted to get as close to her as possible. I couldn't get close enough. She toyed with me, and I floated away on the sensation. It was incredible to feel the slow and deliberate motions and I almost forgot my own mission in touching her.

I don't know how long we were connected, lost count of all the ways I received and gave pleasure. I didn't lose consciousness, but I was not quite present either. I was with her on some plane or wherever you go when things feel so incredible you aren't sure they are real. When I came back to reality, I was on my side, and she was behind me with an arm around me. I don't remember ever feeling so at peace. I think even my hunger had taken the night off. Her hand was in mine, and she was kissing my neck. I was still slightly out of breath, so it hadn't been that long. I could feel the echoes of an orgasm still tip toeing through me.

"Would you like a drink?" she asked me. I didn't want her to go anywhere. I wanted her close.

"No thank you. I'm good." I said. I was. Better than I could imagine. I wanted to stay in this bed for the next few months. Just live off of passion and sex. I could do it. I'm sure I could. Then guilt, even guilt for just considering it crept in. And a voice rang through my head, "Don't blow it Tisa. So many people would love to be in your place. Don't blow it." I hated that it took me away from this moment with Jane. It sobered me up. I had relented at the restaurant and had one sip of wine. "I have to go soon."

"I know." she simply said. It wasn't a snarky comeback. It was solemn and it was followed by a kiss that made it a little better. I turned around to face her, and she put her arm back around me and pulled me close.

"I don't want to go. But I have to."

"You do have to. It's the best for you." she concurred.

"I don't know when I'll be back. I don't know if I'll be back." I put my head on her shoulder nuzzling her neck.

"I know." she said again and paused. Her hand was rubbing my back and the sensation made me sleepy and content. "I want to see you again, Tisa."

"I would like to see you again too." I responded. God did I.

"Then it will happen. Because we want it." She pulled me in and locked her arms around me tightly. I got on one elbow and looked at her.

"Yeah?"

"Yep." she answered confidently, before her hand stroked my hips and grabbed my ass. "You have to go soon?"

"I have to go soon."

"How soon?"

"I don't know. Half an hour perhaps?" I looked at her. "Why?" She smirked. I should have known why.

After, as she was getting dressed, I grabbed her t-shirt off the floor.

"I'm taking this." I stated. It wasn't a request. She knew that. I put it on, and my hoodie over it. We both looked at my own t-shirt. Then she picked it up, and while looking me deadpan in the eyes, put on. It was tight. Way tight. I need to step up my game in the weight room. I looked at her. She looked at me. Then we cracked up. She looked ridiculous. Ridiculously sweet. She grabbed her keys and headed to the door. I gave her a look as if to say 'seriously?' She just smiled at me. I was about this woman. We rode down in the elevator together, hand in hand, through the lobby, with reception staff making confused eyes at her brand-new inadvertent crop top as we walked back to her car. As we drove towards my place we held hands. I didn't want to let go. We sat in the car a few minutes outside my house.

"I'll text you. A lot." I said. It felt like I was off to an arctic expedition with little hope of survival or return. I didn't want to cry, because it felt like it would be too much drama.

"And I'll text right back." she answered, kissing me, her hand on the side of my face, a gesture I took to wholeheartedly. I opened the door as she pulled away and squeezed her hand.

"Bye." I said.

"Until next time." she answered. We both smiled.

Inside my house, dad was asleep. I went straight to my bedroom, pulled out my sweat suit, put it on, and slid back out the door. I had half hoped Jane would still be sitting there in her car by the curb, but she had gone. I don't know what I would've done if she had. Probably something stupid. Instead, I made the sane choice. I went for a run, to work off that sip of wine and the salad.

Chapter 15

*L*eaving sucks. Who knew the random New Year's Eve woman from the bar would end up being so intriguing. Instead of exploring that further, kissing, going on dates and getting laid incessantly, I'm driving the Alaska Canadian highway. Actually, dad is driving the Alaska Canadian highway. I'm sort of running across North America. In the mornings before Dad got up, I'd bike or do the elliptical in the hotel gym, or swim in the pool. Then when he was stirring in his room I'd sprint off alone down the highway like Forrest Gump. *Run, Tisa, Run.* When my dad would catch up later in the day, he scooped me up off the side of the road. Then we drove for a while, taking in the scenery until noon where it was time for us— and by us I mean him-- to eat lunch at a truck stop or restaurant. I couldn't and wouldn't eat that food. Both because of the show and because I actually liked not dying from food poisoning. My dad apparently didn't care. He liked to live dangerously on things like egg salad sandwiches from vending machines. I lived almost exclusively on low sodium lunch meat and protein shakes I had packed in a giant cooler, which I filled with fresh ice every day from the hotels. A lot of people ditch their diets and exercise routines when they're traveling. Not me. If anything, I took this to the next level, with hours of daily workouts in my sweat suits in the middle of August heat. During the evenings, I would text Jane, and dream of me running the other way, back to what that might turn into. I felt like that was where I belonged, and I wondered when I would see her again. At night, I would go to sleep in the t-shirt I had stolen from her at the hotel before we said goodbye. I'd usually take it off soon after, because I preferred to sleep naked, and missed that habit at the Spa because I had a camera in my room 24/7. But I started the night in it because it felt like I had a little time with her when I was in bed in her shirt.

8/23/2015

We arrived in New Hampshire after me running my way across the continent. I found a small place to stay and a job teaching aerobics at the local Athletic Club. This enabled me to workout up to eight hours a day, under the guise of teaching other people and make money to keep myself rich in protein shakes. The job meant I could work out, without anybody thinking much of it. I noticed my dad looking at my excessive working out with a reserved frown while we were traveling. If he noticed it was excessive then other people might too. I needed to be careful. I got into a routine pretty quickly—wake up, text Jane, run, text Jane, go to work, text Jane in the breaks between classes, work out by myself after, go home, text Jane, sleep. It went well for a few days. My season had started airing on TV and because the target audience for the show largely corresponded to the people in my aerobics classes, I'd started to become something of a pseudo-celebrity. The pressure to eat less –I was barely hitting 1000 calories per day—and lose even more weight by the finale intensified exponentially, with the amount of attention I got from people. Word of mouth travelled and I saw more and more people in the gym. I wondered if this was the plan from my employers all along. Good plan on their part, if so.

I was between classes and trying to get an additional workout in on the treadmill, when three women lined up in front of me and began dissecting my appearance as if I were an animal behind glass at the zoo.

"She's so much bigger in person," one cried.

"I thought she'd be less fat by now," another responded, arms crossed while studying me intently.

"She doesn't look that great. She could be working a lot harder," the third agreed.

"I can hear you," I snapped.

8/30/2015

Days being in a routine became a week without my noticing time passing other than to mark how many workouts I put in, and my birthday was drawing closer. I didn't have any set traditions for my birthdays since I had moved around a lot as a kid. It was always decided when the time came. I felt kind of cooped up in New Hampshire. It was a place new to me and I didn't know anybody really. Dad had left and gone back to Maine again almost as soon as my last box was unloaded. I slept, worked out, worked and texted Jane. It wasn't really a routine that leant itself to lots of social interaction unless you count my three new friends from the treadmill incident at the gym. I decided to go to Las Vegas for my birthday for three days. Why not, right? I had a friend in Alaska whose birthday was close to mine, so we decided we would co-celebrate it in Vegas with another of our friends. I told Jane I wanted to go to Vegas for my birthday when we texted before bed.

"I've decided to go to Vegas for a few days, for my birthday."

"It's the place to be for a good time for sure." she responded.

"Have you ever been?" I hadn't actually ever been, so this was extra exciting for me.

"I went once, when I was like 16. My dad and I drove through, and we walked around the casinos just looking." she said.

"Aren't you supposed to be 21 to enter them?"

"I was tall for my age." I imagined her as a 16-year-old girl. She must've been super awkward. It made me miss her more.

"I'm gonna go with some friends. You met one of them after the bar."

"Amazingly enough with all the alcohol I had onboard, I do remember her." she replied. "I'm sure you guys will have a good time." I was sure we would. I almost regretted having made the plan now while texting her about it. I genuinely would rather be going home to Alaska to see Jane.

9/2/2015

The days seem to move so fast right now. I work out and I've cut my rations—as I had taken to calling the food I do eat—to the bare minimum. On the flight to Vegas I had water, declining the pretzels. It was an early flight but I still managed two hours on the elliptical beforehand with that *don't let everyone down* voice ringing through my head.

9/3/2015

In Vegas while everyone else was getting hammered and stuffing their faces at the buffet, I carefully rationed my measly calories so that I could have vodka, diet soda and vegetables from a cold-cut plate we ordered at the pool. Last night, I danced at the club until three a.m. but as everyone slept off their hangovers, I arose at six a.m. and worked out for three hours in the hotel gym. It's been about a month since I left the Spa, and I'm down a lot more weight. I'm not going to fuck up in Vegas and ruin my progress. I know that not sleeping or eating and drinking a bit with all this cardio is probably sketchy, but I look good —it's not like I'm emaciated —and production loves my weight numbers when I have to check in via email. Plus, I only worry briefly when I get dizzy if I stand too fast, or when my stomach hurts but that's easily killed off with more cardio. Exercising is healthy, so who cares if you do it nonstop until your skin rubs off from your sports bra? I just won't wear a bra. Problem solved. It is Vegas for fuck's sake, no one cares.

9/4/2015

Last night, we went out to a bar we found that had good music and a decent dance floor without too many annoying people. We bought drinks and danced. I was exhausted but powered through, because Vegas. The next thing I knew, Britta was shaking me awake in our room, looking anxious.

"Tisa. Tisa. Are you all right?"

"Yes, I'm fine. What are you talking about?" I looked at her, confused.

"Are you sure?"

"Yes. What's the matter?"

"I came back to the room and found you on the floor like this." I looked around. I *was* on the floor of our room.

"Uh," I started. I tried to remember what had happened. "On the *floor?*"

"*Yes,*" She stopped shaking me. "Are you *sure* you're okay?"

"I am," I sat up. I didn't feel more pain than usual anywhere. "Are *you* okay?" I don't know why I asked her that.

"Never mind me, Tisa. Do you remember anything?"

"Um, no," I racked my brain. Last thing I remember was being at the bar, dancing and drinking. Holy shit, I have no idea what happened since then. I've never experienced anything like this. For a second, I was mortified. Oh God, I am the human version of an after-school TV special, complete with heartfelt violin music and people who cared for me and didn't want me to get hurt. I wanted to melt into the floor and disappear.

"You said you were going back to the hotel gym because you wanted to run a bit before bed. Sound familiar? Nothing?" Britta asked.

"No," I looked down at myself. I was still in my heels and outfit from the bar. "How long ago was that?"

"A couple of hours. We just got in," Britta looked worried. I got to my feet, took my shoes off and went to the bathroom. I looked haggard. I had a glass of water before I went back in.

"Are you dizzy? Sick? In pain?" Britta kept asking me.

"No, I feel surprisingly fine. Must have been the alcohol knocking me out," I laughed it off nervously. I was a little worried, but I didn't want her to be. "I'm good. I should probably sleep though."

"Sounds like a good idea," she agreed.

Blacked out in Vegas. I'll add that to my list of accomplishments. At least they had carpeted floors in my hotel room. I still managed to wake up and do two hours of cardio before the flight home.

9/5/2015

When I got back from Vegas, I dumped all my stuff on the floor, shed my clothes and stepped on the scale. As I feared, despite managing to work out every morning in Vegas, I hadn't lost as much weight as I wanted. I blame alcohol and processed meat and regret going to Vegas. I should've gone to Alaska and had sex instead of drinking and eating. I ran and got my workout clothes to drive to the gym—breaking several traffic rules in the process. I didn't even greet my co-workers when I got there. Just rushed to the treadmill and started running. I had perfected the run and talk technique anyway, so I could answer questions like *how was your trip?* And *did you gamble?* And *did you get drunk and married to George Clooney on the Strip one night, oh my god why wasn't I invited?* while on the treadmill. I felt mildly panicked, almost feverish in my effort to work more weight off. I hadn't eaten since I blacked out on the hotel room floor almost two days ago in Vegas but I powered through because I know I need to lose more weight. I can't let the people who didn't get this opportunity down. I can't let my family down. I miss Esther. I miss Debbie. I miss Jane. I miss me.

9/6/2015

After I got back from my morning run, my phone rang. It was the show.

"Tisa, we need footage of you working out," a PA said, sounding like he was fresh out of high school.

"All right?" I responded, suddenly on alert. When. Where. What if I hadn't lost enough weight?

"We'll fly you to Alaska to film it. Next Monday."

"Okay, that works," I said, trying to sound cool and laid back. My insides were exploding in a mix of exuberance and wild uncontrolled panic. I was pretty exalted at the thought of seeing Jane. The thought of working out in front of a camera again made me nearly scream with anxiety however. What if they saw me and were shocked I hadn't lost more weight. What if I hadn't done enough? Did they know I just went to Vegas? Would they be mad?

"We'll film for a couple days. You'll get the details when you get there. We've arranged a pick up for you," he said.

"Thanks, but that won't be necessary. Just let me know where I need to be and I will be there," I responded, banking heavily on Jane picking me up. I'd prefer that, instead of another faceless driver/PA combination. Seeing somebody who actually gave a shit about me would be a nice change of pace from an anonymous driver or PA.

After I hung up, I paced the apartment feeling distraught. I texted Jane, that I was coming and asked if she would pick me up. Her reply was simply "Fuck yes!" It made me smile and eased some of the tension in my chest. I can't wait to see her. It seemed so far away all of a sudden. I nearly cried in frustration at everything. I needed to do better and to do that I realized I need a trainer who can get me that extra lost pound. The gym I work at has several available trainers, so I rushed to my car and drove there immediately, in hopes of catching one of them so I could start immediately.

Amber was just finishing up with another client when I arrived. I hung back for a few minutes until she was done, then pounced on her.

"Amber, I need to employ your services," I said, as I walked up to her.

"Oh, hi Tisa. What? Services?" she asked, looking surprised then confused. Probably not that often trainers asked other trainers to train them so abruptly.

"I am going back to Alaska to film and I need to up my game before I go," I hoped I didn't sound as desperate as I was. I didn't want concern or sympathy. Just her services in pushing me harder.

"You want me to train with you?" she asked, still confused. It was annoying me a little my patience is in short supply lately. My moods are actually all over the place, and I found people-ing difficult, but I needed her help.

"Yes. Just for this week. At least for starters," I said with some urgency. I wanted to get started right away.

"All right, Tisa. When do you want to start?"

"Well, now really, I guess," I looked her dead in the eyes, no flinching. I wanted to impress the importance of this on her.

"Uh, right. Well we can do that," she shuffled with some papers on the counter between us. "I'm free for a bit."

We started off with a few questions, mainly about my routine and diet. I dodged around the pitfalls because I wanted to get started with a program and not have to go over minute details about what I ate or didn't, and how much I worked out. She seemed to accept it, and my plan for losing some more weight before the shoot. This wasn't out of the ordinary. She saw me on TV and like most other people, she believed I was under dietary supervision on the show and given adequate tools to manage it after I was sent home. What she didn't know was, I practically counted calories in the oxygen I breathed and was scared of drinking water, lest I retain too much and gain the weight. She also wasn't at the gym all day, so she only saw me working out at small intervals. To my great relief, she didn't get too inquisitive and we went straight to work spending the rest of the day with her occasionally finding me in the gym between clients, to push me onwards. The last two hours she was practically one of those obnoxious guys at the side of the road during a marathon, who drunkenly and abrasively cheer for everybody as they run past. A welcome addition. I pushed myself and when I drove home, I felt beat. It hurt and I was dizzy but the feeling of really doing something was there and it was what I lived on now. I fought the urge to run laps around my living room until I passed out when my phone rang.

"Tisa, hey, it's Amber. I'm calling because I know I beat the mess out of you in the gym today but some of us from work are going out dancing. I know how obsessed you are with getting in cardio and thought you might want to come with?" she inquired. She was right, I needed something to distract me from my manic pacing. An activity that was cardio but wouldn't seem like working out might be just what I need. "Sounds good, I'm in. What time and where should I meet you?" I replied. I was going dancing.

9/7/2015

Amber dropped me off safely and without concerns because I guess the couple of drinks I did convince myself to have didn't concern anyone and I wasn't acting strange. I wasn't slurring my words or stumbling but I knew I was drunk. I haven't really been eating and I think coupled with all the cardio it caught up to me. A few minutes after Amber left I couldn't stand up anymore and I knew I was going to be sick. I had to crawl to the bathroom. I didn't make it, I started projectile vomiting in the hallway on my hands and knees at the threshold to the bathroom. I managed to drag myself to the tub after vomiting into the toilet but I was vomiting so hard that I shit myself. I couldn't stop. My whole body was wracked with cramping spasms of puking and defecating. I tried to pull myself into the tub to minimize the mess and I passed out.

I woke up this morning covered in my own filth with vague memories of dancing, a few drinks and a lot of badness when I made it home. I couldn't stop shaking. I don't know if that was from the lack of food or dehydration. I looked at the scene in the bathroom and began to cry. I was still feeling too weak to stand, so I pulled myself from the tub then stripped my ruined clothing off my body. The smell was terrible. I crawled to the hall closet to get cleaning supplies and spent the rest of my morning scrubbing the entire bathroom, taking breaks to sip water from the sink when the shaking and dizziness abated enough to stand. I finally managed to shower off the vomit and shit still stuck to me and had to throw away my clothing and bathroom rug. They were ruined. I crawled back to my bed and went back to sleep ashamed and scared.

9/8/2015

Over the next couple days, Amber was by my side for way more than she was charging me. She kept switching me up on machines and doing squats and push-ups. She tried to get me to lift more but I wiggled out of it. Cardio was my thing. I didn't want to start packing on muscle—the show practically forbade that strategy in women. It was about as much weight loss possible as quickly as possible and while muscle may be great in the long run. Building muscle would hypothetically make me stronger and burn more calories eventually, but building it would mean adding weight, I don't have time for that. This is a weight loss competition not a health competition, it's short term. More of a sprint goal not a marathon goal. Do what I need to do to cut weight not build a long-term healthier body.

I was at the gym running, when Amber showed up and still running when I promised to lock up at night after she left. I taught classes along the way but every spare moment I had, I was doing cardio. My feet were bleeding but filming was only days away and they had bled before while I was at the Spa so, I'm not worried. I promised myself I'd ease up a bit as soon as we had filmed. On Friday morning, Amber came in and I was on the treadmill already.

"Tisa," she said cautiously. "I noticed yesterday, when I got back from my afternoon clients, you were in the same spot I left you at four hours earlier. I checked the security cam footage and you didn't move at all. When are you eating? *Are* you eating?"

"No," I said, before I could stop myself. Stupid honesty instinct. "Not yesterday, no," I said trying to cover my blunder.

"And the days before?" She fixed me with a stern and concerned gaze. At that moment I loved her and hated her at the same time. It was nice to feel somebody giving a shit but I really just needed to lose weight for filming and don't have time to explain it all.

"A little," I said.

"Today?" She was hopeful, but I think she knew the answer.

"No."

"You *have* to eat. I know you don't think you do. I didn't know anybody could survive on sheer determination but you certainly seem to be trying. However, I won't train you anymore, unless you eat." For a moment I considered calling her bluff but she was good to me. She did this because she didn't want me to get hurt. I know that. Also, I wanted to keep her helping me. I needed her.

"Okay. I'll eat something," I said, hoping she'd accept that I meant I'd eat something when I got home. Which was a lie.

"I wasn't born yesterday, Tisa," she laughed. "You aren't getting away with it that easily." She walked to the staff desk and grabbed a protein bar. She handed it to me but I was running, and nearly tripped trying to reach for it. She looked at me accusatorily, then she cracked up again. "Tell you what. Here," she unwrapped it, broke off a piece and handed it to me. I ate it. She repeated this until I had finished the whole bar under her strict supervision.

"Thanks Amber," I said with all the snark I could muster. She knew I was sincere somewhere under my layer of resentful bullshit, even if I didn't.

I didn't eat more but it was important to her that I had something nourishing, however small, and I really was grateful for the gesture. Even if I went home without eating anything else. I texted Jane a screenshot of the countdown timer I had made in my phone with her name on it to remind her of how excited I was to see her again just before bed. I fell asleep stomach growling with the aid of a sleeping pill I'd managed to get from a local doctor because I was struggling to sleep through the hunger pains now.

9/9/2015

I woke up feeling like I was floating on air. Today I would get to see her again. I could barely finish the run I managed to squeeze in before I drove to the airport, because every few minutes I lost my concentration when she snuck into my mind. I had packed a lot of clothes because I wasn't sure what they were expecting, and if we'd be doing other shoots. You never really knew and while they'd sometimes provide outfits for shoots, ok, not really, unless it was sponsored by some brand, it wasn't a guarantee. My huge suitcase was checked for free, even though I was supposed to pay for it because the clerk had seen me on TV. I was mildly shaken by this as I moved toward my gate. I'm not ready for strangers to recognize me. Though I did enjoy the free luggage checking. As I sat at the gate, I surveyed the walkways around the airport and considered running laps on them while I waited for boarding to begin. I decided against it though. I was pretty sure that would set off someone's *there is a crazy person* alarm and mess up my travel plans.

The flights were long, even with a layover in Seattle where I was annoyed they didn't have a gym at the airport. I walked by a news stand that carried a magazine with me, Esther and Debbie on it. It was surreal and I looked around half hoping somebody would see it and marvel that I was there next to a magazine cover of myself, and half wishing nobody would ever see it, ever. It also made me miss Esther and Debbie all over again. I logically understand the show rule that we can't contact one another, but emotionally? I wondered if they felt a little lost without me too.

On the flight to Anchorage, I sat next to a lady who recognized me and spent almost the entire flight chatting about diets and *clean* eating. I wanted to rip her larynx out. I tried reading but she ignored it. Earbuds too. I felt like I had to smile and nod along to her crazy shit, because I was on TV and that's what people on TV are expected to do. Famous people do that, I think. Actually, real famous people probably have the money to insulate themselves from these weird interactions. I sat thinking about how strangers knew who I was. Or thought they knew who I was anyway. It's all sort of eerie because being filmed obviously meant I would be on TV but I don't think I got that it would mean people seeing me. I know how stupid that sounds, but I had just adapted to the idea of cameras just being there at the Spa not what the result of that would be.

When we finally landed, I rushed out of the plane before this lady could tattoo her contact details on my arm in an effort to connect more over how little we had each eaten that day. I envisioned lunch dates with her where no one actually ate and we discussed how many burpees it would take to burn off the full fat dressing the beast at the table next to us dare order. It felt like she wanted to be friends, to collect a pseudo-celeb friend. Get me the fuck away from that. As I exited the gate area, I saw Jane standing there and almost dropped my handbag running to her. She closed her arms around me and we kissed, and it felt like the breath of life blown into my body. A big cloud banished from above my head. I wanted to stay in that moment right there. I also wanted to get laid, however, and unless we found a slightly secluded spot in the parking garage, we should probably get to her place immediately, and make that happen. I pretty much exist solely on thoughts of sex, masturbation and, with any luck this trip, actual sex. It's all I have left. It's amazing how much sex seemed to be a substitute for food or sleep in my life now. Once at her place, she almost forgot to turn the car off and lock it, because we rushed in. We tore clothes off each other as we made our way to her bedroom. It was amazing to feel her hands on me again, and hear her breathing intensify as she ran my pulse up unlike any running ever could.

Hours later, after catching our breath and losing it again several times, as we lay naked together, Jane noticed the bruises on my thighs.

"Are you okay?" she asked, looking at me with genuinely concerned eyes. She brushed her fingers over them carefully.

"Oh yes. I bruise easily. It's just from working out," I reassured her. I did bruise easily, even if this was out of the ordinary. I had gotten so used to bruising at this point, that I had forgotten they were there. She seemed to accept it. I didn't want to get into this whole thing just then. I had to film tomorrow. I just wanted to be close and absorb as much of her as I could, while I had the chance. We ordered food, of which I had none, and spent most of the day touching and talking. Guilt over not working out before filming tomorrow was ever present in the back of my head, but I kept it together without freaking out. Eating wasn't an option though. I'm glad she didn't notice the newly formed bald spot on the right side of my head. I keep my hair short so when it started to fall out it took me awhile to notice it too, but my vanity had me thinking about it as we laid next to one another.

9/10/2015

I woke up at five a.m., with the sun shining brightly outside. We had stayed up late and had sex all night. I stretched. My body felt sore in the best way for once. It was nice to feel that kind of work out. I snuck out of bed, found Jane's keys, and snuck outside to the back of her car. I was wearing just a towel and only hoped it was still too early for anybody to be up and looking out their windows. My suitcase was still in the back of her car. We had been in a rush to get inside yesterday. I found my workout clothes, put them on under the towel, stuck the keys just inside the door, and started off on a run. It wasn't the longest run, because let's face it; a naked hot girl was in a bed, possibly waiting for me. It did quench a bit of the guilt I felt for not working out though. Back at her house, I saw my phone had an unanswered call. It was probably from production. Jane was up, and let her hands wrap around me from behind, as I was checking my phone.

"Later today, you should probably do that more." I said.

"Later today, I would probably want to." she answered. I smiled and enjoyed the remnants of her touch on my skin, as she went to the bathroom. I called the number. The adolescent who called me the other day picked up the phone.

"Tisa, we're filming at noon today." he said. At least he was concise. He gave me details on where to be and briefly what would happen. It was going to be at the park in Anchorage. I shuddered at the thought of being in front of cameras again, but a small part of me did feel that weird compulsion I remember from the Spa, at being on the show again. When there are cameras, I need to seem amazing and infallible.

"Where do they want you to go?" Jane asked, as she came out of the shower to dry off.

"Park strip downtown." I said.

"That's close to work. I'll drop you off and leave the car with you. You'll probably be done before I'm off work."

"How will you get to work?" I was genuinely concerned.

"I'll just walk. It's two blocks. I'll have coffee on the way. It's perfect." She smiled, and I wanted to jump her right then again. "I'll text you when I'm about done, and you can pick me up. I'll take you to dinner." That sealed it. I was jumping her.

After causing Jane to need another shower, we arrived in the parking lot of the park. I recognized the crew right away. They had several vans (even a few of my old friends the church vans) parked with lots of crew members milling about. We both got out and she came around to my side of the car, gave me the keys, and kissed me. I briefly hoped Daniel was on the crew today and saw me kissing this gorgeous wonder. Yeah, I'm still that petty. After Jane had strolled off, I went over to survey the crew and check in. I didn't see Daniel among the ten or so crew members and I assumed he had stayed far away from any outings to Alaska. Another PA recognized me and came running up.

"Tisa, good to see you," she said. It was pretty obvious she didn't mean it. "We'll be working out today on the field here."

"I had assumed as much," I replied, trying to look where production was set up on the field. The PA looked annoyed at my remark for a second, then regrouped.

"Did you bring some clothes? We want this to look casual." she mentioned, and looked around me, like I might have a spare wardrobe concealed about my person.

"Yes. In the car," I indicated half assed with a thumb. She stared behind me. There was a sense of urgency about her, which annoyed the shit out of me.

"All right. We have a changing area set up inside that van," she said, pointing to a church van.

"I thought you wanted to keep it casual," I said, then smiled sweetly. She pretended to be super busy with her clipboard and ignored me.

"You'll be working out with a group of people, so it looks like you're their instructor. We just need you to look like it's something you do all the time."

"Well that's easy. I do *do* it all the time. It's my job."

"Your job?" She looked confused like there was no way she could imagine me doing anything outside the context of this show.

"Yes, you know. What I do in exchange for money," I was super annoyed with this woman. One thing I have learned on this show—besides you do your crying in the shower—is how an instructor screams at a group of people to get them to work out and didn't need her pointers. While I don't teach aerobics that way, I knew what she wanted for the camera.

"Yes obviously," she said, as if she had known exactly what I meant all along and was just pulling my leg. I wanted to grab her clipboard and smack her. She looked at me, nodded and mumbled all right, before leaving me. I went to the car, got my suitcase out of the trunk and dragged it into the van. It was a very make do changing area, obviously, being a fucking van. It smelled like I always imagined the guy's locker room smelled in high school. Dank. I saw several people milling about, looking weirdly frightened or nervous. I locked eyes with one and she appeared to bow her head in reverence. Like I was a god walking among ants, and if you looked at me too long, your eyes would burn. I realized, that she, and the others, were some of the ones I would be training today. I wondered briefly what they had been told by production to induce this weird subservient attitude. Probably that they were lucky to be a part of this video and if they did well, perhaps they could be a part of the actual show next. I pitied them, whatever they had been told because it was most likely bullshit.

I changed into workout clothes and tried to keep it pretty homogenous in appearance. I knew they'd balk if I did something extravagant or crazy. My party girl show persona still couldn't pull off rainbow shorts and a pink top with shooting stars on it. Oddly, they provided someone to do makeup. At the end of the parking lot a folding chair, a mirror and a makeup table were set up. I walked down and was whisked into a seat immediately. I don't know what kind of makeup they were opting for, if I was going to be working out. I never wore any myself, whether I was working out or not. Not out of any devotion to looking natural, but out of pure laziness. A woman buzzed around me for a while, appearing to look busy, but when she was satisfied with her performance, urged me to look in the mirror before moving out onto the field, I could discern no difference in my appearance.

On the field, I was met with 20 people in matching outfits scattered around the little group of production assistants. When I was close enough, one of them came over to me.

"All right, Tisa. We want you to drill these people," she said.

"Drill them?" I was confused.

"Yes, you know. Give them a hard workout. We want you to appear to have brought some of the techniques home with you," she said, and looked around the place, like she was noticing it for the first time.

"Can't I just do it my own way?" I asked.

"Uhm, sure." She looked at me fleetingly, the kind of look I knew only too well from the Spa. It was the look you were given when they didn't want to tell you flat out no, but really wanted you to do what they said without personal influence or opinion inserted. "But perhaps utilize the techniques your trainer taught you."

"So, yell at them and threaten their lives while I look into a mirror? Got it." She chuckled at this. Clearly, she had experienced Shea, who was noticeably absent today.

"Something like that, yes." She stormed off to bark instructions at someone. I didn't really know if she was aware that our trainers hadn't taught us much of anything, except how to feel miserable beating up your body every day. Thirty minutes passed, where I stood around watching twenty confused people in matching outfits not really know what was happening. I felt like a grizzled TV veteran. I now knew that reality TV was ninety percent just waiting. Waiting, sweating and crying. These poor bastards I was "training" didn't and they looked baffled. Finally, someone called everybody to attention. Every one of the twenty people perked their ears like eager college freshmen on their first day hoping to hear something useful or not wanting to miss any information. They were given instructions to follow my lead and do what I did. Some of them shot me furtive glances before averting their eyes again. It felt ridiculous. They were distributed on the field in front of me and somebody indicated it was time for me to do my thing. I pretty much ran a standard workout from the gym in New Hampshire. One I had run many times. A few times production yelled at me to be harsher but I just didn't care. I hadn't ever bonded with Shea, so I couldn't channel her chi or whatever the hell they wanted me to do. A few of these twenty people looked like they were about to pass out and I didn't want anybody's death on my conscience. As I should have expected, no water had been brought out for these people (or me, for that matter, but I was used to it and didn't need it) and I felt awful for them.

I worked the folks over for some time, hoping they had some semblance of fun in the process. After they had been debriefed by a PA, no doubt warned not to say anything lest they would forfeit their lives and die from not being skinny, the PA from earlier came up to me again.

"We'd like to shoot some footage of you working out by yourself too."

"All right. I can run some laps if you want." I wasn't even really suggesting that for them as much as for myself. Teaching for the cameras hadn't much resembled a workout for me, and I needed to get some done soon. It was making me antsy.

"No. We'd like to drive you outside of town, by the mountains, and film you running a trail." She looked like she was afraid I would hit her with her clipboard. I couldn't blame her.

"All right. As long as you don't leave me out there to die," I managed a chuckle. She smiled, and I was pretty sure, if it was up to her, I wouldn't make it back. I'm not sure why really, because I had been on my best behavior all day. I wondered if the PAs had a betting pool going on the winner and she had bet on Farrell or something. I hung around for a while, as they packed up everything and stuffed it into the vans. I was grateful I didn't have to sit in the church vans, even if Alaska was significantly cooler than the Californian desert. They weren't comfortable vehicles. Finally, the PA indicated I should join her, and we walked to her rented car, a pretty standard Ford. As I was pretty sure this lady hated me, and I didn't care much for her, it was a silent thirty-minute drive to the outskirts of town, at the foot of mountains. Just one church van had made it there, and the camera people were already setting up and coordinating with sound. I got out and joined the crowd.

"We just want you to run," another PA told me. Finally, somebody made some sense.

"I can do that," I said. "I'm ready now."

"Oh, hang on a second. Let's just set the last part up," she replied, and rushed off to get people going. I waited for ten minutes doing nothing before we were finally ready. I ran back and forth with them shooting different angles, then did a few squats and some other bullshit for the cameras. They seemed happy with my performance, even if I felt like I was phoning it in. After about an hour of horsing around at the foot of the mountains, it was time to endure another fun thirty minutes of silence in the car as the PA took me back to Jane's car. She dropped me off in the parking lot, and I think I almost heard wheels spin on the asphalt, she was in that big of a hurry to get back to the airport. God help her if she had to spend one extra minute in Alaska or near me. After she had driven away, I realized I was left without a church van to change in, and I wasn't keen on driving in

Jane's car all sweaty. Fuck production. This was classic. I got into her car and drove to her house. There were still a few hours left before I had to go and pick her up, so I decided to go for a real run. The working out had been less than satisfactory today, and I wanted to run off some of my crazy before meeting with Jane again. I needed to lose more weight, and I didn't have Amber pushing me.

I stood outside the house for a moment after the run, trying to cool off a little more, and let the sweat dry before going inside. I was checking Facebook to waste a little time while I cooled off. I saw a message pending and half hoped it was Jane even if there wasn't any reason she would message me there instead of just text. It was from a name I didn't recognize. I figured it was somebody from school reconnecting like most of the people I had on my friends list. People you didn't particularly like in the first place, now pushing their social media lives on you and expecting the same in return. It wasn't anybody from school. It was somebody who had seen me on TV.

I hate your fat ugly crying face in that show and your stupid retarded family. Why don't you just do everybody a favor and drop out. That way the world doesn't have to look at you. Go cry by yourself you stupid bitch. You're annoying, I hope they vote your fat ass off if you won't quit.

I read it twice, not quite sure what I was seeing. I felt a lump in my throat and my breathing was suddenly troubled. If I hadn't been outside already, I would've had to step outside. Hate mail. This is a first. I have always prided myself on not caring too much what others think of me, mostly I tried to care what I thought of me. It still stung though—being told I'm an ugly crier—even if it's by some completely random stranger. I tried to figure out what the hell this was all about and realized the episode where I got greetings from my sister's kids had just aired. Some rando felt the need to take time out of their busy life to tell me I was ugly and refer to my special needs niece and nephew as retarded. Classy. I was shaking slightly and wanted to be anywhere else but standing in a driveway smelling of sweat and reading this message. I wished Jane hadn't been at work. I didn't feel comfortable disturbing her during office hours, and I wasn't sure I wanted her to know about this yet. I was embarrassed by it, and it annoyed me, because I shouldn't be. On the bright side this fucker was going to be quite disappointed when I made it to the finals.

On the way into the house I started critically analyzing the day and felt woefully inadequate in my work out segment. They kept interrupting it, and wanting more, Shea style but I didn't deliver. What if my performance wasn't good enough? I hadn't lost a lot of weight since I flew out of New Hampshire, and the fact that the number on the scale hardly budged was getting to me. Add my new hate mail in the mix and I was stressed. I had managed to excuse my lack of weight loss with flights and water retention but it was nagging at the back of my head.

I was feverishly moving about Jane's house, torn between working out for the third time today and trying not to flip my shit when she texted.

"Are you still out?"

"No. I'm back. Thought about going for another run. When are you done?"

"In about an hour. I'm hitching a ride with a co-worker, though, so you don't have to come all the way down here again." This pleased me. I'd like to get the extra minutes with her but the less driving and more running time was better as far as I was concerned.

"Good. I'll see you soon," I almost started running before I was out the front door. I needed to zone out, and running was my escape.

An hour later, I was back at the house, as sweaty as I had been at the work out filming. I stripped naked, and walked around Jane's living room on the carpet, curling my toes. It was a trick I had learned when I was a kid, to combat anxiety. It helped very little today. I went into the bathroom to shower. The water was heating up as I stood standing in front of the mirror staring and picking out my flaws. All the loose skin and oddly placed pockets of fat on my new body mocking my work in the gym. It felt like my body was sneering at my restraint in barely eating *nice try fatty you'll never be perfect.* I noticed a scale at the side of the counter. I debated whether or not to step on it. I knew I couldn't resist but I desperately tried to fight it. I wanted to spend my time there with her, not obsessing over pounds and ounces. I stepped on the scale. The number showed and my heart sank. I stepped off and looked in the mirror again. I was completely naked. No clothes I could drop. Nothing more I could shed. I hadn't lost any weight since Friday. I don't understand it. The scale was still showing my weight. I stepped on it again, in disbelief. The same weight showed. I felt desperation well up inside me, and my hands clenched. Why the hell didn't I drop more weight? How was I going to win, if I kept stagnating like this? I must not be working hard enough. Tears formed in my eyes, and I hated that they did, but I was overwhelmed. My knees felt wobbly. I stepped off the scale and stepped into the shower without having to think about what I was doing because muscle memory from the show guided me. I know the shower is where you cry. Tears were streaming freely, mixing with the water and I sank to the floor while sobbing hysterically.   My sobs in the shower were so loud I didn't hear the front door or Jane calling out to me. I had locked the door to the bathroom out of habit and being in a new place. Jane nearly kicked it down, trying to get to me. Not until she turned the water off and was crouched in front of me, putting her hand on my shoulder, did I really notice. I couldn't articulate what was wrong, and she didn't ask me. She just wrapped a towel around me, half picked me up and carried me to her bed, where she put me under the covers and got in next to me. I sobbed quietly against her, as she rubbed my back and stroked my hair until I dozed off, exhausted. Exhausted by so many different things.

I woke up hours later, by Jane entering the room with a tray. At first, I was confused by where I was and the fact that I was immediately aware that I was naked. Then I remembered I was somewhere I *wanted* to be, and that being naked was the best possible state of being for where I was-in Jane's bed-and I sank back down on the pillow.

"I know you don't eat a lot," Jane started, diplomatically, "But I thought you should have a little something. I think you were exhausted." She put the tray down, and it had a small selection of meats and cheese, accompanied by some avocado. There was also a protein shake.

"When did you get this?" I asked, as I looked at the veritable cornucopia of goodies.

"I bought it when you said you were coming up. I wanted to have something for you," She smiled at me, and stroked my cheek as I looked at her with what I'm sure could only be described as dreamy eyes. I didn't know if I would eat any of it, but I really liked how she had thought of me. She laid down next to me and grabbed a piece of cheese. I had calmed down significantly, in no small part due to her presence next to me. She was like human Xanax. Her hands on my skin was like balm on my soul. I took a sip of the shake. She wasn't watching me like a hawk, and I really appreciated that.

"Thank you." I said, as I put the tray down at the foot of the bed.

"You're welcome." she responded, as her hand ran down my spine. It gave me goosebumps and made the last of my anxiety dissipate. I leaned toward her and our bodies melted together in that instant. This was the kind of workout I never got tired of.

I got out of bed, sweaty for the fourth time today. I really did want a shower this time. Jane was in bed, propped against pillows, catching her breath. She smiled at me as I walked around the bed towards the bathroom. A few steps away from the door, I paused briefly and she noticed.

"I hid the scale," she said, not taking her eyes off of me.

"You *what?*" I squeaked, unsure I had heard her correctly.

"I hid it. I figured it was part of the problem earlier," she said, fixing me with a warm look. Her pleasant smile told me she took me seriously and that she had done this for me. "It is tough to be here, I'm sure, and be split between what you have to do and what you want to do and I felt like hiding the scale might make that choice a little easier for you."

My initial reaction was panic and a flash of anger. How dare she try to control what I was doing. Then I realized I wasn't even in control of what I was doing, so maybe the hidden scale wasn't such a *bad* idea.

"That's very thoughtful of you," I said, and rushed the rest of the way to the bathroom before I let my starved mind confuse me into lashing out in anger instead. "I mean that," I shouted from the bathroom, having realized me rushing off might've felt insincere.

"There is a certain amount of selfishness involved." she chuckled. "I don't deny wanting as much of you to myself as possible when I can."

"Well, you can have as much as you want. When you want," I replied, and turned the water on, leaving her to reflect on what that might entail.

9/13/2015

The next days in Alaska were spent mostly in her bed and running when she was at work. She got up early and left for work, as I went out running. She took half the day off so she could be home earlier. I ran for a few hours and showered before she got home, and we jumped in bed again, had sex and talked. She ate plates of various things. It could've gone on forever as far as I was concerned but I had to get back to New Hampshire and get serious. More serious. I had to lose more weight. Jane took me to the airport, and we sat in the car for a few minutes at the curb. Neither of us wanted to say it, but we both felt it. It was rough to leave somebody you never wanted to be without. She squeezed my hand a final time, and we got out. She pulled my suitcase out and put it on the curb before she pulled me close and kissed me.

"Until next time," she said and smiled at me. I didn't want her arms to loosen their grip.

"Until next time," I repeated. Getting on the plane sucked. I missed her immediately. Also, I was so hungry. That didn't help.

9/16/2015

As soon as I had landed in the airport, and dropped my stuff off at my place, I went to the gym, and found Amber. Playtime was over. It had been ages since I left the Spa and I hadn't lost nearly as much weight as I had thought I would. I'm sure this was my fault for wasting time on trips to Vegas and romance.

I was going hard at it from early morning until late at night, teaching my classes in between working out myself. Amber kept prompting me to eat, so sometimes I would grab a protein bar when she was looking and take a bite as I went to the staff room then spit it out as soon as she couldn't see me anymore. I'd spit it into a napkin and fold it up, in case somebody went through the trash or passed the trash can and saw a half-chewed bite of protein bar. I feel guilty even drinking too much water. Coffee is the only beverage I allow myself on a regular basis. I eat sugar free gelatin at night when I get home, just before I pass out with my phone, vibrator and texts from Jane in my hand. I'm back in my routine and feel like I'm getting somewhere.

My phone rang while I was working out.

"Tisa, have you seen it yet?" my sister said, as soon as I picked up the phone. I was just getting off the treadmill and was still out of breath.

"Hello to you too sis, have I seen what?"

"Your medical records. They're posted online." She sounded freaked out. I wasn't sure what she was talking about. Why would my medical records be posted online? That made no sense.

"What are you talking about? My what?" I said, annoyed. She sighed sounding exasperated instead of just telling me what was up, and it felt like she was playing this for drama.

"Somebody accessed your medical records and posted them online," she said, speaking rapidly.

"Are you fucking kidding me?" I screeched, and my head started spinning.

"No. It's real. Go check it out."

I said goodbye, and immediately searched the internet. It took me a few moments, but there it all was. My medical records from the hospital in Alaska, going back literally to my birth for everybody to see.

As I read the post I realized that a wretched woman working at my OB/GYN's office had accessed my medical records and posted it on the Internet all because she hated me. She had never even met me. She hated the me from TV. I stared at everything in my medical life laid bare for the world. Complete strangers could see I had broken my arm at twelve, they knew I had an abortion as a teenager, they even knew what I weighed at my last doctor's visit. I thought I might black out from hysteria. My first thought was to call Jane. She picked up the phone on the first ring and was immediately aware that I wasn't okay.

"What's the matter?" she said, almost shouting to be heard through my sobs.

"Somebody accessed my medical records and posted them online," I said, managing to put together a full sentence. I was in my car in the parking lot at work, huddled in the back seat where I could remain somewhat hidden from view.

"Are you shitting me?" she asked, clearly pissed off on my behalf.

"No. Everything. My whole life. Posted for everybody to see." There was a moment of pause, where my sniffles were the only sound. Then Jane spoke and her voice had changed from the soft warm voice I was so fond of, to a cold collected one, where anger was lurking menacingly just under the surface.

"Tisa, I will handle this. Go home and don't do anything about it until you hear from me, all right?" I nodded, before I remembered she couldn't see me. I clearly couldn't handle this, I didn't even know if I could drive I was shaking so badly. I needed to be told what to do here. I felt so fucking violated. Of course I would do what she said, I don't know what else to do.

"Ok, I will."

We hung up, and I searched around the internet for a while because I couldn't stop myself. It wasn't everywhere but the woman had posted them to some forum, and it had been picked up by a few outlets. The woes of being a *star* I guess I thought bitterly. I finally was able to get behind the wheel of my car and drive home. For once not focused on obsessing over needing to work out more. This exposure of my life to the world is new to me, and it's scary. I got home and crawled in bed. It felt safe and I lamented the fact that Jane wasn't there with me. Everything felt better with her close. I dozed off, as I laid there and was woken by the phone still in my hand. It was Jane.

"It's handled. Obviously, the records are irrevocably out but for what it's worth, the lady responsible has been identified and will be fired. I'm sorry I can't physically remove it from the internet. I've called an attorney friend to make sure that the privacy violation gets reported to the government, he assured me both she and the office will be investigated."

"Thank you so much," I said, and broke into tears of relief. Not that the immediate problem had been solved—having somebody who cared enough to handle something I couldn't right now was comforting. After so many months on the show basically trying my best to stay afloat with people pushing me down all the time, it was weird having somebody selflessly take time to combat something that wounded me because I was unable to fight back against it on my own right now.

"I'll stay on it and follow up with the attorney. He will be calling you. And if you trust him, he will handle it. I also know a woman in the hospital administration connected with the office, and I'll keep her primed. This shit will not stand," she sounded steely still, but I could sense some of the warmth return to her voice and it brought me peace. "This lady who released your medical records is clearly way too invested in reality TV and ignored her patient privacy training. Like I said, she will at the very least be terminated but I am hoping for more."

"I just don't get it," I said. I didn't. Was I so easy to hate just from being on a TV show? What motivates a person to dislike someone they don't know so much that they would expose their most personal information?

"There isn't much to get, Tisa. She is a shitty human being, who can't grasp the consequences of her actions. She'll pay for it."

"Thank you again. I really appreciate it," I said. I would've loved to fall asleep in her arms right then.

"For you? Anything," she responded. I knew she meant it. It brought me calm to know somebody out there had my best interest at heart. We said our goodbyes, and I got up. I was having an increasingly hard time keeping my shit together. Being near Jane helped. But in lieu of that, I really only had one thing that gave me peace, and that was running. I drove back to the gym and got on the treadmill. It hurt but at least the pain overshadowed the dread I felt at the thought of people wanting to hurt me and the further grief having my medical records released online was sure to cause me.

9/18/2015

My phone rang. I live in a bubble with very little social life outside of the gym, so the phone ringing was unusual. I was on the treadmill when it did, obviously, and it made me nearly face plant from shock when I saw the name on the display. It was Shea. She called to inform me that Farrell was *kicking my ass* and to *step it up*. Thanks for that added pressure. I guess she imagined I was coasting along here, not a care in the world. Producers already required not only frequent email check-ins with my weight and a list of food I was eating, they were also sending me propaganda messages like, *You can be the first female to have a shot at it*. And *don't let everyone down*. Just in case I wasn't taking things seriously. My temper is on full blast and my nerves are shot, a powder keg when you also have an empty stomach and constant scrutiny. Apparently, in addition to hating me enough to put my medical records on blast for the world the internet tells me people think I'm ugly when I cry, and mocks the most vulnerable members of my family just for the fun of it. Now Shea calls to tell me I'm not doing enough. Cool. I have no idea where I'm going to find the energy but I have to step up my game. I don't want to let anybody down, not my family or all the people at home who don't have this opportunity, and least of all Jane. She sees me as strong, I can tell. I don't want to be weaker than she's already seen. The shower crying and medical record breakdown are cringe worthy enough when I ruminate on them.

I emailed a PA on the show and pleaded my case about why the scale wasn't moving, what more could I do? I was desperate. Amber was pushing me physically, but I couldn't share the nutritional tips I had gotten from the show with her, because they basically consisted of *Don't eat. Don't drink. Don't even think about it.* and she would be outraged. Something had to give though because if Farrell was kicking my ass, I needed to do better. The email was long and went over all my considerations and thoughts about food and diets and weight loss. I waited on the response with great anticipation, hoping they would have some cool insights that would tip the scale, literally. The response I got was short and useless, and I cursed myself for ever expecting anything else.

"Try dipping celery in water as a meal," the PA wrote back.

Great, thanks for the tip, genius. I'm starving. Everything on me hurts. I'm covered in bruises; my hair is falling out and my period has decided it's done with me. Every joint and muscle in my body hurt. But I can't stop. Bullshit PA advice or not. I'm losing the game by not losing weight and will have wasted a chance many other more deserving people wanted. I'll figure something out.

Chapter 16

Being back in New Hampshire feels lonely and empty. It's amazing how fast I got used to being near Jane, and how much not being close to her leaves a void in my life. On the flipside not being with Jane means focusing full time on getting the scale moving again.

After weeks of working out between six to eight hours a day the scale still wasn't moving as much as I wanted. After my meltdown in Jane's bathroom in Alaska, I had gotten my scale-phobia under control and now I am worried I've gone too far in the other direction. I know it's becoming an obsession but I can't afford to not monitor every ounce of weight I've lost in real time. I'm weighing myself between five and ten times a day. Sometimes I pee then get back on the scale to see what I weighed afterward. It's making me more anxious but I can't stop myself. Production still emails me daily asking me for my weight. When they don't like it, I have to send an email detailing everything I ate and how much I've worked out. They were getting increasingly frustrated about my lack of weight loss. I can tell in the snippets of messages in the email chain from the different PAs that whoever had been assigned to me was taking it personally that the scale wasn't moving. In addition to all the fans I'm now personally affecting some strangers job with my inadequacy to lose weight.

The next email I received just says *take a free day*. What? Production wants me to not work out at all and to go eat everything that I've been told not to eat for months? How will not working out or counting my calories help? No, no, no that's out of control. I don't think I can do this.

I responded to the email and production could tell I was freaking out and am not about taking this fucking free day. They must have called in the big guns because Shea called.

"Hi Tisa, it's me," she said, when I picked up the phone, in her most cheery voice, like we were longtime friends reconnecting after years of wistful longing.

"Hi Shea," I said, trying my best to match her cheerfulness. I'm pretty sure I sounded like somebody who would've preferred not to be on the phone with her. Which is exactly what I was.

"I'm just calling to hear how my favorite contestant is doing?" I don't know if she cringed when she said that but *I* certainly did. I'm pretty sure she knew I knew it wasn't true.

"I'm not doing well, Shea," I said, quietly holding back tears. I'll be damned if I break down on the phone with Ms. Perfection on the other end of the line. But I am overwhelmed and Shea does feel like a small familiar oasis in the desert of pressured weight loss I was staggering through. "I can't seem to lose more weight. I work out hours and hours every day and do all the other things you taught me."

"Sometimes you just need a little boost," she said.

"Yes, but what? Production told me to take a break and eat a lot. I don't know what that would do. It sounds weird."

"Well actually, production is totally right, Tisa. Take a free day and eat a ton of calories to jump-start it again."

I had hoped that Shea would be helpful. I don't know why I hoped that. I had forgotten who she was and what I was doing for a moment I guess. My heart sank. All right, free day it is. Nothing else is working.

I don't want to eat loads of food– I'm terrified of food. But I'm desperate to shed more pounds and scared of letting anyone down. I clicked off the call with Shea and drove to the closest grocery store. I bought a bag of snickerdoodle cookies and a quart of milk. I ate it all as quickly as I could.

Holy shit, what have I done? Oh God, all those carbs. The milk was full fat. Oh no. Oh no. Oh no. My stomach hurts but I ignored it while I ran back into the store. I chose the biggest box of laxatives I could find. I took all of them. They tasted like chocolate.

I laid on the floor of my apartment in a heap crying, my stomach still hurting and I knew all that food was a mistake. I wanted to call Esther or Debbie, they might understand but we aren't allowed to contact each other. No one else I know will understand and I can't tell them because they might interfere. They don't understand how important it is that I lose this weight. I picked up my phone and tried a suicide hotline. Weird choice but I was having trouble thinking straight through the pain in my stomach and my panic. I told the guy who answered everything I could think of, jumbling it all together.

"I weigh myself after I pee but that doesn't take enough weight off and I don't know how many calories were in all those cookies and it was a whole quart of milk my stomach hurts and I don't know how to make myself throw up and my parents are going to be embarrassed and disappointed and I'm ugly when I cry plus the whole world knows about my last pap smear" I kept rambling practically screeching until I just sort of petered out because I didn't know what else to say and was exhausted.

He was stumped.

"I'm not equipped to deal with food issues," he said. "Only suicide."

"Oh."

I think I *am* killing myself just slowly. I hung up.

To add to my absolute horror today, almost immediately after hanging up the phone it rang again. Production called to tell me I need to be at the airport in the next four hours. I've been booked on a last-minute flight back to Alaska. They had contacted a dog mushing team family and wanted me to drive down to a remote town in Alaska to film me training with the sled dogs. I felt like I had just gotten back from Alaska and while going back to see Jane was the only positive thing I could think of in my life right now, the thought of the trip there with airports and flying and driving was killing me. I stayed laying there on the floor of my little place in New Hampshire, thinking about the absurdity of having just eaten an entire bag of snickerdoodles and a quart of milk with a laxative chaser and how I now had to catch a cross country flight to go work out with sled dogs. I laughed. It was an empty almost maniacal laughter but it's all just so ridiculous. My life is absurd. Laughing is a welcome change from crying, which seemed to be my resting state these days. So, I'll take it. I got up, got my shit together—pun intended—and texted Jane.

"Guess who's coming to Alaska."

"For real? When?" I could just imagine her surprised smile.

"Today. Yes, you read that right, today."

I'm going to Alaska.

9/25/2015

Travelling after downing an ill-advised number of laxatives is nerve wracking to say the least. Airplane bathrooms aren't exactly known for their comfort, and stalls in airport bathrooms don't leave much up to the imagination. Thankfully I completed every step of my trip without emergencies or accidents. I was starting to think the laxatives might not be working at all. Jane picked me up at the airport in Anchorage, and I hadn't even felt a rumble in my stomach yet. Perhaps they really didn't work? I briefly forgot about it as I drove home with Jane and we talked, laughed, and she touched me. That touch felt like a source of energy, perhaps my only one at this point. Well, that and remembering how much I don't want to let anyone down by not doing enough. That was constantly fueling me. As soon as we were in the house, we were about each other. I managed to let myself drift away on pleasure with her for a moment. Orgasms have a way of filling your head and blocking out negatives. As we lay close together afterward, however, I felt it. The laxatives. I extracted myself from the bed, as gracefully as possible, and rushed to the bathroom, without making it obvious I needed it badly. I felt comfortable around Jane but I wasn't sure we were quite at taking *laxative imbued shits with an open door* comfortable yet. I got to the toilet, sat down and it was like the floodgates of hell had opened. Pretty sure I lost consciousness in brief flashes but my stomach felt relatively steady afterward, and I chanced a return to bed. She was half asleep as she put her arm around me. I spent a good while laying perfectly still, listening intently with my inner ear, to any rumblings from my stomach. After a while I dozed off too, feeling considerably easier about everything. Sleeping in her arms felt like the recharge of my batteries I had needed even while on somewhat high alert for stomach rumbles.

9/26/2015

As luck would have it, the day after a laxative chaser is even worse than the hours immediately following. I managed the flights home to Alaska without desperately rushing to the bathroom every five minutes and had actually thought that maybe I'd eaten so little the past few weeks that the bathroom ordeal the night before might be all I had to endure. I was wrong.

After waking up and opting out of more sex—for fear of my intestines revolting mid coitus—I went to meet production feeling lighter than I had in a while. Literally and figuratively. The surprise return trip to Alaska was for more *hometown* filming. This time, it involved driving four hours to Sterling from Anchorage with two producers to shoot a segment where I worked out with the Smith family—the repeat winners of the famous Iditarod dog sled race, and their sled dogs. We had been on the road for about an hour—with the three of us sitting in stilted silence—when, much to my chagrin, the laxatives kicked in again in a big way. I cursed under my breath but there was no way around it. It was kicking my insides' ass.

"Uhm, guys. Could we stop?" hoping they would just oblige without questions. Of course, they didn't.

"What? For gas?" one of them said, as she checked the dash. She looked at me in the rearview mirror like I had told her my species wanted to bring her back on my spaceship for probing. The other production assistant turned with a quizzical look.

"No. I need to go," I said. Come on fuckers, you think this is a game?

"We're in the middle of nowhere, Tisa. Just hold it a bit."

"You don't understand. I ate an entire box of laxatives. I. Need. To. Go." My movements were erratic and my voice strained and they understood the urgency with which this needed to happen. She pulled over to the side of the road, and I burst out of the vehicle before it had come to a complete stop. I realized subconsciously that there was no time for vanity so I pulled my pants down and went. I can't even imagine how this must have looked. Not pretty, that much is for sure. I managed to finish up and clean myself up somewhat. I didn't need that left sock anyway. Back in the car, we had driven maybe twenty minutes, when I felt it again. Fuck. Thank god I've always been a two socks wearing kind of gal.

I spent the entire trip basically shitting alongside the scenic Seward Highway. I shit so much, I swear I saw my birthday cake from 1st grade. Weird how no one asked to film that.

When we finally got to Sterling, I wasn't sure my lower intestines were even in my body anymore. Perhaps this was the way to get the scale moving? Shitting out vital organs. I looked so rough the Smith's asked if I was hungover and needed a shot before we started filming with the dogs. My production crafted *party girl* TV reputation preceded me. Awesome.

After clearing up the fact that I was in fact not hungover or spent all of my days doing nothing but drinking alcohol and living it up, I went to train with Nick. He was a really nice member of the family who spent most of his time caring for the dogs and running the Iditarod race along with his brothers and father. Despite shitting like I was trying to set a world record, it turned out to be a pretty cool day. We filmed me running alongside the dogs and hanging out in the family home. They were an amazing family that welcomed me to their home and were very kind about everything once I cleared up the fact that I was not in fact going to throw a rager in their living room or binge drink with the sled dogs. At some point during the day I had a moment alone with Nick and we got to speaking. His family had done a lot of filming for different reality shows in Alaska already. He told me I looked absolutely miserable and he wasn't surprised because he had shot with people from another reality TV show. He said that show was one that looked like participants traveled all over the world and were experiencing all these different adventures when in actuality every place they went if they weren't filming they had been locked in their hotel rooms. I told him I could relate to everything and he just looked so incredibly sad for me. When it was all done he gave me a hug and told me to keep my chin up and that he wouldn't be watching the show because he had met me in real life and that's all that he needed to know. It was kind of a sweet moment and I wasn't shitting myself anymore. Feels like a win.

During the trip back to Anchorage, I tried to explain to the PA and producer that I was starting to worry that I might be sick.

"Guys, I'm a little concerned that my hair's falling out, my period stopped, I'm more bruises than skin and I can't sleep more than three hours a night. I have read some stuff on Google about over training and it seems like maybe I might be not ok."

"Tisa," Anne the producer who was in the passenger seat started, as she turned around to look at me. She looked so concerned, I thought for a moment that I had finally broached the subject with the right person. "That sounds awful. Like, that seems like some really stressful things affecting your progress. How about we save this conversation for when the cameras are rolling?" Ah, that makes sense, the concern was real, it just wasn't concern for me, it was for the product. I nodded, shut the fuck up and hoped I would never see either of these two people again.

We arrived at Jane's place, and it felt good to be back. The PA and the producer who was concerned I *save it for the camera* dropped me off and I strolled in to find her sitting on the couch watching TV. I went straight over, straddled her and just hugged myself tightly to her. She put her arms around me and we sat there being close for a while. It was pretty much what the doctor would've ordered, if he were a doctor that disregarded all the possible medical things that were clearly not ok with me right now.

"Did you eat?" she asked me after a long comfortable silence. I didn't move my head from her shoulder.

"You know I didn't," I said. Then I remembered that she might not know that, and I wasn't sure she should know that. "It's been a busy day and I haven't had time," I corrected myself.

"Would you like to?" She stroked my hair with one hand and held on tight to my lower back with the other.

"I don't know if I can but I'd like to watch you cook." I really wanted a glass of wine while I watched her prepare delicious foods that we then ate naked. I wasn't going to *actually* consume a glass of wine to make that fantasy a reality though.

We stepped into the kitchen and I sat down on one of the chairs by the counter as she turned on lights and opened cupboards looking for ingredients and seasonings. She turned around, looked at me, and I noticed her eyes widen slightly at a fixed point on the side of my head. I've grown so accustomed to not looking at myself that I didn't realize how different I must look to Jane. I'm covered in bruises, have black circles under my eyes and a newly formed second bald spot. I realized then that she doesn't see me a lot outside of the bedroom or in a car where her attention is otherwise engaged. Her reaction when she saw me though, made me immediately self-conscious. I'd worn a baseball cap to hide it practically all the time. But in my joy at seeing her and getting comfortable in her place, I took it off without thinking or rearranging my remaining hair first.

"Damn, Tisa," she said. I felt like a deer in headlights. "Are you feeling all right?" She stepped over to me and I wasn't sure what she was going to do. I remained still like somehow she might forget it right away. This tactic worked with T-Rexes. Surely it also would with new girlfriends.

"Oh yes. I'm fine," I said, and could hear how unconvincing my voice was.

"Your hair is falling out here," she said, as her fingers caressed the side of my head carefully. "That doesn't seem all right to me."

"Oh, it's just a temporary thing. It happens sometimes." I knew I was in deep shit now. It was like I could hear myself lying but at the same time I really believed it. I had to make it to the finale, that was all I needed.

"I don't want to see you hurt. I really like you," she said, then ran her hand over my cheek. She smiled. It wasn't a smile filled with pity but it stung a little anyway. I really liked her too. I kind of wanted her to be concerned about me but I was also outraged that she questioned my judgment.

"I really like you too." I forced a smile, which turned into a genuine one. I really *did* like her and I did like that she gave a shit. I forgot what that felt like sometimes and I was grateful that she reminded me. Even if it also reminded me that my body was sending signals to me that things were not okay. Yes, not having a period had its advantages but it wasn't normal for me. I knew that. I just had to make it to the finale.

9/29/2015

With only spending limited time in Alaska I relished every single moment I got to spend with Jane. She was amazing at planning things for us to do and trying to accept my life for what it was right now. She would take off from work and we did things like drive out of Anchorage just to talk and enjoy the scenery. We stopped at a little coffee shop to have lunch. She had food. I had coffee. Winter was already upon Alaska in full force and the snow covering the landscape conjured up warm fuzzies for me from my childhood. It was a lovely day.

When we arrived home later in the afternoon and I was about to just hang around the house. Jane, however, had different plans.

"Are you an ABBA fan, Tisa?" she asked, as I slumped into the couch. It took me by surprise.

"Uh. ABBA?" I looked at her. I knew who they were but I wasn't sure why they were brought up or if I could remember a lot of their tracks off the top of my head.

"Yes. I'm not a big fan either. That's why I got us tickets to the Dancing Queen: ABBA musical tonight."

"You did?" I almost screamed, as I jumped out of the couch. "I'm not a fan of ABBA per se, but I do love me a musical."

"I thought as much," she said, and pulled tickets out of her back pocket with a flourish normally reserved for magicians' final prestige. I laughed. Amazing.

"When is it?" I surveyed her with hungry eyes. If it was a lot later this evening, I was probably going to jump her. I had been in the mood all day. When I don't eat, cravings for sex are more intense. Which further explains all the conversations on the Spa about food and sex. I briefly wondered again how I managed all that time at the Spa without sex. Also, cameras around the clock meant I didn't handle things myself either while I was there. Having a crazy lady scream at you from morning until night probably robbed me of any libido, leaving only enough energy to talk about it.

"It's actually in like forty-five minutes," she said, shifting uncomfortably on her feet.

"Forty-Five minutes? Holy shit, we gotta get going." Oh well, I would have to wait until later. We hustled through showers and got dressed. I pondered aloud what kind of clothes I'd go for, since I hadn't packed much in terms of dresses or anything formal. She shrugged it off with *a who gives a shit attitude*, and I donned my trademark jeans and a hoodie. Perfect. We raced through Anchorage and praised our luck in finding parking. Normally something that requires small miracles, we got a spot not a block away from the venue. Pretty sure I saw Jane fist pump. We walked briskly hand in hand and were inside with minutes to spare. Our seats weren't amazing but it mattered little. The fact that she had gotten them at all, correctly predicting my innate love of music and dancing, ABBA or no ABBA, meant a lot to me. I was not out of my wanting to jump her from amazement moment quite yet, so when she put her hand on my arm, as we had settled into our seats, I inadvertently jumped at the immediate goosebumps from her touch. The hubbub of all our fellow patrons quickly settled, as soon as the lights were dimmed, and the show began. I put my hand on hers, and it felt proper date-y with her again all of a sudden. Dinner and a show. Sans dinner. Because, I eat only coffee.

"You want something to eat?" she asked me, after we had stood around a few minutes watching people buzz around buying drinks and food.

"I really just want one thing," I said, as I cast her a coy smile. She chuckled.

"Yep. Me too." The first call back bell rang and I started moving back towards the theater, when Jane put a hand on my shoulder, and stopped me. I looked at her with a confused expression. She winked at me and I felt that spot just above my stomach just below my chest stir like somebody had tossed a firecracker into my ribcage. She grabbed my hand and pulled me in a different direction. "Do you want to go home and get naked instead of watching the rest of this show?"

"I thought you'd never ask," I responded switching direction to match her now mid-stride. She didn't break traffic laws going home but we got there fast. I dropped my clothes on the way through her living room and practically sprinted toward her bedroom.

"This was really nice," I said, as we lay on the bed in the dark, thoroughly spent. It was an understatement.

"Yes. ABBA is pretty damn fantastic," she replied, laughing. "You are something else," she followed up, now serious. "I hate that you have to leave. You should just stay. All the time."

"I would like that. A lot," I said. I really would. But I couldn't. "I have to be in New Hampshire. I have to work on this."

"I know," she said, dejected. "Stay for a few more days though? We'll find a gym here you can use."

"You want that?" I asked, my eyes lighting up.

"I do," she said, smiling, stroking my shoulder. "Very much."

"I don't have to work necessarily so they'd be ok with me missing a few days. It was kind of a deal when I signed on to teach at the gym." I thought about other things that might be demanding my presence. My goldfish was no longer in my life, so there really wasn't anything else yet, law school was looming but I had to get through the finale first so it had been delayed until next fall. Nothing pressing was back on the east coast. I was a little concerned about taking up my weight loss routine in full force again with someone constantly in my space but being near Jane just felt…better. "All right. I'll stay."

10/2/2015

"Plans? Sure," I said, she had mentioned these plans for the night, just as I was heading out for a second run. I thought back on the last plans she had as a surprise, and how they had ended with us in a hotel room and it had been pretty perfect. I looked at her with puzzled eyes after committing.

"You'll see tonight," she said, and flashed me a mysterious smile. I hated and adored her at the same time just then. On to the run though.

When I got home, we hung out. She had bought donuts (that she ate) and coffee, and it was lovely to just be around her. I felt bad about not working out as much as I should even if I kept reminding myself that sex burned off some calories. I fought the urge to do something and I know she noticed my slightly manic look and movements every so often. By evening I had managed to clean her apartment from top to bottom in my inability to stay still while she watched something on TV. She finished the last episode of whatever, turned off the TV, got up, and asked me if I wanted to get ready to go. After showers and getting dressed we headed to the car and were on our way. I was getting confused, because instead of heading downtown she drove toward my best friend's house. I didn't want to ruin any surprise she might have planned so I didn't say anything. I hadn't even realized that they were talking with each other. Obviously, I knew that they had met. I also knew that Britta and she got along well and Jane had become pretty good friends with Britta's boyfriend Sanjay in my absence. He works as a personal trainer and I figure he had bonded with Jane over a mutual love of lifting heavy things. They had even lifted together at the gym, but I was still a little taken aback that she was comfortable enough with them to be taking me to their place as a surprise when we pulled into the driveway.

"I thought we were going to dinner?" I asked as she put the car in park.

"I think I need you to come with me," she responded, and while her eyes were friendly and her smile pleasant, I felt a weird urgency in her demeanor that put me slightly on edge. I trusted her implicitly already, and besides it was the house of my best friend. I had been there hundreds of times before, so I pushed the unease away, and followed her into the house. Britta and Sanjay were sitting in the kitchen. I could see Britta had her phone out and on Facetime.

"What is going on?" I asked, at this point more genuinely curious and confused than anxious. "Are we all going to dinner?" I only subconsciously registered the faces on the phone at first but once I was focused on it, I did a double take as I realized it was my mother and my father.

"Tisa. We are all very worried about you.," Jane said, as she stepped in front of me and looked me in the eyes.

"What? Why?" I tried to process all this and fight off the feeling of ambush.

"Because you are killing yourself slowly," she said, fixing me with a loving gaze. "And we are scared you might succeed. This is an intervention."

"An intervention," I laughed in disbelief. Not quite maniacally but close. It was a frustrated, relieved, confused and mirthful laugh all in one. An intervention? Are you kidding me? This shit is for famous people who can't stop doing cocaine not a woman who maybe spends a little too much time at the gym and drinks too much coffee.

"Please sit down. Everyone is here for you, Tisa," she said, as she directed me to a chair facing Britta and Sanjay and my parents' worried faces on the phone. Then Jane spoke.

"I know how much you work out, Tisa, and I know you don't like me to know. I get that. I also know that you work out way beyond what your body can take. Your hair is falling out in clumps. You sleep only about three hours a night. You're bruised for no reason. And you don't eat. *Literally.* I saw you jot down in your food journal, that a cup of lettuce is 100 calories. It isn't. Your body is caving and we are scared you're going to let it, all for this show." Everybody looked at me, with concerned expressions. It was surreal. I didn't need a fucking intervention.

"We don't want to see you get hurt," my mom said. "We love you." I'm pretty sure she was, or had been, crying. My dad looked somber. I wasn't sure my dad would notice me not doing well until he was identifying my body at the morgue. Even then he would suspect I was just being lazy. All the more impressive he was involved in this. "As your mom and a nurse, I hate to see you hacking at your body like this. It isn't healthy."

"I concur," Britta said, she was also a nurse. "You are killing your body." I found this kind of ironic, since if it hadn't been for her, I probably wouldn't have been on the show to begin with. She's been on approximately eleven billionty diets in the time we've been friends. When I lived with her, her "goal bikini" hung on the damn kitchen wall for four months. This is what she wanted for me—to lose weight, and that's what I was fucking doing. I tried to let my frustration with her slide because getting defensive would just confirm all their suspicions and I wanted to be left the hell alone.

"Your workout regime is too extreme," Sanjay said. I begrudgingly thought he might know what he was talking about, being a personal trainer. "You need to cut down and structure it differently. Less can be more."

I took it all in, trying to process my anger while looking at each of their faces. They looked scared, worried and hurt. They meant well and I knew they had rallied together with my best interest at heart. I let go of how pissed off this all made me.

"What happens now?" I whispered. I decided not to fight it. They were right, whether I wanted to admit it or not. Even though my immediate reaction was a flash of anger at the ridiculousness of this whole thing, and there was still a residue of that anger in me, this stupid stunt had actually given strength to that nagging voice at the back of my head telling me something wasn't okay with me. The little voice that had gotten me to call the hotline during my laxative low point.

"We will get you a trainer to oversee your work outs. And we will get you a doctor and a registered dietician that understands disordered eating. You need a therapist to help you get through this. It's wearing you down mentally as well as physically," Jane said, with everybody nodding their agreement.

"You need to eat more," Britta said. My mother concurred.

"And work out for only three hours a day," Sanjay chimed in. "When you get beyond that, the effect really is negligible. Instead maximize the time you do spend."

"And we'll babysit you the whole time, if that is what it takes," my mom said. I couldn't imagine that. I've lived on my own for almost a decade now and here were five adults talking about babysitting me.

"All right," I conceded, validating their intervention. It contradicted all I had learned at the Spa and I was still struggling internally with getting that sorted. Perhaps a therapist *was* the way to go. "Thank you."

"For you, anything," Jane said, and she was visibly relieved. Couldn't be particularly fun staging an intervention for that girl from the bar you've only been dating for a few weeks. I smiled at the others too. My dad had remained largely silent until then. Uncharacteristically silent. Then he spoke.

"Well, I'm glad you're listening because it means you're going to live, but you aren't going to win."

I think his comment was meant to get me to put my priorities in order but all I actually heard was, "You have let everyone down." Fuck.

Perhaps I wasn't going to win, and perhaps I should be okay with that. I'm not okay with that yet, though, not really. I don't say that aloud to anyone though, I know better.

On the way home in the car, after we hung out with Britta and Sanjay a bit—and said goodbye to my parents—neither Jane nor I spoke for a while.

"Are you upset with me?" she finally asked. A legit question. I wasn't. I mean I had been but now I was actually just kind of impressed with a side of resignation.

"No. I'm not upset. I'm surprised and I don't usually like surprises. I don't know if I liked this one but that doesn't mean I can't see the validity of it."

"I don't want to assume I have any idea of what you're going through. I couldn't. I do, however, assume an interest in you because I really like you. I hope you know that." She looked straight ahead as she spoke, trying not to look directly at me, as if she were scared I would vanish into thin air from her words.

"I do," I said then spent the rest of the drive back to her place staring out the window wondering what not disappointing everyone was supposed to look like now.

10/3/2015

Today, for the first time in months I heard from the shows doctor's office. The actual medical office; not production. The nurse practitioner that had talked to Esther and I months ago telling us that she was worried that we might have Stockholm's syndrome because we were begging for ways to stay on the show and in the game. She called to check in with me. After my initial confusion about who she was—and my joy at having a healthcare professional from the actual show to talk to—I explained to her that my family was concerned. She asked why and I recounted the concerns my family listed at my intervention (that still sounds absurd to me, I had an intervention): I'm covered in bruises, I have black circles under my eyes, my hair is falling out, I haven't had a period in a couple of months, I can't sleep and I pass out sometimes when standing up. There was a long silence and I heard her sigh before she spoke.

"Tisa, I need you to understand that production does not care about you. This is not about your health or wellbeing. This is about making money and producing a product. *You* are that product. I understand you want to lose weight and you're trying to save your life but please understand that the people here are not looking out for you. That's up to you. *You* need to look out for you. It sounds like from everything your friends and family have done, you are starting to look out for yourself. Ignore the show. Ignore production. Ignore their advice and please, I'm begging you, look out for your health." It was a lot to take in and my reaction was pretty stock at this point, part exuberance that somebody gave a shit about me as a person and part annoyance that somebody interfered with my chance to win and prove I deserved to be chosen.

"I will. Thank you," I said. "But I made a promise that I would do the best I could and there were 200,000 other people in line behind me who really wanted this opportunity. I can't just waste it. I'm not going to just give up now. I'm not going to stop trying."

"I'm not asking you to stop trying, Tisa," she said. I could almost feel the desperation in her voice. "I'm asking you to please stop and think about everybody you're surrounded by. Think about the people that are talking to you that genuinely care about your well-being and what they're saying versus the people talking to you that are making money off of you. That's all I'm asking. Understand that this is a TV show. That's *all* it is"

I got off the call more conflicted than ever.

10/4/2015

I'm not sure I'm completely on board with the whole eating more, working out less thing. I don't understand how they think working out three hours a day is going to be enough for me to beat Farrell at the finale. I agreed to make sure somebody was around when I was eating and Jane decided my first meal back to actually eating stuff was going to be at a local restaurant that catered to the bodybuilding community. She woke up early and I went for a run before we decided to go to breakfast. I surveyed the menu for a while, before finally settling on half a cup of plain oatmeal with 1/4 cup of blueberries and scrambled egg whites.

"That's a lot of food," I said when the waitress put my plate on the table in front of me. I felt genuinely scared. Not fearing for my life scared but a cornered animal scared. Jane just smiled at me, as I poked at it a little with my fork. It seemed like an impossibly large plate of food. "Did you ask them to make it bigger or something?" I asked, looking at Jane who shook her head slowly. I took a spoon and tentatively scooped up some oatmeal. I hadn't really had food outside of a few pieces of processed meat, iceberg lettuce, and the occasional protein shake since longer than I could remember. Jane was eating her food too. I took a bite of the oatmeal and chewed it slowly. It felt like it was growing in my mouth, like it was repelled by my stomach. I forced myself to swallow it, and my eyes teared up. Jane was looking at me and took my hand.

"I know, Tisa. I really do know that this is hard for you."

"I don't know if I can do it." I said, tears now running down my cheeks.

"You can and you will. I'll sit here with you, even if it takes us two hours, I'll be here. You need to eat every bite." I didn't argue. I had agreed to this and I was going to follow through. It did take me two hours. And I cried through all of it. But I managed to eat it. *Every bite.*

I also agreed to cut my working out back from six to eight hours down to three hours. Tonight, as I'm getting ready to go to the gym for my second hour and a half of the day that I've been allotted, my phone rang and it was Shea. It was odd to have her checking in on me since it wasn't something she had done at the Spa, and the only other time she had called was when production made her so I was a little suspicious.

"Hey Tisa, what's going on? How are you doing? How're things going?" She littered a barrage of questions in my ear, and before I could get a response in, she continued. "I get your email updates from production and I see that the scale's moving again but it's moving rather slowly?" I explained everything that's been going on to her. The intervention my family staged, how I was struggling mentally and physically, and told her I was exhausted. She told me she completely understood and much like the nurse practitioner who told me I needed to look out for me and stop worrying about the show, Shea completely agreed. It was the first moment I felt like a human being instead of a fitness robot was talking to me when communicating with Shea. I was pretty relieved and after getting off the phone I walked into the bright gym from the dark and snow and put in my hour and 1/2 of lifting. That's right, *lifting*. I'm lifting weights because I really want to try to worry about my health and not just the scale. Scary stuff not doing just cardio, but I'm doing it.

Sanjay trained me and it was a workout I was proud of completing. After we were done, he sat there with me as I had a protein shake. He was sympathetic even when I didn't want to drink it and much like Jane, he told me he'd sit there until I finished the whole thing. I left the gym still feeling pretty concerned about the fact I wasn't working as hard as I needed to be absolutely certain I wouldn't disappoint everyone. As I walked to the car though some of that concern dissipated when I realized I wasn't as exhausted as I been lately and it felt kind of nice to actually have food after a workout—like I had seen Shea and Chad do for themselves at the Spa. Once I was in the car I saw that I had a voicemail from Shea.

"Hiiiiii Tisa, it's me again. I just spoke to production about everything going on with you, and I feel really bad saying this but I need you to suck it up and get your ass back on the treadmill. Farrell is still beating you and it would be too bad to throw all that hard work away at this point. You are so close. Anyway, keep at it, Tisa. I'll talk to you soon. Toodles."

I sat in the car for a while, processing the voicemail. It was a 180 from the conversation she had just had with me and I felt betrayed. Betrayed by a grown ass woman who ended a voicemail with *toodles*. I was so frustrated, I started crying. Sitting in the parking lot outside the gym, alone in my car, crying.

10/5/2015

The next morning, after I did my first allotted hour of running, I got a call from production. Since I had decided to stay with Jane as much as possible, I had dropped the idea of going back to New Hampshire for another few days. Of course, that joy wasn't going to last either. Apparently, in addition to all of the milk drinking I didn't do at the Spa, I now had to fly to New York and not drink it while shooting a print ad for it. Super surreal. I would be doing a milk mustache ad. A picture of me, some nobody girl from Alaska, holding a glass of milk with a milk mustache. Jane and I both laughed at the idea. I wondered if I'd see the other three contestants. I was kind of curious to see how they were faring. Soon my curiosity was overshadowed by a new worry. Flying was a huge problem for me because I know that every time I fly I retain water and I gain weight. When I get on the scale after a flight I flip out. On top of that I have a really hard time figuring out what to eat every time I fly and go through airports. Normally I just wouldn't eat but I was trying to listen to Jane, Britta and my new registered dietician who wanted me to eat more along with cutting back on my workouts. Cutting back on my workouts isn't going to be too hard since I'll be flying for hours to get there and staying in a hotel that I'm not sure even has a gym. The eating thing is really going to throw me off though.

"I'm sorry I have to leave early," I told Jane.

"No worries," she said, with her arms around me. "Perhaps you'll come back after and show me your model face?" I flashed her a smug smile, as dirty thoughts crossed my mind.

"I would like that."

10/6/2015

Getting to New York was an incredibly long trip and the hotel is like nothing I've ever experienced. The hotel stay is being covered by the company shooting the photos. I have anxiety because I'm staying in a room where three nights cost more than my rent for an entire month in Alaska. I feel like I'm in some other surreal world I can't afford, was accidentally admitted into and someone is going to discover the mistake at any moment. All the pressure to show I deserve this is almost crushing. This is a life I didn't know other people lived. I won't blow it.

10/7/2015

I woke up early and looked around the crazy hotel room. I had texted Jane the night before as I was looking out the window at New York. I wasn't ever a big fan of cities, especially cities as big as New York but I couldn't deny there was something mesmerizing about the millions of lights twinkling, and thousands of people going about their lives forty floors below me. I wished she were there with me. Not least of all, because I would've liked to have sex with this view as a backdrop. In the burgeoning light of morning though, New York felt different. It seemed more antsy and anxious, perfectly reflecting how I felt being here, like a stranger in a strange land. I tiptoed around the room like somehow my feet would dirty the floor. I thought about ordering room service but I didn't want to eat, and I didn't want to incur more charges. I felt bad enough for just the price of the room already. I decided to take a shower instead.

As I lay on the bed after enjoying hot water in one of the most lavish bathrooms I had ever been in, I texted Jane about my morning and the day ahead. I had just started relaxing, when somebody knocked on the door. Typical. I got my robe on and opened the door. It was a PA, "Tisa, take a shower and be ready in thirty minutes. Don't worry about makeup and hair."

"Never do," I said, and saw her confused look, before I closed the door.

I was in the lobby in my hoodie and jeans ten minutes later, feeling crazy out of place. I'm pretty sure this was the kind of place Macaulay Culkin conned himself a room at in *Home Alone 2*. Thankfully the confused PA from earlier came up to take me to a black sedan they had waiting outside before I embarrassed myself by asking if anyone had seen Donald Trump lately. The drive to the photoshoot was stressful. The PA gave me little information—which wasn't new—but there was traffic, cars, bikes and pedestrians everywhere. Our driver had to make a few sudden brake slamming stops on the way. When we finally made it, I was happy just to be alive. The lobby of the building is what I imagined every stale soulless office building of New York looked like—high ceilings, marble everything, one woman behind a desk way too large for her. She didn't even look up as we walked through. The studio was on the tenth floor and whereas the lobby had been serene and empty, the studio was abuzz with activity. People walking every which way, some carrying photo equipment, others with clipboards or just focused expressions. The PA led me up to a short haired woman in her 50s who looked like she would keel over if she raised the monstrosity of a camera she was holding further than waist high. She barely glanced at me because she was focused on getting things right for her shot and I went to find wardrobe and makeup.

Makeup took a good forty minutes of little pen strokes across my eyes and cheeks and served as a perfect reminder of why I never bothered with applying it myself. Who had time for this every day? I moved on to wardrobe, where a woman was picking out dresses for me to try on. I got through a few dresses, she looked thoroughly unimpressed with me.

"The guys were really a lot easier to dress," she said, with a laugh. I looked at her in shock.

"Wait, they have been here already?"

"Uh…" she stuttered, realizing perhaps sharing that information wasn't appropriate. Not with *me* at least.

"They have, haven't they?" I pushed. "It's okay. I won't tell anyone."

"They have. Yesterday and the day before. We have to shoot all three of you, because we don't know who is going to win yet," She spoke rapidly, like it had been weighing down on her for a while, or perhaps she was just scared of getting caught. She kept shooting fleeting glances at the door and the familiar feeling of being in a spy movie I remembered from the Spa snuck up again.

"The three of us?" I asked, looking alarmed. She looked alarmed too and clasped her hands in front of her mouth. "Why are there only three finalists? Who is missing?"

"Uhm, I don't think I'm supposed to say," she started but I was fed up with all the secrecy.

"Look lady, you've already fucking said it, so just spill the beans. I'm not gonna tell anybody you said anything. You can't just say shit like this and expect me to pretend I didn't hear it." I didn't mince words. Perhaps I was hangry and my only food substitute was thousands of miles away. Perhaps I was just about done with this production. She looked like I had pointed a gun at her.

"Esther isn't in the running anymore. She suffered some kind of injury and they can't get her back on track."

"Well shit," I said, mostly to myself. "They got her to work herself to injury. Isn't that just awesome," I said in my most sarcastic tone, my heart hurt for Esther. The girl fidgeted uncomfortably with the dress she was holding.

"I think this one," She handed me the dress, red with thin straps. It was actually kind of cute.

"How were Brody and Farrell doing?" I wasn't done with her. For the first time in ages, I had access to a little information. I was anxious to know how they were, mostly afraid they were doing better than me and sort of hoping they were.

"I've only seen a few pictures from late in the show of Brody, so I can't say how much he's changed but he doesn't look like he lost a lot of weight since then," she started, and hoped I would be satisfied. I *wasn't*. I've known damn well Brody isn't my real competition for winning this whole shitshow since the last week at the Spa. It's Farrell.

"And Farrell?" I asked, trying to sound nonchalant in my interest as I pulled the dress on. She looked extremely uncomfortable.

"I think he's lost a lot of weight. I think he is doing really well." She looked like she had just told me my entire family had been killed by a supervillain. "I'm so sorry."

"Why? It's not like anybody died here," I said, acting aloof while my mind was spinning. I turned and looked in the mirror, deciding I'd let her off the hook and change the subject. "This looks good, I think," She agreed, visibly relieved I hadn't pressed for more information. I felt like a big fist had punched me in the gut and then started to panic again knowing that I wasn't good enough for this whole opportunity. A little voice that sounded like Jane piped up, "It's okay to not win this. You have *you* to worry about." That little voice didn't cancel out the dark booming cloud of anxiety eating at me but I was glad it was there. I tried to hold onto that voice while posing with my milk mustache for the cameras.

10/8/2015

After spending another night in that luxurious hotel room, I was both looking forward to flying back to Alaska and dreading the trip. I had spent the night before looking out at the city again texting Jane and imagining that she was there with me. I briefly considered going out, just to see what was going on. When in Rome, right? I already had my hair done and the makeup on but I decided against it because what the fuck would I do? I was a mess. I missed my girlfriend. I wanted to work out but the hotel didn't have a gym. I wasn't about to jog around the city at night in late October. I've lived in Alaska for over a decade and still get lost there, I would be hopeless here. Just, no. I admired the view and went the fuck to sleep.

The trip back was long and cumbersome, and I could feel the water retention happening and adding weight to my ass. I hated it. I tried eating something in my layover airport but it made me want to throw up. When I finally landed in Anchorage, I was physically and emotionally spent. I just wanted to lay down, close my eyes and not open them for weeks or months. Perhaps not until the finale. Jane was there to pick me up. We barely spoke on the way home. I just didn't have it in me. But the silence was a comfortable one.

At her place, she took my suitcase in, as I walked straight in and threw myself on her bed. I was crying quietly when she came in and got down next to me. Her arm slid around me and she tried pulling me to face her. I pushed against it. I couldn't deal with facing the wreck I was right now.

"Tisa," she said with a voice softer than I knew she was capable of. "Tisa, look at me," Her hand applied gentle pressure on my shoulder again, and I let it spin me this time. I didn't look up for a bit, but when I did, I met her eyes. I knew she wouldn't think less of me. I broke down sobbing. She pulled me into her, while I cried with her arms tight around me, listening to her heart and feeling her body as she inhaled and exhaled calmly.

"Talk to me, Tisa," she said in the same quiet voice. It wasn't commanding, or patronizing.

"I'm so scared of letting people down," I said, between sobs. "My head is fucked up. I feel like an imposter, like I'm on the show under false pretenses. All those other people who really wanted my spot, and I got it, and I'm not doing enough. What if I'm not doing enough?" It poured out of me now. Jane hugged me closer, and absorbed all my anxiety and worries.

"It's going to be fine, Tisa," she said, and stroked my hair while her other hand pressed me against her. I needed that. I needed to be hugged tight. She touched my neck and her hand held my face as she kissed my forehead and looked at me. "It's going to be alright," I trusted her words. She kissed my nose and I wanted her lips on mine. My face was still wet but I kissed her—small tentative kisses first then closer and deeper. She held me so tight, I could feel the heat from her body flow through mine. I closed my eyes and let myself ascend into the feeling of her proximity. Her hands slid over my back as we kissed and she touched me in all the places and ways that alleviated my fears. I wanted the ultimate closeness. I wanted to feel her close and become anchored in the moment. No regrets about the past or worries about the future. Just be right here, right now. We fell asleep wrapped around one another in a knot that I would be perfectly happy leaving tangled forever.

10/31/2015

I stayed in Alaska long enough to celebrate Halloween, my favorite holiday. Halloween signals the start of the whole holiday season for me and I am *crazy* about the holidays. Since I practically lived with Jane now, I had taken it upon myself to decorate her place. Nothing extravagant. She wasn't into Halloween like I was so I was pleased to find her engaged in my project, placing fake spider webs here and there for me. She asked if I wanted to go out to celebrate all dressed up, and I had happily agreed. Who doesn't want to go out in costume on Halloween?

We took a cab downtown to a bar we both knew had a large dance floor and usually played decent music. Lots of people there were in costume too, and while we were by no means the stars of the night, we did draw a few glances in our costumes. She went as a chicken and I as an egg. My goal was to dance as much as possible because dancing means partying while also sort of working out. I figured I could dance the calories in my drinks off right away and come out with a zero balance.

I stepped onto the dance floor after sipping my first drink and to my great joy Jane followed. The music thumped and we were both sweaty as we danced close. More drinks. More dancing. I almost forgot to be worried about calories for the rest of the night. We laughed and joked around in the cab on the way home. A fun night. I hadn't eaten, of course but I had managed a few glasses of water and a protein shake I had brought with me. Not a bad night out.

I woke with a sharp pain in both my thighs. I sat up instantly, moaning from pain and clutching my legs. Jane stirred from the movement and sound. I was cramping up and the pain was searing. I didn't scream but I almost cried in pain. What the hell was this? I didn't even know you could get a charley horse in your thigh. Jane was suddenly on her feet next to her side of the bed—confused and still half drunk—asking if I was okay when I tilted and fell out of the bed. Jane rushed around the bed to get to me and just as she kneeled next to me, I threw up from the pain. There were tears, snot and vomit everywhere. She didn't seem to notice, just tried to help me stop the pain. The cramps subsided slightly and I was down to sobbing quietly suddenly aware I was on the floor. Jane helped me to sit and got down next to me as we both leaned back against the bed. My thighs felt better but the thought of the pain was almost enough to nauseate me again.

"Tisa. This isn't good," Jane said, as she pulled me closer to her.

"I'm sorry about this," I said, indicating the puke on the floor.

"I don't care about that. I care about you. You aren't doing well." She was right, I wasn't. I had trouble seeing it when things were just moving along. This was quite literally a wakeup call.

"I'm not. I want to be though," if I wasn't already crying, I would've been by now. I thought I had cried myself out at that damn Spa yet here I was again.

"You have to take our agreement more seriously. I know you are trying but you are still killing yourself," She was right. I didn't have the energy to muster my usual annoyance at someone telling me what I should and shouldn't do regarding the show. I was tripping myself up, I'm covered in vomit and crying while Farrell was still beating me. So, what was the point really? Waking up in pain and throwing up on your girlfriend's floor seems like an awfully shitty price to pay to prove I was worth it .

"I will. I promise," I responded. I meant it this time. She hugged me tighter.

"Come on. Let's get you cleaned up. Also, we should get you some potassium, I read that helps with muscle cramps," she suggested, then helped me to my feet. As I was in the shower she cleaned up the puke. I stood there for what felt like hours and hoped the hot water would wash away some of my embarrassment and anxiety.

11/14/2015

Before flying back to New Hampshire, leaving Jane yet again, knowing I wouldn't see her again until the finale in Los Angeles, we decided to go out to breakfast. We chose the local restaurant where I ate my first meal after my intervention. The waitress recognized me when we sat down at our table and was all excited about my progress on the show.

"Oh, you're doing amazing, girl," she said, and smiled so wide I thought perhaps we were old friends and I just didn't remember her. "We're all really very proud of you here in Anchorage."

"Thank you," I said, still unaccustomed to having random strangers talk to me or recognize me. It wasn't a completely awesome feeling. I ordered my usual —a plain half a cup of oatmeal, blueberries and an egg white omelet. She seemed pleased with my selection. When Jane gave her order of chicken fried steak smothered in gravy with extra hash browns covered in cheese, it was a different story.

"Are you really going to eat that in front of her?" she asked with a look of disdain so severe I wasn't sure if we should hide the cutlery. She pinned Jane with a disgusted look.

"She's a grown woman and yes, I am going to eat it in front of her, every bite, I promise," Jane retorted with a snarky tone in her voice and I stifled a laugh. The waitress returned to the table and gently placed my food in front of me while damn near throwing Janes plate at the table. Jane looked at her, smiled smugly and we both ate our meal. I realized mid meal it was getting late and I wanted to get a workout in before I headed to the airport to catch my flight back to New Hampshire. I flagged down the waitress.

"Is it possible to get our check I need to hurry up and get to the gym."

"Of course," she said and handed me the check with a sugary smile. Then she looked at Jane. "Will you be going to the gym as well?"

"No," Jane replied, with a tone of barely controlled rage in her voice. "I will be going home to slow roast a pig then eating the entire thing alone, if that's all right with you." The waitress looked at Jane in horror and rushed off embarrassed. I giggled, out of awkwardness and genuine amusement.

In the car heading to the gym, neither of us spoke a lot. She had her hand on my thigh—like she almost always did—keeping a tangible link between us and my hand on top of hers. We both dreaded this but there was no way around it now. I had to get back to New Hampshire and get into a routine again for the final sprint of time until the finale. As much as I enjoyed spending time with her, I couldn't do what I had to do in Alaska. I wasn't focused enough here. I had my suitcase in the back, and she helped me take it out at the gym. I would shower and take a cab to the airport after working out. She took me in her arms, standing in the parking lot next to her car, and hugged me.

"I'll miss you," she said, as she held my face in her hands and kissed my forehead. I wanted to disappear into her eyes and stay there.

"I'll miss you too. I already can't wait to see you in L.A." I dreaded going back to L.A., her being there would help.

"I will be there…for all of it," she said. I appreciated that more than I could articulate.

"I'm going to need that…need you." I said. I worried about how I was going to survive finale night.

Chapter 17

've been desperately trying to find the golden middle between not letting everybody down and making a good showing at the finale—while also really keeping my word to Jane, my friends and family. Learning how to eat like a *normal* person and learning how to exercise without hurting myself seemed like an insurmountable goal. As someone who spent months with an irate lady screaming in my face that I wasn't good enough until I was bleeding, throwing up and writhing in pain—I knew this wasn't going to be an easy balance to find. Exercise doesn't *count* if it doesn't hurt.

I had spent the last couple of weeks back in New Hampshire doing nothing but working out and thinking about what things were going to be like in L.A. at the finale. I was not particularly fond of L.A. after living at the Spa. Going back sounded like misery.

I could pretend my aversion to L.A. was because Daniel had broken my heart there but that really wasn't how I felt. He had been a fuckstick, true. And I didn't particularly want to run into him at the finale, even if it was probably inevitable. But with distance I realized my intense infatuation with him while on the Spa was a time filler—an escape from the fake reality I was participating in. I'm embarrassed by it, but it's true. The feelings were manufactured by the intensity of the environment and the isolation. Plus, Daniel was *production*. That didn't make him inherently evil or anything, but it does mean that he's part of this whole machine that feels like it's grinding me to pieces. Also, he had probably cheated on a girlfriend with me, which is generally considered a dick move. In L.A. or anywhere. L.A. with or without Daniel is just a mishmash of miserable memories for me. Church vans, immense heat, pain, anxiety, crying in the shower and not being able to pee without some guy listening in.

I spent a lot of time on the phone with Jane talking about how much I missed her and how I couldn't wait to see her again. Coming home at night and eating the little food I allowed myself while on Facetime with her (it was the work around my family came up with so someone was making sure I was really eating even if I wasn't in the same state) was the bright spot in winter days that grew increasingly darker, both literally *and* figuratively as I ruminated on the upcoming finale.

Everyday has started to blur together. Day in and day out, the same thing. Trying to make myself eat. Making sure I have enough calories so that I'm not passing out. Limiting my workouts to just three hours a day.

A lot of my time is spent on social media. I have to distract myself so I don't keep returning to the gym and overdo workouts. I'm still not able to sleep well and my attention span is broken. I used to be able to read whole novels in a day and I can't seem to process more than a few lines of reading at a time anymore so social media is good for all of those issues. My mother had called a few times in or close to tears because she had been looking at social media too and read some random nasty thing someone posted about me. I told her she should try and ignore it but it was hard to say with a straight face. I wasn't doing so well at it myself. My heart breaks for her when she reads posts about what a terrible person I am and how my mother must be an awful woman to have raised me so poorly. It hurts her so much. I've been doing everything I can to convince her to stay off social media for the last couple weeks until the finale but it's not working.

"They hate you, Tisa," even over the phone I could tell by the thickness of her voice that she was choked up or had been crying. I hate hearing her cry because of choices I made. Even if it *wasn't* really my fault weight loss reality TV obsessed trolls exist.

"Mom, have you been on social media again? I told you, don't go on there. People are assholes."

"I just don't understand why? Why are they so angry?" she cried. I wish I could tell her why but the truth is, I have no fucking clue. I mean, I get that I come off as detached or shitty sometimes. Who doesn't? This kind of hate for the version of me as seen on TV though? I don't get this shit. These people have never even met me.

"They don't know me mom. They're just talking out their asses. Try not to pay attention to it. It's not important."

"How are you though, honey?" she was trying her best to be supportive while it was tearing her up to see the vile things people called me. My mom didn't ask for this, my dumbass did and she was suffering.

"I'm good, mom. Just trucking along, biding my time before the finale," I put on my *brave* voice, hoping I wouldn't alarm her any further. I wasn't doing as bad as I had been—the intervention actually helped me but I'd be lying if I said I was doing *well*. "How is Thanksgiving dinner coming along?" I decided to use the old diversion tactic. It worked like a charm.

"We're getting there," she said, sounding considerably less burdened by grief over my situation. "Your dad bought a huge turkey. I don't know how we will ever manage to eat all of it," She chuckled drily.

"Aren't you having people over? I'm sure they'll help." She never thought all the food would get eaten, and every year all of it *was*.

"True, we are having guests, that will help. I wish you were going to be here this year," she said, sounding somber again.

"Me too, mom. Me too." I wasn't sure I really meant that. Sure, it would probably beat anxiously working out by myself in the dark and cold but there were other places I'd rather be right now, like a beach in Fiji without Wi-Fi. We hung up with me feeling considerably less happy thinking about the people who hated me that might attend the finale, and my mom, hopefully, feeling better about my well-being.

11/28/2015

When I wasn't working out with Amber supervising me (this time with her savvier to my hidden agenda) I had weekly sessions with a therapist. I had promised the people who loved me I would, so I did, even if in my head I kept going back and forth between *I don't need this* and *God I need this*. That mental split made the sessions tiresome and an irritating element of my weeks. My therapist was a nice enough middle-aged lady, who did her best to help me sway my allegiance from the show's diet and exercise regime to a more easy-going approach. There were moments where I loved her sessions but mostly I feel like I'm bullshitting my way through. I say all the right things, "Yes, self-care is important and I'm focusing on healthy choices," while she smiles and nods at me then I get to leave. I really do know I have to eat a little bit every now and then and I can't live and breathe in the gym, but it's not forever. I only have to stay hungry and tired until the finale. I'll have plenty of time to eat and sleep after the finale. I don't want to let everyone down or publicly humiliate my family any more than I already have because I'm too lazy and have no willpower.

12/5/2015

I woke up in the middle of the night dry heaving and shaking. I don't think I had enough food today. I crawled to the kitchen. I had four raisins. I don't want too many extra calories. The dry heaving stopped but the shaking didn't until I fell asleep on the kitchen floor.

12/6/2015

The upcoming finale feels like I have to give a huge presentation in front of hundreds of people on a topic I've never heard of before. It feels like years since I said goodbye to Jane. I miss her arms around me and talking to her in person. I also miss sex. I miss it a lot. Sex is a substitute for food. When I was with Jane—if we weren't actively having sex, I was thinking about having sex with her. Now in New Hampshire by myself with the finale getting closer, my food intake dropping and my workout hours climbing along with my anxiety I don't have sex as a release. Instead I masturbate. *A lot.* The little sleep I get almost always came after an orgasm. When I wake in the mornings, I'd often wake up with an orgasm followed by coffee. When I get back from running, I'd masturbate again before hitting the shower. I have no social life because making new friends feels like a minefield now that the show is airing and I don't want to be questioned about how much I am working out or if I am eating by people I already know. I don't eat, and I spend all my time working out. Orgasms are all I have to take my mind off the agonizing hunger pangs and the shame I feel about not doing *more* to lose weight in the little time I have left.

12/8/2015

I am a jeans and hoodie kind of girl. I had even entertained the thought of wearing jeans like Shea's as my finale reveal outfit. So, when production called today and I made the suggestion, they made it very clear that would not be happening. Just like I wasn't allowed a full shirt until I lost enough weight, I'm not allowed a pair of pants at the finale. Dresses only for the women. Everything is such a fucking fight with them.

I know I am not going to be comfortable in a dress. I'm just not. I need something to make me feel comfortable. I hate everything about my body right now except my face. I'm going to stop working out long enough to go to a local salon and get my eyebrows done. I always feel weirdly better when I like my eyebrows. I'm feeling good about doing something not directly related to losing weight. I'm pretty sure this is an actual self-care thing and not in the bullshit way I tell my therapist. I'm going to focus on my face. I am going to interact with people I don't know and I am going to be normal. I can do this.

Once I was at the salon I felt like the old chatty and upbeat version of myself that I hadn't seen in months. I was comfortable enough with the esthetician and confident enough in my people-ing skills today that I started talking about the finale because he had recognized me from the show and asked for details. I was blathering away about how I needed a dress for the finale and figured I could just grab something inexpensive online.

"No, no, no, please don't do that," the woman next to me interjected. "Please do not buy a $20.00 dress to wear on national TV," she added pleadingly. The esthetician and I both looked at her, confused about her agitation. She was a middle aged posh looking lady, and one of two other patrons in the salon. Being weirdly quasi-famous because of reality TV for a couple months now had made me a little wary of people I didn't know inserting themselves into my conversations. It usually meant they had an unwarranted opinion about the show or me on the show, and they absolutely had to share it, thinking I would faint from joy. I hadn't fainted from joy yet. This lady looked like she might know what she was talking about though, so I decided to go with it.

"For twenty bucks on Amazon I can get a dress and still have enough left over for dinner I won't eat," I quipped. She wasn't having it.

"You are a stunning girl. You need a beautiful dress that emphasizes you. Brings out that beauty." Well how could I possibly argue with that?

"I don't know anything about it, obviously," I said, laughing. "I would show up in a hoodie and jeans if they hadn't vetoed it." Her face looked as though she had just witnessed me murder somebody.

"Oh no. No. That won't do. I will help you," she said, with the authority of a cop commandeering a vehicle. "This is what I do for a living," she explained. Turns out she was a professional stylist and insisted on taking me shopping. After they finished with my eyebrows, I hopped in this complete stranger's Mercedes (She made me call my mom first. She said it was her duty as a mom to make sure I let someone know where I was. Moms are weirdos.). She drove us to a boutique where we spent hours choosing a beautiful dress then she told the clerks precisely how to tailor it to my body. We then chose some heels to go with it and undergarments. I would have died not knowing the importance of good bra and underpants, if it wasn't for this random lady recoiling in horror at my ratty old bra and deciding it wouldn't do.

My next problem presented itself immediately, when I put on the heels. I don't spend a lot of time in four-inch heels. Just standing in front of the mirror with my new friend and the clerks looking at me I felt nervous in these heels. I hadn't even moved in them yet and was panicking about wearing them. I was going to wear these. On national television. When I took the stage at the finale in these things there was a very real possibility that I would fall flat on my face and be the ridicule of the nation. Well, *more* of a ridicule anyway. I stood there looking in the mirror imagining me crashing through my Fat Tisa poster to a cheering audience, landing on my face then coming up with blood, tears and make-up smeared everywhere. Anxiety is fun.

"Go on, Tisa. Twirl," my new stylist friend said. I didn't know if I could. I tried. She immediately saw my struggle. "All right, let's try walking instead." How was walking going to be easier? I walk in heels like I'm a newborn baby giraffe. Falling is a real possibility. After a bit of staggering, I got kind of a decent flow going. I mean it's not like I'd *never* walked in heels before, but it had been a long time. Society doesn't generally make wearing heels all that easy for a fat girl with wide feet.

12/10/2015

New dress and heels in tow, I was finally on the way back to L.A. to see how it was all going to turn out. I stopped eating solid food completely about six days ago. I was focused on not letting everybody down and putting in my best showing on that scale. I had cut my water back too. No one was really onboard with this plan except production but I wasn't going to be deterred this close to the finale. The only thing that I was really allowing myself to eat was sugar free gelatin. I had packed several of them to take with me on the flights to L.A. I had a bunch of single serving packets of sugar free gelatin and I was clinging to them like a security blanket. I had to stop myself from handcuffing them to my wrist.

After checking in for my flight, I arrived at TSA and the agent looked confused about my sixteen single serving sugar-free gelatins in a Ziploc bag.

"Ma'am, you can't bring this through security," he said, holding up the bag with a tired look on his face.

"What? Why not?" I asked, already in a state of mild panic.

"Because we don't allow liquids or gels over 3.4 ounces or 100ml," he said, with the monotonous voice of someone who probably says those words in his sleep. "I'm going to have to confiscate this," He waved the bag back and forth a few times.

"I need it though. I need it for the cookies and peanuts," I wasn't prepared to let my sugar free gelatin go. I was starved and tired and anxious and this felt like a last straw kind of thing.

"Cookies and peanuts? I'm sorry, ma'am, I don't know what you mean. But I can't allow you to take it through this checkpoint," He was looking mildly annoyed now.

"Look. I haven't eaten in like eight days or something. I need these for my trip. I can't eat anything else."

"Are you allergic, ma'am?" he asked, now with genuine, if baffled, curiosity.

"What? No," I said, like he had offended me.

"Then why can't you eat anything else?" People behind me were getting irritated at me; the crazy lady with the sugar free gelatin. I didn't care.

"Because of the show. I really want to bring this. I can't eat the cookies. I can't have the peanuts. I just can't," I was crying now, and the poor guy looked horrified. I'm sure he had seen a thing or two over the years but probably never a lady crying feverishly over a Ziploc'ed bag of sixteen servings of sugar free gelatin.

"I'm sorry ma'am. I can't let you bring them. It's policy. Has been for years now," he said, looking legitimately sorry now. "I'm going to have to ask you to throw those in that bin and move along. I'm sorry."

I moved along through the scanner booth, tears streaming down my face with people looking at me like I was insane. They weren't wrong. I went on to the gate, quietly sobbing and feeling like I had no idea what the hell I was doing. I texted Jane, but she was also in transit and couldn't reply. It was stupid but the loss of my gelatin felt like a cataclysmic event, and I felt alone sitting between all those other people waiting to fly to L.A.

The flight was long and shitty because I couldn't do either of the only things I used as coping mechanisms—work out or masturbate. Don't think I didn't consider both. I sat next to an old white guy who kept trying to strike up a conversation, even when I had earbuds in. I could hear his voice faintly through music and I'd take them off occasionally and go *"pardon me?"* and he'd repeat the most boring conversation starters known to man one after the other as I replaced my ear buds. It was a fun game. Finally, he dozed off and I was allowed peace to try and do the same. I managed to dodge the cookie and peanut distributing crew members by shaking my head in a way that I'm sure resembled someone trying to put a fire out in their hair. I couldn't muster the mental energy to use my words. The little sleep I did get was welcome, even if it was the broken half-dozing airplane kind.

I rushed off the plane as quickly as possible after landing. I nearly knocked a kid over, as I barged out and away from my seatmate. I had a mission. Sugar Free Gelatin. Also, see my girlfriend. Everything in me just wanted to be near her—and go shopping for sugar free gelatin. I stalked along the walkway, trying not to run and cause alarm but also making it out before people cluttered things up. I turned the last corner and spotted her further ahead. There she was, with a bouquet of flowers. I stopped short and just stood there, stunned at the sight. She turned her head and saw me as well and broke into a smile. I couldn't move I was so happy to see her. She started coming toward me, against the flow of now annoyed people. I felt like I was in a 1980s teen movie. She wrapped her arms around me and kissed me on the head. She stood back, gave me the flowers and I almost crushed them when I hugged her again to kiss her. I was distracted by a man staring with a weird intensity at us. He started walking toward us and I got a sinking feeling in my chest that this was production fuckery.

I was not wrong.

"Hi. Tisa?" he asked with the voice of somebody who knows the answer to the question but is asking it to be polite. Also, I think he was painfully aware that he was interrupting a *moment.*

"Yes?" I asked, still in Jane's arms and my bouquet of flowers in one hand.

"I am Andy. I've been assigned by the show to be your personal assistant the next few days before the finale," For fuck's sake. The universe is a funny fucker. I have a babysitter. I'm pretty sure this guy was sent in as a metaphorical kick in the face lest I get too happy. Great. The three of us head toward baggage claim, get my suitcase, and head to the curb.

"What are you driving?" I ask Jane.

"I rented a car. It's in parking here," she said, and pulled the key out. We both looked at Andy.

"I have a car here for you," he said, looking kind of sheepish.

"Can we meet you somewhere or something?" I asked as Jane went off to get her rental and pull up.

"Uhm. Well, I'm not supposed to let you out of my sight. I can't let you drive off too far," He looked super uncomfortable, and I almost felt sorry for him. Couldn't be an easy job.

"Did they book you in a double room with me or something? Because I'm telling you now, that room is full already," I shot him an accusatory look. He cleared his throat.

"No, not at night. Just when you are out of the hotel."

"Good," I said. "That could've been awkward. Or interesting, depending on Jane," I was resorting to jokes because of the absurdity of having this man babysit me.

He explained he had been hired specifically for the days leading up to the finale to do nothing except watch me. The reason he had to watch me was because I was not allowed to talk to or interact with any of the other contestants. The thought process was that it would ruin the reveal moments at the finale if we knew what one another looked like beforehand. While every other contestant got to spend time together again, I and the three other finalists (Farrell, Brody and Esther) were to be completely isolated. I didn't actually know if Esther would be here or not. I hadn't pushed that poor girl in NYC for information about Esther skipping the finale but I doubted production would let her skip this spectacle.

Andy explained each finalist had somebody assigned to them making sure there was no unsanctioned communication between any of us. Andy seemed like he was a nice enough guy but there is something incredibly weird about being an adult who has somebody assigned to watch my every move. Don't get me wrong, my friends and family had been watching me and looking out for my well-being the past two months as best as possible but they were motivated by concern for me. This guy was concerned with the sanctity of a reality TV reveal moment. Jane pulled up and rolled down the window. I looked at Andy.

"I need to go to the grocery store and I'm going to ride with my girlfriend. Can you follow us or something?"

"Uhm," He seemed to consider it but resigned himself when he saw that I was dead serious. "How about this, we can all use the car the show provided and I'll make sure Jane gets rides wherever she needs to go too? I mean, she doesn't have to spend money on a car that way and you guys don't even know where you're going to find a grocery store right?" He was right, we didn't. I told Jane I needed to go get sugar free gelatin and she agreed to leaving the rental. We googled for a supermarket on the road to my hotel while Andy helped me with my suitcase.

In the car with Jane, I lamented this babysitter development. It was uncanny how this show had a knack for casting me in spy movie scenarios. A nanny following me around L.A.? What a joke. I briefly thought back on all my shenanigans at the Spa and realized maybe I couldn't fault them. The truth is I would've barged into the rooms of the other three finalists and asked every question I could if given the chance. Even so, this still felt ridiculous. It's reality TV, not nuclear launch codes. I would've preferred to pick up sugar free gelatin and head straight to the hotel to have sex, because it had been a month and a half and I hadn't eaten in days. Instead I would get to spend time with my new friend Andy. I heaved a deep sigh, leaned back, and let Jane's hand on my shoulder be the best I could get for now. We got to the grocery store and I had the pleasure of shopping for sugar free gelatin with two people awkwardly following me around. It turns out there was a coupon sale for sugar free gelatin.

"I guess they knew the finale was this week," Jane said, and even Andy had to crack a smile at that one. The coupons offered sugar free gelatin purchasers a chance to win free tickets to attend the finale. I wonder how they would react if I won and claimed the tickets?

Back in the car, we drove straight to the hotel while I inhaled a sugar free gelatin and Jane looked back and forth between Andy driving and me with an expression of part amusement, part worry. I cared not at all. I had been needing that gelatin badly all day and having it mitigated my anxiety a bit. When we arrived at the hotel, Andy followed us inside. I checked in, went back, gave my key to Jane and asked her to take my suitcase up to my room. She did, and I turned to Andy.

"Look dude. I know this is your job, so don't take this the wrong way, but you're a pretty big pebble in my machinery right now. I know you can't leave me alone before the finale, so here is what's going to happen. I need to get laid in the very foreseeable future, or so help me I'm going to be extremely difficult to deal with the next few days. Unless you want to watch, can you give me thirty minutes of alone time here, so I can have sex? After, I'll go along with whatever you have planned. Deal?"

Andy looked like I had asked him to solve peace in the Middle East or I would have his family murdered. After a moment of suspended animation, he collected himself.

"Uh, yes of course I mean sure. I'll be, uh, I'll be here I guess. Waiting," he stuttered and looked around for a chair seemingly befuddled and not realizing there were three right next to him. I was happy he hadn't called my bluff with the offer to watch, because I was beyond caring but Jane probably wouldn't have appreciated an audience. I left him trying to find the chairs located right next to him and rushed to the elevator. I was antsy while going up to the 7th floor, feeling tempted to push the button several times, you know, to make it go faster. I used my second key to open the door, close it and lock it. Jane was standing by the bed and I nearly bowled her over when I got to her.

"Fuck me," were the only words I had enough wits about me to utter. Super romantic of me. She was game. I had fantasized about this for weeks. She handled me in ways that put all those fantasies to shame. It was a run for orgasms and it was precisely what I had hoped it would be. After I had come down to Earth again, I could fully appreciate having her close. I wrapped myself around her to maximize the surface area of our bodies touching before I settled a little bit.

"We have ten minutes before we have to be downstairs again," I said, heaving a sigh. My body said stay and sleep, everything else be damned. My mind, however, was already starting to dart off elsewhere, and I hated it. I was in

L.A. again and like darkness, it crept back into the small crevasses of my mind. I wanted to be in Alaska with Jane, having sex and perhaps even take a stab at eating. Instead I had a personal babysitter and a date to be on national TV. Jane kissed me and let her hands banish the Los Angeles darkness from my mind briefly with another orgasm before we both showered and got dressed quickly.

Andy was dutifully sitting in a chair looking like he had been twiddling his thumbs for thirty minutes. He remained composed but I feel like I saw a brief knowing smile flash across his face before he got up to meet us.

"All right, Andy," I said. "I'm all yours now, as promised," And thus I was whisked away from Jane once again, on this *magical* journey through Tinsel town with my new friend Andy, who was to go with me everywhere I went. He filled me in on the schedule for the next couple of days. During this day I was to do some photoshoots of publicity stuff for the show. Then I had a meet and greet with press and fans, pretending to be the socialite I never wanted to be in the first place, plastering a big old smile on my face and shaking hands with a lot of people I didn't give a shit about. There was a day in the schedule to spend at the doctor's office, reliving all the same testing that I went through in the first week that I was brought out to L.A. Not an experience I was looking forward to. I was relieved Jane wasn't allowed to go with me on most of these outings. Andy was nice enough to suggest that she might want to spend time with the other contestants that were allowed to meet with one another. They decided after taking me to the doctor's office in the morning, in yet another church van, Andy would take Jane to a different hotel to spend the whole day meeting other contestants. The people she'd seen once on television and heard me tell stories about. I was briefly worried for her but luckily, she's a strong enough personality that she can handle her own in a room full of strangers. Then another day of interviews was scheduled and similarly themed bullshit, before it was finale day and time. The most dreaded night. I felt more and more like I was going to crash out on that stage, fall on my face, have the dress somehow get ripped off my body, then lay there naked on the floor with a bloody nose on national TV. I can't wait. I kissed Jane goodbye and went with Andy into the car.

I spent the rest of that afternoon and early night doing whatever Andy could come up with from his clipboard. It was a blur after the second hour of faces, hands, flashes and smiles. I hadn't eaten anything since my one gelatin, and I wasn't about to—especially because I knew I wouldn't have the opportunity to work out again. When the tasks finally ended, I was ready to crash but I knew the rest of my family had arrived, were hungry and waiting for me back at the hotel before going to get dinner. When Andy took me to the hotel, I was greeted by my parents and my older sister who were very excited to see me and eager to meet Jane when she returned. They were all asking questions and talking loudly. All I really wanted at this point was to crash in my hotel room while waiting on Jane. That was not going to happen. Instead I was going to In-N-Out Burger with my family. I couldn't bring myself to even drink water except in the smallest of sips this close to the finale so I sat at In-N-Out burger watching everybody else eat and drink. It was better than sitting by myself though, I reasoned.

When Jane returned to the hotel, it was almost nine p.m. and I was in our room. Andy having graciously allowed me privacy for the rest of the day. I was all over the place, physically and emotionally. I was pacing the room when she walked in, counting my steps.

I had cut my water intake almost entirely because I was keenly aware that the weigh-in for the finale was actually decided at tomorrow's weigh in at the doctor's office not on the giant TV scale. I knew tonight would be my last push to get as much weight off as humanly possible. I had searched the hotel and found a sauna. I decided I was going to spend the rest of the evening in and out of that sauna. Jane was pissed I was doing it and refused to participate. She didn't plead with me not to do it, realizing it would have been futile, but she didn't want to be an active participant in it either. My mother, a nurse, knew I wasn't going to be talked out of it and did the best she could by monitoring me. She kept checking my blood pressure throughout the insane process.

It was strange having her and Jane meet for the first time in person while I was deliberately dehydrating myself while both of them tried to help me in their own way. My mother made one last attempt to argue with me to convince me not to, but I insisted.

I spent six hours getting in and out of the sauna every fifteen minutes trying to take off the last little bit of water weight that I could. It worked. The combination of the sauna, cutting my water intake and not eating the past two weeks dropped the scale twenty pounds. I got back on the scale every time I went in and out of the sauna and my mom looked terrified. She was literally wringing her hands but I couldn't be talked out of it. I wasn't that worried because production knew what I was doing and my dropping dead would probably be bad publicity so I figured they would've stopped me if it was *really* a problem. Andy had said I needed get spray tanned earlier today but I postponed it, pissing production off. I told them they could spray tan me if they wanted but it was going to be incredibly streaky and look like shit because I would be spending the evening in a sauna. They postponed the spray tan.

By the time I returned to the room, Jane was asleep. I pondered waking her for sex but she hadn't been completely happy with me and my sauna stunt. I didn't want to pick that conversation back up. So, I took a hot shower then passed out from exhaustion.

12/11/2015

Waking up next to Jane again was delightful and touching her first thing in the morning was bliss. The impending doctor's visit quickly brought back my anxiety though, and I was out of bed before I touched her as much as I really wanted. Jane watched me stroll around the room, half engaged in tasks nobody, including me, really understood. I was like a headless chicken. Andy told me last night before leaving the hotel he would get ahold of me early in the morning so we could make it to the doctor's on time. He called not long after I woke up, saying he would pick me up twenty minutes later. I felt immediately rushed and after storming around like a rat in a maze for five minutes, Jane caught me and held me tight.

"It's going to be alright, Tisa," she whispered in my ear. "I can't be with you today but I will be with you in my head."

"I know," I whispered back, as I clung to her. I was crying. Not that I noticed anymore, it was such a regular occurrence. This time my tears were sheer frustration with everything—mostly myself—and because I felt out of control. Jane held me for another few minutes before letting me go and asking what she could do to help. I managed a smile and told her she was already doing it.

The spectacle of the doctor's office was much like the same spectacle in the very first week I was in L.A. —it feels like that happened years ago. Basically, the same routine, being poked and prodded, put in a giant machine that looks like a copier where they scan my body to show how much body fat I had. There were classics like peeing in a cup. Coughing so they could listen to my lungs, all that fun stuff. This time though I was accompanied by my mother and everything was done as though it were the Secret Service carrying out my tests. They were afraid that I would bump into one of the other finalists who were also in the building at the same time. If we did bump into each other, apparently that might cause a rift in the time space continuum or cause cataclysmic reality TV events that would end the world as we know it—or at least reduce their revenue stream somehow. My mother happened to get a glance at Farrell and started to tell me how he looked. I was so overwhelmed that I didn't want to hear it. I didn't want anything to do with it. I just wanted the doctor to finish sticking me, forcing me to pee and weighing me, then let me get the hell out of there to be done with this entire travesty. After I was done with this enjoyable experience, they rushed me out of there like the paparazzi were going to be waiting outside. Production literally formed a human shield around me and got me back into a church van with my mother who looked just emotionally exhausted by the whole situation. I was happy to be out of a medical gown again.

I was in the room again when Jane returned from spending the day with the other contestants. She was in shock.

"Tisa, you have no idea the amount of crazy out there," she said.

"Worse than *me*?" I asked.

"You're a model citizen compared to some of the things I witnessed and heard about today. Get this, one lady peed in a Ziploc bag, then inserted it into her vagina, before they tested her for dehydration."

"What?" I asked, in shock and amazement. "How, what, how would that even work? What would it do?"

"I've no idea. But it fucking happened," She said. I looked at her in awe as I also wondered how the hell I managed to pass the tests for dehydration. As I understood it, the limit to go with no water was somewhere around three days. I had been pushing it by just taking minimal sips of water when I couldn't stand it anymore for almost a week now. Not only had I not had any liquids before the doctor's visit, I had been in a sauna off and on for six hours, flown across the nation, and had sex. I was almost proud. "They treated Bruno like shit because he *only* lost seventy pounds and Dawn has gained most of her weight back. She was lamenting how she weighed more than when she left the Spa, and she took a diuretic before the weigh-in, Tisa," Jane said after a moment's pause. Many of these names came flooding back into my memory. It had been so long since I had thought about them but of course, they were still real people somewhere out there.

"It sounds like a madhouse. I'm glad you made it out alive."

"Yes, apparently that isn't a guarantee. I spoke to Farrell's wife. She is worried for him."

"What? What for?" I was suddenly keenly interested. Farrell was my only competition really, as Esther was out and I never seriously considered Brody in the same league. I felt kind of bad relishing the possible misfortune of Farrell but we were so close now and I couldn't even keep my head collected enough to feel truly bad. He had fucked me over once, after all.

"After the doctor's visit today, he wanted Mexican food, and proceeded to eat nachos, two burritos, a taco and two margaritas before he became violently ill. According to his wife there was a considerable amount of vomit then fear of refeeding syndrome."

"Montezuma works in mysterious ways," I said flippantly. Jane chuckled, even if we both knew it wasn't particularly funny. I was making jokes out of fear of what I had done to myself. I was still too scared of food to eat after the doctor's office but since the final weigh in was now done, I was drinking water like it was going out of style. Was I going to be violently ill when I ate something?

12/12/2015

We headed down to the breakfast area of the hotel and it was clear production had rented most of the rooms there. People with clipboards and A/V equipment were milling about left and right, obviously connected with the show in some capacity. My family was already there and took Jane to the breakfast buffet while I sat down in the lobby area. I requested some granola with soy milk because eating again came with a side of extreme trepidation. As they walked off, I spotted Daniel entering the hotel. He saw me right away and walked toward me, his face lighting up like we were old friends finally getting back together for a chat. I stood up to greet him and just as he was about to say *hi* I passed out. Just fell out on the fucking floor. I came to, what must've been seconds later because he was holding my head up. He helped me back to my chair. Great, this is totally how I wanted to see this guy again.

"How are you?" he asked, looking concerned for obvious reasons.

"Peachy," I responded. "Clearly doing well."

"Of course," he said, an awkward silence followed. "I broke up with my girlfriend," I looked at him. It's been six months, buddy. Even if I *had* cared at any point, six months probably isn't a good amount of time to wait before you tell somebody you're single.

"It doesn't matter, Daniel. You missed your shot," I considered telling him about Jane but really I didn't have to. I had come to this conclusion about Daniel before Jane was even a thing in my life. She had no impact on the decision not to try to contact or go back to Daniel when returning to L.A. It was my own decision. "Please have a good life but move along out of mine."

He looked at me with great sadness, for which I felt no real sympathy. Part of which was probably lingering embarrassment at being picked up off the floor by the guy. He slowly nodded as he got to his feet again, then he wished me good luck and went on his way. He didn't try to persist and respected my decision. I appreciated that, I'm sure he had production work to attend to and I was no longer his *job*.

After I ate breakfast, thankfully without mishap, I kissed Jane goodbye once again and wished her luck. She would be spending all day with my interesting family—after having just met them—so she was going to need every ounce of luck she could get. For me, the rest of the day passed with endless interviews. If I had to answer one more question about what my favorite low calorie, low fat snack was, I was going to lose my mind. Apparently, celery dipped in water wasn't the right answer because production started answering for me. Who knew I loved blueberries so much? Production did, that's who.

At night in our room, I again considered having sex, and a naked Jane did nothing to dissuade the thought—hot damn this woman was stunning. We started fooling around but I was weirdly exhausted before even getting going. After a bit we agreed to abandon the project. I was out of breath and felt light headed. Sleep seemed like the smarter idea.

"Jane wake up. I think somebody's at the door," I said with a start, scaring myself in the process. "I hear somebody knocking at the door."

"What? What?" she responded, still halfway between reality and dream land. "I didn't hear anything."

"No Jane I'm sure of it," I was mildly panicked now. Who would be at the door in the middle of the night? "I thought I heard somebody knock."

"Tisa, it's two a.m.," she said, looking at the clock through squinted eyes. "There's nobody at the door."

"Could you please just go check? Please," I had the weirdest feeling somebody had knocked. Jane got up and went to see if there was anybody at our door. There was no one there. She told me as much, and I realized I must've imagined I heard something. Jane came back into the bedroom of the suite and turned on the light by the bed. When she looked over at my side of the bed, she gasped. I looked down at myself. The entire side of the bed and I were covered in blood. She looked down at herself too and realized she had blood down the side of her torso and one leg. There was blood everywhere and she started to freak out.

"Oh my god, are you hurt or is something on you hurt? What is going on? Are you okay?" she yelled as she stormed around the bed and pulled the covers off of me.

"What do you mean?" I asked confused. I didn't feel hurt, I felt okay. Then what I was seeing clicked in my brain. I was covered in blood. It looked like a scene out of a horror movie on this bed. I clasped my hands over my mouth to stifle an accompanying straight horror movie scream. I started shaking. Jane was now furiously checking my body for whatever—gunshot wounds, or stab wounds, or Alien abdominal exit wounds, I don't know. She calmed down a little bit when I appeared to not be actively bleeding from my torso or legs but was still looking concerned. It took a moment for it to register to either of us, but it turned out the period that had eluded me for months now, had decided to come back with a vengeance tonight before the finale. I had no idea what was going on with my body. I was still shaking and couldn't stop again. Jane got on the room phone, called down to my parents' room, asking my mom to please come up in a hurry because she was worried about me. Moments later my mother was in the room and her eyes turned huge when she saw all the damn blood. Realizing immediately what had happened, my mom helped me clean up and get into clothes. I was still shaking but not as badly.

"I was just here," she said, after housekeeping had been called and had helped us with a new mattress and linens, surprisingly efficient at three a.m.

"What?" Jane asked, not sure what she was talking about.

"I was just here. Outside your room before you called. Knocking on your door." Her voice was weirdly ethereal and I had to pinch myself to question if all of this was really happening. I looked at Jane, not even having enough energy to be cocky that I was right about the knock, just mouth agape in amazement.

"What were you doing knocking on our door at two a.m.?" she asked, always the rationalist.

"Your little sister called from the East Coast," she replied, and looked back and forth between us like that explained it all.

"Okay? What was she calling about from the East Coast this early?" I asked, annoyed that the information wasn't flowing freely at this point.

"She was worried about you, Tisa," my mother said. "She said she woke up after a dream she had where you were sick and she knew that you needed something or somebody to check on you. She called me and woke me up and I got up to check on you. It looks like she was right."

I looked at my mom, unable to speak. Then at Jane, who looked like she didn't know what to say either. My little sister and I had had a bond like this forever—like she always sort of knew things before other people did and we just never questioned it. She has a great sense of intuition and she always trusted it.

Tonight, she knew I was in trouble and that I needed her. My mom took my blood pressure and my vitals and monitored me. She stayed up with me for almost the rest of the night and well into the morning until it was time for final finale prep to make sure that I was going to be okay. I just looked at her desperately.

"It's almost done, mom. It's almost done. We're almost there," was all I could say to her. Over and over. My mom looked so sad.

Chapter 18

My mom got a little bit of sleep during the late morning when I was led downstairs to eat and meet with a few producers about what was going to happen during the day. My head was everywhere at once. I got a bullshit spiel about us having to go to the Spa and film some homecoming schmaltz and was briefly told about when we'd go to the venue for the show. Nothing about how it would actually be, of course, just that I would be doing it. Finally, I was told my spray tan appointment would happen in half an hour. I could hardly wait. I'm sure it will be as fun as watching paint dry, on my body. I ate a granola bar while people talked at me, and I wondered where the other three finalists were and the rest of the contestants. I hadn't spoken to any of them in months. Debbie in particular I was looking forward to seeing again. When I got back to my room, Jane was on the bed reading and I told her about the plans for the day.

"How are you feeling?" She asked, as I sat down next to her, unsure of what I was supposed to do but with the distinct feeling that I didn't have time to just sit around.

"I don't even know how to answer that," I replied, and flashed her an apologetic smile. "Like, focused and confused at the same time? Like I really just want to get this over with but also I am a little scared what will happen once it is done."

"I see your point." I knew she didn't see all of it, that she couldn't but I appreciated her for even being here. She could've cut and run at any point doing this madness.

"I'm sorry I'm so much trouble," I said, but she stopped me.

"No. You have nothing to apologize for, least of all to me. I'm not here because I think it's some noble thing to do. I'm here because I want to be, for you," She reached out and rubbed my back; that little bit of contact felt soothing. "I also meant how are you doing physically?"

"I think I'm good. Not bleeding any more at least," I said and snapped my fingers jauntily.

"I should think you'd have no blood left to bleed after last night," she replied, and we both laughed. "You can do this, Tisa. I believe in you."

"Thank you," I said, as I leaned over to kiss her. She pulled me down on top of her in a hug. "I might not win," I said after a minute in her arms.

"I don't care about that. I'm proud of you for being here at all. Not because of what you accomplished through the show, but because this whole machinery is crazy beyond my wildest imaginations, and you're holding up through it all. That's strength." She squeezed me tight, and neither of us said anything for a while. I found peace in her embrace, and I could have dozed off, if it hadn't been for my mom knocking on the door. She looked trashed when I opened it, but at least she was up and I appreciated her checking on me. I told her I was getting spray tanned soon, and it was happening right in my room. Jane took the hint and said she'd go and grab something to eat. Not that having her watch me get spray tanned would've been particularly harrowing, but with my mom and some stranger there too I figured it'd be easier for everybody with a smaller audience. As she opened the door to leave, a man was just getting ready to knock. She let him in and disappeared down the hallway.

"Hi. I'll be spray tanning you today," he announced in a voice all too chipper for somebody who was putting down a large piece of plastic on the floor. I stripped on his command and stepped on the plastic. Pretty weird to be sprayed with tan, naked, by a complete stranger, while my mom watched. I spun in a circle to get it even, before I had to let it dry off a bit by just standing, still naked, on a piece of plastic. I was getting nervous. Not because I was getting chemicals sprayed onto my body for no real reason, but because today was the day I'd find out the final results. Was winning a real possibility? My mom kept bolstering me to be positive.

"Just be positive and don't worry too much about the result but about the process you went through." Which was another way of saying she was afraid that even though I said I was okay with not winning I might not be. "Doing the right thing *always* pays off, Tisa," she kept saying, like somehow that made it more valid. Pay off how, though? What exactly *was* the right thing here? Did I even know anymore? I felt like Alice through the looking glass again. Was what I had chosen to do, eating more—though I sure as hell hadn't done that the last two weeks—and working out less, the right choice? Or should I have continued doing what I had been told? I would know today.

We had all worked out until we vomited, our clothing rubbed our skin off and we bled through our shoes. We worked out with injuries, including sprained ankles, bursitis, and torn calf muscles. The entire world would see if we, and of the most concern to me, I, had wasted this opportunity.

I was allowed to put on clothes again after the tan had dried, and he fitted me with a piece of plastic over my shoulders, so he could do my face too with some weird tiny specialized air brush. Jane came back some time in the middle of this process and sat down next to my mom.

None of us were really about the spray tan look on me. I'm not really about a look that would require this much time and maintenance. Plus, being mixed race, I'm already dark so spray tanning felt superfluous. A beat passed, my mom got up, and said she'd leave us alone for a bit to go check on my dad and sister. I was sort of surprised my older sister who had made it to L.A. for the finale wasn't all over my room. She had a way of inviting herself along with everything. To be fair, she also always showed up for me no matter what the event. "How are you feeling?" Jane asked, when my mom had left.

"I'll get by, I guess," I said, truthfully. I was, but I sure wasn't adding more pleasant memories of L.A. to my already shitty catalogue. "Can't wait until it's over."

"Me neither," she said. I looked at her curiously. "I hate what it does to you."

"Oh," I said, and smiled. I like that she cared.

"And this spray tan business isn't my favorite thing either. You look orange more than anything," She said, as she got up and carefully touched me. I laughed, and it felt like a small liberation to be able to. "If it was any other day, I'd insist we ruin it on that bed," We both looked at the bed, and suddenly I wanted little else than to get naked again and do just that.

"I wish we could," I said, and kissed her carefully. "The moment this is over, you should," She smiled and nodded agreement.

"I'll be in the audience when you come on stage. Look for me, if you need me."

"I don't know if I'll even be able to correctly say my own name at that point," I said. "But thank you. That means a lot."

The phone rang and it was production telling me twenty minutes before I had to go to the Spa. I called my mom and told her. She said she was on her way up.

"I'm going to head out and do a little sightseeing of whatever L.A. has to offer." Jane said. "While I'm finally out of Alaska, I might as well be constructive."

"You'll hate L.A.," I said. "Have fun," I laughed again. She did too.

"Good luck tonight, babe."

"Thank you. For everything," I said. We moved in for a sort of hug but our mutual fears of smearing the tan or something made it this awkward back patting spectacle. We chuckled.

"Later," she said, referring to the hug. Then she kissed my hair and left.

I was looking at myself in the mirror as my mom entered the room, which Jane had left open for her.

"You look beautiful," she said, joining me in front of the mirror.

"I have you to thank for that," I replied, smiling at her.

"I wish. You have your grandmother to thank for that," she said, and chuckled. We were still standing there, when a knock on the door indicated it was time for me to head to the Spa. I dreaded the finale later but I was pretty ambivalent about going back to the Spa.

I was met by a PA in the lobby again, after looking around for familiar faces and seeing none. I briefly pondered the amount of personnel needed to keep, what I assume was, fifty people separate from one another. In only two hotels. The logistics of that seemed impossible. We ducked into a car with the PA immediately and were on our way soon after. It was with trepidation I noticed the buildings become fewer and further between, and the Californian desert open up ahead of us. Flashes of all the horrible bullshit we had done at that Spa flashed in my mind. The PA asked if I was okay, and I realized I was sweating in a car kept so air conditioned I could've juggled ice cubes without getting my hands wet.

"I'm all right. This just brings back some memories, and they aren't all pleasant," I said. She looked at me like I was an idiot. All right then. The desert was as featureless as deserts often are but I still managed to recognize a few landmarks as we got closer to the Spa. All the trips in church vans had given me, if nothing else, the time and opportunity to study and memorize all the nooks and crannies of the desert by the road leading to the Spa. Soon we were driving down the entranceway and I saw the usual mishmash of sound guys and camera people mixed with PAs of all kinds. I also noticed a car similar to the one I was in and somebody standing next to it. It looked like it could be Farrell and my heart skipped a beat. Some people next to him noticed our car and he was rushed in, and the car sped off as we pulled up.

"Was that..?" I started, but I was cut off.

"Somebody else, yes," the PA said disdainfully, as she exited the vehicle. I looked at her back with eyes that could've frozen fire and decided if I was willing to risk losing this whole show just so I could stab her. As I got out, I was first surprised at the relatively mild temperature in the desert. It was winter but I still had this idea that it was permanently scorching out here. I was led toward the house and kept remembering all the times we had walked back toward the house from the church vans, after a day of what was no doubt full of bullshit. It had felt horrible and yet now that I was here again, I felt somehow more horrible. The smells were the hardest part to get over and they fucked with me as I was led toward the gym where they wanted to shoot me coming back and reminiscing. They wanted me to be all teary eyed as I talked about how amazing it was to be back. I couldn't do it. Just no tears at all. I was in shock, walking around seeing things without really seeing them. Even through my hazy thinking, I felt a familiar urge to get on one of the treadmills and just go for hours. They took me out to the hallway and asked me to look around in wonder as I walked up the stairs and talked about the good times I had there. I was overwhelmed. I was weirdly staccato when speaking and I kept getting the timing wrong because I wasn't invested. It was clear I hadn't had a lot of good times to talk about. I wasn't able to focus properly and after ten minutes my PA was exasperated with me. She went over to a group of crew members, and they all debated back and forth, gesticulating wildly and her gesturing towards me several times. I just wanted to get the hell out of here. It felt like they were arguing about letting me live or simply taking me out behind the tool shed for execution. Finally, another person strolled into their midst and pointed at his watch. We were out of time presumably because the next finalist was on his or her way to film the same bullshit I had just attempted. My PA dragged me back to the car, got in and we drove off with perfect timing to not allow us to pass too close to the other car. My PA didn't say a single word on our way back. I looked out the window but I could still feel her shooting me annoyed looks, like I had somehow caused her personal distress. She should come home with me and I'll put her through six months of gut-wrenching bullshit so she knows what personal distress is. We drove to the hotel, where I was escorted to my room before being left alone. I was wondering what the PA's problem was, when the phone rang and informed me it was already time to head to the finale. Why the fuck they didn't just take me straight there, I'll never know. I went to the bathroom to see if I could pee off some more liquid because even if I wasn't weighing in, I was getting in front of cameras. I had to wear the spandex and tank top weigh-in combo on national TV today, so I really wanted to get the last of it off of me. Somebody knocked on my door while I was in there and they were on the phone trying to call the room, when I finally opened the door.

"I was… never mind," I said, and grabbed my bag with my dress and shoes, and followed her downstairs. Outside a familiar, if not welcome, sight greeted me. A church van picked me up at the hotel and took me to the finale stage. I really had not missed these uncomfortable pieces of shit. This one even had the added fun of having all the side windows blacked out—presumably to keep my identity secret. The lengths to which these people went to guard pretty unimportant secrets about us was insane. Who gave a shit? There are real famous people in this town, no one cares about a reality TV person. The drive was eventless and boring, traffic usually is. I was a little taken aback that they hadn't gotten the full presidential car escort to cart me through. I did have the human shield circle again when I got to the venue though as they led me past confused people waiting to enter for the finale.

I sat in my dressing room alone. I knew Brody was in the next dressing room because I had seen his name on the door in passing and he knocked on the wall to say hello. That small comfort helped —otherwise I felt completely alone. I thought about devising a clever knock routine with Brody, so we could talk but just as I was about to knock on the wall to alert him to my idea, the door opened and the makeup lady came in. More shit I had to sit still for when what I really wanted to do, was pace the floor ceaselessly just to do something. My stomach was turning upside down, and with no remnants of food in there to flip around, it was weirdly noisy and upset. She seemed to take forever doing my make-up, though she was sweet and kind so I relished the company. For me, more than five minutes doing my makeup is an obscene amount of time. I tried my best to not be a fidgety pain in the ass. The next person to enter was a lady for my hair, and I think I saw her die a little inside when she took a look at me. A few bald spots and short hair. I'll give her credit, she actually managed to do a pretty decent job with what she had to work with. I looked in the mirror after and was amazed at how hard the bald spots were to see if you weren't deliberately looking. When she was finally done, another lady replaced her to help me with my dress and shoes. I wasn't sure what help I needed, it was a dress and a pair of shoes. I was, at least for all intents and purposes, an adult. She insisted on helping me though, so I had to strip in front of yet another stranger. I've determined that show biz mostly means feeling like shit about yourself and then getting naked in front of others. Fun times. I got the dress and my shoes on as she fussed around me five more minutes tugging and pulling and brushing the fabric without, it appeared to me, actually doing anything. Gotta look busy to earn her keep, I assumed. Throughout the pampering by these three people the door opened a few times with other members of production popping their heads in giving us time updates. Every time they did, I could hear the roar of the audience in the distance or Cynthia's voice going on about whatever. Finally, I was left alone again and the tension in the little room was rising steadily. I wanted this shit over with but I feared having to do what I needed to get it over with. Just as I was about to pick up the knocking scheme again, the door opened, and A.C. Moss poked his annoying rat face through the door.

"Hi Tisa," he said, and waved cheerily, like he expected I had been hoping he would take time out of his busy schedule to grace me with a visit. He came into my dressing room and smiled so wide, I was scared he might sprain his cheeks.

"Hello," I said, smiling curtly. I was in no mood for this bullshit. It was like the tormentor coming down for one last warning talk with his victim.

"You are so close Tisa," he started and held up two fingers that were, in his defense, pretty close together. "So very close. Anything is possible tonight." It was complete Jedi mind-trick fuckery. Was he threatening me, encouraging me or chastising me for giving up too soon? After all my body had been through, could it be possible that I was going to disappoint millions of people? How in the world could this body, with the bald spots, perpetual hunger and all the bruises clad in this beautiful dress and heels not be good enough? We didn't say much more, because somebody else opened the door, and said it was time.

Finale Time

Finally, it was my turn. I had tried so hard to make the right choices, even if I wasn't ever sure there were any. I was desperate to show people I was worthy of being selected for this opportunity. Now, here in this moment, about to walk out on that stage, listening to the very people I worked so hard to not let down, boo me, nothing felt right.

With the stinging *boos* of the crowd ringing in my ears I burst through the poster of fat Tisa and faced a crowd of hundreds in the studio and millions at home. I'm on the stage and shit is bright and colorful, and to my eyes it's like a blur. The crowd is making noises I can't comprehend. Their booing is still resonating with me. I walk to one side of the stage and give them the *what were you saying that's right I thought so* pose. I go over to Cynthia who starts on about how amazing I look.

"Thanks. It's all an illusion."

"What?" she goes on, looking confused.

"Yes, look," I scrub furiously as my face, and the makeup comes off showing the black circles around my eyes. "See?"

"Uh," Cynthia says, and looks around her for help in understanding what the fuck is happening.

"Yep. And that's not all. Check this out," I mess my hair around so the bald spots are clearly visible.

"Tisa, I'm sure you're just kidding around," Farrell said. I hadn't seen him on stage until just then.

"Oh hi, Farrell. You of all people should know that I'm not," I said, and snatch the microphone out of the hands of a stunned Cynthia. "In fact," I turn to the audience, "I'm dead serious. None of this is real. We aren't this happy to be on the show. We're beat up. Abused. By the show and ourselves because the show has told us we should be, that nothing in life is good unless you suffer for it. Losing weight is a war of hate against your body. I haven't eaten in ten days, ladies and gentlemen. Until this morning. I was so afraid that I might gain an ounce and fail. Fail at showing you all how amazing an opportunity this is. I sat in a sauna off and on for six hours the other day, trying to lose water weight before getting weighed for the finale. This scale you're about to see, fake. Fake. Fake." I walk over to the huge scale on stage, and notice people waving furiously behind the scene, trying to cut to commercial. I ignore them. "This scale is not real. It's just here for show. We were all weighed yesterday, just like on the show. You're being fooled. All of you at home, it is a sham. Don't do what we did. It doesn't work. I may look like *great*, but I hate myself, I hate my life right now and I hurt every day. I bled like the hallways in The Shining last night. They don't tell you that," I turn to backstage again. "I see you A.C. waving at me. You're in this as well, so don't even try to excuse it. You too, Cynthia. Farrell, Esther and Brody, and the rest of you contestants, it's okay to say no. It took me a long time, but this is it. I'm sorry mom and dad, but I'm done," I drop the mic on the floor, flip off the cameras, turn to a crying Debbie and give her a hug. Stunned silence radiates from the audience. Then cheering erupts. People are going nuts. Crew members come rushing out from the side of the stage to tackle me, and I see Jane rushing from the audience in slow motion to dive in front of me. From somewhere in the back somebody on a cell phone is desperately screaming for a commercial break lamenting why they didn't incorporate a time delay.

Fun right? Nothing like complete chaos to end this farce.

It would've been, if I hadn't just made all that shit up. That was the best-case scenario. Real life, however, is rarely the best-case scenario.

In reality, I crashed through Fat Tisa and was suddenly on a stage having hundreds of people in the studio and millions of people at home judging my body again—like the rest of the show except this was happening with a live studio audience. I was near euphoric with adrenaline and craziness. I pulled off a metal devil horn finger salute and stuck out my tongue, because that's what people expected. They had just seen me on screen in an edited montage being the party girl who finally realized partying just wasn't going to cut it. The audience had just watched me cry bitterly about having a drink with my friends instead of working out and lamenting how I was a horrible person for it, in a segment actually filmed days after going out. I stalked back and forth on stage showing myself to the audience, before I went to Cynthia. Brody was already on stage, so I hugged him. I didn't really want to let go. I wanted to just disappear. When we let go, Cynthia talked to me but I wasn't really aware what she was talking about. I wanted to find Debbie and Esther. That was really all I cared about. I looked around and spotted all the people who had been voted off the show. Debbie was there, in the crowd, waving at me. I answered Cynthia, without really knowing what she had asked. I couldn't form coherent thoughts. It didn't matter. This was all insanity anyway. I could've been brought out in a coffin, and people would've still cheered the show on as long as I was thin. Brody looked so thin now. Did I look as thin as he did? I didn't feel it. My introduction on stage was relatively quickly done with and Cynthia moved on to introducing Farrell. We saw his segment and I thought about running to Debbie to talk but Cynthia kept me back by firmly grasping my arm. The segment ended, and Cynthia introduced Farrell, who burst through the Fat Farrell poster to thunderous applause. He was clearly the fan favorite. My mean girl persona the show played on so heavily had worked. They hated me. They really hated me.

He pranced around the stage, then came down to us and I just looked at him. He was so thin, I couldn't believe it. How had he done that? How had he lost that much weight? Had he gone the distance and just had organs removed? I could barely recognize him, and I stood right next to him. He looked like a mix between somebody who just won Olympic gold, and somebody who just tripped before the goal line and was trampled by the other runners for last place. He spoke to Cynthia but I heard none of it. I was mesmerized by his transformation. There was no way I beat that. No way. Was he thinking the same about me? I doubted it. Finally, it was time to bring out Esther. Cynthia had prepped everybody that she was out of the game. I was looking forward to seeing her and envied her being out of this already. She crashed through her Fat Esther picture and made the same peculiar display of poses for the audience I did. Ones that clearly show we don't really know how to handle all this weirdness. She walked down the same stairs I managed to traverse on my heels without falling on my face—something I'm suddenly grateful for. I hugged her tight.

"I'm so hopped up on painkillers I barely know where I am, Tisa," she whispered in my ear, before we broke the hug and she was accosted by Cynthia for the post-segment chat.

"Tell us what happened at home, Esther. You were fine when you left the Spa," Cynthia belted more to the audience than to Esther. What the hell was she talking about? Esther was far from fine leaving the Spa.

"I tripped over the garden hose at home and tore my ligaments in my left knee. The show's doctors deemed it unsafe for me to go on," she said with a huge smile. I had no actual proof but I was fairly certain that wasn't at all how things had gone or that the shows doctors were in any way part of this. Cynthia turned to the cameras and announced that we would get to the weigh-in right after a commercial break, and we cut filming. I was next to Esther immediately.

"Did they really sign off on your injury?" I asked in a hushed voice. Everybody else was milling about, busy setting things up for the next segment.

"No, Tisa," Esther responded laughing bitterly. "Production tried to force me to go on. I am not even sure they informed the actual doctor and I had no way of connecting with him. I got my actual doctor to protest. It was a travesty. I have to use crutches right now but they refused to let me come out here on crutches. It wouldn't look good, they said."

"Are you fucking kidding me?" I said out loud and a few heads turned. Esther shook her head. "I envy you. I know you're injured so that sounds terrible but I'm so fucked up, Esther. I'm so scared of letting everybody down. I'm scared of food now." She put a hand on my shoulder but before she could say anything, somebody came up to us and pulled Farrell, Brody and myself off the stage. We had to change into our weigh-in outfits—spandex shorts, a shirt and flip flops. When we came back on stage, all the other contestants had been moved to a huge scale that I could only assume would've been used for truck load weigh-ins, if it had been real. I knew it wasn't. We were called back from commercials and Cynthia started talking about the goal for the collective weight loss all fifty contestants had agreed to before doing the show. 4,000 pounds. She asked the four of us—three of us in weigh in outfits—to get on the scale with everyone else. We reached the goal and then some. Whoop de doo, who cares. Just get this shit over with.

They shimmied all the at home and voted off contestants off stage and raised the stupid fake weigh in scale we had been on so many times during the show. I shivered looking at it. My fucking destiny. I was standing next to Brody and Farrell in my spandex shorts and shirt, looking thin but feeling right back to the first day. It gave me chills or maybe the chills were because I was cold. I was cold a lot now, so I couldn't really tell. Cynthia was talking about Farrell getting to choose who went first and he picked me. I took a step up towards the scale and took my flip flops off before ascending all the way. Moment of truth. The whole weigh-in part with numbers going up and down on a screen meant nothing. That was just for show. I knew exactly what I weighed, and the percentage. It all came down to Farrell's weight. Even if Brody looked a lot smaller than he had at the Spa, he wasn't anywhere near me. The scale blinked and displayed a number. People cheered and I flashed another two fingered horn salute and stuck my tongue out. I had to do something and I had no idea what the appropriate response to this bullshit was. I stepped down, and Brody got on the scale. Same procedure. He hadn't lost nearly as much weight as me, as I had suspected. Then it was Farrell's turn. I sort of hovered around Cynthia, unsure of what to do or where to look. It was a cacophony of noises, and things were sort of moving in a blur. He took his flip flops off and got on the scale. The screen flashed numbers and settled. He lost way more weight than I had. Way more. And his overall percentage was well above mine too. I wasn't even really close. I felt like screaming in sheer frustration. Both frustrated joy and resentment. I had lost. I had let everybody down. I had not been good enough. I looked out into the audience and found Jane's face in the crowd. She looked at me intently, and our eyes locked as confetti was starting to rain down over everybody. I was ready to faint as I clapped and cheered for the guy who had just beat me. Seeing Jane's face gave me a tremendous sense of relief, which just flooded over me. A huge weight off. Pun intended. I had lost but it didn't really matter.

Cynthia rounded off the show, now that everybody had been weighed there was very little else to do, and somebody yelled it was a wrap. Jane got up and rushed the stage immediately, as did a lot of journalists. It was a tornado of people. She got to me fast and was holding me up as I clung to her shoulder when somebody stuck a microphone in front of me.

"Tisa. What are you going to do now?" the woman asked me. I looked at her and at the microphone, and I felt delirious.

"I think I'm gonna do Playboy with a new set of boobs, maybe a full body lift, some butt implants," I said, and the girl stared at me befuddled, perhaps rightfully so. "Then I might go and find myself a job with Star Search, somewhere I don't have to think so I can focus exclusively on being attractive to look at because I was so goddamn worthless before. Now that I'm pretty enough to look at without people turning away in disgust," I was going bonkers and the woman was just staring at me still.

"You probably shouldn't print any of that," Jane told the reporter, who just nodded slowly. "Thank you," She walked with me off stage, and back behind the scenes toward the back exit. I still clung on for dear life, barely able to walk anymore from sheer exhaustion. Jane busted the door open and the scene from the Bodyguard played in my head, where Kevin Costner carries Whitney out of the venue, only I was staggering next to her. Plus, I was way too paranoid to actually let anyone lift me off the ground. No matter what I look like, I'm still pretty sure my bones are made of adamantium and make me unfathomably heavier than the average person. She hailed a cab and got us both in. We rode to the hotel as she held my hand and hugged me close.

At the hotel, Jane walked me into the almost empty lobby and sat me down in a chair saying she'd go and get a bottle of water for me from the front desk. As I sat in the chair slowly regaining my faculties, letting the relief of this being over fill me, a woman walked over. I vaguely recognized her as a producer on the show.

"You should've won," she said a little curter than I thought was perhaps warranted. "They set you up to win, and you fucked it all up."

"What are you talking about?" I asked, confused why she was antagonizing me, and peripherally aware that I had ditched my entire family at that finale stage and probably should let them know where I was.

"We would sometimes *save* your weight losses if we needed to," she said, still pretty aggressively. "For example, if you lost ten pounds one *week* but only needed an eight-pound loss to stay safely out of the possibility of being eliminated, we would call your loss eight pounds and carry those extra two pounds over to the next weigh-in. That way, if you only lost four pounds at the next weigh-in we would call it six with the extra two from the week before. So easy. We practically tried to hand you *first female winner* but for the finale you had lost so much less than Farrell that we couldn't make it work."

"Well, all right," I said, having absolutely no idea why she was even telling me this. Jane came back with a bottle of water. The producer barely noticed her.

"I hope you're happy. You've let women everywhere down," she said with contempt in her voice. Jane was next to me, about to speak up, when I jumped to my feet.

I finally lost it. "Guess what, *bitch*, I'm not on your show anymore, so you can go fuck yourself. Nobody gives a shit about your opinion," I said, inches from her face. She looked shocked. Jane put her arm around my shoulder and led me off. I was shaking with rage. I'm pretty sure I saw Jane flash a grin in the elevator door reflection. In our room, things were already all but packed. She had apparently handled that before she left for the finale.

"I figured we'd want to get out of here as soon as possible," she said, when I looked at her questioningly. She wasn't wrong. I sat down.

"I lost," I said.

"You did and thank heavens for that."

"What do you mean?" I asked, genuinely surprised.

"Well, you made it out alive and you don't owe them shit. You don't owe anybody shit. If you took this hard a hit, I don't even want to imagine what Farrell had to do to win. If you *had* won, you'd still be there and they'd want to exploit you further. You'd be preparing for a *victory* press tour. Can you imagine months of talking about how great this was? Losing this was the real winning, Tisa."

I sat for a while and pondered all this, while she sat on the bed and did the same. I sipped my water and felt my mind slowly spin down and my sight and hearing return from hyper drive mode. There was a knock at the door, which Jane answered. It was my parents and sister. My mom was next to me immediately asking how I was doing. I assured her I was doing as well as I could be expected to. She knew this meant I felt like shit but considerably better than this morning. They were leaving too but wanted to come by and make sure I was all right first. I hugged them all goodbye and closed the door behind them. Then I turned around and looked at Jane. She held out a hand to me.

"Jane, the only thing I want right now is to be left alone," I said, as I took it.

"I know, babe," she said, as she picked up my suitcase. "Let's go home."

12/31/2015

I ended up in the hospital after I couldn't stop throwing up for four days. Turns out my immune system had crashed. Who would have thought? I also had thrush and it turned out I was so dehydrated I needed an IV. The doctors were so alarmed, they asked if I had anything that could be suppressing my immune system.

"Tisa, the thrush infection in your mouth is concerning us as much as the dehydration. Your immune system is not doing well and we need to figure out why," the doctor said. He was a kind man with a pained expression on his face.

"Uh ok," I said, trying desperately to find my old aloofness at the harder emotional situations but coming up short. It was hard to be aloof when you were in a hospital bed and you had thrown up almost nonstop for four days.

"Your body is having trouble fighting, that's why you have thrush. Usually when an oral infection like this occurs in adults, it is a symptom of HIV, leukemia or uncontrolled diabetes," the doctor said. "Your body is struggling and your immune system has been weakened by something. You need medications to kill the thrush, along with the IV for hydration. We also need to look at why your body is crashing like this," he said as he left to order more blood work.

Suddenly, my eyes were opened. I realized what my family had known for a while and tried to tell me. I had fucked my body up. I was crying and Jane took my hand. I looked at her and must have looked so miserable.

"Look, Tisa," Jane started, as she sat down next to me and held my hand. "I don't know how you happened to come into my life, and I don't know what I did to keep you around me but I do know that I am impressed with what you've done every day. You need to focus on getting well. You need to ignore all the hate spewed on the internet and in real life at you right now. Those people don't know shit and you don't owe them anything. You are an amazing person and I will be by your side no matter what, as long as you want me there. Getting healthy is a thing that will happen."

I looked at her for a while. My God she was beautiful. I didn't know how she had happened in my life either and I didn't know if she would really want to stay. I pondered these things with my hand in hers. I realized I really liked her taking care of me but that I needed to be the one taking the best care of me. I needed saving but it wasn't by somebody else taking my problems on. It was by me. No place like the hospital while vomiting profusely with an oral infection to make you really take stock of your life choices. I looked her in the eyes.

"I am very happy you feel that way. I appreciate what you have done for me. You have cheered me on supporting me no matter what and that means a lot to me. But," I saw slight alarm in her face at the word but, and continued, "I don't need a savior to descend upon my life and pull me up out of the filth. I know I leaned on you in that way through all of this but I don't want somebody else doing my dirty work. I'm strong enough to get through whatever it's going to take to get to something resembling sanity and health. I understand we met during absolute chaos and I understand it's harder to maintain a relationship when all you've known together is crisis so I need to take time and space to analyze if this is something I really want. Please understand, though, that I am going to be okay, with or without you by my side. I don't need approval to be healthy. I need to learn how to clap for my damn self. I don't need to be attractive. I don't want to be reduced to something pretty to look at anymore. I am powerful. I am intelligent. I am wise. I have the blood of hundreds of strong warrior survivor women who came before me coursing through my veins. I won't allow myself to ever be mistaken for merely decorative again. I don't want a relationship where you're constantly propping me up or holding me together. I can stand on my own. Okay, well, maybe not physically in this moment, because I'm dehydrated but you get my drift. I would be honored if you were willing to stand next to me while I do this though and hold my hand as I stand on my own but I think we need to begin again, and slowly. I can't guarantee where it will go, how it will look or who I am. The thing is, this person, me right now, I am not the same me I knew before all of this. I won't be the same me when I finish working through all of this. We have no idea if the me I actually am works with the you that you are. I've been selfish, self-centered, obsessed with my own life and I barely know your middle name Jane. I know your moral compass, I know your compassion but I have also placed you in this role in my life where I never experienced the depth of who you are. I have relegated you to a plot device in my own story. Let me please figure out who I am and learn all the facets of who you are but slower and without the *tragic fake famous sick girl* thing tainting it all. I know I am asking a lot of you after you have given me so much but you deserve more. I deserve more. I would like to be more, more me." She stared at me silently for a moment.

"Tisa, I love you."

In response I promptly vomited off the side of the bed and all over her as she caught me and held me up.

I hate New Year's Eve.

12/31/2016

I never felt lesser or hated my body before the TV show. I mean, I was teased as a kid, and dealt with never being able to find clothing that fit, not fitting in seating at events. I attended all the usual bullshit that every fat person experiences but I had such a full and fun life. I taught aerobics, I kicked ass at school and was happy with ME. I've spent days and weeks this past year just loathing what I see in the mirror. I can go into any store I want now and buy right off the rack but I also spend hours looking in the mirror at everything wrong with my body. The weight I still need to lose, the size of my breasts, how my skin sags. Just a litany of all the things wrong with me. I did the same thing during the show, with each pound I lost I found something more that was wrong with my body. Weight loss reality TV did that to me. Diet culture did that to me. I'm in therapy now, really working it this time instead of bullshitting everyone around me just to be left alone to starve myself or workout until I bled in peace. I'm learning to be gentle with myself and I know relapse is part of recovery.

Sometimes I feel weak, then I remember that I survived this, I'm still surviving it. The hate mail I still get. The accusations of being a "fame whore." The random strangers asking me what I weigh now. People at grocery stores in my small-town checking what's in my cart to make sure I'm being a "good fatty," appreciating the "gift" that reality TV gave me and not wasting it by gaining any weight. The occasional person who wanders up to my table and asks me "Should you be eating that?" at a restaurant. I'm surviving it all. I'm also talking about what I went through and what I've learned with other people. I get booked for speaking engagements because of my fake fame, and I think they expect me to sing the praises of the show and react like I slaughtered Santa Claus in front of them when I tell the truth. It's worth it though when someone comes to me privately afterward and thanks me for telling the truth because it saved their lives. I've told it all over social media and the show has threatened to sue me twice this year but all I have is my student loan debt, so they can try it if they want.

I've found fat activism spaces that have taught me about intersectionality, how all the things I've faced as a fat woman are compounded by other layers of my life- my queerness, and my Chamorro heritage. I've found activism spaces that don't grasp that fat phobia is just as pressing an issue as misogyny, and I've learned how to push back from those spaces. I've found my voice and I have a feeling I'm going to be needing it more than ever after this past November. I'm loud as fuck, I have White passing and thin privilege that I intend to use. There is power to be found even now. In myself. I am a disruptor.

I've been galvanized by what I've been through, not victimized, though make no mistake I was a victim of a huge money-making machine and diet culture but I find no shame in that, only strength.

I don't want to change my body, I want to change the world. For tonight though, I'm going to crawl in bed next to the love of my life and fall asleep.

Happy New Year.

Acknowledgements

This book came about after ten grueling years of being told no and not wanting to deal with the emotions of writing it. It also came about with the assistance of many people, both directly involved in the process, and peripherally attached as physical, emotional and/or academical support. In no particular order, I would like to extend my personal and professional gratitude towards the following people: Dr. Moore for letting me work on his research team, Chavese Underhill Turner for her work in and with BEDA/NEDA being an inspiration, Lizabeth Wesley whose body positive fight against weight stigmatization gives me hopes for a brighter world, other former contestants for their support and contributions to reserach, JD Roth for being the epitome of the sentence "My shoes are worth more than your life", Andrea and Doug for being a small but sane spot in an otherwise completely discombobulated time period during the completion of this book, my parents for chuckling at my scribblings while secretly hoping I'd get a proper job and finally Stella for never giving up the dream of catching that squirrel. My deepest apologies to anyone I missed.

About the Author

Kai Hibbard is former contestant on The Biggest Loser, a licensed social worker (LMSW), body acceptance activist, motivational speaker, and writer. When not providing individual and couples therapy, or publicly combating mass media hypocrisy and body shaming, she uses her voice to give presentations promoting body positivity and to shed light on the issues close to her heart.

After finishing her stint on Season 3 of The Biggest Loser, she realized the negative impact the show had, not only on her own life, but on society in general. Vowing to be part of the solution rather than part of the problem, Kai fought, often as the lone voice, against the unrealistic and damaging message regarding our bodies the show represents in the media. Over time that struggle has been featured in countless magazines and newscasts, both domestically and internationally, and Kai's honest, straight forward approach to her own story never fails to shine through.

Outside of writing, Kai explores living healthy and happy with her body in a society that inundates people with the message that she shouldn't. Through well researched and empirically backed discourse, she encourages people to think independently and critically about the messages they are being sent in the media. She urges people to be comfortable in their own skin, embrace who they are, and own the space they take up in the world with both the good and the bad that follows, knowing this to be the best first step towards a happier, healthier existence.

Sometimes people on the internet like to call her a "Fame Whore" and her mom gets upset, but speaking your truth comes with consequences so it'll be ok.

She can be reached at KaiHibbard@gmail.com but please don't message to call her names.